Ruthless

Ruthless

Book 3 of the Raptor Castle Series

SOPHIA JOHNSON

Ruthless

Cover design by Delle Jacobs
http://www.dellejacobs.blogspot.com

Typesetting by Hale Author Services
www.haleauthorservices.com

Visit the author's website at www.sophiajohnson.net

Dedication Page

Gloria Paugh Kohler (1941 – 2012)

Gloria first wrote to me on February 26, 2006, after reading *Risk Everything.* She was my first fan. From then on, every time I turned on my e-mail, I scanned the list of addresses looking for Dragoness83. My husband did the same on his PC, because he'd send her the funny things he found, just to make her laugh.

She always told me the truth about a character or plot and I never disregarded her advice.

This past year, I didn't write often. Gloria didn't either. I had no idea she was so ill. I thought she was tired of hearing about my problems. Instead, I should have been writing to tell her how important she was to me.

I regret that with all my heart.

Many special thanks to Valeri Sperry for her excellent job of keeping me upbeat while writing *Ruthless.* Also for calling when she finished reading and hollering, "What! I didn't want it to end. Where's the next book?"

Chapter 1

Loch Rimsdale, Scotland, 1124 A.D.

MAGNUS OF CLIBRICK CASTLE stood tall and unflinching, his shoulders squared, his back stiff as he dipped his fingers in the pewter bowl and painted the left side of his face. He must hurry, for as blood cooled, it made his task more difficult.

His chest tightened, awaiting the fiery stab of an arrow sent flying from the army of warriors facing him. At first sight, their appearance was much as he would expect them to have been when Vikings first raided Scotland.

Taking a calming breath, he steeled himself to swirl his fingertips in the thickening blood twice more afore he completed the task. Finally, he nodded.

Though he could not see what he had done, 'twas like peering into a square of polished steel for Feradoch, son of Olaf of Kinbrace Castle, stood across from him copying his every move. Blood covered the left side of their faces while blue woad painted the right. Thunder rumbled in the distance while they traced a bloody line below their Adam's apple as if a blade had slashed there. They chanted the vow, each using the other's name, which bound them, heart and soul for the remainder of their lives.

"*The sun shall light my deeds for all to see I mean no harm to Feradoch, son of Olaf of Kinbrace. No action by me will bring harm upon him or those of his blood, nor by inaction will I allow harm to befall him.*

"*Should my brother be felled by treachery, I am honor bound to hunt his attacker and deliver justice. All shall ken I will fulfill my vow. This I swear to ye.*"

Their fathers handed each a pewter horn and nodded. Magnus held his breath and steadied his hand as he raised the horn to his lips and drank his own and Feradoch's blood thinned with red wine. Though he felt the need to shudder, his muscles tensed iron-hard to prevent it.

Once done, Magnus pressed his lips tightly together to stifle any disgraceful sounds of sorrow or regret from passing through.

He was seven years old.

The Morgan and Gunn clans faced each other beside the cold waters of Loch Rimsdale, a spot chosen for its equal distance between their castles. Behind each Chief, long rows of warriors sat astride their horses, their restless hands fingering their weapons. Their mounts sensed the tension of their riders, making them stomp and sidle, anxious to spring into action.

The two clans had been mortal enemies for centuries.

Angus of Clibrick Castle, Chief of the Morgan Clan, stood beside his eldest son Magnus. When the boy reached his prime, he would be his father's image. Angus was taller than most men, trim of body with thick black hair, dark brown eyes, firm lips and an iron jaw. Temples streaked with silver were the only signs of aging.

Prepared for treachery, Angus wore a claymore slung across the forest green, black and blue wool covering his back. A short sword hung from a sheath on his belt. Strapped to his thigh, a dagger peeked from beneath the bunched wool at his knees. A round leather shield protected his chest. He stared at the Chief of Clan Gunn, knowing this harsh man would be raising Magnus. Swallowing his regrets, his voice was cold, the words uncaring when he spoke.

"We are pledged then, Olaf?"

"Aye! For better or worse."

Olaf of Kinbrace Castle was equally as large with hair a

reddish-blond worn long and shaggy. A heavy beard hid his lower face, making his blue eyes startling. Animal pelts covered his shoulders and a thick leather belt decorated with pointed iron studs held the heavy skins around his waist. Brown boots covered stocky legs up to his knees. Turned down at the top, they exposed the soft fur inside.

Feradoch in no way resembled his father. Long blond hair fell to his shoulders framing a face as pale as his Danish ancestors. Where the father appeared crude, the son bore himself with grace.

'Twas only when Olaf took their family's ancient Norse helmet from his own head and placed it on Magnus' that Feradoch showed any expression.

Feradoch's lips flirted with a sneer; hate flashed from angelic blue eyes.

Surely, Magnus had not seen aright.

Chapter 2

Blackbriar Castle, Southeast of Kinbrace, 1141 A.D.

S WEAT STREAMED FROM BENEATH the ancient helmet to trail down his forehead, burning the warrior's eyes and blurring his vision. By the time Blackbriar fell, Magnus would not be inclined to be lenient.

A sennight earlier, he had disregarded safety and ridden Odin, his great white warhorse, within shouting distance of the castle's barbican tower. Lord Baldor stood in a crenelation above the barbican gate holding an oblong shield to protect his chest.

"Baldor!"

Magnus' bellow was so earsplitting even a man who had lost his hearing must have felt the vibrations of his voice.

"Devil's spawn! Tuck yer tail betwixt yer legs and hie back to Kinbrace like the mangy hound ye are!" As his temper mounted, spittle flew like a rain shower from Lord Baldor's lips.

"Yield now and I will spare all but the men who butchered our villagers and patrols," Magnus demanded.

"Fool! I'll see ye in Hades first!"

"Ye leave me no choice. Concede defeat within three days. If ye dinna, ye will condemn every man at Blackbriar. Yer own life will flow into the river of their blood when I break through yer walls."

He waited for the space of three heartbeats. Frost could have formed from the breath of each word he next spoke.

"I will give no quarter."

Magnus sensed someone watched his every move. 'Twas not the eyes of a man or warrior. He was used to their stares. As his gaze swept the parapet, a woman stepped behind a merlon on the corner tower.

Lord Baldor's response was a whistling shower of arrows, which fell short. Some struck the ground with enough force they quivered back and forth. Others flew with little speed, falling like leafless branches blown from small trees during a summer storm. Magnus had expected Baldor's wordless reply. He waited calmly until the last arrow struck the earth then brought Odin up on his hind legs and wheeled him to gallop away.

Muriele of Blackbriar studied the man who rode the huge warhorse up to the barbican. In the weak sunlight, his helmet flashed with a blue tint. The rounded helm and cheek flaps protected his head down to above his lips. Two rounded sections were open through which his eyes could see in all directions.

Ancient Norse designs and patterns decorated the intricate gold-plated bands dividing the two sides of the helm from the back and up over his head and down to his nose. Another rounded the helm above his eyes. A veil of riveted mail hung from the rear of the helmet and protected his neck while leather ties on the cheek flaps shielded his jaws.

All she saw of his face was the flash of cold, black eyes, firm lips and a chin and jaw, which appeared rock-hard. She shivered and rubbed her hands on her upper arms, chasing the chill bumps there.

'Twas the man known as Magnus the Ruthless.

She sensed he had earned the name. He was relentless and powerful when he issued his ultimatum. Her stepfather was a fool not to heed him. And he would pay with his life. 'Twas right that he should.

Muriele would not waste one tear mourning his death!

She'd thank God instead.

When she straightened her shoulders, she winced with pain and steeled herself to walk tall and straight to where her mother and the women of the castle waited.

"I have seen this Magnus. He has given Baldor three days to yield," she told them when she slipped back inside the solar.

Her mother's sad gaze swept over the women in the room. "Do you think he will kill us all?"

Some women bit their lips or clasped their hands over them to keep from crying out, others wailed with despair.

"He has said he will spare all but the men who rightly deserve to die for killing his villagers and their families."

"Baldor willna yield. He is so bloated with self-worth he can not believe he could fail." Her mother shook her head in frustration.

"Then, this Magnus will give no quarter." Muriele sighed. "I canna believe a man who would go to battle to avenge the killing of his village's women and children would put to death more innocents."

"Aye. He may spare the women and children, but I dinna think *we* will be with them." Her mother gripped her hands in her lap and closed her eyes as if seeing something too horrible to endure. "He will put to death anyone related to Baldor."

Muriele swallowed and nodded.

The women listened to all Muriele and her mother said about Sir Magnus the Ruthless and clung to the hope he would be merciful.

Old Grunda, the spaewife and healer from the village, was the first to speak up. "Even though Sir Magnus may spare the women and children, as our lady said, he will be honor bound to put to death anyone related to Lord Baldor."

"Have you seen this in one of your visions?" The cobbler's wife asked.

"Nay. Since fostering with the Chief of the Gunns, he has learned their ways of an eye for an eye, a tooth for a tooth."

A young maiden cried out, "But both ladies are related by marriage only."

Cook's helper, wearing an apron streaked with soot and

mud from slipping in puddles in her haste to reach the safety of the room added, "Aye. But a short six months ago!"

Muriele shook her head. "Fury and revenge may shatter all reasoning in his mind."

"But if he canna find ye, 'tis naught he can do," Grunda added.

She went to the corner of the room where she had stored her basket of medicines, concoctions and many other mysterious things. After hunting through it, she brought several things over to the washstand.

"They know our lady and her daughter have an unusual hair color." She busily measured and stirred an ugly mixture together. "By the time I am through with this oak bark, 'tis a muddy brown their locks will be."

As Grunda rubbed the dark concoctions through Ragnhild and Muriele's hair, the women called out ways to disguise the two. One took her life in her hands when she ran down into the bailey and dodged burning debris and rubble from the bombardment to scurry back with a pewter cup of dirt. Her red-faced friend stopped crying long enough to help mix the right amount of water into the cup to make a light-colored mud.

They giggled when Grunda dabbed bits on their ladies faces and hands to make them appear unwashed for many days.

"My lady, ye look like the goose girl last summer when the old drake pecked her legs and made her fall in the mud pile!"

Muriele stared at the polished metal square hanging over the washstand and burst out laughing. As the day faded into evening, her shimmering hair became a dull brown.

The castle women, chamber maids and cook's helpers all did their part to disguise their mistress and her daughter, for after Lord Baldor came to the castle, the two women had tried to make their lives easier. Now, the faithful women helped them dress in worn clothing and two tattered cloaks with hoods. Once they decided not even the most discerning eye could tell the women were the mistress of Kinbrace and her daughter, they coached them how to appear being of the common class.

A chambermaid clucked her tongue and advised, "Ye canna stroll, my lady. Shuffle like ye are bone tired."

"Aye. Hunch your shoulders forward like you have carried baskets of dirty laundry for many years," a laundress said.

Back and forth they walked, practicing their shuffle and rounded shoulders. Still, something was missing.

"I dinna know why, my ladies," a knight's wife said. "Beneath it all, your breeding still shows."

"How can we still look like ladies of the keep when we are covered with mud and our hair straggles limp from beneath our scarves?" Muriele asked.

"Ah, I think I know what 'tis," Grunda said. "Yer height. No other woman here is as tall as ye are. Sir Magnus will check for lasses who come up to a man's chin."

"Huh! What are we to do?" Muriele was beginning to despair. "We canna shrink like wool cloth boiled in water."

"Aye. But ye can walk with yer knees bent. And if ye would be lowly servants, dinna respond with anger if someone touches where he should not."

Grunda pointed to five of the women and told them to walk two ahead and three after Ragnhild and Muriele.

They shuffled around until they felt confident in their deception.

Chapter 3

DAY AND NIGHT, HEAVY stones from the catapults bombarded the castle walls. Between the missiles meant to break through the walls, trebuchets threw balls of fire flying over them. No one within could rest or sleep but were under constant stress putting out fires.

Finally, as dawn broke on the seventh day, the last several barrages opened gaping holes in two of the castle's walls.

Magnus and half his army swarmed through the west side like hungry ants attacking a day-old corpse, while Sweyn, his first in command, assaulted the east with as much fervor. Amidst the screams of the frightened, the injured and dying, the castle fell.

The conquering army did not see so much as a glimpse of Lord Baldor. As the fighting waned, the Gunn warriors searched for him as they gathered the women and children to send them from the castle. The least-injured Kinbrace warriors would guard them.

Magnus sat atop Odin and studied the women who cried and clutched each other as his men led them down the keep's stairs into the bailey. Sweyn stood in front of him and peered at each woman's face as she went past. If she walked with grace or dignity, he signaled her out for special scrutiny. He had already stopped several and pulled aside their scarves or hoods to bare their heads, only to find they had hair of any color but what they searched for.

Magnus knew he would recognize Baldor's wife and daughter. Bards sang of the beautiful women with their tall and willowy bodies and hair the color of ripe wheat.

He found no signs of them.

Muriele felt the huge devil's eyes rake over every female as they descended the stairway to the bailey. When ordered to walk single-file, Grunda shoved Muriele and Ragnhild in front of her, and with a sharp nod and twitch of her shoulders, reminded Muriele to stoop.

Feeling the force of his eyes as he studied her, Muriele hazarded a glance at Sir Magnus through lowered lashes, feeling much like a wary mouse peering out a small hole chewed in a barn wall.

Today, he was their conqueror. Power radiated from him even in the way he sat his horse. Together, they seemed a statue hewn from granite.

Hard. Silent. Unmoving.

Sparks of tightly held emotion sizzled around the man. The hair on her arms lifted every bit as much as when she found herself outside in the midst of a lightning storm.

What caused it? His fury?

She nearly halted. What right did he have for fury? It was their castle destroyed. It was he and her loathsome stepfather who caused it.

"Sst!" Her mother hissed in front of her, the sound barely heard.

Muriele looked down. If her mother had sensed her feelings, then so could someone else.

When the devil's commander reached out to snatch away Muriele's hood, Grunda stumbled and cried out, bringing their attention to her. Ragnhild halted and bent low to help her. With the old woman's curses and rants, the man let them through without further scrutiny.

Outside the keep, the soldiers herded them into the front bailey like so many sheep. Muriele near ruined their disguises when a smelly lout prodded her mother's back and ordered her to hurry. Had Ragnhild not grabbed Muriele's wrist, she would have cut him with the knife strapped inside her woolen sleeve.

They no longer heard the moans and cries of the wounded within the castle walls. He had meant it when he warned he would *give no quarter*. The women's sobs and wails drowned out most sounds.

Muriele was all out of tears. She'd had much to grieve over.

Cursing and scuffling filled the air as the last stragglers passed through the keep's huge doors. Four men grappled with Lord Baldor as they pulled him out into the open. A man followed carrying Baldor's shield and weapons.

"We caught the bastard hiding in the storage room like the blustering coward he is," the last man said with disgust.

"I yield! Ye canna kill a defenseless man."

He held his empty hands high in the air. Magnus snorted.

"Yield? When ye refused my offer four days hence, ye sacrificed yerself and every man within the castle's outer walls."

His fingers twitched with the urge to strangle the fool for causing such useless slaughter. By Magnus' code of consequences for right and wrong, Baldor must die by his hand. Keeping his eyes on the loathsome man, he threw his right leg over Odin's back and slid to the ground.

As Magnus leisurely took his shield from his squire, Baldor foamed at the mouth. 'Twas an insult to act like the coming fight was of so little consequence he was in no hurry to don his arms. When the squire held up a fighting flail, Magnus grinned and nodded. The long, leather-wrapped handle held two chains, a morning star at the end of each. The wicked, spiked iron balls could wreak havoc. With a hearty swing, he could generate tremendous force and wrap the balls and chains around a weapon, wrenching it from an attacker's hand.

The flail and sword would be his only weapons, his shield his protection. He wrapped the chains around the flail's handle and tucked it in a sling hanging behind his right hip, the morning stars secured against a tough piece of leather which kept the spikes from puncturing his back.

Finished, he widened his stance, yawned and stretched.

"Let Baldor arm himself."

He watched with amusement as Lord Baldor's face purpled with anger. Magnus had pricked him on purpose. An angry man was a careless one. The eejit seethed while he should have calmly thought on how to save his sorry arse.

Even so, Baldor surprised him with the speed with which he grabbed his war hammer and slipped it beneath his belt. Gripping his shield in his left hand and arm, the man hoisted his sword. Magnus knew he would need all his skills and more to defeat him when Baldor sprang at him, his sword slicing the air between them with such unexpected agility and mastery.

Muriele noted the guard's excitement as suddenly, the sharp screech and clang of swords again filled the air. Sir Magnus was in hand-to-hand combat with her stepfather.

If Sir Magnus won the match, her stepfather would die.

If her stepfather won, Sir Magnus would be dead.

Whatever way the fight went, Lord Baldor would die. The men who fought under Sir Magnus would see to it.

'Twas possible her life would be easier if both men died. But Muriele could not wish it to be so. For just a moment when she had passed Sir Magnus sitting so still on his great horse and spied his sensuous lips framed with the precise short beard, her skin had quivered. A spark flashed through her straight to the pit of her stomach. There was something more to him than mere danger.

After so many sennights of hearing the terrible booms and shudders of hurled missiles, the swarming sounds of arrows flying overhead, and the shouts and cries of men fighting and dying in a castle under siege, how could the shriek of two swords striking together seem even more ominous?

The guards began yelling and placing bets afore the combat had started. Magnus and Baldor had not wasted time testing each other but went straight to battling for the kill.

"Ah, I can see why ye send men to do the killing for ye," Magnus said as he sidestepped out of Baldor's reach.

"Coward! Stand and fight like a man," Baldor shouted. His face turned redder and he grunted as he made a vicious sweep with his sword.

Magnus's sword shrieked as he repelled the thrust.

"For certs, I hear yer men hold your opponents so ye can skewer them without risking yer lily-soft hands," he taunted.

Shock swept through Muriele remembering her stepfather's men holding her betrothed's arms behind his back while Baldor plunged a blade into her beloved's chest. Though Magnus may have meant to taunt her stepfather, did he realize how true he spoke?

When Baldor's teeth ground together, Magnus lunged forward as if aiming for his right side. Baldor shifted his great iron shield to the right, leaving a small opening on his left. Magnus' sword found an opening between his chain mail and leather padding. Blood soon seeped through.

"Did ye know ye bleed like a stuck pig, Baldor?"

"Bastard!"

"Nay. I am the image of my father." He waited a breath then added, "I hear ye can sire no sons."

Baldor thrust his sword high, trying to go over the top of Magnus' shield and strike his head from his body. Magnus raised his shield in time though the force of the strike near knocked him off his feet.

"Nor even daughters." He continued to mock Baldor. He turned his blade parallel to stop another downward strike. "E'en a weak man can swell his wife's belly with puny girls."

Soldiers guarding the women became more excited with their betting. Men ran back and forth to spread word of how the battle fared to those who could not see. Whenever the guards were engrossed in the scene in front of the keep, she took her mother's hand and edged the slightest bit backward toward the broken walls.

Grunda kept her head lowered as she whispered to Muriele

and her mother. "Travel northwest to the forest of Kildonan. Afore I came to Blackbriar, my father had a cottage near to the northern end. He has long been gone, but if fortune follows ye, it may still stand. They willna think to search so close to their own lands."

"The next time excitement o'ertakes them, we'll slip into the woods," Muriele whispered.

Baldor barged forward with his massive shield. The two men near locked together. Magnus stopped his taunting as they hacked and thrust at each other. Soon, all one could hear was the loud, resonant sounds of their blades clashing and screeching as they fought.

How could two men battle so long? By now, surely they must be wobbling on their feet. Both were bloodied aplenty from the long siege; both were bone-weary. Magnus' right foot slid on the blood soaked cobblestones. As he caught his balance, his shield moved slightly. The opening allowed Baldor to score a strike low on the firm flesh aside Magnus' rib cage.

"The bastid's sword struck Sir Magnus under the arm!" A guard shouted as he shoved the women out of the way.

Muriele peered around him and noted Sir Magnus did not take his gaze from her stepfather's eyes and face. Was he searching for signs of weakness? He kept his own face expressionless.

Now, Magnus' lips lifted in an amused, wicked smile.

"Yer leman whispers to everyone she canna tell if ye are swiving her with yer finger or yer cock."

With a vicious snarl starting deep in Baldor's body, he swept the air with his sword. Magnus ducked beneath the whistling blade and struck upward. Blood spurted from Baldor's armpit.

"I will nail yer wee cock to a post for all to see ye couldna pleasure a woman with such a pitiful weapon," Magnus promised.

The guards paid little attention to the women in their excitement to get a closer view of the fighting. Keeping a wary eye on them, Muriele and her mother edged backwards through a gaping hole in the castle wall. The castle women quietly filled the space they had left.

If Magnus didna end the battle soon, he feared his own strength would desert him. 'Twould bring him shame if he didn't make a clean kill. Though the Highlanders had rightly named him as ruthless, 'twas not for causing undue pain.

Too furious to put words together, Baldor responded with curses and screams. With the iron shield protecting most of his body, Magnus couldn't get in a killing blow. Finally, he spied a likely way to defeat him. Never once had the burly man spared a quick glance behind him. Magnus lunged and struck with all his might, forcing him back.

Seeing Sweyn from the corner of his right eye, Magnus tossed his sword at his commander's feet. Turning slightly to the right to protect his side with his shield, he yanked the flail from his hip and spun it, unwinding the chains in swift movements. With great, arced swings, he battered the iron shield. Shattering shock waves from each contact swept through his shoulder and back.

Baldor thrust out with his sword when Magnus made a sweeping backswing. Fresh blood flowed from Magnus' underarm. Gritting his teeth, he brought the flail forward, wrapped the morning stars around the steel blade and wrenched the sword out of Baldor's grip.

The man screamed, cursed and grabbed for his war hammer. Magnus continued beating his flail against the iron shield. Each blow forced Baldor backward.

Magnus maneuvered him to where his men had collected weapons from the fallen warriors. With Baldor's next backward step, the flail flew around the edge of the iron shield and sent him sprawling. The spikes held tight. Grunting with exertion, Magnus wrenched the shield and sent it clattering across the bloodied cobblestones.

Baldor struck at Magnus' legs with his war hammer. When the heavy head cracked into Magnus' left thigh, it threw him off-balance. He lurched to the side as Baldor sprang up, hefting the hammer, preparing to thrust the iron spike atop the hammerhead into Magnus chest.

The men shouted and cursed at the top of their lungs.

Magnus swung again.

Both morning stars struck Baldor — one between the eyes, the other at his temple.

"There goes Baldor," men shouted.

Baldor toppled and crashed much like a giant tree struck by summer lightning.

A roar rang out, rolling on like claps of thunder. It drowned out the sounds of Muriele and Ragnhild running through the dense forest.

Chapter 4

MAGNUS' MEN WADED INTO the painful task as they searched through the fallen and retrieved their wounded. Honorable knights carried a misericord to spare a mortally wounded comrade an agonizing death. Without hesitation, they used the thin bladed daggers to deliver the finishing stroke.

Archers patrolled atop what was left of the wall walks of Blackbriar.

Since the warrior's barracks had burned to the ground, the bulk of Magnus' army returned to their tent camp outside the castle walls. It would take days to bury the dead.

Once the sad chore was finished, he would allow his men to claim a certain amount of spoils, depending on rank, from the castle.

'Twas a shame a man like Baldor had become its lord. He grimaced with disgust.

After the healer Grunda tended his wounds, he ordered the women counted. As he expected, the total was two less than the original reckoning.

Baldor's wife and daughter had been there.

Somewhat relieved, he shrugged. He had not truly decided what to do with them. Early in his first years at Kinbrace, he had learned to keep his thoughts to himself. He didn't believe women should pay for what some lout of a husband had done. He had no doubt Olaf would have sampled them himself then thrown them to the men before he finally slit their throats.

With Sweyn at his heels, Magnus wandered around the keep, hiding his pain and fatigue. He propped his back against the doorframe of Baldor's bedchamber and eased his weight off his badly bruised leg as he gazed around the room. Chairs with heavy tapestry cushions sat on either side of the fireplace. Two straight-backed chairs stood close to a beautifully carved light brown table. Tapestries on the walls gave the room a feeling of warmth, as did clothes chests with forest scenes painted on their lids.

He groaned on seeing the canopied bed with its scarlet draperies. He would sleep well this night on its thick, featherbed mattress. Alone. He thought of the tall, slender woman said to have hair like wheat, silky skin and soft brown, almond-shaped eyes. Had he not so many stitched cuts and swelling bruises, he would set out to recapture her. He grimaced. 'Twas fortunate for her he was too pain-wracked to track them down.

Stilling his face to hide a wince, he pushed away from the doorframe and looked once more about the room. He couldn't imagine a hulk of a man like Baldor in such stately surroundings. An unwanted tinge of pity for Ragnhild swept his mind, for her first husband had obviously been a man of a different sort — one of refinement.

He passed through a door on the right side of the bedchamber into the lord's solar. Its furnishings were much like the previous room. Without the bed, from the looks of it. Blackbriar must have had a master carpenter.

Noting another connecting door, he went over to turn the handle. Locked from the other side, it did not open. Curious, he went out through the door leading onto the landing and found another entrance ten paces away. The women's hasty exit had left the door ajar.

Inside was a smaller bedchamber, equally as neat. Surely the Lady Muriele's room. Had she reason to lock her door into the solar? 'Twas not surprising. Baldor had likely wanted both mother and daughter. Bright-colored smocks and kirtles spilled over the sides of an open chest. Others strewn about the floor looked as if someone searched for a particular garment but did not find it.

Beside the bed stood a small table cluttered with the many things all women liked. Ribbons shimmered in a silky heap, and without thought, he picked them up. Enjoying the silky feel and the sight of the brilliant colors, he spilled them from one hand to the other. He gently put them back where they had been, then studied the small bits of jewelry beside them. Naught but some ornaments with small combs attached to sweep hair off the face, several decorated circlets to place around the head and a pewter pin with a likeness of Blackbriar etched on it. He twirled it around and around, before deciding it likely held a lady's draped plaid to the shoulder of her kirtle.

A stoneware pot painted around the outer sides with birds of brilliant colors caught his eye. He found it filled with a soft soap smelling of fresh apples and spices. He closed his eyes and breathed in the scent.

An image of the girl formed in his mind. A graceful lass lounged back in a steaming tub as her long, elegant fingers scooped out a portion of the soap.

He pictured her as she lathered moist, naked breasts, stroking her nipples 'til they hardened and jutted, awaiting the next touch. Her head fell back spilling golden brown hair over the tub's rim until it brushed the floor. When she opened heavy-lidded eyes filled with searing passion, she reached out her hand and beckoned to him. Water dripped off her arm and spilled onto the floor. His stones grew heavy and heated; his cock swelled and throbbed. As he pictured her naked woman's place framed with golden hair floating in the clear, warm water, his demented cock jerked upward and near bruised his belly.

He snapped his eyes open to keep from spilling his seed.

Lucifer's horned balls! Too many days had passed since he'd swived a woman. Frustration filled him, for he would not allow himself to sample any of the women. What he denied his men, he denied himself.

He snorted. 'Twas not much of a sacrifice. He didn't want just any woman. He wanted a woman with fine taste. One of softness and beauty.

Forcing himself to ignore his aching stones, he went to the corner washstand. Pots and combs stood beside the basin. A small clay bowl caught his interest. Inside, little remained of a foul-smelling paste. His nose wrinkled. What was its purpose? His answer came when he spied a comb stained brown with the same mixture.

Huh! The women had been wise. 'Twas why he didna see their light-colored hair. He should have been more observant and checked for such a ploy. He shrugged. No matter. They would not live long in the wild.

When he turned to leave the room, he hesitated, looking at the soft finery strewn about the woman's clothing chest. He turned to Sweyn, patiently waiting in the open doorway.

"Have a squire ask amongst the women and find the ladies' maidservants. Have them gather the finery here. We will take it back to Kinbrace."

"What are we to do with Blackbriar when we leave?" Sweyn appeared loath to hear Magnus' answer.

Magnus' teeth clanged together so hard he near bit his tongue. He stared at his commander for a moment then forced his face to relax.

"This morn, I had but one wish. Burn it to the ground!" Looking around the room, he sighed.

"You've changed your mind, then?" Sweyn's solemn face brightened.

"Aye. 'Twould be a terrible waste. Though we destroyed much, the next baron can rebuild it. We'll leave enough men to see to its safety until King David appoints Blackbriar's new lord. He would not take kindly to us leaving him an empty shell."

Satisfied, he used the tip of his sword to retrieve a deep blue-green kirtle tangled with a soft silver smock off the floor. The faint hint of spiced apples drifted from the soft cloth. Ah, the tall, naked lass of his mind had worn it.

His cock again burst to life beneath his kilt, shooting pleasure through his battered body. He shook his head in disgust.

The long battle had left him brainsick.

CHAPTER 5

Kildonan Forest, Five Months Later

HEAT CAUSED MURIELE TO gather her skirts between her legs and secure them in front with a thin cord. Leaving her mother behind in the old hut, she went out to hunt.

Magnus' wrath had spared Blackbriar's villages, for they had not participated in the castle's defiance. Far from it. Lord Baldor had locked the gate and left them to fend for themselves.

From the earliest Muriele could remember she went with her mother to bring extra food, clothing, and medicines to those who needed it. Her father kept watch over their homes and farms, and provided aid to repair huts and thatched roofs. Her parents never ignored any plea for help.

After Lord Baldor arrived at Blackbriar, he forbad giving aid to the villagers. It did not stop the women. Hiding their supplies in a cart, they went as often as they could. When Baldor kept too close a watch on them, Grunda took their place. If a warrior came close to her cart, the old spaewife yelled chants and made spastic gestures, arms and legs flying. They did not venture closer.

Now, the villagers did what they could to help Lady Ragnhild and Muriele. They kept watch, fearing Sir Magnus would return and find the women whom he'd searched for after the siege.

Since he'd taken Grunda to Kinbrace Castle, her mother was the only woman knowledgeable enough to aid them. They put aside their fears of Magnus's patrols whenever the fevers, the bloody flux, or any number of other ills took them.

Before the sun rose, an elderly woman came on behalf of her grandson. The boy was careless while thrashing wheat and suffered a festering wound. Muriele's mother did not hesitate but grabbed a cloth sack of herbs for healing concoctions and hurried off to help the boy.

Muriele's arrows had flown true all day, and she now had more than enough meat for a sennight. 'Twas near dark when she stepped out into the small clearing before their hut. No plume of smoke rose from the hole in the thatch. Usually, her mother had hot water ready for Muriele to prepare the day's kill.

Inside, she filled a pot from the water barrel in the corner, and kindled the fire. By the time she completed her chores, she had vegetables and a plump hare stewing. A sickening feeling roiled in her gut. Every crack of a twig or rustle of leaves caused her to run outside to check the woods nearby. Her mother always returned at night, using the moon as guide.

She did not sleep but waited for the darkness to fade to gray. Throwing a woolen shawl around her shoulders, she set out on the paths leading to the village. Halfway there, she cried out. At a bend in the path, scavenger birds circled.

Muriele ran. She tripped over a bundle of herbs and her mother's cloak. Scrambling to her feet, she pushed through brush until she burst out into a small clearing. Ragnhild lay naked, on her side with her knees forced up and tied to her elbows. Blood covered her thighs, her woman's place. Her pale hair, shoulders and chest, the ground on which she lay, were dark with blood. Her throat gaped from ear to ear.

A wail, long and piercing, warbled from Muriele's throat. Pulling a knife from the sheath at her waist, she cut the rope bindings and stretched her mother out on her back. Tugging off her shawl, she wrapped the body then gathered her into her arms and cradled her on her lap. Tears flowed down on the unseeing face, beautiful still though bruised and cut. Muriele rocked back and forth, unable to stop keening.

"Will ye look at her? Ain't she a bonnie one?"

How had she become so careless? 'Twas the Kinbrace patrol. They'd heard her cries and returned, knowing they'd have more sport. The men slid off their mounts and circled her.

"This'n be younger, too."

Hands reached to grab her, pulling her away from the limp body. Muriele fought, hate for these human beasts gave her strength. Blood smeared their clothing. Her mother's blood. She kicked, scratched and bit anything within range.

"Aye. Me cock's ready to crow again," one man said, leering at her. His breath wheezed from his throat when her foot landed a blow to his ballocks.

She near bit the ear off a surly, stinking lout trying to pin her arms to her side. Another darted close to slip a rope over her head. He tightened the loop until the need to breathe forced her to grab it. She used all her strength to keep it from strangling her.

Still, she fought on with her feet. After what seemed an eternity, the man holding the rope spoke.

"I be tired. Let's take her to the castle. Ridin' will rest us." He snorted a laugh. "Runnin' will tire the witch out."

He pulled her over to his horse and mounted. As he signaled his horse to a trot, she craned her neck to look back at the still figure on the ground. Tears blinded her as she ran. If she fell, she did not doubt he'd pull her along the rough forest path all the way to Kinbrace Castle.

"How many times over the years have we crossed this spot, Feradoch?" Magnus looked over at his blood brother who flashed him a wide grin.

"The tally stands at thirty and four, one coming and one going for each of seventeen years."

"Aye. After ye spend this fortnight at Kinbrace, 'twill be the last of our yearly month together. Next spring, ye'll return here for good and I will go to Clibrick. Graemme will be pleased."

"Your brother is far too soft. I can still hear his snivels

when we pledged."

"Soft?" Magnus chuckled. "Graemme was five years old at the time. Eight days past, he near beat ye with the war hammer. Had ye not thrown dirt in his eyes, ye would have needed to forfeit yer shield for the sennight."

"He'll learn to keep his eyes darting from face to hands. He won't make the same mistake again."

Though Magnus had been gone all these years, Graemme still greeted him with as much gusto as he had the time he returned for his first fortnight visit. Magnus wondered why Graemme had never formed a brotherly affection for Feradoch.

'Twas strange. Feradoch was pleasant company. A good warrior. A number of lasses at Clibrick frequented his bed. At Kinbrace, he had a leman he'd sworn he first took when he was twelve years old. He'd offered Magnus her services while he was gone, but Magnus had the feeling had he availed himself of the offer, his blood brother would have resented it.

He spotted the towers of the castle beside Loch Badenloch and settled the Norse helmet more firmly on his head, knowing Olaf would scowl if he did not. Over the years, he had determined his own father was too soft. Though the Morgan motto was *With a Strong Hand*, he preferred *Either Peace or War* of the Gunns.

He had oft learned the truth of it. Whenever an outlying clan had a dispute, Olaf took Magnus to squelch them into obedience. He enjoyed a good fight. The day he heard his reputation in the Highlands had earned him the name Magnus the Ruthless, he'd shrugged.

They spurred their horses into a gallop, racing to be first to enter the barbican. Side-by-side over the wooden drawbridge the horses' hooves pounded so loud Magnus couldn't hear his own laughter as he burst ahead into the dirt of the front bailey.

After waves of welcome, the guards atop the battlements turned eager faces toward the ground in front of the stables. He saw why when he and Feradoch slowed their mounts to a walk.

"Have they naught else to do than gawk at a simple fight?"

Magnus cocked his head. Chief Olaf was as oblivious of

their entrance as the men crowded around five men who were fighting. Not amongst themselves, but with a lone opponent. Curious about the uneven bout, they edged their horses closer.

To his surprise, it was no warrior but a woman the men were trying to force to the ground. By the looks of her, she was not just *any* woman. She was tall. Beautiful. And as wild a woman as he had ever seen. Strange-colored hair, neither light nor dark but streaked with both, fell around her face as she crouched. Her hands gripped a rope tied around her neck. Blood splotched large areas of her worn clothing. From the way she moved, it wasn't from her own veins. Men cheered when the warrior holding the end of the rope yanked her off balance.

Muriele fell to her knees in the dirt but sprang upright and kicked out with hard blows to the soft belly of whoever ventured too close. With agility and strength, she kept the louts from finding a knife strapped to her thigh.

Her eyes scanned the area around her, spotting the two men who rode into view. They swept their horses heads to shove men aside until they were on the front line.

One man wore a beautiful silver helmet decorated with gold. When he lifted it off, he revealed hair and eyes as black as a raven framing a face as harsh as granite.

Shivers prickled through her. 'Twas Magnus the Ruthless. The foster son who was harsher than the hated Olaf. She had seen him in action at Blackbriar. The other man was bareheaded. The breeze lifted long pale hair to fly about the face of an angel. 'Twas the true son of Chief Olaf, fostered to the Morgans.

Her opponents laughed with delight when the top of her ragged kirtle slipped off her right shoulder. The breeze on her naked breast shamed her. She ground her teeth together. Her breast would have to stay bare. 'Twould be fatal to drop the rope to cover her flesh.

She was more than tired. The memory of her mother kept hate roaring through her veins, giving her strength. She kicked out at a fat lout's tarse bobbing above his blood stained, hairy ballocks. He went down, clutching his sex and howling like a gutted boar.

"Lucifer's scum! Come near again and I'll cut yer tarse off," she yelled at him.

The black-haired devil rode his horse between her and the men.

"Hold! Have ye men no balls? What sport is fighting a tethered woman, five to one?" Magnus' harsh voice rang out over the noise of the cheering men.

"But she be the witch's lass what lives in the forest," one man called out.

"If yer quibble be with the witch, why dinna ye take it out on her?"

"Did that. Was right good sport. But her blood spilled too easily." He stopped to take a deep breath. "This one be hardier."

Magnus frowned and looked around at the men. "Since ye have already rid yerselves of breeches, I see ye dinna have a hearty set of balls betwixt any of ye. Ye are down to four men now. Drop the tether. 'Tis more sporting."

For one brief moment, he stared into Muriele's eyes. She caught her breath. In his, she saw a flash of puzzlement as he scanned her body.

Magnus pointed his sword at the leader. "Drop the rope else I'll drop it for ye. 'Tis no way for a man to fight."

The moment she felt the rope slacken, she grabbed and yanked it back to her. Magnus backed his horse to where he had been. She snapped the rope, lashing it like a whip. When it hit bare buttocks, the men leaped out of the way. Finally, she opened an area open enough she could reach beneath her skirt. In a heartbeat, she had her knife. At every opportunity, she lashed out at the men then quickly looped the rope over her shoulder.

"Ack!" Whenever a man tried to grab it, Magnus shouted and pointed his small sword.

Muriele nicked more than one man's hand or arm when he drew too close, but she was exhausted. She gasped for air, her breathing ragged. Her arms ached and a stitch in her side caused her to limp. Her feet were raw and bleeding from her long run. She tried to ignore them.

She screamed. Someone had stolen behind her and kicked her behind the knees. She toppled onto her stomach. Strong, beefy hands gripped her wrist and wrenched the knife away.

Cold air spread over her lower limbs as a man threw her skirts up over her head, baring her naked buttocks. Others grabbed her ankles and forced her legs apart.

She shrieked, loud and shrill.

Fury at being a helpless woman sent all fright away.

Chapter 6

MAGNUS FROWNED AS THE men called shouts of encouragement to the swinish louts who had gone too far. 'Twas one thing for a man to claim a woman he captured. But all of them? And by the stirring of his blood, he knew she was not just *any* woman but one who would not easily be broken to a man's hands.

Disgust filled him looking at the filthy man who stepped between her beautiful legs, his cock bobbing and so engorged it wept.

"Get yer pox'd hands off her. Now!"

The men ignored his bellow. When the man knelt and tried to position himself, the flat of Magnus's short sword landed across his hairy buttocks. The lout yelped and fell forward atop the struggling woman.

A filthy hand landed in the dirt beside the woman's face. As fast as a feral cat, her teeth locked around the beefy wrist. The man screamed. Blood smeared aside her mouth where her teeth punctured his skin. Magnus grabbed the man's shoulders and hauled him off her back.

"Open yer mouth, woman!"

Her jaws strained even harder.

Magnus reached beneath her chin. He dug a thumb on one side of her jaw, his fingers on the other and squeezed.

Harder.

Finally, her mouth opened. The man pulled away, cursing and holding his injured wrist.

Magnus narrowed his eyes in a cold stare at the filthy men still trying to hold her legs. They released her and backed away.

With her face pinned to the dirt, he shifted his hand to the base of her skull. He rose and hauled her off the ground as easily as if he lifted a child. Her fists lashed out at the nearest man, who scurried backward, his feet slipping on warm horse shite. He landed with a splat. Chief Olaf barked with laughter.

"Stop fightin', lass, else I'll throw ye atop him."

Magnus' harsh tone tinged with menace would have made a burly man heed his words; only a daft person would dare defy him.

Still, she struggled. Though she was tall for a woman, he topped her by two hands. None too gently, he stalked over to the nearest horse trough. As the crowd opened before him, her dangling feet aimed backward kicks to his shins.

"I said stop!"

His nostrils flared and the muscles in his jaw twitched with suppressed fury. Never had he encountered a woman with such foolish disregard for an order.

He threw the lass into the trough. Water erupted out wetting everyone who hadn't jumped away. Holding tight to her neck, he kept her head submerged until her struggles lessened. He pulled her up, shaking her like a wet dog. She gasped for breath and lashed out again.

He couldn't believe she still dared to defy him! It seemed to amuse Chief Olaf even more. Shame filled Magnus. The woman was making a fool of him.

He gritted his teeth. His temper flamed.

"Do so again, lass, and I'll beat ye!"

One hand on the back of her head, the other at her hips, he shoved her back beneath the water. Her thrashing created even more waves until so much water had sloshed over the sides a muddy puddle covered the ground.

Magnus was as wet as she was. The next time he hauled her up, he stood her on her feet and scowled his disapproval. The bedraggled lass coughed and spluttered then finally caught her breath.

Looking into his wet face for the first time, her eyes widened with fright as if she peered at Lucifer himself.

As soon as Chief Olaf strode over to cuff Magnus' shoulder in pride, everyone quieted. His voice boomed above the noisy yard.

"Well, now. Magnus is the only man who can control the wild witch's get. Not a scratch on him." He chuckled and looked down at Magnus' legs. "Your shins might be a wee bit sore."

"The fools should not have given her such a long lead in the first place," Magnus muttered.

His hand went to her throat. She backed away until her knees bumped against the wooden trough. He narrowed his eyes in warning. If she didn't halt, she would have an even longer dunking. She read him correctly. She stilled, one hand clutched her torn clothing over her breast as water dripped off her hair, down her nose and off her chin. No longer grimy, the soft beauty of her face was startling.

With the wet cloth clinging to her body, she was as willowy as ripe wheat swaying in the summer breeze. True, a little thin around her face. But her shoulders, arms and legs had muscle aplenty.

"She's yours." Olaf said, laughing. "If she gives you more trouble, beat it out of her." He looked around at the seething men she'd made fools of. "None of these weaklings could even plow betwixt her legs."

"Taken." Magnus nodded acceptance of the gift.

He knew if he had refused, Olaf would turn her over to the warriors as a plaything. She was too fine a beauty for such a short life. Once someone took hot water and soap to her, she might serve him well.

Glaring at Olaf, she ignored Magnus' hand on the rope around her neck.

Proudly lifting her chin high, she spoke in a haughty voice.

"I am not yours to give to any man!"

A voice rang out to their right. As a woman stepped around the corner of the stables, her words became stronger with each footfall. 'Twas the spaewife Grunda, the seer of the future and the healer they had brought from Blackbriar. She pointed a gnarled finger at the crowd.

"Ye will rue this day. Lady Ragnhild appeared to me on the rays of the sun. She told me what was done to her. She wails she will have her revenge. If those who foully mistreated her are not punished, she will come amongst ye in the darkest shape of the moon. Yer cocks will fall limp. They will be covered with weeping sores, as useless to a man as fingers without bones."

With eyes opened wide seeing something only *she* could, she threw back her head. As she raised her hands to the heavens, an unseen wind began to whip her clothing about her body while no one else's garments moved. She rocked back and forth as if the great wind blew her off balance.

"If ye bring harm to this lass of her blood, I see what awaits in time to come." She swept her arms wide to include them all. "The two Clans will suffer. Fathers will fight sons. Brothers will fight brothers." Grunda's voice rose to a shriek "All will be split asunder!"

Magnus no more believed in witches than he believed he could jump from atop a mountain tree and fly across the valley below. But the use of one name had immediately caught his attention.

"Ye said Lady Ragnhild? Of Blackbriar?" Magnus hand tightened on the rope around the lass' neck.

"Aye! Her killers will curse the day they laid hands to her!"

Turning to the lass, he took a lock of hair and stretched it out to its entire length. About two-fingers wide from her scalp, the hair was a soft gold-flecked color. The rest of its length was murky brown. Unwashed for many moons from the likes of it, for brown water colored his hand.

He tipped the lass' chin up to stare into eyes shooting shafts of hate at him.

"Ah. This wild lass who fights like a crazed cat is Muriele of Blackbriar."

'Twas not a question but a statement.

Magnus stared down at her, a hard glint in his eyes. "When I conquered Blackbriar Castle, ye were part of the spoils of war that belonged to Clan Gunn. Ye are mine, now. I canna have my new servant trailing a rope behind her as she goes about her duties," he said with an evil chuckle.

The woman hissed like the cat he'd referred to.

"Hold still if ye dinna want yer neck's blood to join the water."

She did as he said. He grasped the rope and studied it. Seeing the crude knot had tightened from her struggles, it was easier to cut through part of it. Likely, it would open easily and fall free. His fingers slipped between the rope and the fine skin of her neck. When his flesh pressed the pulsing vein there, a jolt flashed through him setting his heart racing.

'Twas not an unpleasant feeling. Far from it. More like the excitement of a wild summer storm. He stared down at her to judge if she had felt the same. She had. At first, her almond shaped eyes were near golden. He watched their slow change as sprinkles of gold darkened to amber flecked with brown.

The rope fell free. The back of his hand stroked the length of her silky neck then dropped to his side.

"There is great evil here."

The words floated from Grunda's lips, her voice near a whisper. She studied Feradoch's face then stared into his eyes. She blinked and took a quick, startled breath; her eyes clouded and appeared sightless. She turned toward Magnus.

"As months pass, evil will rule and spread to Clibrick Castle. Ye must right a great wrong."

Magnus shrugged. "Humph! Enough of yer caterwauling, Grunda." Turning to Muriele, his gaze held her prisoner. His voice deepened. "Ye are mine now. Serve me well and I will treat ye the same. But know ye this. If ye dare to leave Kinbrace, I will hunt ye down. Ye will be most sorry for causing me the effort." His eyes turned sinister. "Again."

Muriele's hand went to her throat as she swallowed.

"Grunda, ye have room in yer bothy for the lass?"

"Aye. Enough for another pallet.

"See she washes the filth from her hair and body. After first light, bring her to me. I'll decide on her duties then."

Muriele watched as Grunda studied Magnus. She took her time on his face. She looked deep into his black eyes then stared at the harsh set of his lips. His face tightened under her scrutiny, making him even more forbidding than before.

Unconcerned, the spaewife walked around to view him from all angles. When she again met him face to face, she nodded, satisfied.

Satisfied? Why did her mother's old friend seem pleased by what she saw? He didn't look to have any softness in his entire length. Even men feared him. She sensed they listened to him even over his foster father.

"Old one, if ye are through judging me like a turnip ye plucked from the ground, tend to her. Her feet are raw and cut from her run here." He frowned as he gazed down at Muriele's kirtle then into her eyes.

"Do ye have any other weapons hidden about yer person?"

"Nay."

"Best check, brother, else a blade might seek your ribs."

The beautiful blond man stood behind Sir Magnus' right shoulder. Her gaze flew up to meet his and found naught but a warm, kind light shining from clear blue eyes. He gave her a small, regretful smile, his lips turning up slightly at the corners. He nodded at her then explained.

"I would have no harm come to my brother because he trusted foolishly."

Magnus snorted. His gaze roamed over every inch of her. She followed where he looked. Embarrassed, she saw her nipples thrust against the wet cloth she'd clutched at her breasts. Down further yet, she blushed hotter. Over her belly, the kirtle clung to her skin until it met the springy curls on her woman's place. The lush hair there thrust the light cloth away from her flesh.

Muriele lowered her other hand to shield it.

"Huh. Ye worry for naught, Feradoch. Even the smallest flower petal would be easily seen."

His black gaze swept quickly upward to tangle with hers. Where she steeled herself to see hot need, she found emptiness.

"See she wears proper clothing," he said and nodded to Grunda.

He turned, ignoring her presence as he pointed one finger

at the five bloodstained men who had attacked her.

"Ye dared lay hands on two noblewomen." His face turned grim as he motioned to his man standing nearby.

"Sweyn?"

"Aye, Sir Magnus?"

"Hang them."

Chapter 7

"Tell me of yer mother, child," Grunda ordered as she scrubbed Muriele's long hair. "Last eve, I felt a coldness in the air as the moon began its rise. I suspected 'twas Ragnhild's spirit."

Muriele crouched in the wooden washtub, her knees drawn up under her chin. She swallowed and recounted the horror of finding her mother's body.

"The boy Mother came to aid?" She tilted her head back to look at Grunda and held her opened hands at her forehead to reroute the soapy water away from her eyes. "Did it not go well?"

"Nay. The family was most grateful."

Grunda stood and tapped the back of Muriele's head for her to lower it then emptied a bucket of warmed water over her. "Now ye'd best get out of the water afore yer skin has as many wrinkles as me neck." She laughed with good humor, the sound no more alike the wild cackle in the stable yard as a dove's cry was to an owl's screech.

"The lout ye kicked in the stones lived in the hut beside the boy's family. He knew yer mother was there. The evil scum must have watched the forest roads waiting for her to go back that way."

"I must return to the woods and bury her."

"Huh, lass! Dinna try to leave whilst he's here. He came by the name Ruthless by honoring his vow to track down enemies and end their lives. Should ye flee, he would make ye as sorry as he vowed. Did ye not hear Chief Olaf give ye to him?"

"Aye, but he canna be serious. I am not a common woman to be given to another."

"Child, dinna ye ken? Maybe not amongst civil, gentle people. Even more than what the Chief decided, ye'd best pay heed to Sir Magnus. Ye heard him order his man to hang the louts. Not a person dared say him nay."

Thinking of living behind castle walls as a servant was stifling. Hot fear near closed Muriele's throat. The man had ripped Blackbriar apart like a castle made of twigs. If not for him, her mother and she would still be there. Granted, life would be difficult amongst the ruins, but this Magnus had made sure they could never return.

"... dinna trust such sweetness," Grunda muttered.

"Eh? Forgive me. My mind gathered webs instead of thoughts."

"The Chief's son. The yellow-haired one."

"Aye, I noted him. He looks to be filled with kindness."

"His eyes and face show sweetness and light. Yet when he looks at Magnus, the heat surrounding his form tells of tightly held secrets."

"How can ye tell he has aught to hide?" Muriele stopped drying her hair to study Grunda.

"The struggle to keep his thoughts hidden makes him so tense I can hear the blood pounding through his body. Ye ken? 'Tis a sound like plucking the deepest sounding string of a lyre."

"'Tis because ye see and hear things no one else can."

Muriele sat on a stool close to the small fire, clutching the drying cloth around her. "Why did ye nod when ye walked around Magnus?"

"His face be made of stone. I canna read it. But when I stepped behind him, his body remained calm. Confident."

"Aye, why would he not be? He is a massive warrior."

"All else believe I am an old woman to be feared. Even Olaf blanched when I talked this day."

"I see."

"Magnus has changed much from the boy of seven. These past months, I have talked to the women. His first year at Kinbrace he was like a Peregrine eyas, a young hawk not out of the nest, hiding his fear. Chief Olaf's wife tried to nourish him. Olaf stopped it saying it would make him soft.

"Olaf believed 'twas no way to train his future protector. If Magnus showed any weakness, any kindness, his foster father was swift to beat him. Now he is as Olaf wanted. A hardened raptor. He can slash and tear the life's blood from a man then laugh and drink wine with the chief as if naught had happened."

Someone scratched so lightly on the door as to be furtive. Between the cracks, they saw a tall woman standing close on the other side. The hinges creaked when Grunda opened it to allow her to walk through.

Muriele thought her most unusual in looks. Black hair, long and full with waves and curls, framed a lean face with sun-kissed skin. The woman's high forehead rose above striking black brows, slightly slanted dark eyes with thickly-lashed eyelids. A thin nose and wide, red lips accented her angular jaw.

Deep brown eyes studied first Grunda then Muriele. A hesitant smile flirted with her full lips. She carried a beige smock and brown kirtle draped over her arm.

"I thought this may have belonged to you?" She handed the clothing to Muriele and glanced uneasily at the door. "We are near alike in height. I was told to discard it afore the next sun."

"Thank you. 'Tis most kind to return it to me. I feared I'd have to stay wrapped in a blanket until my kirtle dried enough to mend it."

Grunda stared at Muriele as if she saw something far away then scowled.

"*He* is a fool, Esa."

Esa's gaze darted to Grunda and back, but she ignored the blunt statement as if she had not heard it. She looked hopefully at Muriele.

"Perchance when this fortnight ends, we might talk together?"

The sounds of a male striding past outside made her stiffen and back against the wall. She held her breath until the footsteps passed the hut. When her gaze returned to Muriele, Esa reminded her of a hare lifted into the sky with a raptor's claws piercing its back.

"Aye. 'Twould be most agreeable." Muriele felt drawn to the woman who seemed in dire need of kindness.

Her words barely faded before the girl glanced though one of the door cracks then opened it to slip silently out and disappear in the shadows.

"How strange. Why was she so afeared of someone seeing her here?" Muriele rubbed her hand over the familiar clothing, remembering the smooth feel of it. 'Twould be comforting to again wear something soft and finely made.

"She lives in a small room in the keep's north tower. Away from the others." Grunda shook her head. "I believe 'tis the golden angel she fears, though I have never seen him with her. 'Tis whispered most of the year she is happy and outgoing. When he arrives, 'tis not long before they dinna see her at all. The first few days after he leaves, she wears clothing which covers her skin from neck to toe."

"Perchance it is the Ruthless one who mistreats her?"

"I thought the same. But never has anyone seen Magnus near the north tower. During last year's visit, the blacksmith's daughter returned through the postern gate late of a night. Hearing the tower door ease open, she ducked behind a tree. Moonlight glinted off a man's pale hair."

"Could it not have been one of the men here? Many look like their Danish sires from long ago?"

"Nay. Only *he* strides with such arrogance. Any other would walk calmly away."

Grunda banked the peat fire and they moved to sit at the small wooden table to drink cups of hot broth.

"We must rise afore the sun if ye are to receive yer new duties. The master will go with the early patrol at first light to show all the villagers his sons are here."

They unrolled the two pallets and placed them close to the cook fire for warmth. Though it was summer, the Highlands were never warm of a night. Exhausted, they rolled tightly in their blankets and slept.

Olaf lounged back in his seat at the high table with Magnus and Feradoch, the two young men he had forged together to protect Clan Gunn for the next generation. Everything had gone as he planned. Since the blood oath, the Gunns had prospered, adding more and more of their neighbors' lands to their own.

It was quite canny of him to have arranged for the powerful Morgans to be at his beck and call whenever he felt the need for extra warriors. Of course, the casualties of war were mostly from the Morgan ranks for he placed them in the most dangerous positions.

Olaf always reported to Magnus' father Angus that as many or more of the Gunn warriors were lost in battle. To make sure the Morgan chief never learned the deceit, he had those 'lost' men stay hidden until after the Morgan warriors returned to Clibrick.

Never did he let Magnus know of his deception.

Now, he watched and studied the men drinking with him. Feradoch did not fool him with his golden smile or his praise of all Olaf did. When Feradoch gazed at Magnus, deep in his son's cold, blue eyes, Olaf saw his soul.

It worried him.

This son of his loins had not grown into the man he had hoped he would be. 'Twas Angus' fault for not beating him regularly.

As Chief of the Gunns, he was proud of Feradoch. As a man and father, he knew better than to trust him at his back.

Magnus, on the other hand, was so alike himself he near forgot he was not of his own blood. After those first years, the boy had stopped thinking like a Morgan and became a Gunn. He learned early that Gunn justice was all that mattered. There was one way to judge all things. 'Twas either white or black. If it benefited his foster family, then it was good. If it did not, he dealt swiftly with it and had no regrets.

Olaf knew Magnus would be forever loyal.

The Morgans should be afeared.

Feradoch would not heed his oath.

"How fares your family, Magnus? You have not told me of

Graemme. Has he reached your height?" Olaf said with a sly glance at his son. "Feradoch tells me he is much like a lass in his ways?"

"He not only has the height but the muscles, too. Hm. A lass?" Magnus narrowed his dark gaze to stare at Feradoch, who returned the look with an innocent expression. "In what way do ye think my brother womanly?"

"He spends much time with the women of the keep, laughing and coaxing them." Feradoch's lip twisted in a sneer.

"Aye. He spends time with bonnie lasses, to be sure. 'Tis his nature to find laughter with them. Huh! I found their eyes followed him whenever he was in sight. They seem to particularly admire his arse." He shifted in his seat to study his blood brother's face.

"He is never at ease around me. I have offered to share women, but he never agreed." Feradoch squared his shoulders. "I believe he fears his cock a wee hapless thing when likened to mine."

"If he said nay to sharing, 'twas because he prefers his bed sport with one lass at a time." Magnus's throaty laugh filled the room. "Graemme has no need to be ashamed of his cock. I can tell ye with all truth, he has a mighty weapon. I came upon him unawares one day. The lass was happy, to be sure."

"No lass needs happiness to be good at swiving. All I require is an obedient one who keeps her legs wide and her mouth shut — except when I fill it." He made an obscene gesture with his middle finger tapping and sliding between his lips and deep into his mouth.

Magnus did not care for talk about bed sport. What he did with a bonnie woman was his own concern, not something to brag about in the company of men. At first, he'd had trouble coaxing women to his pallet. They were afeared. Over the years, his reputation as a considerate lover had provided him ample partners.

"I placed the woman Muriele with Grunda. In such a short time, she has become as wild as the forest creatures she lived amongst. Until I find out what womanly skills she has, I have not yet decided how she will serve me."

Feradoch glared at his father. "Ye should have given the woman to me. 'Tis my right as natural son. The captured noblewoman should be mine to do with as I see fit."

"Huh! Ye didna capture the castle and all within, did ye?"

"Nay. But had I been here, I would have."

"Lady Muriele belongs to Magnus. He can keep her or kill her. Matters not to me."

Feradoch shrugged and turned to his foster brother. "You provided us with fine sport when you ordered the men hung. They twitched and turned, legs lifting and kicking the air like they did a heated sword dance."

"Though ye may find amusement in it, 'tis never to my liking to watch a man die."

"They well-deserved it for not bringing the women to me." Yawning, Olaf stood and stretched then scratched his naked groin beneath his kilt. "We go early to inspect Badenloch's waters."

"The villagers are still plagued with thieves?" Magnus frowned.

"We've had tales aplenty about them along the loch's shores. We need workers for the crops of they're strong. It should not be too hard to capture the louts. If they dinna want work, we'll leave their bodies to fatten the boars in the forest."

Muriele spent a sorrowful night. Way afore first light, she rose from the pallet and put on the beige smock and dark brown kirtle. She brushed out her long hair and braided it from her temples until it met in the back then tied a leather strip to the ends to keep it out of the way.

During her sleepless night, she could think only of her mother's unprotected body in the woods. She gritted her teeth knowing she had to delay tending to her burial until after meeting Magnus and doing whatever he required of her. Since Grunda had been her mother's sole friend, surely she would agree to help her. They would return to the castle before the patrol did.

Magnus could find no fault in that.

Could he?

She stoked the fire, found a cloth bag of oats and had porridge simmering when Grunda stirred. A sad smile twisted the old woman's face when she opened her eyes.

"Deep circles beneath yer eyes deny ye had a restful slumber, eh, lass?"

"Aye. But I had enough."

Muriele busied herself rolling her pallet and tucking it into the corner where she'd seen Grunda retrieve it. The hut's ceiling was higher than most, enough for bundles of dry herbs tied with cord to hang from the roof-beams and under the eaves to dry. At the far end of the room, crude shelves covered the wall holding earthenware pots, jars and flagons of all sizes sealed with wax or cloths dipped in wax and tied with strips of leather.

"Have ye done all this since coming here?"

"Most. They took me from Blackbriar because their healer had died o'er a year ago." She shrugged her shoulders and shook her head.

"How could they wait so long for a healer?"

"They noted little difference. Their old one knew stitching and festering wounds, but naught of common ailments so many die of."

Muriele walked beneath the drying herbs, pinching a leaf here and there, smelling and identifying it.

"'Tis peaceful here alongside the gardens. I grow most of what I need. All else is in the nearby woods. Yer mother supplied me with herbs and medicines found along the shores of streams, those growing amongst wet roots or such herbs like Mandrake. The Chief does not want it readily at hand." She shrugged. "He fears anything which can be used to poison him."

Muriele raised her brows. She had not thought Chief Olaf would be afeared of anyone poisoning him. Who would be so bold?

After they broke their fast, Grunda walked with her to the keep and left her at the entrance. 'Twas the first time Muriele had been inside Kinbrace's great hall. She didn't like the size of it with so many people in one space. It appeared cramped alongside the great hall at Blackbriar.

"What kept ye so late, lass?"

The resonant voice split the air like unexpected summer lightning, startled her. Magnus strode from the high table, looking ready to ride out. His squire hurried behind him, carrying his helmet.

"A servant has already freshened my bed. This day, ye will tend to all atop my clothing chest. See ye mend and wash it. Have it ready for the next morrow."

His eyes looked as black as his wavy hair falling loose to brush his shoulders. Padded leather looked to be beneath his chain mail. Atop the mail was leather shoulder padding attached by straps to a thick leather vest. His short sword hung low at his hip.

"I thought to ask ..." She got no further. He had already turned away and was halfway to the keep's heavy doors. His squire sprinted ahead and tugged the doors wide for his master to stride through.

'Twas just as well he'd left before she could finish asking for help burying her mother. She and Grunda would be enough.

By the time a servant directed her to Magnus' bedchamber, she heard the screech of the drawbridge lowering and looked out his window. Below stood a most impressive sight.

Chief Olaf led the warriors, with Magnus and Feradoch on either side. All three men had claymores strapped to their backs.

The sun rose and flashed on Magnus' shiny helmet, sending shards of bright light. She raised her hand to shield her eyes. Magnus stiffened and slowly turned to peer up at her. Though she couldn't see his eyes beside the nosepiece, she felt their hard stare.

In that brief look, she remembered his resonant voice of yester eve warning her.

If ye dare to leave Kinbrace, I will hunt ye down.

Since she intended to return afore he did, Sir Magnus would never know she had disobeyed him.

CHAPTER 8

'TWAS FORTUNATE MURIELE HAD learned to wash clothing these past months, else she would have had to rely on watching the other women. Dried mud covered a pair of breeches. She frowned, for they appeared to be the pair he'd worn the day before. She did not recall Sir Magnus kneeling in the mud.

She tackled his dark brown tunic first. The men must have had skirmishes on their trip from Clibrick to Kinbrace, for blood aplenty had dried into the linen.

As soon as she put his garments to soak in the large tub of soapy water, it turned the suds a dirty pink. She stirred the clothing with a heavy stick then used it to lift them out.

After tossing out the water and refilling the tub, she rinsed and laid all but the tunic out to dry. Kneeling beside the stream, she beat the cloth against smooth rocks until her knuckles were red and sore. Finally, she nodded her head, satisfied to see the last hints of blood fade away as cold water rushed over the rocks.

Had it been merely blood on the cloth, she would have thought it belonged to some hapless lout so foolish as to interfere in his journey to Kinbrace. But the stains spread out from a rent in the garment. Only a sword could cause such a sharp rip.

She stood, holding the dripping tunic up high to where it would have reached Magnus' shoulders and studied the tear. Aye. If she judged his body aright, the wound would be on his right thigh.

From the unflinching way Magnus walked, he didn't seem to bear any unhealed injuries.

Remembering yester noon, her eyes widened. When he had

hoisted her by the nape of her neck, she had kicked backward with her feet to strike his legs. Thankfully, her height kept her blows to his shinbones. If she'd kicked a healing wound and angered him further, he'd have kept her head below the water until her last breath.

Once she twisted the last drop of water from the cloth, she spread the tunic over a coarse-limbed bush to catch the sun and anxiously attended to the rest of his clothing. A thin white shirt needed reinforcing on the holes through which cords pulled the material together over his chest.

The sun was getting well into the noon hours. Anxious to finish with the chores he had set her, she decided the tunic was dry enough for her to get on with its mending. When she finally placed the last stitches in the dark brown fabric, she hung it over her left shoulder and gathered each piece of clothing she had washed and dried. Once she'd folded them, she hurried back to the keep.

From the looks of his large clothing chest, he must have clothes aplenty. She placed the stack of clean garments atop the chest and spread the tunic on the bed to let any lingering dampness dry.

"His chores kept me overlong, Grunda. We must hurry if we are to return before the men." Muriele spread soothing salve on the soles of her feet then wrapped them in strips of cloth. She laced her shoes tight to hold the bindings firm.

"I dinna think it wise, lass, but I know ye won't change yer mind. Ye will go alone if I dinna come with ye." Grunda clucked her tongue, her eyes clouded with worry.

"I can't wait any longer. The thought brings sourness in my belly to flood my mouth. Mother must have a proper burial."

She slung the sack holding the shovel and spade Grunda used in her work with the herbal garden over her left shoulder. She hadn't time to eat but gulped down water she'd poured from the pitcher beside the window.

While she swallowed, Grunda hurried to the door. "I'll go first. If we leave through the postern gate, it's possible no one will note us."

Grunda slipped out the door and skirted around the garden's edges, taking advantage to hide behind each tree she came across. Muriele followed.

Soon, they pulled away vines growing over the latch on the gate. It took both their efforts to force the old wooden gate open and drag it closed behind them. She prayed when they returned they'd be able to open it again.

Once they reached the forest path, they lengthened their strides and moved quickly. When Grunda began to breathe heavily, Muriele felt ashamed and stopped.

"Dinna cause yerself an injury. I will run ahead to where she lies. When I hear ye coming close on the path, I'll call out."

She waited to assure herself the old woman was all right then wrapped her arm around the bag of tools. If she kept them from flapping against her side, she could run in a steady lope. Each footfall was painful, but she closed her mind to it and ran ahead.

Reaching the tramped down brush alongside the road, her heart pounded with dread knowing her mother's ravaged body lay beyond. Saying a quick prayer that she'd be strong at the sight, she took a deep breath as she burst out into the clearing.

A scream ripped from her throat.

Olaf wiped his brow and pulled back in the shade, letting his foster-son take the lead. Magnus patted Odin's neck, easing not only the horse's tension but his own. He always enjoyed a good fight. He could not judge today's as one of them. It did not take long for the Kinbrace men to subdue the raiders. But some louts were more cowardly than others. Three such men stood together, the one in the center slightly ahead like a spear. Each man clutched a villager's child against their chest to escape the two-bladed axes he and Feradoch wielded.

He edged forward as he fingered his weapon's long handle. His mouth tightened. Noting Feradoch's black Thor stamped and snorted, ready to burst forward, he motioned his foster brother to hold back. He stared at the first lout backing away. His left arm clutched a young boy's waist so tightly his frightened face turned red.

"Put the lad down."

He led Odin a step closer. The man snarled and tightened his hold even more as he took another backward step.

"I willna tell ye again."

He was bone tired. Heat from his helmet near made his head steam. His lids narrowed as he decided. The young boy was a brave lad, trying hard not to cry. He stared at him until their gazes met.

"Lad. Obey."

The boy gave the slightest nod.

"Bend at the waist. Now!"

Magnus' bellowed command demanded obedience. Quickly, the boy did as Magnus told him and folded over the louts arm — just in time.

Whoosh!

The speed of the two-bladed axe as it sliced the air created a breeze.

Blood spurted. The man's face froze in shocked surprise less than a heartbeat before his head flew through the air to bounce along the hard ground in front of the hut.

At first, the dying man's arm convulsed then slacked. As hot blood showered over him, the boy's shrieks sent birds from the trees into flight. Screaming, he broke free and ran. Unthinking in his need to put distance between himself and the twitching body, he near overtook the rolling head until an old woman blocked his path and caught him up in a tight embrace.

The other louts took but one look at Magnus and Feradoch's faces and read their fate. They dropped their human shields, turned and made a mad dash for the woods beside the huts.

The thunder of Odin and Thor's hooves, along with Feradoch's wild laugh were the last sounds they heard.

Olaf left with several men to return to the castle, but Magnus did not leave the village until he talked to the men and women and learned what they needed. He found the old woman who had helped the young boy. She guessed his age as near twelve years old but said he was smaller than most because he had little enough food. He had been a newborn when dropped off at the village in the dead of night, wrapped in a cloth still wet from the birthing.

The woman who took him in named him Gille. She had died of a fever this past winter. Since then, the other families fed him what they could, without starving their own bairns. Magnus thanked her for her kindness and gave her a coin.

He promised the villagers wagons of thatch to repair their roofs, a dozen chickens and a cow to replace the one killed by a wayward axe. It did not take long to see things set to rights.

Still, he would not leave. One last duty remained. 'Twas a deed that always caused Feradoch to shake his head with disgust and call him a weakling for it. Magnus and his men helped the villagers bury their dead, though Feradoch fumed at the duty.

Magnus never left a battle with slain men above the ground who had fought honorably. He had no such qualms about cowards. For them, he had the men haul their bodies with ropes tied to their ankles deep into the woods.

Soon after the noon hour, they left the village. The boy Gille sat on Odin's haunches, his thin arms clutching Magnus around the waist.

Frightened by Muriele's anguished screams, forest creatures scurried away. Frantic, she ran around the clearing looking for signs of her mother's body. Loud sobs tore at her throat. Had wild animals already feasted on her loved one? Would she find bones and pieces of her scattered around the forest? She fell to her knees and rocked back and forth, keening. Time had denied her this last act of kindness for a well-loved mother who had given her the best of care.

Grunda, gasping and stumbling, crashed through the brush and stopped. Her gaze scanned the area looking for the cause of such dire keening. Nothing threatened Muriele. Puzzled, she knelt beside her and stroked the young woman's hair.

"What is it? Has some strange creature threatened ye?"

Never before had Muriele cried where anyone could see her weakness. She had been stoic these past days, holding back her grief until she was alone. Shaking her head, she put a hand to her mouth and choked back a sob.

"Nay. Mother's body. It's gone!"

"Ye are sure this is the right spot?"

"Aye." She pointed to a flattened area ten paces ahead. The disturbed ground and darkened stains on the crushed grass and leaves proved the louts had murdered her there.

After Grunda walked around the whole clearing and searched beyond, she came back, shaking her head.

"No signs of animals. Only horses and men have been here. But they could be from when the patrol found ye."

"Aye." Muriele whimpered and gazed up at her with grief-stricken eyes. "What can I do?"

"Naught, child." Grunda held out her hand and urged Muriele to her feet. "Come. Let us go to the bothy. Ye will want Ragnhild's things about ye."

Muriele nodded. She would collect her mother's comb and brush, and the pewter clasp that swept her mother's hair back from the sides of her face. After they fled Blackbriar, Ragnhild had hidden two rings and a silver chain in a small box in the ground beneath where she slept. Ragnhild's wedding ring from Lord Colban was a silver band with twisted gold around the rims and two gold trinity knots with a blood-red stone between them. He'd said it symbolized his heart.

The second ring was Lord Colban's given to him by King David when he made him Baron of Blackbriar. 'Twas heavy gold carved with Celtic designs and set with a large bloodstone from Iona.

Once Lord Baldor arrived at Blackbriar, her mother had hidden the rings.

Her only other treasure was the soap her mother made because Muriele favored the scent of apple blossoms. On the first sunrise of May, her mother had worked her spells beneath the wild apple tree. It was in full bloom, its scent sweetening the air. When Ragnhild made the soap, she'd added a hint of spice-scented oil to the blossoms to add mystery to the scent.

When they reached the hut, Muriele calmed her breathing before she entered the familiar room. Built much like Grunda's hut, they had used it mostly for sleep and the making of potions. She moved aside the pallets and taking a small garden trowel, quickly unearthed the box. With tears streaming down her cheeks, she secured the chain and rings around her neck. The feel of them between her breasts made her feel her mother and father were watching over her.

Time passed quickly as they collected those medicinal things that lost their potency if left too long. They would take them back to Kinbrace with them.

Muriele tied her belongings into a small bundle, her treasures safely locked in the center. She and Grunda would carry the bundles slung around their shoulders and backs. 'Twas only when they heard the soft huff of horses and the creak of leather they realized the day had sped faster than they had reckoned.

Muriele grabbed her spare bow and quiver of arrows she always kept beside the door. She nocked an arrow, ready to speed it through some churl's throat. Had she not moved back several paces, the door would have swept her to the floor when it crashed open.

Magus was furious. Nary a man at Kinbrace dared to disregard his orders. Yet a mere slip of a girl defied him the moment he turned his back!

Nay, he corrected himself as he glared down the length of the arrow aimed at his throat. She was not a mere slip at all, but sleek and long-legged. Her rigid body spoke of tension ready to explode. Curly, wheat-colored hair fell wild around her face.

Puffy and rimmed with red, her almond shaped eyes stared back into his. He watched their near-golden flecks darken to deep amber, spitting fire at him. Muriele looked like a cornered animal ready to kill.

Humph! He spied the bundles beside the door. Whatever she'd cried about before was as nothing compared to the reason she'd soon have. She belonged to him

His lips quivered with the snarl rumbling up from his chest. He had expected her to drop the bow when she saw who faced her. She didn't. She stood, resolute. With full lips pressed together, the muscles in her shoulders and arms taut, Muriele was a picture of stubborn determination. Magnus' eyes narrowed further at this display of strong will.

"Ye disobeyed me." His words seemed to bounce against the walls of the small room.

"In what way?" She widened her stance, balancing herself firmer.

Her throaty, sensual voice stirred something in his gut. He snorted at her reply.

"Ye fled Kinbrace after I warned ye I wouldna allow it."

The arrow quivered a trifle. She started to shake her head then thought better of it while she was trying to keep her eyes on her target.

"She wasna fleeing Kinbrace," Grunda said as she walked over to stand beside Muriele.

"Pfft. Her bundles are beside the door."

"'Tis to take back to the castle. Potions and salves will spoil without looking after them. Some personal items and such, is all."

"She could have asked for them to be brought to her."

"She had a more personal matter to attend." Grunda stopped and looked at Muriele, giving her a chance to speak.

"I came to bury my mother." Muriele spoke slowly, the words forced through her stiff jaw. "I couldn't leave her for forest creatures and animals to ... to devour." She halted and swallowed. "I came too late."

To his surprise, silent tears trailed a path down her high

cheekbones. She blinked them away, appearing shamed, and clamped her teeth tight seeking composure.

His anger eased, though he still planned to punish her for disobeying him. If he did not, she would believe him weak. She was a woman who would defy him at every chance.

"Ye should have sought my permission."

"I tried this morn. Ye didna let me."

"Put the bow down."

Magnus waited. Though Muriele looked undecided, she didn't obey. She shook her head, the movement so slow he almost didn't see it. He took a deep breath to cool his temper. And lost.

His bellow near scattered thatch off the roof.

"Put the bow down!"

Chapter 9

M AGNUS' RIGHT HAND WHIPPED out. Steely fingers clamped around hers on the bow, locking the arrow there. His teeth clamped so tightly together the muscles in his jaw jerked. Staring into her defiant eyes, he pried her hand from the weapon. His first instinct was to break the bow over his knee. He thought better of it and tossed it to the ground.

"Come!"

Instead, Muriele backed away. He grabbed her by the scruff of her neck and forced her ahead of him. She flailed her arms around trying to break his hold. When she attempted to pry his hand from the base of her skull, she may as well have tried to move fingers forged to her skin.

Magnus snorted. Unlike the day before, he left her feet on the ground to do their own walking. It seemed the only way this woman obeyed an order was to grip her neck and force her. He ignored his men on horseback as he propelled her around the left side of the bothy.

"Did ye think to look in yer own surroundings?"

He led her thirty paces through the trees until they came to the apple tree growing wild and lonely. On the ground beneath stood an oblong mound heavily covered with stones and rocks to discourage animals from digging.

Muriele let out a lonely cry then burst from his hand to fall on her knees beside the cairn. She leaned over to pat the stones then spoke rapidly in the language of her Celtic ancestors, saying prayers for her mother's soul.

Grunda knelt opposite her, echoing her words in a soft, strong voice. At the end of their prayers, Grunda spoke.

"Bend yer head for me, lass."

Muriele did.

Grunda pulled a small knife from a sheath in her worn kirtle. The maker had made the hilt from a rowan tree and carved into the wood the Pictish Double Disc symbolizing the two worlds, the here-and-now and the 'otherworld.' The knife cut the cord of life leading from mother to child after birthing. Magnus strong hand gripped her wrist before she could move.

"Dinna fear. I would cut a lock of Muriele's hair to leave with her mother."

Magnus eased his hand away but remained watchful. Grunda took seven long hairs from the curls falling down Muriele's back and followed them up to her scalp. She covered all but the very tip of the blade before cutting the hairs close to the skin. Asking Muriele to hold them at the top end, she carefully braided them together.

Once Grunda finished, she searched for a long, thin stone and wrapped the hair twice around before knotting it tight. Chanting as she did so, she stood and held the stone high, facing north, east, south and west then back to north.

She fell to her knees at the head of the cairn and began moving stones until she reached the dirt below. With great care, she scratched out a shallow basin, then put the rock in it and covered it with grass, leaves and dirt. When she replaced all the stones atop it, she stood, satisfied.

"No matter where ye be Muriele, yer mother will always know where to follow and protect ye."

Muriele nodded, gave the stones one last pat and stood.

"How did ye know someone had buried her here?" She asked Magnus in a hoarse voice.

A bark of laughter split the air, and for the first time Muriele must have realized he had not come alone. Feradoch stood, his shoulders propped against a tree, grinning at her. His face looked as pure as a newborn bairn despite having as much blood splattered over his clothing as was on Magnus.

"Ye did this kindness?" she asked.

"Me? Nay. A dead body doesna know or care what happens

to it. He pushed away from the tree and straightened. "'Tis a dafty compulsion of your master. *He* canna leave a body aboveground. He and Sweyn saw to it last eve whilst we grown men were swiving."

"Enough, Feradoch. I grow tired of yer yattering."

Feradoch's eyes heated. He'd been subtly prickling Magnus since he had gone to Clibrick Castle for his fortnight there. Magnus didn't know what the cause was. Could he be testing his loyalty to see if he could provoke a fight between them?

Yestereve, he had studied Feradoch's face when Olaf asked his son if he hadn't had manly training at Clibrick. When Feradoch asked why, Olaf grumbled Feradoch's body was not as muscled as Magnus'.

Feradoch's pale blue eyes had turned murky gray.

Magnus stepped back from the women.

"Come. We leave now."

He waited to see if the woman obeyed.

Muriele looked one last time at the cairn then turned back to the bothy. She made haste to keep up with his long strides through the woods to the hut. She didn't want to give him an excuse to grab her neck again.

'Twas a strange thing. When he had forced her to the horse trough the day afore, he had hoisted her in the air like she weighed no more than a fowl about to be axed. A small quiver went through her. Today, his strong fingers on her neck had not felt cruel. She knew he could have tightened them enough to break the bones there if he chose. His hand had been firm to make sure she went where he led, but not so harsh they bruised her flesh.

When they came back to the hut, he pointed to two men and ordered, "Take the bundles beside the door and tie them to yer saddles." He waited until they did as he asked before he pulled the door tightly closed.

He nodded to his commander, "Sweyn, Grunda will ride

behind ye."

Taking Grunda's waist, he hoisted her up to sit behind the man. She settled herself and grasped Sweyn's waist, avoiding his weapon's belt. Magnus nodded satisfied the old woman would be secure.

He looked at Muriele and debated on tossing her up behind Feradoch's squire but saw the lust shining from his eyes when he looked at the lass. He could take her up behind himself. If he did, he wouldn't be able to wield his weapons if someone attacked them. Before he could speak, Feradoch did.

"Give the lass to me. I will keep her safe if any brigands be in the area." His blue eyes held no expression, nor did his face.

"Come, girl. We have tarried long enough."

Magnus wrapped his hands around her waist. For truth, she was slender, for his fingertips near met each other. It took no great effort to lift her to sit behind Feradoch. The horse, Thor, sidled, near upsetting her until she grabbed Feradoch around the middle. Feradoch smiled and took her hands, pulling her closer. A flash of heat from his eyes told Magnus he relished her breasts against his back.

He regretted giving his blood brother that pleasure instead of himself.

Muriele held tight, for the horse pranced and stomped and seemed to dislike carrying the extra burden. Feradoch didn't seem to mind and let the beast have his way. Once Magnus started ahead, the rest fell in line behind him. Though they traveled fast, the gait evened out and she felt more secure.

Now she wasn't afeared of falling, she tried to pull away so she didn't fit against him like a second surcoat. He didn't let her. One hand moved to clamp over hers, keeping her in her place.

It was not unpleasant feeling the muscles playing across his back. Far from it. Her breasts hardened and she wondered what his hot, bare flesh against hers would feel like. She brought herself back to reality when she realized his hand moved hers lower against his stomach. The blood on the surcoat was still wet. Sticky.

Repulsed by the feel of it, she began to note the odor as well. The mingled smell of blood and sweat sickened her. She turned her head, lifting her face as far away from him as she could, welcoming the fresh pine scent of the forest. He felt her movement.

"Ye best get used to the stench of blood around Magnus. Did ye know he can lop the head off a man with one swift stroke and yet on the return swing chop off another's?" Feradoch laughed when she startled in surprise. "Aye. His double-headed axe is as a second arm to him. And ye must have seen the fighting flail he used to defeat your stepfather."

"And what is yer favorite weapon?"

"My claymore when not fighting ruffians. With rabble, I favor the hooked spear."

To her eyes, she deemed Feradoch's clothing and horse more blood-soaked than Magnus'. She had not realized the broadsword was bloodier than the axe.

When they rode into the front bailey of the castle, Magnus began barking orders.

"Collect yer clothing. Be quick about it."

Muriele startled and looked up at him. His voice seemed filled with ire, and with the look he gave her, he blamed her for his temper.

Instead of swinging her to the ground, Feradoch was up and off the horse in one easy movement. He stood with arms outstretched. His hands brushed against her breast when he caught her beneath her arms and plucked her off Thor's back.

Holding her close, he lowered her slowly against his body. Her breath caught at the lust in his eyes. She could not mistake the long hard shaft pressing into her belly before her feet touched the ground. Trying to put distance between them, she pushed at his chest.

"Feradoch."

The sound at her back was just above a whisper.

Feradoch grinned and winked at her. What ailed him? Did

he not hear the menace in Magnus' cold voice? 'Twas far more than if he'd bellowed the name.

"Get what clothes ye need, lass, and bring them to my bedchamber."

His black gaze swept over her, causing her to edge away.

"I wish to bide with Grunda."

"I dinna wish it. I canna trust ye when my back is turned." Magnus' eyes slanted at Feradoch, letting him know he realized what he'd been doing. "Ye will be within my sight until ye learn to obey."

"I wasna running away."

Hands on her hips, Muriele frowned and backed away. She didn't want to share his room. He was a man. Her mother had warned her, men didn't have a woman in their room unless it was to keep them handy for bed sport. She'd no sooner allow him to force her than yestereve's louts.

"Dinna argue. Ye thought to disobey me without any consequence. By rights, I should thrash ye for it. When ye prove I can trust ye, I will allow yer return to Grunda. Collect yer clothing and be there, else Sweyn will do it for ye."

Magnus waited until he saw the men hand down their bundles to the two women then motioned the warriors to the stables. He wheeled Odin, giving her no more chance to argue. If she had, he'd be sorely tempted to treat her roughly.

When they arrived at the stables, Gille came to wait beside him as he dismounted. Hesitantly, the boy looked at the great white horse and held out his hand to take the reins, eyes wide with fear. Magnus was pleased the lad wanted to prove his worth, but there were duties other than handling the big gelding.

"Brian will take the horse, lad." He turned to his squire. "Have him help ye with washing down Odin so the horse will get to know him." He looked at the boy and noted how dirty he was. How long had it been since he'd had a good washing? "Do both horse and lad at the same time. I canna tell the color of his hair. Find him clean clothing, too."

"Aye, I will, my lord. I can place a pallet beside my own in the warrior's tower, if it be your wish."

"It is. The lad has courage. I'd like to see if we could turn him into a warrior over time. Ye can start with teaching him to clean armor and weapons."

He hoped Brian could do for Gille what Sweyn had done for him.

Since the day he fostered with Olaf, Sweyn had honed Magnus' skills at the practice field. When Magnus turned twenty, he named the red-haired giant his first in command. Sweyn had proved himself a staunch companion, someone he could trust at his back in the fiercest battles. He also stitched wounds. Though he'd had plenty of practice over the years, every scar stood out from Magnus' skin as if he'd left his mark there.

Brian tied Odin's reins to a loop attached to the wall, then turned to help Magnus remove his stained armor and outer clothing.

Once done, Magnus nodded and strolled across the grassy area between the stables and the outer bailey. His body felt free. 'Twas a relief to be rid of armor and leather which sometimes felt like an unwieldy body clinging to his flesh. One that was heavy and stifling.

"Have hot water sent to my bedchamber," Magnus ordered the first servant to cross his path while climbing the stairs to the front door of the keep. By the way she scuttled away, you'd think she had seen a beast.

He reached up to shove away a hank of hair pestering his eyes and saw his stain-covered hands and arms. He turned his palms up then over and shrugged. He couldn't blame her. He looked like he'd bathed in blood.

He scowled. When he'd first returned from subduing the raiders, he had noted his clean tunic spread across the bed. He'd hooked a finger under its hem and lifted it to the light to see if she'd repaired the sword's damage. The gash had made him bleed like a gutted hare but he'd seen no reason to have it tended. Sweyn's stitches left puckered scars, for they hadn't easily healed. He'd mend faster without them.

He'd noted Muriele's stitches and nodded with approval. Never had he seen such precise mending. Hmm. From now on, he'd have her stitch his flesh. When he'd sent a servant to order her to attend him, he found she'd fled.

Suddenly, the stench of blood and sweat caused his nose to wrinkle and his lip to curl. 'Twas overpowering. He jerked open the keep's heavy doors and strode into the great room.

Olaf, sitting beside the fireplace in a massive armed chair, looked up and waved a horn of ale at him.

"Ah, come sit and tell me of the fun. You hardly began when you found out the girl was gone. Did you hunt her down? Such a tasty bit. 'Twould be a shame to miss swiving such a lush piece of flesh."

"The hunt didn't take us far. She'd gone to bury her mother."

"Eh? Did you beat her?"

"Nay."

"Why not? Feradoch tells me you wasted your time last eve depriving the forest creatures of food. 'Twould have been better to throw her body off a cliff so it wouldn't be offensive. Then you had to go chasing after the daughter."

Magnus sighed. "Beating draws blood. I dinna want a bleeding woman in my bed. I wish to rid myself of the smell not create more of it. I'll sit with ye later."

He raised his hand and brushed it through the air as if ridding it of the questions. He heard the Chief chuckle as he took the stairs two at a time to the upper floor.

When he slammed open the door to his bedchamber, he didn't see Muriele within as he expected. Seething with anger because she had disobeyed him, he turned and near knocked her off her feet. How had she come up behind him so quietly?

"Where have ye been?"

"I came as soon as I collected clean clothing."

He noticed she carried a small bundle close to her chest. He nodded, his temper cooling.

"Get me a clean tunic. A bath will be here soon."

Muriele nodded and went to retrieve the tunic she'd

washed earlier.

"Ye will tend my clothes each day. Go through the chest to see if any need mending."

"Yes, my lord." Without looking at him, she folded the tunic over the chair beside the fireplace.

She seemed tense. Was she afeared he'd beat her? Servants arriving with buckets of hot water distracted him. He pointed to a spot in front of the fireplace where they placed the tub. Squatting before the banked fire, he added kindling and squares of peat to bring it to life. Once it was blazing, he noticed the servants pouring the water as slowly as they could, one eye on the girl as she bent to place a drying cloth and a pot of soap on a stool.

Did she stir lust in everyone who set eyes on her? It pricked his ire.

"Get on with it," he snapped. "Afore ye empty those buckets, the water will be cold."

His ill temper soon had them splashing water into the tub and hurrying from the room. Ignoring her, he sat on the bed and jerked off his boots. Standing, he bent and grabbed the end of his shirt and pulled it over his head then tossed it to the floor. The filthy thing stank as it swept against his face.

Unlacing his breeches, he hooked his thumbs in his waist-line. After pulling them over his hips, he stopped to untie a bloodied cloth from around his right thigh then bent to tug his breeches off his feet.

A strangled cough sounded behind him. He frowned and looked over his shoulder at Muriele. The creamy skin on her face had turned a mottled red.

"What ails ye girl? Are ye ill?"

Muriele couldn't speak but shook her head. She knew what made a man's body different from a woman's. Growing up at Blackbriar, she'd seen couples tupping in the keep's alcoves, behind the stable and any other place providing scant privacy.

What she'd not learned from her own observations, the other young girls at the castle filled in the gaps. Men seemed to have many names for the things dangling between their legs. Though there were three, they called the two which were alike anything from stones, to ballocks to balls. She had told her mother ballocks sounded more likely for large beasts such as bulls, but not a man. Stones sounded uneven. How many stones did ye see side-by-side that were the same in size and weight? Aye, she'd thought balls the proper name for the smaller ballocks belonging on a man. Now she wasn't sure.

And the other single part? It was supposed to be a prick, a staff, a hammer, a rod, a tarse or even a cock. Though why a man would call a part of his body after a small, male fowl she didn't understand.

When Magnus had leaned down to pull off his breeches, her eyes widened. And her stomach had a rather strange feeling much like her mother had spoken about. 'Twas most interesting, for when he moved, his, er, things swayed. They were rather large. Perchance she was wrong about ballocks?

She near giggled then slapped her hand over her mouth and tried to swallow it back. Oh, saints help her! He had heard. She looked up at the rafters, her fingers twisted together and pressed to her stomach. He was so quiet she feared to move. Hearing the soft padding of bare feet on the floor, she chanced a quick look.

Her gaze clashed with near black eyes that didn't seem cold any more. Was there a hint of laughter in them? She blinked. It was. Magnus stepped into the tub with one foot then slowly lifted the other to join it. She noticed a startling change. What was limp and unimposing before now commanded attention. It had thickened. When he moved, it bobbed as if nodding.

Ah! Was the motion why they called it a hammer?

Nay. 'Twas more a staff now because it stood upright. She squeezed her fingers together so tightly she feared she was about to break a few. She stood between the tub and the door. If he made any threatening moves, she would be out the door before he lifted his foot from the tub!

Never would she be any man's vessel for bed sport. Her mother had warned her about men when she had her first time of the moon. A lass easily coaxed into bed without being handfast was doomed to spend her life going from one vile churl to the next.

Better to live alone in the forest or make her way to an abbey or convent and beg to take vows.

She heard water splash and knew Magnus had lowered himself to sit in the water.

Chapter 10

MURIELE FELT MORE CONFIDENT now Magnus sat in the tub with everything safely out of sight. She tried to look unconcerned as she walked to the bed and pulled back the covers, fluffed his pillow and did all the little things she did to her own pallet of a night.

"Come. Wash my hair."

It was not a request but an order. She knew better than to deny it. She composed her face and went to stand behind him. Unsure about how to wet his hair, she hesitated. If she poured water over him and it got in his eyes, would he be angry?

"Why are ye waiting?"

"It's dry. How do I wet it?"

Magnus snorted. As he lifted his legs and slid down until his knees were over the end of the tub, water surged and splashed. He leaned back, closed his eyes and submerged his head in the steaming water. Muriele felt her face heat, for he was no longer covered. His tarse bobbed atop the water as if filled with air. It no longer faced his feet but now pointed at her. She lowered her lids to take it from her sight.

When he surged up again, he tossed his head like a wet dog and swiped the dripping hair from his face. He scowled seeing she barely had her eyes open.

"Ye canna wash me without looking at what ye are about, girl. I want this stench gone from my body. Tend to it!"

"I had something in my eye, 'tis all." She grabbed the small pot of soap and dipped her fingers in to take out a goodly amount. His black hair was thick and healthy. As sweaty as he was, it would take a good scrubbing to get it clean again.

She spread soap over the top of his head and the hair at the back of his neck. The soap had a woodsy scent. Perchance Grunda had not only shared her recipe with her mother but with the head laundress at Kinbrace?

"Scrub harder. Ye'll nay get my head clean if ye only tickle it with yer fingers."

His tone sounded so irritable she applied all her strength into scrubbing his scalp. His head bobbed at first, but then he held his neck firm. Sighs of pleasure slipped from his lips and she glanced down and over his forehead to see his face. Eyes tightly closed, a slight smile played over his lips.

She might as well wash his face and beard while she was at it. He leaned his sudsy head against the back rim as she brought soap around to lather his face. She liked the way he trimmed his facial hair. She had thought it would be stiff and wiry but it was soft and silky to the touch. Kept very short, it shaped his jaw from ear to ear. A neat moustache came below his nostrils around his lips down to meet his beard. It too was short. Judging from the stubble beginning to grow there, he shaved his cheeks each morn and the small area from his lower lip down to the hair framing his chin. It gave his face a neat appearance and went well with his thick brows.

Wetting a cloth in a nearby bucket, she wiped the soap from his face and eyes then pulled back.

"If ye sit upright, I'll rinse yer hair."

He nodded and straightened with a reluctant sigh. Careful not to waste the water, she slowly poured it over his head as he ran his fingers through his hair.

"'Tis enough. We'll get what's left in the last rinse."

She handed him the cloth and he wiped the water from his face then returned it.

"Scrub my back and I'll finish the rest."

She sent a silent prayer of thanks that he didn't expect her to bathe him like a bairn. Washing his back was no hardship. At first. She lathered the cloth and started over his broad shoulders, liking the feel of the muscles beneath. From his shoulder blades on down, his skin roughened. He leaned forward to give her access, baring his flesh to the candlelight in the room.

Muriele bit her lips. Crisscrossed scars so rough she felt them through the cloth, marred his back. Who had taken a stick or whip to him? She couldn't believe any man would have the nerve to try to beat him. But what about when he was a youth? Had Chief Olaf been so cruel to a young boy when he first came to Kinbrace?

When she hesitated, he stiffened, guessing her reason.

"They have long since healed. They are from well-taught lessons in obedience. You would do well to learn from them."

He shrugged and reached behind to take the cloth from her. She moved back out of the way of flying water droplets as he bathed his chest and arms with quick efficiency. When he thrust his foot in the air washing it and creating a lather down his long, hairy legs, she stared at the muscles in his calves. Her body was well honed, but the lines of his hardened legs were sleek. More powerful.

Why couldn't she stop staring? It was not as if she'd never seen a naked man before. For truth, it was just yestermorn. Of course, they were warrior scum who felt masterful by preying on unattended women or travelers.

Men were men. One didn't change much from another, did he? When Magnus stood to wash what had been beneath the water, she turned her back and pretended interest in folding her own clothing into a neat pile beside his clothing chest.

She heard his snort of disgust.

What ailed the girl? Ha! She'd seen men with their pants dropped the day before. Had he not intervened with her attackers, she would have cut the stones off the nearest man when she had the chance.

Why had she appeared surprised on noting his cock resting in the water? She'd not seemed shy when the filthy lout's rod was near spitting with need as it bobbed with every step the man took. Nay. Far from looking shy, she'd been ready to kill.

Shrugging, he lifted his cock and pressed it against his stomach to scrub the underside and his stones. He'd sweated all day in the saddle, his heavy chain mail and clothing near bringing his body heat to boiling. He paid particular heed to the gash inside his right thigh, midway between his groin and his knee.

It hurt more today than yestermorn when he and Feradoch were ambushed by hapless ruffians. Not too hapless, though. One had landed a lucky thrust with a rusted spear. The bleeding had all but stopped. He pressed around the wound, causing dark, yellowish fluid to ooze from the center. Likely debris remained within the cut.

"Rinse me, Muriele."

She turned, her eyes averted, as she went to pick up a fresh bucket. He motioned to the stool, meaning for her to remove the towel and stand on the stool.

Muriele carefully clutched the wooden bucket to her chest as she stepped onto it. Lifting the water as high as she could, she slowly poured it as he turned around several times. He stopped her before the bucket was empty.

"Save the rest. I noted yer neat stitches. I have need of yer sewing to close a wound." He took the bucket from her and put it on the floor as she got off the stool.

"I thought ye had an injury when I sewed yer tunic, but I see none." She handed him the towel and curiously looked at his legs.

"'Tis on the inside of my leg."

"I will have need of medicines and cloths from the supply we brought back with us today."

Magnus wrapped the drying towel around his waist and went to jerk the door open while bellowing for a servant.

A maidservant carrying a tray of goblets stepped through the solar door and hurried over to him. "Aye, my lord?"

"Go to the spaewife's hut. Tell her to bring salves and supplies to cleanse a wound."

The woman looked relieved as she raced off to the stairwell. Had she seen him all but naked and thought he wished to swive? He snorted. He didna want a woman he must plow in the dark, else his cock would shrivel and cower against his balls for protection! He shut the door and turned as Muriele bent over to gather his clothing from the floor. On studying her shapely hips and supple back, his cock was far from shriveled.

It stirred in interest.

He ignored it.

The girl busied herself doing nothing but moving the clean drying cloths to the table beside the window. She stood back, stared at the table, the bed, back to the table. What was she thinking?

She grasped the table and tried to tug it over beside the bed. He stifled a laugh when she looked surprised, for although the table was plain and serviceable, it was made of sturdy wood.

"Why do ye move the table?"

"So I can put the things I require close by the bed. I canna run back and forth to work on yer leg." She frowned as if she thought he could have figured it out for himself.

Magnus cleared his throat so she would look at him. She had been gazing everywhere in the room except at him. He stood beside a small table in the right hand corner. A conical shaped piece of wood to hold his helm stood atop a post and sturdy base. Twas empty now until Brian cleaned and polished the gold-plated helmet and the chain mail attachment that protected the back of his neck.

He stood the wooden stand on the floor, picked the table up and crossed the room. "Where do ye want it?"

"Here, please, my lord."

Muriele kept her gaze high, avoiding looking at his naked chest and legs. He would have laughed, but he was too tired and had much to do afore he could retire for the night. Thankfully, Grunda called outside the door.

"Enter." He settled the table about two hands away from the bed.

Grunda carried a square basket of supplies. Muriele edged past Magnus, careful not to touch his bare flesh. She took the heavy basket and put it on the large table.

"My lord, we must see the wound to know what is needed

to heal it."

He walked over and stretched out on the bed, not caring about the drying towel twisted around him. He watched as Grunda went to the door and took an iron pot of hot water from a servant who had followed behind her.

Uncomfortable from the bunched cloth, he tugged it away, baring his body. Twisting his right leg to the side so the women could tend it, he held back a grimace. When Muriele gasped, he didn't know if 'twas from the sight of his flaccid sex or the angry look of the wound.

He preferred it was his cock.

Both women came close. Muriele reached out then drew her hand back. Her face flushed. Finally, she reached for the cloth and slid it across his stomach and down over his left leg. Once his bared sex no longer seemed an obstacle, she touched his flesh with interest.

"You rode out without a proper dressing over it?"

"Aye. 'Tis yer doing. I would have sought care, but I had to hunt for a wayward girl who doesna obey orders." His hard eyes blamed her for the festering wound.

She bit her lip, likely to keep back a foolish reply. He watched as they busied themselves setting out soft cloths, smelly ointments and bottled decoctions from the basket.

"A hot compress of woundwort will draw out the evil," Grunda muttered. Taking some betony leaves from a jar, she crushed them between her hands then placed them in a small earthenware pot. After she poured hot water over them, she left them to steep.

Muriele leaned close and gently tested the inflamed skin around the wound. "Pus. Flakes of rust. Do ye think we can flush them out?" She asked but didn't expect an answer, for she grabbed the drying cloth off him. "Lift, please, my lord."

Muriele no longer felt reluctant to touch him, for he became as any other hurt animal she had helped. When he lifted his leg, she slid the cloth beneath and packed it against the sides of his flesh. Selecting one of the clean cloths laying on the table, she ripped off a small piece. Holding it with her fingertips, she dipped it in the hot water then flapped it in the air until cool enough she could fold it to where there were four sharp corners. She placed it on his bare belly.

As Grunda held his flesh open, Muriele held a knife blade alongside the lip of the small pot of betony-soaked water to hold back the leaves while she poured the warm water into the open wound. Grunda worked the flesh around, spilling the thinned pus from it. After several soakings, Muriele used the tips of the cloth to pull the dislodged rust away. Magnus gritted his teeth as she dug to get the last piece.

She sighed. "'Tis as clean as I can get it." She looked up at Grunda. "Ye can stitch it now. Do ye think a compress with harebell roots and woundwort will staunch the blood and clear the infected fluids?"

Magnus brought her attention back to him.

"Ye do the stitching; Grunda can do the compress making."

Why, she had been so engrossed in what she was doing she near forgot she was working on a man.

"I have never stitched a man. Or woman. Only animals." She shook her head at him. "Grunda must do it."

"Dinna defy me, woman! If ye can stitch my clothing, ye can stitch my flesh. 'Tis no difference."

What if she hurt him and he knocked her to the floor? Sometimes pain-riddled men struck out at their healers if someone didna hold them to the bed. She gulped and jumped back.

"'Tis painful. Who will aid ye? Grunda isna strong enough to hold yer leg still."

"Do ye think me a nithing of a man? Get back here and do it."

"You trust the witch's get to work on your flesh, brother?" Feradoch said from the doorway.

"Her mother was Lady Ragnhild, nay a witch. The girl knows where her fate lies. She wouldna dare cause me harm." He turned his hot glare to rest on her.

"Ye sew and I will cut the thread. 'Twill be faster," Grunda said as she handed her the needle already threaded and waiting.

"For the lass' safety, should I hold you down?" Feradoch

stepped over to the bed.

"Keep yer hands to yerself."

"Best get on with it then. Father is impatient. He sent me to fetch you." He folded muscular arms across his chest and lounged against the foot of the bed.

She took a deep breath and tried to think of the leg as part of a wounded animal. But an animal did not have bronzed flesh with soft hair tickling her hand when she moved.

She held her breath taking the first stitch. When he didn't lash out at her, she felt more confident. Every now and again, his flesh quivered.

"Best not be so clumsy, lass," Feradoch warned.

Muriele dared not look up but worked as fast as she could. Her needle no sooner made the knot than Grunda's knife tip cut the thread and she was on to the next one. Once the last stitch was in place, Grunda handed her the poultice and helped spread it over the wound. She moved back for the old woman to wind the bindings around his leg and secure it.

"Ye did much better than Sweyn. No doubt it will heal sooner with no dirt left behind." Magnus swung his legs over the bed and stood.

Muriele's eyes widened. Dirt? Did his squire not know to clean dirt from a wound? No wonder he had so many ridged scars on his body!

Feradoch picked up the clean tunic and tossed it to Magnus. He snatched it out of the air and over his head in one smooth movement. He took only long enough to pull on his boots before they left without another word.

"I think ye will have made a friend in Sweyn, lass," Grunda said, grinning.

"Why?"

"Ye saved him a blackened eye." Grunda laughed at Muriele's look of surprise. "Aye. Sir Magnus refused my aid when I was brought here saying Sweyn needed to learn the skill for after battles. But he always lashed out at him."

"Is Sweyn clumsy, then?"

"Nay." She shrugged and chuckled. "Except he needed to be deep in his cups afore he could get near Sir Magnus' flesh."

They had no sooner put their supplies back in the basket than a servant appeared with a rolled pallet slung over his left shoulder. Relieved to see it, Muriele placed it in the far corner until they could get the room back to rights. After he left, she closed the door and looked at the tub.

Magnus had certainly needed a bath from the looks of it! The cooled water left scum along the wooden sides. Wrinkling her nose, she went to the window and looked below to see a cobblestone path with grass on either side.

"No one seems to be about. I can empty the water out the window." She grabbed the nearest empty bucket and dipped it in the tub.

"Nay, girl. Let me." Grunda reached around her and took hold of the braided rope handle. "Warm water is left in the rinsing bucket. Best take advantage of it now whilst he is gone."

A small washstand stood in the far left corner with a polished metal square hanging above it. She knelt and found her soap then hurried over to pour warm water in the basin. She bathed as fast as she could, listening for the slightest sounds. When she finally slid the beige and brown garments over her head, she sighed with relief.

"Ye no longer need me here," Grunda said as she hugged her. "Be abed afore he returns. Likely, he won't notice and will crawl between his sheets. Warriors sleep quickly. He'll be snoring afore ye know it." She collected the basket of supplies and slipped out the door.

Muriele shut it, but instead of it giving her a sense of security, she felt imprisoned. She shivered and tidied up Magnus' shaving table, making sure to place everything exactly as he left it. She looked around for anything she had forgotten to do. Grunda had emptied and wiped out the tub before pushing it against the wall. The floor dried, aided a bit by blotting with his dirty clothing. She made a bundle and put it out of the way for washing the next morn.

After replacing the small table in the right hand corner

where it belonged, she put the helmet stand on top. She looked around again, making sure she hadn't missed anything. 'Twas a big bed for one man. The fat feather mattress looked inviting as she straightened the sheets and fluffed the pillows he'd propped himself against. Smoothing the sheet and blanket, she folded them back at the corner so he needed only to sit and pull them over himself.

Nothing seemed out of place. Except her rolled pallet. Where could she place it so it wouldn't be obvious, yet be as far from the bed as possible? The space along the wall between the helmet table and the clothing chest seemed the safest spot.

Her stomach grumbled when she unrolled the bedding. Too late to think about food now. Ah, well, it was not the first time she'd gone without eating. And it likely wouldn't be the last. She slipped off her shoes and debated about taking off her kirtle. Nay. 'Twas a cold room and the thin blanket and pillow rolled inside the pallet wouldn't be enough to keep the chill away.

She sat on her bedding and brushed her hair as she thought over these last horrible two days. Once done, she made one long plait to the side and stretched out. Shivering, she wrapped her hands in the blanket and drew it tight under her chin. Seeking her mother's comfort, she cupped the treasured rings through her clothing and waited on the bedding to warm. Once it did, she sighed and slept.

Magnus, bone tired and sore, wanted nothing more than to return to his bedchamber. His leg felt afire. Once he'd told the Chief about the raiders, he settled back to drink until it dulled his aches.

The men broke up their bouts of swigging by feats of strength. He had arm-wrestled with the Chief and Feradoch, and to do so, he'd had to plant his feet firmly on the floor, tightening his muscles to lend strength to his back and arm. Feradoch had near beat him the last time. He was insisting Magnus body-wrestle with him when Sweyn mentioned

Magnus had new stitches on his thigh. The Chief frowned and put a stop to the evening.

Feradoch's disappointed look brought home the coming changes in their lives. No longer would they spend a month together each year. With time, would they lose the special bond between them? The unspoken loyalty? He hoped not.

He felt uneasy about returning to Clibrick. Though Graemme seemed to welcome the event, would he miss the man who had been more of a true brother by living there these past seventeen years? An ancient Clan belief claimed, *A man is affectionate to his kin, but a foster brother is the life blood of his heart.*

When he reached his bedchamber, he clutched his sheathed short sword under his left arm then shifted his helmet from his right to his left hand and opened the door. The glow from the rushlights at the top of the stairwell spilled into the room. He spied his empty bed and snapped the door shut with his heel. Walking over to put his cleaned helmet on its stand, his right foot stepped on something soft. A startled gasp caused him to hop and shift his weight to his left foot.

Chapter 11

BENDING, MAGNUS FELT THE edge of his boot to find what was beneath it. 'Twas a braided rope of hair. He lifted his foot, took the hair in his hands and followed it until he reached the woman's head. When his hand cupped her jaw, the clouds moved from the moon. Its light spilled over her face, making her skin glow like a yellow stone polished by a rushing stream.

His fingertips stroked over a warm cheek and soft lips and stopped to explore them before moving up to stroke the silky hair of her temple. Her eyes, wide and startled, met his gaze.

He remembered their look when she had concentrated on stitching his flesh. Worry. Compassion. She had tried hard not to cause him added pain.

"Why are ye awake at this hour?"

"I was not. Ye near yanked the hair from my head."

"I'm not yanking it now. Get to sleep."

He jerked his hand back as if her flesh scalded him, and then stood. Feeling his helmet pressed against his left side, it reminded his ale-fuddled mind why he was there. He dropped the helmet in place. His leg ached like Lucifer's moldy horns ripped into his flesh and jerked on it.

Going to his bed, he slammed the sword atop the extra pillow then tugged off his clothing. Finally, he threw everything across the chair and stretched out on the bed. Grateful he wasn't wrapped in a plaid and sleeping on the hard forest floor, he sighed and rolled over, pulling the blanket with him as he closed his eyes.

Muriele's muscles cramped from her efforts to remain so still she'd be inconspicuous. With her back to the wall, she wanted to change position but feared Magnus was not asleep and her movements would remind him she was there. Finally, when he began to snore, she relaxed enough to drift off to sleep.

During the night, every time Magnus turned, squeaking bed ropes awakened her. Her gaze probed the darkness until heavy breathing told her he still slumbered. 'Twas likely his leg ached and he needed to move it to a more comfortable position.

What if his wound festered? Would he blame her? Though he had not struck out when she stitched his flesh, what if he went out of his head with fever? His fist would likely break her jaw.

Clutching her arms around herself, she thought over everything she'd done from the time he stepped into the bath. If the wound began to fester, hot water and soap would help draw bad humors from it. And he *had* scrubbed his legs vigorously.

'Twas a good thing, wasn't it?

Ah … but what about the sweat-soaked breeches he'd worn all day? Not to mention the dirt and blood from other men had washed off his body into the water.

'Twas a bad thing, wasn't it?

She reminded herself she'd cleansed the wound with the betony water and had added harebell and woundwort to the dressing. If his skin looked inflamed come the morn, she'd best put a hot poultice with herbs on it to draw out the infection.

If he allowed it.

As darkness started to fade, she fell asleep, exhausted.

Muriele snapped awake. What had changed? Something was about to happen, but what? She stopped breathing to heighten her hearing. Soft murmurs came from outside the door. Its latch slowly lifted. The door eased open. Two shadows stood framed in the open doorway, one huge the other smaller. They hesitated then slowly moved forward. They carried something in their hands.

"Beware!"

The shout left her mouth as she scrambled to her feet, feeling on the calf of her right leg for the familiar sheath there.

Her hand touched bare flesh. Magnus erupted from his bed and before his feet touched the floor, he had drawn the short sword and stood balanced to spring.

He was visible in the faint light from the hallway. 'Twas a warrior ready to kill, crouched with a sheet wrapped around his left arm, his right hand gripping his weapon, ready to strike.

"My lord! 'Tis Brian and Gille."

"Lucifer's rotted arse, woman! Why did ye scream?"

"They entered so quietly I thought someone meant to skewer ye while ye slept."

"I am most sorry, lady," Brian said with laughter in his voice. "Each morn I bring hot water for my lord to shave. He usually awakes before I open the door."

Muriele's heart slowed to a steady beat, but her face flamed. Embarrassed by the attention, she pulled her kirtle into place where it had twisted as she slept. Out of the corner of her eye, she watched Magnus pull on his breeches and boots. He winced when he first bent his leg, but once he'd laced the clothing at his waist, he did not look to have trouble walking.

After Brian built up the fire, Magnus stared at the young boy.

"This is Gille? The lad must have worn a mountain of dirt. His hair is light with shades of red. I thought it dark brown."

"Aye, it was. Several dunks in the pond got the muck off him afore I even gave him soap." Brian chuckled.

Magnus studied the boy in the growing light. Clean and attired in proper clothing, he did not appear a varlet's son. His eyes were gray with a hint of blue. He had too-fine features to be a peasants' get.

Could he be one of Olaf's bastards? If so, why send him to a remote village? He had spawned other children amongst the servants and placed them in huts along the castle grounds. Why hide this one? He shrugged. His back crept with a prickly reminder. 'Twas not his right to question Chief Olaf. He'd learned not to from an early age.

Less than a fortnight after he'd come to live at Kinbrace, he found a newborn pup amongst a hunting hound's litter. The stable master had said it would be dead within a few days because it was too small to survive.

Chief Olaf had come up behind him then. "Smother the weakling. The strongest pups need the bitch's milk to grow into hunters."

"But, my lord, the pup can eat when the others sleep," Magnus reasoned.

"Smother it!" 'Twas a harsh demand.

Olaf turned and left, expecting him to obey without a thought. The little animal squirmed in his hand and looked up at him, all big, brown eyes in a small head. He couldn't do it. Instead, he put it back in the box with the other pups and carried it to the stall at the end of the stable. The mother followed him. 'Twas out of sight and unlikely Chief Olaf would see it.

"Magnus!"

Days later, Olaf's shout near made him shite his breeches. By the time they met at the front stalls, his knees wobbled.

Thunk. Dust puffed. The lifeless puppy landed at his feet. Its neck was broken.

The fact hardly registered before blows across his back near felled him. His eyes had widened in disbelief, for never once had his father at Clibrick taken a whip to him.

"This is for the trouble you put me through by not obeying orders!"

The next blow sent him to his knees. He curled over, protecting his head. When the Chief's arm grew tired, he threw down the whip.

"When I tell you to do a deed, do it without thought."

Vomit and tears covered his face when he'd lifted it. 'Twas the stable master who came, murmuring soft words Magnus couldn't understand because of the pain streaking across his back. He carried him to the keep where his foster mother gave him potions that eased his pain and rubbed ointments on the stinging welts on his back. It was three days afore he could wear the tunic she had mended for him.

Those first years, Lady Asleif tried to protect Magnus, for Olaf was determined to change everything his father had taught him. When she could not, she was there to soften the pain of

Olaf's lessons. She died from a deep cough when he was ten.

Thereafter, any time he tried to befriend a creature or person, something happened. He'd learned being alone wasn't unpleasant or even lonely. 'Twas easier not to form attachments.

Aye. He would not seek to learn the boy's beginnings. It mattered not.

"Gille cleaned my sword last eve?" Magnus turned the blade around and around, looking at it. Not a sign of blood remained from the battle the previous day.

"Aye. He has a fine eye for spotting smudges," Brian said as he poured hot water in the basin then stood back so Magnus could tend to his morning routine.

He splashed water on his face then cleaned his teeth with mint and hazel twigs. He kept an eye on Muriele as she rolled her pallet and started straightening the sheets on his bed. When he finished shaving, she was done and was looking through his clothing chest for anything that needed mending. It pleased him she had not forgotten.

"Break yer fast afore ye tend yer duties. Yer empty stomach's rumbling kept me awake most of the night."

Brian opened the door wide for his master to precede him and waited.

"Ye will keep my room clean from ceiling to floor. Mend and wash my clothes and help with my bath. When time permits, ye will trim my hair. It has been too hot of late." He frowned and started to leave. "And see what ye can do to help Cook. I grow tired of stews and soups. We have not had decent meat in way too long."

"Aye, my lord."

She was relieved to see he did not limp or look to favor his right leg. Young Gille followed Brian. His eyes watched every move Magnus made as if he was a god come to earth.

It was not yet full daylight when she went down to the great hall. She looked around not knowing where she was supposed to eat. She felt a light pluck on her kirtle and turned to see Esa's strong face with a slight smile on her lips.

"The color suits you," she said, nodding at the brown kirtle.

Muriele smiled a welcome at the woman then paid particular heed to the high table. Magnus sat to the right of Chief Olaf, Feradoch to the left. Olaf's commander was there and a dozen knights. The Chief and the two brothers seemed to be arguing about something and paid no heed to the others.

"Come. Let us find a bench afore all are filled."

Muriele smiled and gladly followed her. Though several benches in the center of the room were near empty, Esa led her to the last row along the wall. Muriele, too, preferred no one could walk behind her.

Perchance she was wrong on the reason the woman chose the spot. She saw her look toward the dais and sigh, as if with relief. Muriele wondered why until she, too, glanced toward it. Ah. She could not see it. When the woman relaxed beside her, she knew she avoided someone at the high table. Was it one of the men?

Servants walked through the room placing steaming bowls of porridge at the center of the tables and hot loaves of brown bread. Before long, she was blowing on her spoon of porridge, impatient to eat it.

"Esa, at the high table, why do the women sit separate from the men?"

"Each morn, they talk of their war plans or about their conquests from the night before. They dinna want the women hearing, so they are not allowed. At the noon meal, they resume their rightful places."

"They argue more than anything else." Muriele had noted the tense set of Magnus' shoulders and the way Feradoch stared at him.

"Aye. Magnus must see to the disciplining of the warriors. When Feradoch comes, he claims his foster brother is too harsh. He doesna feel men should be punished for certain things."

"Oh? What would they be?"

Esa shrugged her shoulders and ignored the question,

appearing uneasy with it.

The crowded room soon became uncomfortable, for they sat far from the large entrance, the only source of fresh air. Muriele was grateful when they finished eating. She went above to take the laundry to the stream where the women gathered to do the washing. She felt uneasy and kept to herself, though she liked hearing them talking and joking with each other.

She did as the day before. While the clothes were drying, she sat beneath the swaying green canopy of a willow tree and repaired his clothing. 'Twas while she was stitching a torn pocket in a blue linen tunic when they heard a commotion. Curious, the women stood and looked to the right. The front gate and drawbridge was quite far, but they could make out men galloping their horses into the front bailey, calling out for help.

"'Tis the hunter's men," one plump young woman said, her fingers going to her lips in a worried gesture.

"Aye. Something's happened."

Muriele saw Grunda's figure hurrying across the bailey, the heavy basket slung over her arm. Without another thought, Muriele put her mending aside and held the hem of her kirtle high as she took off in a loping run.

When she reached the grassy area beside the stable, Grunda was crouched over someone on the ground. She hurried over and stopped so quickly she near lost her balance. One look and she knew a boar's tusks had ripped a gaping hole in the man's stomach. His bowels bulged from the opening. Blood and gore covered his clothing. Grunda reached out to softly stroke his eyelids shut.

A woman's shrill shriek made her flinch. Grunda quickly took off her cloak and laid it over the dead man from neck to toe, shielding his mangled body from his wife's eyes.

A cold voice quieted the horrified murmurs of everyone gathered around.

"Dinna waste time on him. It is more likely you can save the other hunter."

'Twas Feradoch who spoke.

Two men were lifting a second man from the back of a

horse. He clutched his bloody, right arm across his chest. His face was pale. Someone had knotted a cloth just above his elbow. She helped Grunda to rise then grabbed the herb basket for her.

"Take him to the warrior's tower," Muriele said to the men helping him walk. "We will stitch him there."

They hurried ahead, calling out for someone to bring hot water. When they approached the tower, the guard at the door held up his hand, denying them entrance.

"Move, ye ignorant churl! Would ye rather the man died on yer doorstep from loss of blood? Ye can move him after we stop the bleeding." Grunda shoved the man who was so startled he moved out of the way.

A table close to the entrance seemed a perfect spot. Muriele took her arm and swiped everything onto the floor, not paying heed to the men's grumbling.

As Grunda prepared what they would need, Muriele cut away the man's leather shirtsleeve. While men fed him wine, Muriele studied the damage. The large gash went from elbow to wrist on the top of his arm. She knotted a clean rag above the one already there and twisted it with a small piece of wood.

"Hold this tight. Dinna let it go," she ordered a man standing at her elbow. Taking a thick clean pad from Grunda, she pressed with all her might on the ripped skin while Grunda cut away the blood-soaked cloth tied too close to the wound for them to stitch. Blood quickly soaked through the pad then slowed.

As she worked, she asked questions. They were the castle's main hunters who provided game from the forest.

"How could ye make such a mistake as to get between the wind and the boar? Did ye not see signs of one close by?" Muriele scolded. Likely, they had been too deep in their cups last eve and became careless. She didn't catch the answer because she was too busy to care.

Once the bleeding stopped, they worked quickly. Several men surrounded the table, lending their hands to hold the injured man steady. It took far longer to repair the arm than it had Magnus' leg.

When Grunda no longer needed her, she backed away and

hurried back to the stream. The clothes she had strewn on the bushes were gone! She panicked until she noted a neat bundle beneath the willow tree at the stream's edge. She looked around for someone to thank but everyone had gone.

Until then, she'd had no idea it was well past the noon hour. Everyone was probably eating in the great hall. After she returned the clothing to Magnus' bedchamber, she'd visit Cook as he had ordered. She might be able to get something to eat then.

Hurrying, she made her way across the castle yards to the front bailey. She slipped inside the keep and hurried up the stairway, her soft shoes barely making a whisper of sound. She was just steps away from Magnus' bedchamber door when her nape prickled. The next thing she knew, a large hand flashed around her head and clamped over her mouth.

Muriele fought like a wild barn cat. The carefully folded laundry flew out of her arms when she grabbed at the thick fingers pinching her face. She couldn't get her mouth open to bite, but she used her feet to kick back hard as she could. It didn't seem to faze the man. He grabbed the hem of her skirts, yanked them to her waist and shoved his right leg between hers.

Slamming her against the wall, he pinned her there with the weight of his upper body then fumbled with his tunic. Grunting like a hog taking a mud bath, she felt him tussling to pull the clothing from between them. Hot and heavy, his shaft pressed against her nether cheeks. When he tilted his hips back to position himself, she used all her strength to shove against the wall and pitched sideways.

He released her mouth and scrambled to grab hold of her. She let out a scream loud enough to startle the dead awake. Cursing, he struck her behind her right ear. Her forehead slammed forward against the wall.

As if boneless, she slid to the floor in a heap.

Chapter 12

WHEN MAGNUS ENTERED THE great hall, he didn't feel Muriele's presence. Though she had thought he had not noted her this morn, he knew the minute she entered the room. He'd no need to look up. He just knew.

His gaze swept over the tables below but saw no sight of her. Now and again, he glanced toward the far corner table where she and Esa had sat to break their fast.

As he took a sip of cold wine, the distant echo of a throaty scream floated above the noise in the great hall. The diners ignored it assuming one of their comrades was tupping a reluctant servant.

Except for Magnus.

Bounding out of the chair, he shook his head as Feradoch started to delay him. His instincts led him to his bedchamber area. Muriele was lying in a crumpled heap with laundry strewn around her. In the shadows at the far end of the corridor, a man's broad shoulders disappeared down the rear stairwell. 'Twas no use chasing him. He'd vanish amongst the servants below.

"By all the saints! What trouble have ye caused yerself now, Muriele?"

Bending on one knee, he propped her against the wall. When she winced and raised her hand to cushion her head, he ran his fingers around her skull and found a lump behind her right ear. 'Twas not the only one, for above her right eye, an angry red bump began to swell.

"Who struck ye?"

Muriele pressed both hands to her temples, hoping to still the walls spinning around her. They did not. She closed her eyes for a bit and swallowed back a sharp retort to his first foolish question then answered the second.

"I know not."

"Hmpf. Did ye give a man reason to think ye'd swive him?"

"Give a man reason? I have paid no heed to any man at Kinbrace."

He huffed in disbelief.

"Ye went to the warrior's quarters to tend the hunter. Women dinna intrude where men sleep unless they are servants. When there, ye did not give them cause to think ye eager for bed sport?"

Muriele blinked and winced. "Where else would we tend the hunter?"

"Nae in the warrior's barracks."

"On the dirty ground, then?"

Her eyes flashed fire at him. He ignored her.

"The next time ye sustain an injury, *ye* should lie on the cobblestones."

"Dinna be foolish."

"Ha! Men are the foolish ones." When he stiffened, she knew she had gone too far. "Any man who thinks me easy to bed will find a knife betwixt his ribs."

"Brother, you'd best pay heed to her threat. I wouldn't turn my back to her if I were you." Feradoch's voice, though teasing, held a hint of warning.

"Ye dinna have to warn me. The Chief has taught me well to place my trust in no one but the two of ye."

"Aye, Father has the right of it. But your brother's greetings easily drew you in at Clibrick. You may be too trusting with *your* family."

Magnus' brows near met in a warning frown to quiet Feradoch. Grasping Muriele's chin, he turned her face from side to side, noting her eyes when they faced the shadows and when they looked into the lighted stairwell.

"I dinna think ye harmed yerself, though yer forehead will be unsightly for a few days." He leaned back and studied her face.

She hoped he could not read her thoughts, for she wanted

to scream she hadn't banged her own head back and forth on the wall!

"Do ye think ye can get up?"

"Aye."

As he helped her to rise, he glanced around them.

"Ye've strewn clothing over half the landing. Once ye clean up here, see Cook for sustenance. Await me there."

He waited until sure she stood on her own then turned with Feradoch to go back to the front stairwell. He shot one more command over his shoulder.

"And dinna lure men into the kitchens with ye!"

Muriele held a taut rein on her temper. Her hissed reply barely left her lips.

"Eejit!"

"Now what is this warning ye were about to give?"

Magnus stopped midway down the stairwell and stepped into a niche built into the thick walls. He stooped to look out the arrow slit to see a clear, blue sky. Sunlight danced on the blue waters of Loch Achnamoine, inviting him for a swim. The brisk breeze changed his mind. Encountering the cold stone when he sat on the narrow bench, his bare arse tightened with surprise. When his balls cringed and shrank, he thought it wise to stand and adjust his clothing, cushioning his flesh before he sat again.

"I've lived at Clibrick these many years. I've learned much of your family by earning their confidence." Feradoch hesitated and looked reluctant to tell Magnus something hurtful.

"Cease with yer hints. Tell me what ye truly mean."

"I wish to spare you any unpleasant surprises when you return there." He shifted in his seat as if his arse, too, resented the cold contact. "For nigh on seventeen years, Graemme has been as an only son in your father's eyes. The Chief even allows him to believe he will be commander over the warriors."

"Graemme has always known as first-born I will some day take my father's place."

"He reports to Chief Angus he fears you will stir trouble amongst the Morgan warriors. Word came to him you slaughter without purpose."

"He has no reason to think I start combats for the joy of killing."

"Truly? Did you not order five men hanged because they swived one woman who was such a weakling she died? They but sought a night's sport with the daughter."

Magnus snorted. "They were common churls who raped and killed a noblewoman. Dinna forget it."

"Then the next day you led in beheading several skilled warriors because of useless village children? Those men could have swelled our ranks."

Magnus sucked his teeth in disgust. "They were barely above savage beasts."

"An army of such men wins many victories." Feradoch's lip curled with scorn.

"Nay. Their type canna be trusted or trained."

Feradoch shrugged, dismissing Magnus' words. "This killing of your so-called beasts lends truth to their worries you live up to your name."

"My name?"

"Aye. Ruthless." Feradoch shook his head in sympathy. "Tales have spread as far as Clibrick about the blacksmith you hung last winter."

"The man killed his third wife within as many years. I dinna think beating a woman to death because she failed to give him a cockstand was reason to kill."

"'Tis not the way we heard it. Word came to us he did them a kindness by killing them."

"A kindness?" Magnus' brows quirked. He paused and pinched the bridge of his nose, mulling over Feradoch's words.

"'Twas said you forced his wives to swive you while he watched."

"Huh! I have ne'er forced a woman."

"Blood lust fills you after battle." Feradoch shook his head in sympathy. "You truly dinna remember?"

"Ha! I truly *know* I never did such." Magnus studied his blood brother's serene face. "What proof do ye have?"

"I fear it is dead and buried. 'Tis why the blacksmith killed them. He couldna bear to see their shame and released them from their torment. Surely you recall spending yourself then branding them?"

"Your tale gets more foolish by the word." Magnus shook his head in disbelief. "The brand? Was it an 'M' for my name or an 'R' for my character?"

"Neither. An eye opened wide. Staring. Above the springy curls of their pleasure cave." Feradoch nodded and continued. "You spat on the burn saying it would cool the flesh."

Magnus snorted. "And ye believe the blacksmith would make a branding iron for me to use on his wives?"

Feradoch shrugged. "Not ours. Mayhap the blacksmith at Clibrick forged it for you when you visited."

"Ha! Not even an eejit would consider such a thing." Magnus' lids narrowed. As he studied the placid, blue eyes gazing back at him, his lips tightened. "Enough of this. Ye can assure Graemme no such thing occurred by my hand."

As Magnus stood to leave the niche, the back of his neck prickled. Ever alert, he whipped his head to look behind him.

He blinked and the hate flashing like fire deep in Feradoch's gaze had disappeared.

Had he imagined it?

Chapter 13

"*I* caused myself trouble?"

Muriele muttered and kicked a small stone on the floor so hard it flew over a pair of crumpled breeches. She reached down to grab the offending garments and near fell on her face.

"Ohh!"

As the walls spun and the floor pitched, she held her arms out at her sides to steady herself. Great gasps of air kept her from spewing.

Once her stomach settled, she was more cautious on how she gathered the rest of the laundry. Once it was safely in her arms, she entered the bedchamber and stored Magnus' clothing in his chest.

"The fool thinks I tempted some churl to treat me like an animal?"

When had she started talking to herself? Did the twin blows to her head make her brainsick?

She stepped over to peer into the polished steel hanging over the washstand. Studying the throbbing lump on her forehead, she turned her face to the side. Placing her fingers cautiously on the swelling behind her ear, she tried to peer at it from the corner of her eyes.

"Huh! I hope a plump fowl doesn't light on my head and attempt to hatch them!"

She giggled at the silly thought. When Grunda called her name from the open doorway, Muriele jumped.

"Ye would need two hens, lass. One in front and one in back."

She hurried over to examine Muriele's forehead and

muttered a curse on the assailant. He'd probably awake to a tarse no longer than his big toe come morning. With worried eyes, she shook her head and clucked in sympathy.

Muriele grinned at her. "Dinna cluck too loudly, else we'll have a flock of feathered friends hopping and flying up the stairwells."

"Sit!"

She sat. Grunda gently parted Muriele's hair in back and examined the swelling there.

"'Twill be sore when ye sleep this night, but I dinna think the lout caused serious damage."

"Ah. Sir Magnus believes I caused it." She snorted. "He acted like I'd sat on the hard floor and took turns bouncing my head against the stone wall."

"Pfft! Men are fools!" She patted Muriele's shoulder. "Did ye keep yer meal down?"

"I had naught to come up."

"Ye've not eaten since early morn?"

"Nay." She huffed in disgust. "He kindly ordered me to the kitchen. Then he warned I should not lure men in with me."

"Ye best ask Cook for something easy on the stomach. I'll bring a potion for yer head to ease the ache. Come."

Grunda stood to the side watching Muriele walk across the room. "Ye seem to have yer balance back."

Muriele would have nodded in agreement, but at the moment, she didn't think bobbing her head would be wise.

The kitchen stood outside the keep against the right curtain wall, far enough from the Great Hall to provide safety from fires. Though Muriele sat at a bench close to the open doorway, sweat trickled down her spine. On the opposite wall, a fireplace large enough to cook two oxen had a huge cauldron of soup simmering. A second hung on its iron hook far to the right. 'Twas stew from the noon meal kept warm for patrol warriors returning.

Muriele watched Ivar the Stout, the head cook, toss scraps of raw meat into the soup. When he'd cleared all from the chopping block, he looked over the few hares the hunters had provided for the day. He shook his head and frowned, displeased.

From what she could tell, his wife was responsible for making the food palatable — behind his back. Whenever he turned, the red-faced woman tossed a handful of spices in the pot and gave it a quick stir.

"The stew is quite tasty, Ivar. What is yer secret?"

Muriele had tried to identify the contents of the large bowl his wife placed in front of her. 'Twas obvious what had started out as roasted mutton a day or two ago had become stew. She came across pieces of stringy meat that was neither mutton nor hare.

Ivar snorted, not bothering to answer.

"Huh! 'Tis the old rooster what chased him around the well and pecked at his arse one time too many." His wife swatted at two spindly boys who were too slow wielding their paddles to remove round loaves of brown bread from the ovens on each side of the fireplace.

Though lambs and pigs were fenced outside, Muriele looked around the huge kitchen, puzzled at the small amount of fresh-killed deer, wild hogs, hares and grouses.

"The hunters have had ill luck lately?"

"Aye." Ivar threw the plumpest hare onto the chopping block and eyed her with dislike. He near growled when he spoke. "From Blackbriar arrows!" Picking up a huge butcher knife, he slammed it down with vigor, severing the head.

No doubt, he would have preferred her neck beneath its blade.

Magnus strode across the front bailey, unaware of anything around him. Had the smell not alerted him, he would have trod through a pile of fresh horse dung. Hopping in a quick side step, he avoided it.

For truth, light from the arrow slit had played tricks on his sight in the alcove. He hesitated and stared at the tip of his boots, pondering.

He knew of no reason for the silvery flash of hatred in

Feradoch's eyes.

As he entered the kitchen doorway, Ivar's heated remark and the vicious strike of the knife drew his eyes to Muriele. He expected her to freeze, her eyes wide, body stiff.

Instead, with squared shoulders and head held high, she stared Ivar in the eyes. Her courage pleased him. When Ivar turned away, she shoved a lock of hair back from her sweaty forehead and winced on brushing against the purpling bruise.

"Grunda tells me ye were responsible for supplying food while ye lived in the forest."

She had not heard him approach, for she startled and her eyes widened. Just as quickly, calm spread over her face.

"Aye."

"And afore the siege, ye went out with the Blackbriar hunters and supplied as much as the best of them?" He dragged over a tall stool and straddled the seat. If his stones had a voice, they would have sighed in comfort from the heated wood. "I dinna believe ye have the strength to bring down an animal larger than a wild piglet."

"Huh!"

When he pricked her anger, she stiffened and her jaws squared much as a man's would. The intriguing golden flecks in her eyes turned to dark amber.

"Sweyn and I feasted on the hare stew ye left."

She blinked. She had forgotten the food she'd prepared for her mother's return. Her face fell as the memory crashed in on her.

He stretched his shoulders backward. Her gaze skittered away from looking any lower than his chin. Curious, he leaned forward and braced his forearms on his thighs. Feeling bare flesh there, he kenned her problem. From her low chair, her eyes were level with his groin. He ignored it though his cock stirred with pleasure.

"Ivar has scant rations of fresh meat. Tomorrow ye may prove yer skills. Ye will join the hunters when they ride out."

Muriele's back straightened even more and her eyes sparked with interest.

"Dinna think it a chance to run away. I plan to judge this marvelous skill ye are said to have."

He rubbed over his bandaged thigh, pulling her gaze down to his bare flesh. No doubt she worried he would ruin her handiwork. Her face flamed and her glance jerked back up.

"Be ready afore first light."

Instead of returning to Magnus' chambers, Muriele headed to Grunda's hut. She ran her right hand down her brown kirtle, knowing she could not chance ruining what little clothing he had allowed her. Far better to use her old hunt clothing, no matter how frayed and mended it was. It would not matter if thorns tore new gashes in it or if it became mottled with blood.

Thinking of the small freedom outside the castle on the morrow, she didn't see a grubby-faced lad skitter around the corner of the stables. She near ran into his rubbish cart filled with horse shite. From his pinched in nose and the slightly green look on his face, the smell did not sit well with whatever he had eaten for the day.

As she approached the herb garden, she watched her old friend kneeling in the dirt carefully selecting clippings from the plants.

"Ye will need to mend yer old garments," Grunda said without turning around.

Muriele was a good ten paces away. How had the woman known who approached?

"How did ye know 'twas me?"

"By yer footsteps, of course."

"Hmm. But how did ye know I would be in need of my hunting clothes?"

"'Tis simple. In a sennight, the Chief's son will return to the Morgans for the last time."

"What does his return have to do with my hunting clothes?"

"A feast. The keep's servants were airing fine linens for the Great Hall. Listening to their chatter, I learned 'tis their custom to have a feast lasting for days." She grunted then huffed in disgust. "'Tis a good reason to overeat and swill ale until the men fall like oxen hit with the smith's hammer."

"Huh! No wonder he's willing to risk me with a weapon in my hands. The kitchen barely has enough meat for the next few days."

"Aye. I'll need yer help, too. We must prepare barley for tea to soothe their fat guts after the feasts."

"And extra pain killers for those who canna stop drinking." Muriele looked over the nearby rows of plants, mentally noting the ones they would need.

"Pfft. I'd as soon let them suffer," Grunda muttered.

"Aye. But if they are like Lord Baldor and his men …?"

Grunda nodded. "Ye're right. 'Tis best to have aplenty. They canna do harm in their sleep."

Muriele shuddered. In their drunken rages, Baldor's men had taken to beating and raping women and young girls. She, her mother and as many females as they could hide, sheltered in Muriele's room. They locked her chamber doors and pulled heavy objects to block anyone from forcing them open.

She and Grunda worked peacefully together. After gathering the herbs, Muriele startled when Gille appeared at the hut's open doorway.

He straightened his spindly body and studied the top of the doorsill as if seeing the words there. He took a deep breath, puffing out his chest.

"My master says if ye dinna come at the proper time to dine, ye will go without eating till the next morrow," he rushed the words out in one breath. His chest went flat again. As if afeared Grunda would cast a spell on him, his eyes widened.

The old seer grunted and nodded. "Thank ye for telling us."

"'Tis not all." He sucked in another deep breath and began again. "Ye are to help him in his bath first and tend his … his …," he hesitated again and turned red.

"His?" Muriele tilted her head, working her mouth.

He blushed even darker. "I didna know the word. My master only pointed."

"Aye? And where did he point?"

Gille gulped and looked shamed. "Here."

The boy poked his finger at the joining of his thighs, turned and ran all the way back to the keep.

Muriele's hands fisted until she feared her nails would cut into her skin.

"Have ye the knives I left here for safekeeping?"

"Aye. I wrapped them in yer torn clothing."

Grunda turned from the table where she was carefully placing herbs in stoppered jars and went over to the far corner to a small trunk. She lifted the led then reached in for the bundle of Muriele's clothes and held them out to her.

Muriele patted the bundle. Her face grew hot when she laid them out on the far end of the table.

"They're gone!" She went over to kneel beside the trunk and searched through it. "Ye didna mistake the place ye hid Mother's eating knife and Father's dagger?

"Nay." Grunda touched Muriele's shoulder and gently moved her back. "Give me time to feel."

Muriele nodded and rose to stand across the room. She watched as Grunda lowered the lid and latched it then knelt before it. The seer's head tilted back. As she chanted ancient words, her eyes closed. Raising her hands in the air, they hovered over the trunk, still and silent. Finally, she let her hands fall to stroke over the latch.

Lowering her head, she jerked back and opened her eyes.

"Sir Magnus took them."

Magnus watched as servants prepared his bath, impatient to wash off the hours of grime after training Kinbrace's warriors. His routine had made them the most efficient warriors east of Ben Clibrick. Never would he let them be idle for a day, else their muscles would turn to flab.

"Ye did a fine job of washing Odin today, Gille." He looked at the boy anxiously waiting beside the door and glancing over his shoulder.

"Thank ye." His face lit. "He didna try to bite me today.

Not even once!"

"Good. Ye need all yer fingers to become a squire," Magnus nodded solemnly. "And Gille?"

"Aye, master?"

"Ye told the lady to come right away?"

"I did." Hearing a sound behind him, he sighed as if he'd been holding his breath. "She comes now, sir."

"Ye may go."

Gille had no sooner scooted away from the door than Muriele stormed into the room. Mayhap he exaggerated. But she did burst into the room as if a gale had shoved her through the doorway. She didn't say a word. There was no need. Her blazing eyes told what she thought. She carried a small bundle of clothes. He recognized them.

He turned his back and began shedding his clothing, ignoring her. Would she dare argue with him over the loss of the knife and dagger?

Stripping didn't take long. He wore only a sweaty tunic. Even his feet were bare. He felt her smoldering glare on the bare skin of his back. No doubt, she'd like to plunge a blade between his ribs.

Providing her with the opportunity, he took his own dagger from where he'd placed it on the table. After he cut the knot holding the bandage about his thigh, he tossed the knife onto the foot of his bed. He took overlong unwinding the bandage then studied the wound. No pus oozed from the scar's edges or through the closing thread holes.

When he stood and strolled over to the tub, she forced her gaze away from the knife. He felt her fire and anger and knew she used all the control she could muster.

Water sloshed as he climbed into the bath and abruptly sat.

"Come. Tend my hair."

'Twas a harshly given order. Tension charged the air like a sudden burst of thunder on a clear day. What had she been like when her father still lived at Blackbriar? Attired in the bright gowns he'd studied in her bedchamber, she must easily have been the most comely woman in the Highlands.

Had she suitors aplenty? 'Twas surprising she was not already wed. He frowned. Before he left to spend his visit at Clibrick, he'd heard some whispered words amongst the women about Blackbriar. He'd ask the married knights. Their wives always knew the hidden secrets of nearby holdings.

He shrugged and ducked his head back under the water. As he straightened up, he opened his eyes in time to see her hand grab something beside her.

Fast as a raptor's claws, his fingers seized her wrist in a tight vise.

Chapter 14

"**D**ID YE INTEND TO seek yer revenge?"

As he stared up at her, his eyes narrowed to mere slits. "Revenge against what? Filth? Stinking sweat?"

Her tone was laden with scorn. No woman had ever dared speak to him in such a way. He jerked her arm forward. She cried out and tumbled over his right shoulder. Her breasts brushed against his face before she landed pressed to his chest. Water soaked her clothing.

She fought for balance. Bent over the tub rim, her hips in the air, her feet sought firmer ground.

His nostrils flared feeling the softness of her breasts, the whisper of her gasp against his chin. Gazing down, he studied the soft flesh pressed against him. Her nipples hardened through her wet clothing. His eager cock responded.

The ribbon confining her hair slipped free. The silky strands brushed against his nose and lips. He inhaled her clean sent. If he lifted her and suckled her breast, would they taste of apples and spices?

Taking his time, his gaze noted every feature of her face. Her eyes shot sparks. She didn't flinch. Her nostrils, far from pinched with fear, flared. Her lips didn't quiver but remained resolute. Not a flicker of fear anywhere. What he did see was barely held rage. Could he force her to lose control? His heavy stones urged him to.

He grasped her head and held it steady as he sought to soften those determined lips until they either screeched with rage or softened and sighed. He preferred the latter.

His lids narrowed thinking of the heat of her mouth and all

the erotic things those beautiful lips could do. His eyelids near closed imagining them sliding up around his cock.

His unruly member's eagerness near created a wave.

She knew his thoughts, for her luscious mouth clamped together in denial. Holding her firmly, he ran his tongue over her plump lower lip. She had tried to deny him by sucking its softness between her teeth. He chuckled. Had she been immune to his caress, she would have had no need to thwart it.

He traced their outline then nibbled gently at her upper lip. She quivered slightly. He stepped up his sensuous assault, plying his hot lips over hers, stopping to clasp the flesh with his teeth when it softened. He felt her shudder with the effort to withhold her feelings.

He didn't let her. His hand left her head and reached between them to cup her breast. When his thumb scraped over the wet cloth covering her nipple, she gasped and shivered. His tongue took advantage and plundered her mouth, swirling and dancing around as he explored her teeth then probed beyond to slide along her tongue in hot greeting.

When she groaned into his mouth, he lifted his head. Satisfied. He had forced the reaction he wanted. He kept her gaze pinned to his as he raised the hand grasping her wrist to see what she had so hastily picked up.

He stared. Dumbfounded.

Muriele was unable to detach herself from Magnus. Through her sodden clothing, his heated flesh pressed against her. To her shame, her breast betrayed her and became heavy. Her nipples hardened and itched, demanding attention.

Why? She had understood her body when Duncan of Dalbreak coaxed her into an alcove at Blackbriar. His kisses and soft touch had soothed any alarm he arose in her as his wet lips nibbled from her ears down to her vulnerable flesh peeking above the opening of her kirtle. When his hand had cupped and lifted her breast, the lightest touch of his thumb had seduced the nipple to harden and beg.

He had kissed her there, wetting the cloth. When he blew

his hot breath on it, she'd had an almost uncontrollable urge to press her breast closer. He had groaned as he nibbled the turgid nipple, soothing the itch there. Unwanted feelings near made her knees give way.

Was she a slattern? She feared so. Else, why did Magnus' lightest touch cause her to catch fire like summer heat lightning in a forest knee-deep in dried leaves? If the caresses had been by Duncan, someone she loved, aye. But Magnus was her enemy. A warrior who had fought and defeated anyone who posed a threat to Kinbrace. He'd forced Blackbriar to its knees like a castle made of clay.

If not for him, her mother would still be alive.

At first, she resisted when he forced her hand down to see what she had picked up. Once level with his eyes, she quickly squeezed her fist. He stared at her hand then blinked. Bubbles formed between her thumb and fisted fingers. She tilted her head and arched her brow when he finally met her gaze.

He cleared his throat. His face looked flushed with heat. It wasn't from the water.

"Now, if ye are through trying to break my wrist, I'll need more soap to wash yer hair."

Magnus released her and flushed even deeper. Her tone, though tinged with sarcasm, was patient as though talking to a not-too-bright youth.

If she used any more soap on the wretched man, he'd slip and slide when he tried to get out of the tub. 'Twould serve him right if he fell and banged his head on the wooden sides! She'd worked most of her anger out on his scalp before attacking his back. She hadn't the heart to be rough over the scars there.

When he decided he didn't need her help to bathe the rest of his body, she picked up her robe and went to the dark corner beside the door at his back. Before he finished washing his legs, she was out of her wet kirtle, her robe belted with a small cord around her waist. She pulled a chair over to the fireplace and put her wet clothing across the back. Hopefully, it would dry before she missed another meal in the Great Hall.

Sitting cross-legged on her pallet, she started to mend her torn hunting garments. When she picked up Grunda's small scissors to cut her thread, she felt his gaze on her.

"Dinna worry." She waved the scissors at him. "If I were to kill ye, it wouldn't be with this puny instrument. I'd use a blade that cuts deep. Besides, do ye think me such an eejit I would do it within yer own chambers where I couldn't escape?"

She didn't bother waiting for an answer but returned to her sewing.

Though Magnus did not look directly at her, he could see the way she attacked her clothing. No doubt, she regretted not stabbing the needle into his flesh with the same vigor she used on the cloth.

"Hmpf!" For sure, now was not the time to order her to cut his hair. 'Twas strange, the way he felt. Never before had a woman caused him to act like a fool.

Muriele's lids snapped open without a twinge of sleepiness lingering behind. It had been one of those rare nights when she awoke so rested she barely had to stretch sluggish muscles to spring out of bed. A wry smile on her lips, she shrugged. Springing wasn't the right word for someone who now rose from a pallet on the floor.

She sighed and shook her head, remembering the comfort of her feather mattress and pillows at Blackbriar. They had stuffed this pallet only enough to soften the hard floor. The pillow was near flat. After all, if they were plump, how could one roll them together and not take up room? The good thing about her new sleeping arrangements was the absence of ropes squeaking when she got up.

Heavy, even breathing coming from Magnus' large bed assured her he was still in a deep sleep. She slipped out of her robe and let it drop to the floor. Unable to resist a leisurely stretch, she threw back her head, her hands lifted in the cold air, her back arched. During the night, the ribbons holding her braids had come loose, freeing her hair. Wavy locks floated softly across her naked back. Rising to her toes, its sensual whispers over her body made her tremor.

Her muscles twitched with energy. For the first time since the louts had captured her, she was anxious for the day to begin. She had missed riding in the woods, tracking deer and snaring rabbits.

She froze in place. What was different?

She didn't feel alone with the dark any more. As if her limbs could sound an alert by moving too quickly, she eased her arms down. One covered her breasts. The opposite hand shielded her sex.

Was he awake? Hardly daring to breathe, she glanced toward the bed. Had she seen a glint of white? Like his eyes had been watching her?

She couldn't tell. The sounds of sleep were the same. Likely, she had imagined it. Feeling like a small rabbit staring at a crouched fox, she remained frozen. Counted to twenty. When Magnus didn't move, she inched down to take her folded hunting clothes from beneath her pillow.

The men who had captured her had near ruined them beyond repair. It had taken her well into the night to mend them, but she was well pleased with the results. The same small, neat stitches she had used on flesh, now made the garments stronger than ever. Where the men had ripped the cloth by her left breast, she sewed a seam from under her arms across to her breast. After looking at the finished seam, she made a matching one on the right without trying it on.

The other rents and damages had not taken long. She pulled the smock over her head and wiggled her body, helping the skirts to fall free.

She stopped. Held her breath. Frowned. Her imagination was getting the better of her. Magnus had not moved. She would have seen it, for her eyes had remained on him the whole time. Shuddering, she pulled her kirtle on and settled it. Always before, the kirtle had flowed over her breasts with ample room. Now it hugged her skin like hands cupping her breasts. It and the sleeping man made her nipples itch and swell.

She nibbled her lip. There was no time to add a piece of cloth to make her overdress fit looser. She would use the old shawl Grunda had given her. 'Twould hide her too-obvious curves.

After rolling her pallet and blanket, she sat on the floor and prepared to wait for the sun's rise. No sooner had she settled down than Magnus spoke in a husky voice filled with passion.

"Muriele? Now ye've awakened me, ye had best get below by the time I count to five, else I'll put this cockstand to good use."

Magnus vowed if she didn't hie herself off in time, she would be beneath him with his cock buried deep in her hot center.

Her startled gasp must have shaken her whole body.

"One." Her shadow sprang upward and twirled toward the door.

"Two." Reaching the door, she fumbled with the latch. Her ragged breathing matched his own, but for another reason.

"Three." The door slammed shut, but some piece of cloth caught, for it shoved open enough for her to grab it and retreat. 'Twas it the shawl, perchance?

Muriele's feet were going to be very cold, indeed. She was in such haste to escape his rampant cock she'd not taken the time to grab her shoes. He sighed and wished he'd not been so generous. Instead of giving her the chance to escape, he should have blocked her path.

Nay. When she'd stretched up on her toes, he should have wrapped his arms around her naked body and tossed her on the bed.

"Shite!"

His sex stretched and swelled so tight it burned. If it didn't find relief, could the skin on a cockstand split like over-ripe fruit? He closed his eyes and groaned, picturing her in the near dark. His hands moved down, seeking the only comfort left.

He'd sensed the moment Muriele awoke. Already facing her, he'd no need to move. His thick lashes allowed him to peer at her. When she'd arched her back, her woman's mound had thrust out, inviting his hand to cup it. He shuddered imagining her hot, wet sex cradled in his palm.

His lids had widened. She must have seen the glint of his eyes, for she stilled. He thought she'd bolt, but when he didn't move, she calmed.

Now, a long, agonized groan forced through clenched teeth as he arched up from the bed, his seed spurting, his legs straining. After several breaths, he collapsed back, spent.

"Devil's spawn," he muttered. She was his for the taking. Why had he spared her?

"Never again."

'Twas a vow.

"I thought you would look forward to the hunt this day," Esa said as she slid onto the bench beside Muriele.

"I am." Muriele rubbed her feet together, keeping them raised off the cold wood of the floor.

"Then why are you twitching and looking ready to bash someone's head?" She moved a little to the left and peeked beneath the tabletop to see bare toes flashing at her.

"Is something the matter with your feet? Did you injure them? Where are your shoes?"

Muriele looked at her friend. Her heart still pounded, which was no way to start a days hunt. She must be calm and deliberate in all her moves. Could telling Esa soothe her mind?

"I didna have time to don them."

Esa looked at the high table where Magnus sat, a scowl on his face and fire in his eyes as he stared at Muriele.

"He made you come below without your shoes?" Her voice rose.

Two men in hunting attire snickered and made comments about keeping lasses barefoot. 'Twas unlikely they could run fast enough to evade a randy male.

Muriele huffed and sent them a chilling look that would have made the surliest of Blackbriar's servants wilt.

She lowered her voice near to a whisper. "I awoke afore

dawn. Sir Magnus still slept soundly. At least I thought he did. I should have been faster about dressing. It was so early I didn't think he would hear me."

"Nay! Did he force you to his bed?"

"He allowed me to the count of five to leave the room. I near choked when I saw the size of his cockstand tenting the sheet."

Esa looked at her in disbelief. "Ye left?"

"'Twas either leave or he threatened to put it to good use."

Her friend sighed. "Every woman in this room, even the ones already wed, would have dawdled about and made sure she was far from the door when he stopped counting."

Muriele glanced around at the women, puzzled. "Why?"

"You have not been here long enough to know he's said to be the strongest lover in the Highlands."

"How would they know? Does he boast about his conquests?"

"Nay. The women do the praising. He never speaks of it."

"'Tis possible they enhance their tales to brag?"

"Even so, I still wouldn't refuse him."

"He has never taken ye to his bed?"

"'Tis his code. He ne'er takes a woman who belongs ..."

"My Lady?" Gille's soft voice spoke behind Muriele.

Esa's face lost all color. She looked stricken that someone might have heard her.

Muriele turned to see the young boy standing at her shoulder, her shoes and stockings in his hand. He thrust them at her as if he thought the mere fact of holding them was akin to touching her flesh.

"Thank ye, ye are most kind to bring them for me," she said as she took them from his hand and hid them in her lap.

"Sir Magnus bid me to." He looked up at the ceiling the way he had done at Grunda's hut and repeated what Magnus had said. "My master bid me to tell you a woman should always keep her shoes on if she intends to outrun a man."

The lad blushed so red he rivaled the brightest holly in wintertime. He did his own rapid retreat.

Muriele put her head down and peered from the corner of her eyes to see Magnus still watched her, his face taut, his eyes accusing as if she had deliberately seduced him then fled.

"Lean forward and block his view, please, Esa," she whispered.

Muriele turned sideways on the bench and struggled with her stocking and shoes until she got them on. It wasn't until she heard a choking sound of someone snorting porridge through his nose when she looked up. The men at the table's end had their heads beneath the table watching her every move.

Quietly so as not to alert them, she picked up the big spoon used to serve the hot gruel and filled it. Holding the handle with her right hand, she tipped it back with her left then when taut enough, let loose. Her aim was accurate. It splattered over the men's backs. The sharp cracks of their heads on the hard wood pleased her.

"Ow!" One man near fell off his bench trying to straighten up. "That be a dafty thing to do!"

"We was but lookin' for a spoon he dropped," said the other as he rubbed his head. His eye slithered away from the two wooden spoons sitting in plain view.

"Be glad I have no blade, else I would slit yer ears." Her appetite gone, Muriele rose from the table. "Come. I must find Grunda. She promised to prepare a sack for healing to take with me. By the looks of yonder hunters, they'll have need of patching afore the day darkens."

Walking with deliberate dignity and grace, her head held high, she left the great hall. In these last days, she had not failed to note some of the fine garments now worn by the Kinbrace women had once belonged to the women of Blackbriar.

Gille met her at the foot of the stairs leading down to the bailey. He held tight to the reins of a reddish-brown gelding ... if one could still call it such. Other than its height, the poor thing was barely fit for teaching youths to ride. She walked around the hapless animal, stroking and talking to it.

"Puir thing. I will be most careful not to lead ye into danger. For truth, ye could not outrun an ancient hare much less an angry boar."

As she talked, the beast responded to her soothing tone

by standing tall and snuffling as he butted his head against her shoulder.

"Dinna thank me. Ye will be most tired carrying my weight through the woods. But a hunt?" She shook her head in sympathy.

"Ye think the beast isna worthy enough for ye to ride?" Magnus' mocking tone caused her mouth to tighten.

Muriele would not let him bait her. She raised a haughty eyebrow and scanned him from head to toe. He wore naught but his dark green and blue kilt, wrapped around and bunched at his waist, the end draped over his left shoulder. A massive sword belt held it all in place.

Magnus seized her shoulders and held her at arms length. He deliberately mimicked her study, but instead of cold indifference, hot passion blazed beneath heavy lids. Her flesh responded to his intent gaze slowly traveling over her. 'Twas as if he stripped her of her clothing and his fingers explored every inch of her flesh. She used all her will to appear indifferent.

He lowered his cheek to rub it softly against hers; his lips touched her left ear.

His voice near purred. His eyes sparked with promise.

"If Bolt betwixt yer legs is not to yer liking, we will return to my bed where ye can ride a lively cock instead."

Shivers crept down her back on feeling the softness of the short beard framing his jaw. She fought even harder to keep her composure, for his hot breath teased her ear.

"Be that what ye'd prefer? Hmm?"

CHAPTER 15

"HUH!" MURIELE SNORTED AND wrenched from his grasp, ignoring his remark. "Am I to hunt with weapons, or do ye intend I throttle a deer with my bare hands?"

He beckoned and Sweyn came to hand her the bow and quiver of arrows she'd used to keep Magnus at bay in the old hut.

"Thank ye, Sweyn." She slipped her arm through the straps of the quiver. Using her own bow, she had no need to test it, other than to make sure the string was taut. Rolling her shoulders, she settled the bow and arrows until they felt comfortable.

"'Tis dangerous to hunt without a dagger," she said as she turned back to Magnus. "You took my father's from my belongings."

"When ye have need of one, I will return it."

"Hold on, lass, afore ye mount."

Muriele peered around Magnus to see Grunda hurrying and waggling her hands at a burly rooster. The old woman carried the healing supplies tied in a bundle.

"Get away, ye silly creature." She hopped to the side as the fowl flapped his wings to lift off the ground, its head extended, beak open for a quick peck.

When the pesky fowl kept up his antics, she stopped and pointed a gnarled finger at him. He flapped and squawked until she fixed him with squinted eyes and muttered beneath her breath. The rooster let out one deranged screech and scurried away as if a torch was singeing his tail feathers.

"'Tis one thing to hunt with skirts when ye are alone, but wear this so these randy varmints' dinna get ideas." Grunda took an old plaid from around her shoulders and handed it to Muriele.

Magnus nodded his approval and strolled away. Muriele's gaze followed and watched as his long legs carried him over to a strange horse. It didn't surprise her, for only a fool would hunt astride a mount as rare as Odin. No warrior wanted his warhorse gored by an angry boar. When Magnus put his left foot in the stirrup, his muscles pulled taut, accenting their slim muscled strength. When he threw his right leg over the horse's withers, his kilt flew in the breeze, revealing a tantalizing view of naked arse and legs.

She forced her gaze away while she and Grunda wrapped the yellow and black plaid loosely around Muriele's hips and tied it in a knot at her waist.

"Mount now and ye can spread the wool to hide yer legs," Grunda said and patted her shoulder.

Gille came and cupped his hands, his eyes diverted as he aided her to swing up into the saddle. He turned his back while she draped the cloth around her like a blanket. When she was done, he tied the healing supplies to her saddle. When she glanced up from helping him, Grunda nodded at the spot where she'd anchored the plaid near Muriele's right knee.

Muriele smiled her gratitude. Grunda had hidden something in the cloth.

"Dinna take all day, else dawn will see the best game gone."

The bailey was crowded with knights and their squires carrying their master's favorite falcon. They would hunt in one section of the dense forest while other hunters would look elsewhere for the smaller animals. Magnus, leading the last group, would go deeper into the woods.

He had not bothered to tell her what their game would be for the day. The falconers clattered over the wooden bridge out into the cleared field, then turned sharply southwest where the best grouse hunting was available.

Each group of hunters had their special dogs. Some were valued for their scenting abilities and their skill to run the prey down. The men who trained the most robust dogs to hunt wild boars kept them separated from the other packs. Pages too unskilled to be in on the kill carried extra quivers of arrows, spears and cudgels. Varlets and squires hefted boar spears and regular spears.

While Magnus looked over everyone in the bailey, she adjusted the wool as if afeared it would come lose and expose her flesh. She sighed with relief finding Grunda had sewn a pocket on the underside where she'd hidden a dagger near as long as Muriele's had been.

She felt a thrill of excitement when Magnus motioned the dog handlers to start out of the castle. He beckoned her to join him. Though Bolt had seemed too old to be in the hunt, the beast brightened and eagerly trotted close to Magnus. When he reached out to butt his nose on Magnus' leg, she tried to hold him back. He didn't allow it. To her surprise, Magnus reached down and scratched the graying hair between Bolt's eyes and murmured to him, then thumped his neck and motioned him forward. Bolt's head rose high and he pranced like a young stallion trying to lure a shy mare.

Quite some time later, Muriele raised a grimy hand to push the hair out of her eyes. Though she had secured it with a leather strip, each time she brushed against it reaching for an arrow, curling locks made their way free.

A stream of carts and wagons went back and forth. Varlets placed the kills on small carts. Once it contained a goodly number of hares and other small creatures, the driver headed back to the castle. If the carcass was a large animal, they wrestled it onto a low, flat wagon and sent its driver on his way.

Before noon, the hunters gathered at a large clearing beside a stream where servants placed bread, rounds of cheese, hard cooked eggs, a plentiful supply of fruit and dried fish on a long cloth.

'Twas fortunate injuries had been minor and needed only cleaning and binding. Muriele had no need to use her needle and practice her stitching. Freeing her unruly hair, she gathered it again to bind it more securely. She shoved her sleeves up her arm and knelt by the stream. As she splashed her face and neck, the cold water refreshed her.

Since the fall of Blackbriar, she'd never felt better. Using the end of the worn plaid, she dried herself. Though Magnus knelt beside her, she ignored him. He looked like he had eaten soured fruit for his mouth pinched in at the corners.

She stretched and near snickered when she overheard one of the men saying she was as fast at spotting a hare as the beagles were. No one had properly trained the men to hunt the creatures. They preferred bigger game. But hares had been an important part of the food stocked in Blackbriar's kitchens. She supposed they were as important at Kinbrace. Today, she'd bagged more hare than anyone, even more than Magnus had.

"Dinna dawdle, woman. The men are taking the dogs to the best deer hunting area."

She nodded and grabbed an apple, a hunk of cheese and a mug of cider before going over to sit with her back against a gnarled oak tree. Squirrels ran for safety to the highest part of the tree, not trusting the weary hunters below.

Every time she took a bite of food, she felt eyes watching her. If it was not Magnus, then it was Sweyn. Gille, a chunk of dark bread and some strong cheese in one hand and a boar spear hugged tight to his side, glanced around. The boy's shoulders slumped when none of the other squires spoke to him. He shifted from one foot to the other, undecided whether to sit or stand.

She raised her hand and beckoned to him, inviting him to sit with her. Her heart softened seeing his relief. The poor boy likely missed the people in his village. This must be his first hunt. Though it always stimulated her, he might be a little alarmed by the dangerous riding.

Too soon, it was time to start again. When Gille helped her to remount, she thanked him and warned him to be cautious.

Days before, castle hunters had noted where the male deer were. Since it wasn't mating season, they'd be in segregated herds. Within three leagues, the large dogs led them to two beautiful harts, the red male deer. Each had ten tines on their antlers. Muriele avoided looking at their beautiful eyes, hating they were fated to fill peoples' bellies.

Once they felled a deer, they sent it back on the wagons. The hunters rode on through an especially dark section of the thick forest. When the dogs began even more excited baying, the riders hurried to catch up to the handlers, who had cornered a magnificent hart.

They formed a semi-circle and waited as the handlers tried to call off the dogs. They whistled and called their names, cursing when the dogs ignored them. Finally, the handlers grabbed the more stubborn dogs by their thick collars and attached rope leashes to haul them back. This huge hart bore fourteen tines. Though three arrows pierced its flesh, it reared and beat its hooves at the dogs.

Magnus was already out of his saddle. Something wasn't right. As he approached the deer, his sword ready, the hart ignored him, its eyes focused on the forest to its left.

Hackles rose on Muriele's nape. She scanned the dark bushes and sensed something lurked there the hart feared more than man or dog. With one quick slash, Magnus put the creature out of its misery. He turned away from the trees and headed toward his horse.

Muriele's hand whipped up to notch an arrow. She bent the bow to its maximum capacity and let loose her arrow at something about to burst from the bushes. It whizzed past Magnus' left shoulder, its feathers near brushed his ear.

Magnus face turned grim as a hangman securing a noose around a murderer's neck.

His eyes blazed at her. His lips thinned.

"Seize her!"

Chapter 16

MAGNUS' SHOUT BELLOWED OVER the clamor of the dogs and the piercing scream of a wild pig. Sweyn backhanded Muriele, knocking her off her saddle. She hit the ground and rolled. Still crouching, she glimpsed a large boar about to erupt from the darkness. Unaware, men and dogs scrambled after the first beast where her arrow protruded from its eye. Magnus' sword pierced its side, putting an end to its rampage.

She snatched the boar spear from Gille's hand. She did not have the strength to throw it hard enough to pierce the boar's thick hide. Warbling a pagan cry as wild and eerie as a Banshee's wail, she ran, the spear aimed at Magnus.

Nearly at his side, she tightened every muscle, slammed the wooden shaft into the ground and braced it with her feet. Behind Magnus, a beast burst out into the opening, its beady eyes maddened. It lowered its head, its tusks aimed at Magnus' back. Too late, it sensed the threat and tried to leap. It impaled itself on the spear. 'Twas silent.

"Ooof!" The force knocked Muriele to the ground.

The screams of lost souls in Hades could not have been louder. Men were shouting and near falling over themselves.

She landed on her side, thankfully on a thick carpet of leaves.

Gille ran over to his master, so agitated Magnus couldn't understand him.

"My lord! Her spear stopped the boar." His thin arm came up as he pointed behind Magnus.

For the first time, Magnus felt a mighty weight on his plaid and backed up. No spear pinned his clothing to the ground. The boar's tusk held it firm. Muriele's spear was lodged in the beast's heart clear through to its cross guard.

For the first time in his life, a woman had bested Magnus. He didn't like the feeling! He'd thought at first she'd aimed her arrow at his neck, for its feathers scratched his flesh as it whizzed past. Before he knew she'd aimed so precisely to skewer a running pig, he'd ordered her seized.

If that wasn't humiliating enough, she'd kept a maddened boar from sinking its tusk into his blarsted arse!

Had he become too aware of her breasts swaying and straining against her clothing? Her delighted laughter when a hare scurried up behind a hunter, had coaxed a smile from his lips. Hades! He *never* smiled.

The hart had acted fearful, but he'd failed to pay heed. And after the pig charged, even a foolish hunter would have kenned there would likely be a mate for the damned pig! 'Twas Muriele's fault. She distracted him and made him careless.

Two men had piled atop her, locking her to the earth.

"Get up, fools," Sweyn ordered. "She has done naught wrong."

The men sprang up and helped her to her feet, sheepish smiles on their faces. Magnus narrowed his eyes, studying them. They'd both made free with their hands, for their cocks tented their plaids. Muriele waited calmly, as if she knew they'd taken leave of their senses but would regain them soon.

Sweyn quietly searched her for hidden weapons. When he found the knife concealed in the old plaid, he shook his head.

"I didn't believe you to be so foolish, lady," he said.

Magnus scowled. From whom had she stolen it? And why had she felt the need of a special weapon? She hadn't meant to use it on him. She could have relaxed on Bolt and let nature take its course.

He waved his hand at Sweyn, who moved back. Magnus stepped so close the toes to his boots crowded her feet. He ground his teeth together knowing he was a fool to have brought her on the hunt.

He hadn't been himself since lusting after her in the darkness before dawn. Unfulfilled passion made a man careless.

All he'd thought about was his raging cock and sinking it deep into her hot body.

"Where did ye steal the knife?"

Indecision flashed over Muriele's face. When she didn't answer, he took the knife from Sweyn and turned it around in his hand. He gave a brief nod, recognizing it as the old seer's.

He held it, blade upright, close to her face. He waited. His gaze bored into her eyes and willed her to speak.

"As ye slept, I took it from Grunda's hut."

"I would have woken had ye opened the chamber door."

Muriele snorted. "*If* ye had heard me. Ye snore so loud the noise would drown out a rooster's crow. Grunda, too, sleeps soundly. She didna hear me when I took it from her gardening supplies."

"Mayhap I failed to hear ye leave. But returning?" As he widened his stance, his eyes narrowed, gauging every little change in her features.

"I waited outside the door until I was sure ye were still grinding out noises sounding like the grating of the drawbridge chains."

"For certs ye tell the truth?"

"Aye!"

He rocked back on his feet, his face hard. Triumphant.

"Since ye come and go with such stealth, 'tis best I keep ye closer of a night."

His smoldering black gaze traveled over her body from head to toe then back up to hold her gaze. He nodded, making up his mind.

"Ye will be in my bed. At my side."

She swallowed a gasp and near blurted out an objection. Instead, she bit her lip and remained quiet. Thinking of the night to come, satisfaction coursed through him.

"Release her. And Sweyn? Dinna let her out of yer sight."

She had not much time to think, for Magnus decided this last game would be enough. With it added to what the other two hunting squads brought in, they had game aplenty. Feradoch had led the hawkers, for 'twas his favorite sport. His female Peregrine was ever ready to hunt, and being larger than most, brought down the fattest game birds, grouse, duck and an occasional goose.

Once they were winding their way back through the forest, she'd ample time to consider her decisions for today. Why had she interfered in the hunt? If she'd hesitated, even for a second, the outcome would've been different. If not for Magnus, her mother would still be alive. She'd been a foolish eejit to act on instinct. She should've let the boar do its worst. On Magnus' proud arse. A tusk piercing his ballocks and taking that part he valued the most would've caused turmoil. She could have outwitted the warriors and escaped.

Ha! Who did she think she was fooling? Not herself. The man would've had to die instantly else Sweyn would have ensured she cared for his master's wounds. If the boar had gored Magnus between his legs, 'twas possible relieving him of his great, hairy stones would've been the only way to save him. How arrogant would he have been then?

After all, they gelded a stallion to make the horse more pliable. She took glee in imagining Magnus yawning and refusing to do manly things. Would he decline to wear a sword because the weight was too heavy? Or even simper and dress in brightly colored tunics as English courtiers did?

She was so pleased with her imaginings she ignored all around her.

"What mirthful thoughts spring from yer brain, lady?" Magnus harsh voice reminded her he rode alongside. "Ye look as smug as a field cat, a filched boar's ear in its mouth stalking high atop the kitchen rafters."

"Nay, they didna spring from my brain but from my sight."

She should have kept her tongue behind her teeth! Now wasn't the time to goad him.

"Ah. Ye envisioned the shame I would have suffered had the boar's tusk lodged itself in my hide?"

"Nay. Not yer hide."

Holy Saints! Why did she not keep her mouth shut?

Magnus shot her a scowl knowing exactly where she'd pictured it.

"Best ye remember, Lady, a bay dog is clever. He will keep the cat prisoner atop the rafters. It canna live there out of reach. It must come down. The dog will have its revenge."

"Ah. Not if the cat waits until the cur sleeps."

"Perchance he will learn to sleep with one eye open."

Muriele glanced sideways and noted Magnus regarded her with cold speculation. She clamped her teeth together, determined to keep silent the rest of the ride back. Her foolish taunts had only served to spur him into being more vigilant in keeping her prisoner.

Magnus had his temper under control by the time they rode through the barbican and into the outer bailey. Stable hands were there to tend to the knights' horses. The hawkers had arrived before they did and began to compare their hunt's spoils.

As each cart had lumbered into the castle, the drivers gave a total of dead animals and who had felled them. 'Twas Chief Olaf's custom to honor the hunter providing the most game, also the hunters bagging the largest prey. They would sit at the high table for the night's meal.

"My Peregrine brought down a large grouse, heavier than any the archers brought in," Feradoch bragged. "'Tis a fact it is so big the clever bird did its kill low to the ground."

"Well, now, who killed this huge hart?" Olaf tugged the deer's head by its antlers, noting the cleanly slit throat. He thumped Magnus on the shoulder and grinned. "From the slash, I would wager 'twas your doing?"

"Aye." Magnus nodded.

"Who stopped the giant boar? 'Twas good he used a boar spear. The cross guard kept the beast from attacking the bearer. Your kill, also?" Olaf looked expectantly at Magnus.

Magnus ground his teeth, not wanting to tell the tale of how a mere woman had bested him in the hunt. No doubt, Feradoch would piss himself laughing at his expense. Sweyn saved him having to answer.

"After felling the hart, Sir Magnus turned. The boar charged out of the woods. The beastie all but leapt to its death on the spear."

"Which of the knights threw it?" Olaf looked around at the milling hunters then at Sweyn.

"'Twas not thrown but braced." Sweyn said.

"Well, then, what hunter braced it?"

"The Lady of Blackbriar," Sweyn replied.

"You were fools to allow the lady a spear." Olaf's tone was incredulous.

A snarl started deep in Magnus' throat much like one of the hunter's dogs. 'Twas the first time anyone had dared call him a fool. He feared no man. Not even Olaf. Not any more. He fixed his foster father with a black stare fraught with warning.

"Enough! Do ye think I would cower from a woman?"

Feradoch rubbed his chin as one eyebrow climbed slowly. He studied Magnus. Circled him. His blue eyes seemed drawn to the ragged tear in Magnus' clothing.

"By the saints! 'Twas the woman who was the fool. She saved your worthless arse."

Magnus fought hard not to backhand his foster brother and break his blarsted nose. Clamping his teeth together, he walked away. He didn't want to ruin this last two days with Feradoch. But if the man prodded him again, he'd break far more than his elegant nose.

He spotted Muriele and Esa, each as tall as the other, walking toward Grunda's hut. Golden hair and black, side by side, as they conversed quietly. No doubt, Muriele would tell Grunda of today's happenings. Not for one minute did he believe she had stolen the knife.

In Grunda's hut, while they put away the rest of the supplies, Muriele described the wounds she had cleaned and with what she had dosed the men. She stood behind a screen bathing from a large bucket of heated water while rinsing from another. Not satisfied she'd washed the stench of blood away, she had Grunda empty the soapy bucket and hand her another.

The old seer and Esa drank a hot herbal brew, their back to the door. Suddenly, a draft swept the room. Had Esa left? Muriele, her hair dripping water, quickly draped the drying cloth around her. It barely covered her breasts to her thighs as she stepped around the screen. Too late, she saw Esa still seated with Grunda. 'Twas Magnus in the open doorway, legs spread wide, staring at her. With heated eyes and a fierce scowl, he looked mean and ill tempered.

She had thought herself crudely soiled from today's hunt, but Magnus had barely a hand's-breath of flesh on his massive torso unstained. When he'd slit the throats of the biggest deer to put them out of their misery, their blood had spurted in wide splatter patterns.

"Ye cleanse yerself when I have need of ye to wash the filth from my own body? Don yer clothes and come tend to it."

Magnus' penetrating gaze heated as if he peered through the linen cloth. She folded her arms across her chest and opened her mouth to berate him for bursting into the hut. Before she could speak a word, his arm raised. In a blur, Grunda's knife hurtled across the room. Its tip thumped into the hard-packed earth floor — between her feet.

Magnus spoke without taking his gaze from Muriele. His voice became menacingly quiet, almost near a harsh whisper.

"Dinna ever give Muriele a knife again, old woman. Be warned. If ye do, I will see ye turned out of every village for a hundred leagues around."

"I told ye …" Muriele got no further.

"Ye lied. Ne'er do so again."

Magnus had spaced the words apart making them more sinister.

Muriele knew he dared her to speak again, to enter any further excuses. Wisely, she kept silent. He nodded.

"Ye will sit alongside me at the evening meal. And tomorrow's feast."

He half turned to leave, but Muriele stopped him.

"Why? Ye've never treated me as a hostage of rank afore."

The muscle in his jaw twitched as he faced her again.

"'Tis the custom for yer hunting results. I will return one of yer dresses. See ye wear it. It will be on my bed … the bed where ye will sleep from now on."

As his gaze traveled over her, his eyes heated with lust. Again. Before she could retort, he stalked from the hut and slammed the door behind him.

Magnus made his way to the keep. His thoughts brought a menacing scowl to his face. His expression and angry strides cleared a pathway all the way through the milling bailey.

He had no intention of allowing Muriele to get away unscathed for lying to him. Ever since he had entered the bailey the first day he'd returned to Kinbrace, she lurked in his deepest thoughts, distracting him from his duties.

If that wasn't bad enough, of late, sound sleep was nigh impossible. She entered his dreams unbidden, seducing him. Each dream had become more worrisome. Where before he had dreamt of hunting, battling between clans and swiving the bonnie women who vied for his bed, Muriele intruded.

Blarsted Lucifer's bloated balls! 'Twas *his* dreams. He should have mastery over what she did. Yet, she always denied him release for his throbbing cock. Her long legs locked around his back, her hips rose, inviting his swelling member into her slick center. Just as the head pushed through, her body shattered around him in bits and pieces like the thinnest crockery dropped on a stone floor.

Even more frustrating, those pieces turned to ash and floated out the window, carried on a puff of wind. He awoke with a raging cockstand. He huffed, for his plight was no surprise. That he did not leave his bed and seek out a willing partner, was.

Before the Lady of Blackbriar entered his life, the mere thought of the lovely young widow Flori with her red hair and blue eyes, or Ingirid, equally lovely with blond hair, readied him to swive. Their bed sport had been more satisfying than any of his other partners. Since he installed Muriele in his room, his sex failed to quiver when the lasses' pressed their breasts against his arm, inviting him to their beds.

For truth, this irritating, fashious lass had near unmanned him. He clambered up the keeps stairway, his mind intent on the day.

At the hunt, Muriele had sighted the large pig about to burst from the woods. He was closest. Why hadn't he seen and skewered it? Her arrow's aim had been accurate. If its path had not been so close to his neck, it would have missed the animal.

Thinking about the boar, he ground his teeth. Never had he failed to sense danger. He had killed many an enemy who thought him unaware as they stalked him in the dark. His not noting the vicious creature had put him nearer to death than at any time in his life. No one else at the hunt had paid heed, either.

When Muriele charged at him with her chilling, high-pitched Banshee warbling, he'd thought she meant to skewer him. Her screams and his men's shouting had drowned out the sounds of the boar charging out of the forest. He'd pulled his sword from the pig and was preparing to thrust it into Muriele's side when she slammed the spear's shaft into the ground and braced it with her feet.

His carelessness and the humiliation of a woman doing what he and his trained warrior's had failed to do sparked his temper like lightning hitting a field of dried flax. He redirected his anger toward her.

'Twas fortunate she overstepped today by carrying the hidden dagger and saying she'd left the room during the night. He'd known it for a lie. His dreams had kept him from sleeping.

One good thing came of it. Now, he had reason to take her to his bed and finally get her out of his blood. As with all women who'd drawn his lust, one swiving would break her hold on him.

Gille had seen his bath awaited him when he reached his bedchamber. He threw off his clothing and climbed into the tub, motioning the boy to leave. He dunked his head and slung the hair from his face before he leaned back, resting against the high tub end. A man could easily sleep immersed in water. It drew the tiredness from his limbs. Closing his eyes, he calmed his breathing and let his temper cool.

The faint scent of warm apples and spices drifted on a breath of wind. Muriele had entered, though he had not heard the door open. He felt her behind him. As if asleep, he remained still and breathed slowly. His lids opened a mere slit so he would see her hand. When she made her move, his grasp near broke her wrist.

Chapter 17

"Ye honor me with yer fear, my lord. Do ye ken I, a mere woman, am skilled enough to kill Magnus the Ruthless?" Muriele leaned forward grateful she'd startled him. "Do ye intend to break my wrist afore I can cleanse the blood splatters from yer face?"

"Foolish lass! 'Tis the second time ye near caused me to snap yer neck."

"Ye didn't hear me enter? Hm. And yet, 'twas much easier to leave yer room and ease myself back in when ye were snorting and snuffling amidst yer pillows."

"I dinna snort and snuffle!"

"What would ye name such heavy breathing and grunting? I thought ye'd taken a poor lass to yer bed."

He did not answer. His grip slackened and she pulled her arm away. As she spread pine-scented soap over the cloth, she felt the force of his dark eyes watching her every move.

"Hm. Mayhap I'll sleep more quietly once I am betwixt yer legs."

Muriele snorted with such energy it ruffled the hair beside his eyes.

"What now, woman?"

"I dinna intend to share yer bed."

"Ye think I give ye a choice?"

"Ye canna order me to make love with ye."

"For certs, I can." He waggled his fingers, reminding her to continue bathing him. "But then, I did not ask ye to 'make love.' I require someone to satisfy my urges. Since ye will be in my bed, adding another woman would crowd my comfort."

"Ye have not the right."

She slapped a handful of soap on the top of his head then scrubbed furiously, not stopping the soapy water from running down his forehead into his eyes. Instead of yelling, he took his time to feel around for the cloth, wring it out and wipe his eyes.

"Aye. I have the right. By the spoils of conquest."

"Ye conquered Lord Baldor. Ye dinna have authority over Blackbriar's heir without King David's consent."

"Aye. Yer stepfather left no heir. I have privilege over anyone captured during the siege."

"Ha! Then ye have no claim over me. Did ye take me from Blackbriar to Kinbrace with the other women?"

He grew still beneath her hands. For truth, though he knew she'd been there, he and his men hadn't identified her among the captives.

Muriele near heard his teeth grind together.

"Ye know I didna. But ye will still share my bed. I canna trust ye to stay put of a night."

Her hands stopped digging into his scalp and continued in a more comforting way.

"Ye will not force me to swive?"

"Ne'er have I needed to *force* a woman. They seek my bed. Since I have held ye here, they have been most canny."

Canny? Then he was swiving women in some other part of the castle? A painful ache filled her chest. No wonder when he sought his bed he slept as if something had robbed him of all energy!

'Twould be a snowy day in summer afore she would ever *seek* his bed. Wisely, she did not speak. Instead, she distracted her thoughts by using a goodly amount of soap on his back and shoulders then scrubbing fiercely.

"That will do, Muriele."

Magnus took the bathing cloth from her and stood, preferring to bathe himself. He only needed help on his hair and back, not wanting to leave dirt or gore he couldn't see. When he had her bathe his legs before, it was to test her obedience. He pressed his lips together. She was one woman who didn't bend easily.

He propped his foot against the tub's side to scrub down to his feet. He felt her gaze and heard the sharp intake of her breath. He fought to keep the grin off his face. Likely, his turgid sex startled her. She'd best get used to it. Arousal was the state he was most likely in every time she came near.

"Yer stitches are gone. Did Sweyn take them out?"

"Nay. I did. They became bothersome."

"Ye should have sought Grunda's help or mine. The flesh may not have grown tightly together."

She started toward him, her eyes fixed on the long scar. The closer she came, the greater his cock responded. Before, when she'd tended the wound, the pain had kept his sex under control. Now, if she touched him, he'd likely explode. By the widening of her eyes, she could no longer ignore his condition.

Wisely, she stopped.

"The wound is healed enough. Tend to yerself." He nodded toward the bed.

She followed his gaze to see a soft, blue-green kirtle and a silver smock rested atop the covers. Her face froze with a startled look. She stepped backward as if putting distance between her and the clothing. Were they not her own? He had noted them the day he prowled through her room at Blackbriar. It looked to have spilled from the bottom of her clothing chest, as if was the last thing taken from it. He had picked it up with his sword tip and inhaled its scent, picturing the daughter of the castle wearing it even before he knew her face.

"Are they not yer own?"

"They were. I dinna want to wear them."

"Of all yer garments, the kirtle is by far the prettiest. Wear it."

"Nay!"

Her stubbornness pricked his anger. He wanted to see her in the dress. By Lucifer's bloated gut, she'd wear it!

"Ye will. If not, ye'll go to the great hall in naught but yer skin!" Menace tinged his words. His eyes narrowed in a scorching look.

Shudders swept down her body. When she went to the bed,

she stared at the clothing there. Her hand hovered over them, hesitated then drew back.

"Dinna think to thwart me in this." Her hesitation heated his temper. His chin thrust out and he slowly stepped out of the tub.

Good. Her hand finally closed around the garments and picked them up. She paid heed to his command. Once she had them in her grasp, she brought them to her breasts and hugged the garments to chest. She shuddered again before she stiffened and turned her back.

To rob him of his pleasure, the aggravating woman intended to dress in the corner where there was only faint light. He stalked to the fireplace, leaving a trail of water behind him, and tossed two additional squares of peat on the burning fire. While he dried, he studied her. She looked undecided on how to dress with any privacy.

She had none.

While still facing him, she pulled off her brown kirtle. Still in her beige smock, she ignored the silver smock and started to pick up the bright kirtle.

"Nay." He needed but one word.

She looked undecided again as she picked up both garments and placed them atop her rolled-up pallet. Still she hesitated. He could see her difficulty. Should she expose the front of her body to him or her back? Finally, she decided and quickly turned her back.

In a flash, the peat broke into a bright blaze. Its flames spread light to every corner. As she frantically tried to pull the sheer smock over her head to cover herself, he glimpsed her naked back. The beauty of her form so enticed him he near missed something unusual.

Had he imagined a darkness of the skin between her shoulder blades? 'Twas not something solid atop her flesh. More like a smear of color. And her back didn't appear as smooth as her lovely, ivory buttocks.

She hurriedly settled her clothes around her hips and started combing her hair. He puzzled over her back as he pulled a full, white shirt over his head. He loosely pulled the shirt's laces closed at his neck then gathered his green and black kilt around his body. Holding it in place with a wide, black sword belt, he threw the end up and over his left shoulder. He secured it to his shirt with a pewter pin decorated with a likeness of a fist holding a dagger upright.

Muriele's curly hair flowed freely around her face and down her back. The circlet, which went with the dress, was made of silver and gold strands braided around a long ribbon cut from the dress' fabric. The ribbon tied in back, and the ends would trail down her curly hair. She ignored it.

"Wear the circlet."

Her face twitched. She didn't move.

"It was meant to go with the dress. Put it on, else I will do it for ye."

As her hands slowly picked up the beautiful circlet to settle it around her brow, her eyes flamed with hatred.

By all things heavenly! She was even more beautiful in the clothing than he'd thought. Something was amiss. She looked as if she did not want to move and feel the cloth against her skin. He sensed she fought hard to keep her face devoid of any emotion. Why would she dislike wearing the prettiest of all her clothing he had transported from Blackbriar?

He kicked his soiled clothing atop her own she'd dropped upon entering the room.

"Dinna neglect mending the rip in my clothing. Ye have been forgetful of late."

He thought to prick her temper. Force her to lose control of her stony features. He was wrong. She nodded and stood like a woman who wanted to hide within herself.

"Come. Chief Olaf willna be pleased if ye keep him from his meal."

Magnus strode out of the room, wondering if she would force herself to move from the spot where she seemed frozen. By the whispering sound of footsteps, he knew she followed.

The great hall teemed with people. The women wore their most beautiful kirtles and jewelry while the men donned colorful kilts and soft linen shirts.

He stopped at the entry door and waited for Muriele to join him. He reached out and took her hand, placing it on his arm to escort her into the room. Everyone stared at the lass. They had thought her comely in her mended garments. Now, wearing clothing worthy of her station, her dignified beauty struck them.

With the absence of expression in her eyes, the stillness of her beautiful face, she looked ethereal. Everyone stared as if expecting her to disappear before their eyes. As he led her to the high table, he noted a small crack in her composure when they passed by Grunda. On seeing Muriel, the old seer gasped then flashed a look filled with sympathy.

It startled him.

Everyone on the dais made way for her.

"My lady, ye are most bonnie," Feradoch crooned and reached for her fingertips. He didn't kiss the air above her hand but pressed his lips to her flesh.

Magnus' eyes twitched. His foster brother lingered overlong. Chief Olaf cleared his throat and bowed.

"Ye will sit beside me this eve, fair lady."

Olaf insisted on seating her himself. 'Twas not because of honoring her for the hunt. She did not blush or react as if he did anything unusual. Sitting next to the Chief, she was in her customary surroundings.

'Twas her due.

During the meal, Magnus was aware of every little thing Muriele said or did. She conversed with graceful skill to all who spoke with her.

The cook would serve tonight's meal with only three removes, centered on the smaller animals. Ivar the Stout ushered in the first course, featuring fresh herb and cheese tartlets, poached beets with a sour vinegar dressing and a great pie filled with chicken, beef and pork covered in rich gravy. Magnus took care to keep their shared wine goblet half-filled.

After the first platters were cleared away, grouse with onion and parsley stuffing, diced turnips cooked in apple cider and butter, a variety of wilted and buttered greens, spiced pears in sweet wine syrup and sugar glazed currant cookies arrived for the second remove.

Though Magnus picked the most succulent morsels and placed them near her hand on their shared trencher, she ate only when he held something out to her and refused to remove it until she took it between her teeth. She was ever cautious not to let her lips touch his fingers. He snorted, mentally, knowing she would have gladly bitten them.

As the time passed, wine loosened the men's lips until they were soon joking and telling tales about the hunt. They poked fun at themselves because Muriele had far more skill at bagging the elusive hares than they.

One knight sitting to Magnus left leaned forward.

"My lady, how did ye know where to wait for the hares? They seemed to run straight to you." He laughed and slapped the table. "I do swear they begged you to capture them! What is yer secret?"

"I have no secret. 'Tis ye have not noted their habits."

"Habits? What habit do they have," he rolled his eyes and winked, "other than making more rabbits?"

Muriele seemed to relax for the first time since they had left the bedchamber. Should he ply her with more wine? When her head turned toward the knight, he filled their shared goblet.

"Have ye not noted hares seem to run in circles?" Muriele tilted her head and raised her brows questioningly. "If ye chase after one and lose it, be patient. The scamp will circle around and appear again."

"Ah! No wonder ye stood quietly!" He grinned when his wife laughed and poked him in the side.

"Rabbits sound like they enjoy the chase," his wife said.

"They are curious animals. Sometimes they follow after a dog chasing on the tail of one of the hare's less fortunate friends." For the first time this evening, Muriele smiled.

Magnus watched and listened. She seemed wary of the men and kept them at a distance but responded unhesitatingly to the women. She drew them into conversations, asking about their children. More than once, he sensed she longed to withdraw from the room. Each time, he put his hand on her arm, she stiffened and became still again.

By the time the last of the food arrived, she surprised him by readily sampling venison basted with red wine, oil, ginger, salt and pepper. Bowls of cooked carrots glazed with honey, baskets of white loaves of bread served up with platters of sharp cheeses with sugar walnuts, finished off the meal.

Between each course, minstrels sang, pipers played and jugglers performed. While the diners nibbled on cheeses and walnuts, a young troubadour sang a long song about the two young boys who spilled and drank their blood together to form an unbreakable bond. Muriele must not have heard the tale before, for she flinched when the troubadour sang of the chalice leaving their lips and the redness lingering on them.

'Twas late into the night when the men were drunk enough to mention the attack from the great boar. Feradoch was well into his cups and laughed at the telling.

"Yer father will be pleased to hear yer stones are intact," Feradoch gave him an angelic smile as if he praised him.

"Dinna worry, Feradoch. They are as hearty as ever."

"For truth? After all these years, I have failed to note any bastards at Kinbrace with yer hair and eyes," His foster brother hiked a brow at him, looking doubtful. "'Twould be unmanly if ye also failed to sire heirs for Clibrick. Yer brother Graemme doesna seem up to proving himself, either."

Magnus' wanted to spring from his seat and demand Feradoch cease his snipes about Graemme. Tension built around Magnus, near raising the hairs on his arms. A cold draft of air came between his legs and cooled his arse, making him realize he had risen halfway out of his seat. His hand gripped the hilt of his dagger. He forced his muscles to relax and sat.

Could Feradoch resent leaving? He'd seen the way he studied Muriele and near heard his thoughts. If 'twas Magnus returning to Clibrick, he had no doubt Feradoch would claim the woman for his own. He fixed his foster brother's innocent blue eyes with a steely glare.

"Have no fear, Feradoch," Sweyn said, laughing as he passed

a new pitcher of wine around. "Magnus has kept his seed from fertile ground. He will have his children at Clibrick, bastards or not."

Muriele withdrew into herself. Men were alike, no matter whether they were Baldor, Olaf, Magnus or Feradoch. They judged their manliness with how many women they swived in a sennight, or the number of bastards they sired.

At least at Blackbriar, the women were able to leave the table and retreat to their rooms when the men were deep in their cups. From the angry heat coming from Magnus, she feared he would leap on Feradoch.

She wanted to leave, to take off this dress with its terrible memories. And to cry and wail. She could not. Until he allowed her to rise, she must wait. What did it matter anyway, whether she was here or in his bedchamber? At least here, there was no bed where he could command her to join him. She hadn't known him long, yet she knew he seldom drank as much as he had this night. Would he become like Baldor, who lashed out and hurt those within his grasp?

When Magnus finally stood and held out his hand to her, Muriele stiffened. She remembered their strength when he had hauled her off her assailants and dunked her in the horse trough. And when he seized her, thinking she meant him harm in his bath. Until he had ruled she was to share his bed, she had never wondered if they could be gentle.

Earlier, he'd said he'd never taken a woman by force. He was a man who did what he promised, else he would not have spent all these years at Kinbrace until both families agreed to end it. All she had to do was not tempt him and keep a hand's span of open space between them.

She realized he still held his hand out to her. She glanced up through her lashes and saw the determined look on his face. He would wait no matter how long. Finally, she forced her hand to his. Surprisingly, his calloused flesh felt warm.

When his fingers closed over hers, they were gentle.

Though she wanted to flee out into the darkness, she paused

and smiled at those seated around the table, as she would have if at Blackbriar's dais. When she turned to Chief Olaf, he shocked her and rose to his feet.

"Thank ye for a pleasant evening, Chief Olaf." She bent her knee in a brief bow and fought to keep her voice steady. "I wish ye a good eve."

He held out his right hand and waited for her to put her fingertips there atop it. When she did, he bent, and as courtly as any visitors to Blackbriar, kissed the air above her hand.

"Good eve, Lady."

When Magnus led her from the room, she closed her ears to the whistles and rude advice from the lower tables and walked with her back stiff, her head high.

Every brush of the dress against her flesh reminded her of what she had lost. Her feet felt as though she struggled through thick mud. She forced one foot in front of the other until they came to Magnus' bedchamber. A cold draft blew up the stairwell. Someone had opened the great doors to the keep.

Magnus threw the door open and stood back for her to enter. 'Twas strange to be treated with courtesy and not as an object to be ordered about. The room was warm. Gille must have tended the fire in the hearth. Had he turned down the bed, too? She stopped in mid stride. Who had put her favorite sleeping smock across the pillow? She had never favored sleeping bare, though it was the custom.

Grunda was the only one who knew her habits. She shook her head, puzzled. Why did her old friend approve of her sharing Magnus' bed? If she didn't, likely she would have placed a dagger under the pillow.

She would search for it!

Chapter 18

"Come. Dinna dawdle."

Magnus scanned the room and noted the shutters were drawn. Not believing night air let bad humors into a bedchamber, he thrust them open.

Ah! Muriele's pallet was gone. He frowned at the smock on the bed, but the cloth looked flimsy enough to yield to a man's hand.

Ignoring Muriele, he poured a pewter cup of cold water and drank it down. It rid his mouth of the wine taste. He'd consumed more than in the last fortnight and disliked the way it made him feel.

Unsteady and mellow.

Someone could easily persuade a man in his cup into making mistakes. He wanted as clear a head as he could manage — at the moment.

He fumbled with the clan pin and finally pulled it from his shirt. He laid it on the table then took off his belt, letting his kilt slide to the floor. When he rolled the belt and picked up the green and black cloth to drape it on the chair, he saw Muriele stood against the wall, staring at him.

"Ye've seen me naked afore."

He sat on the chair and removed his leather shoes and stockings, then stood again. His heart lurched. By all that was holy, she was beautiful. A streak of desire shot through his groin, startling his balls to life. He looked at her, waiting for her to shed her own clothing. Likely, she'd also had too much wine and needed help. He was more than willing to aid her.

"Do ye require help?"

She shook her head. Why, then, did she not start?

He took a step toward her but stopped when her hand went up to remove the lovely circlet. The beautiful piece suited her. Or she suited it. He wasn't sure which. For truth, her beauty added to the glow of the band.

She carefully laid it on the corner table beside his helmet stand then turned her back to remove the blue-green kirtle. The color was a lovely contrast to her glowing sunlit hair and skin. Never had he seen such beauty and grace. How could he not have recognized it the first day in the bailey when she fought off her attackers?

Muriele looked around frantically, likely seeking a dark corner to finish undressing. Thanks to the fresh peat, there was none. She started wringing her hands. Why? Never had he known a woman reluctant to bare her body. When he invited a lass to share his bed, they usually were sprawled naked on the sheets afore he removed his belt!

"Ye need help with yer smock?"

She backed up. "Nay!"

He watched her carefully fold the kirtle and look for a place to lay it. She finally put it atop his clothing chest. It reminded him to have her clothing brought to the room on the morrow. She'd likely enjoy having her things about her.

He stood, quietly. Could she hear his heartbeat? 'Twas loud enough. At least his cock was silent when it filled and sprang upward, seeming to watch her with as much eagerness as he was. The thought caused a throaty chuckle to escape.

Why did she decide to face him when she changed out of the silver smock? Not that he regretted it. In other women, he knew they did so to entice him further. Not Muriele.

Strange. Why should exposing her back be more threatening than creamy breasts and her tempting womanhood?

In swift movements, she removed the silver smock and tried to don the other. The sleeves tangled in a snarl. Her head shoved futilely against the twisted cloth, seeking the opening. His gaze drifted downward. The blond curls guarding her sex barely hid the cleft there. His lips twitched. His mouth dried as if stuffed with linen. A groan of instant desire rumbled in his chest, masking a sound from her. Closing his eyes, he blocked her inviting body from his sight. Ah! 'Twas a whimper of frustration. He padded over to her.

"Are ye always so clumsy preparing for sleep?"

For certs, she startled easily. Her yelp made his ears ring.

"Be still, foolish lass. Ye're making a fierce mess of yer garment."

Why was she acting as if he was going to throw her on the floor and tear into her flesh? He'd told her he'd never taken a woman unbidden. He swallowed. He was going to be in a deal of pain if she refused him! His balls were so heavy he was thankful he didn't need to mount a horse.

He groaned. Shite. The only thing he wanted to mount was her beautiful, silken body.

He realized her problem. In her anxiety, she'd knotted the sleeves. Impatient with her struggling, he clamped his hands on her shoulders and forced her to turn.

She fought like a wild woman. Naked flesh brushed against him.

He caught his breath. The sight of her bare back did not arouse him.

It twisted his heart.

"Who did this?! One of my warriors when ye lived in the forest?"

"Nay. I incurred Lord Baldor's wrath."

He bent his head closer to hear her voice.

With one hand, he held her still while he ran the other gently over her quivering back. The ridged scars were not as old as his. These were pink. Recent. That someone had whipped her was bad enough. But not the whole of it.

As gentle as handling a bairn, he touched his fingertips to the flesh between her shoulder blades. The cruel beast had branded her with a steel blade.

"Why did ye not tell me before? Does old Grunda know?"

He untangled her smock and helped her smooth it down over her shoulders. Once she felt the cloth shielding her from his sight, her tremors slowed. She took a slow, deep breath.

"Aye. She healed me."

"Does it still pain ye?"

"Nay. It happened a sennight before the siege on Blackbriar."

Paying no heed to his own nakedness, he paced back and forth, his jaw clamped together. He was glad Baldor had fought so long. He'd been in pain aplenty afore Magnus had dealt the killing blow. If he'd known about this, he would have kept him alive after he disarmed him. No torture would be too cruel for anyone who would brand a woman of noble birth ... nay, any woman.

"Come." He led her to the bed and pulled back the covers, motioning for her to climb in. She held back.

"Dinna be afeared. I willna ravish ye."

As she climbed the steps up to the bed and scrambled between the sheets, tension eased from her shoulders. When he got in on the opposite side, he left ample space between them. He no longer feared his balls would explode. One look at her back and he had lost all desire. But not because she was any less beautiful.

He still intended to seduce her, but not tonight. There were many nights before his return to Clibrick. He had time. There was something more important tonight. Before first light, he swore he'd learn her secrets.

He never broke a vow. Not even to himself.

Muriele had forgotten how soft a feather bed could be. Compared to the pallets she'd slept on since leaving Blackbriar, surely a cloud couldn't be more comforting. She feared to move, though. Could she trust him?

All she'd heard about him told her she could.

'Twas said Magnus' word was more important to him than his own feelings. His own life.

She'd not had the chance to braid her hair to keep it out of the way. It was beneath her shoulders. She tried to lift up enough she could pull it out without disturbing him. His eyes, lit from the fire, were watching her. He reached over, gathered it and pulled it to the side.

"Mmm. Apples and spices." The words crooned from his chest as if savoring them.

"What? Ye smell apples? There are none in the room."

"I meant yer scent. When at Blackbriar, it remained behind in yer belongings."

"Ye were in my chambers? Why?"

"Aye. How did ye think yer things were kept separate from the spoils?" He rose up on his elbow and braced his jaw on his hand. "Except for one thing. My foster brother requested a brown kirtle for Esa. Since she returned it to ye, I take it he didna like her in it."

He thumped his pillow, put his left arm beneath it and turned toward her. "'Twas only the knight's wives clothing we shared with our women."

He was quiet. It prodded her to remember her manners, though she was not sure how she should respond to the man who had captured her castle home.

"Thank ye for the kindness."

He nodded. His eyes squinted and a slight frown formed between his brows.

"How did ye cause Baldor's wrath? Refuse to swive with him?"

"Nay."

"Did ye steal from him?"

"Steal? When all he had was taken from us?"

"Then tell me. Ye must have pricked his rage. Refused him something of note."

As he awaited an answer, he continued to stare at her. Her throat ached from her black memories. He looked determined. Would it be best to get it over with all at once? In this past sennight, she'd learned of his determination. No matter how long it took, he would pry answers from her until he was satisfied.

"I refused to wed old Aymer of Corrag."

Magnus snorted. "An unpleasant choice. Yet he canna live long to trouble a woman. Why did Baldor not lock ye in yer chambers with naught but bread and water?" He rose higher to stare at her.

"He did. I still refused."

"Tell me of it. The whole of it so I may judge fairly."

"I dinna know how."

"From the start of what caused it."

Magnus waited while Muriele gathered her thoughts. Once she started to speak, 'twas little above a whisper.

"Soon after my father, Lord Colban, died, Lord Baldor arrived to pay his respects. Once Mother allowed the gate lowered, his men overpowered our guards. His army had hidden in the woods. They fought their way in. The next morn, he forced my mother to wed him.

"After taking over Father's possessions, he learned I was to be betrothed to Duncan of Dalbreak."

Her voice broke as she said the man's name. He waited patiently until she gained control of herself and continued.

"Lord Baldor refused to allow it. He said he could negotiate a more profitable bride price from Lord Aymer."

He was close enough to feel her shudders through the mattress.

"In anger, I yelled no priest would force me to a marriage if I refused to repeat the vows." She took another deep breath and released it slowly. "He tried to whip me into obedience. Grunda helped me send a message to Duncan. He came alone. For secrecy. I met him in the forest in the mid of night. We fled Blackbriar on his horse.

"Baldor and his men caught us afore morn. They held Duncan's arms behind him. Baldor beat him unmercifully." Her breathing quickened. "I grabbed Duncan's knife from the ground. To defend him."

"Ye were foolhardy, lass."

She nodded. "Baldor cut himself when he first struck me. He slammed his fists into my face until I lost consciousness."

She turned her face near into the pillow. Her voice was so muffled he needed to strain to understand her.

"When I regained my wits, he pulled my clothing down to

my waist. He screamed, 'Ye *will* obey me.' 'Twas then he branded me with Duncan's dagger."

Muriele clamped her hand over her mouth. She looked about to spew then squeezed her eyes shut. Magnus kept silent. If she chose not to continue, he would allow it. If this Duncan was in love with her, it must have driven him mad seeing her suffering. As if she knew his thoughts, Muriele spoke.

"Duncan screamed with me. Baldor laughed. He was still laughing when he went over to plunge the hot steel into Duncan's heart. Those last months at Blackbriar, at every meal, Baldor took delight in using it as his eating knife."

Cold rage spread through Magnus. "'Twas unfortunate I didna gut Baldor while he yet lived!"

Muriele curled in a tight ball, her back to him. She pressed her face into the soft pillow then knotted her hand in the sheet and pulled it to her face. He laid there, his body rigid with suppressed fury. And everyone called *him* Ruthless?

But then, no one knew of Baldor's cruelty. He doubted even Muriele realized the extent of it. 'Twas likely Ragnhild wanted to murder him for what happened to her daughter. But what could she have done about the slimy bastard? Had either woman killed him, the law would have seen them hung for it.

He put his hands behind his head and stared at the ceiling. He went over her story in his mind. He'd seen Lord Aymer. The man was an ancient. A few strands of hair. Several teeth. One eye clouded and blind. No doubt, Baldor thought to secure all his holdings when the old man died.

He knew of Duncan of Dalbreak's disappearance. Members of Dalbreak's clan had combed the countryside asking if anyone had seen him. Baldor must have had his men dispose of the body.

He had felt a sharp pang when Muriele said the name with such emotion. For truth, she had loved him. Magnus had met the young man two summers past. He concentrated on remembering his appearance.

The picture of a tall man with light hair ... almost as light as Feradoch's, formed in his mind. His sky blue eyes seemed to laugh at life. A dimple in his chin. A man he remembered because he reminded him of his foster brother.

They met at a wedding festival and banquet for the eldest Dalbreak son. They played the usual Highland games and Magnus and Duncan had been equal throughout. 'Twas at the caber toss Magnus had won — by less than a hands width. The man had laughed and buffeted Magnus on the shoulder. Later, they had sought out willing wenches and fallen into a drunken stupor.

He pressed his lips tight. Muriele's shoulders had stopped quivering. Though she had smothered any sounds, he knew she'd grieved. Now and again, her breath hitched like a bairn's who had cried overlong. Her emotions had exhausted her, for she slept.

What had the dress to do with the story? Surely, it was not the same dress Baldor had wrenched from her shoulders.

He'd not learn its story this night.

In the darkest time of the night, Muriele half-awaked and wriggled back against the hard stones of the wall. Each night, she folded and placed her shawl between her body and the wall for warmth, then anchored her blanket around her front. At first, the cold slipped through, but if she stayed still, her body heat won out.

This night, she awoke to splendid warmth. Strangely, her legs were relaxed and not drawn up to help warm her belly. Never had the wall become so wondrously hot. She sighed and stretched her legs.

And near yelped.

She blinked. Her foot had slid down something hot and solid.

Aye. It was solid all right.

With hair. 'Twas the back of a hard muscled, hairy leg.

She froze. Her heart near stopped when she remembered where she was.

Before she dared move, she took note of all that touched her flesh. During her sleep, she had slid very low in the bed.

Her bare buttocks nestled against the back of Magnus' thighs! His hot arse filled the small of her back. She stifled a gasp with the blanket clutched to her lips. His flesh felt gloriously warm all the way up to her head. His body heat was greater than any warming stones at Blackbriar!

Magnus had kept to his word, for he had not raided her body during the night.

She could not say the same for herself. Had she pressed against him any harder, she would have shoved him off the bed to the floor.

Her only recourse was to ease herself away, bit by bit. She slid first one foot then the other from the glorious warmth. Each time she ventured a move, he stirred. She held her breath and stilled.

Her right leg rested atop her left. She waited then slid them away. When she shifted her buttocks, he sleepily grumbled and would have none of it. He threw his arm backward, clutched her waist and dragged her back against him.

Did he think her a pillow? His sigh of contentment ended with a melodious snore. She had no recourse but to wait until he slept soundly again.

No chance she would, though. Now she was fully awake, other sensations intruded on her thoughts.

She had seen him naked before. She had even touched his bare flesh. She squeezed her eyes tight trying to erase the vision of what pressed against her so intimately.

Her head rested between his shoulder blades. She had bathed the white scars there, had wondered who had caused them. In the tub, he had leaned his head forward and dropped his chin to his chest giving her access to his back. It had been pliable, the muscles relaxed when she massaged them. Now, those same flexible muscles felt taut against her shoulders.

Though he had not forced her to wash his arse, when he stood naked and dripping in the bath, she'd noted his lean hips, his buttocks tight without a hint of softness. Now, pressed so intimately against the small of her back, his nether cheeks were hot, hard.

His long, powerful legs intrigued her. Were they stronger than his arms? Surely they must be. When he clamped Odin between them, he had complete control of the great warhorse without having his hands on the reins. 'Twas a strange contrast, though, to feel the soft black hair growing there.

Experimenting, she rocked her leg gently. Somehow, feeling his leg against the back of her calf was comforting.

Her breath was still unsteady from crying herself to sleep, but strangely, she felt a glimmer of relief. 'Twas the first time she'd been forced to speak about it since Baldor had killed Duncan. It was as if talking about Duncan helped her to finally find some peace, though hate for Baldor still burned like a hot fire in her mind. She wished she had been the one to kill him, to hold him to account for Duncan's murder, her mother's suffering and her own. The man whose warmth she now shared had done her a great service. She was grateful for it. Tension waned and slipped from her as if fading into the feather mattress.

Yawning quietly, her eyes grew heavy. His sensual, spicy scent soothed her. 'Twas like resting in a forest surrounded by pines on a beautiful autumn day.

She pulled the covers to her cheek and sighed as her eyes closed.

CHAPTER 19

NEVER HAD MAGNUS BEEN so close to breaking a vow! If the lass hadn't stilled and fallen back to sleep when she did, he wasn't sure he could have reined in his desires for another breath.

Why did this girl stir a wild lust in him he'd never felt for another? Could it be some spell learned from her mother? He'd heard men claim Ragnhild of Blackbriar drove them mad with desire.

If Lucifer clamped his ballocks in his iron fists and squeezed the life from them, they could ache no more. His cock fared no better. For the first time in his life, he feared it would rip apart. He could do naught to relieve it. He had a new understanding of increasing women. Had a woman's belly ever burst like a bloated sheep's carcass?

Picturing the horrible event doused him in a cold chill, for which he was thankful.

He ordered his mind to think of anything but the soft, warm flesh pressed against him. It was nigh impossible. So instead of her body, he began to think of the lass. After seeing her tonight at the high table in clothing befitting her station, 'twas as if she had three layers of personalities.

His first sight of Muriele was the snarling, fighting warrior woman who could defend herself, if in a fair fight, against any man.

He had no doubt that Muriele, full of grace and beauty in the great hall, could rule over any castle. When she'd had a proper dowry and an alliance to bring into a marriage, she'd have made an admirable wife for men like Duncan of Dalbreak.

Like himself. 'Twas a pity she'd lost it all and had nothing of value to offer a man.

The third Muriele was the hidden lass tonight who crumpled and wept in helpless misery over her memories.

The first two he would have swived without a qualm. But he could not thrust his raging tarse into the heated body of this third woman. Fortunately, grief healed, and she would emerge a strong combination of the three personalities.

He would wait.

Once she became used to her new station in life, Muriele would make him an admirable leman.

"Well, now, are ye planning to sleep 'til the sun is high?" Grunda's voice held a surprising hint of pleasure.

Startled awake, Muriele sat up in bed. Luckily, Grunda grabbed the covers and held them in front of Muriele. Her sleeping smock gaped open and slid off her right shoulder, leaving one naked breast exposed.

"Put the lady's clothing chest beside the master's," Grunda said, glancing behind her.

Two men entered Magnus' bedchamber carrying the familiar chest from Blackbriar. Muriele caught them stealthily peeking from the corners of their eyes as they put the chest alongside the wall. One lad gave her a sheepish grin, but it did not stop him from feasting his eyes on the tumbling hair framing her face.

"Off with ye, now," Grunda ordered, "else I will be tempted to shrivel yer manhood!"

The men shoved the chest against the wall and near tripped hurrying from the room.

"Saints, Grunda! If ye had not come, I fear I would have slept on." She near bounded from the bed, clutching her arms around her breasts for warmth. In swift movements, she changed to the familiar tunic and kirtle and settled it around her hips. She stopped, puzzled when Grunda pulled the covers to the end of the bed. She stood there for a time, frowning.

"What do ye search for?"

Grunda snorted. And shook her head.

"Something which isna there."

Muriele cocked her head, frowning. Slowly, her eyes widened. Her old friend looked for stains of virgin's blood and spent seed! She looked disappointed none was there.

"Hmpf! When ye left the great hall with him, he appeared about to devour a more savory feast than had been placed on the tables." She pulled the bedding tight as Muriele scurried over to help finish making the bed.

"No wonder he was up afore the stars dimmed their shine." She stopped and looked at Muriele. "How did ye stop his taking ye?"

"'Twas my back."

"Eh? I didn't think he was the sort to let a few scars repulse him. His back carries much more."

"Nay. He was most gentle about my shameful scars. He insisted on learning the why of it."

"Ye told him all?"

Grunda's voice was soft with sympathy.

Muriele silently nodded. She'd refused to speak of it from the day she returned to her room at Blackbriar. Bending, she opened her chest to remove the garments and stack them beside her on the floor. Without having to ask, Grunda brought the blue-green kirtle, silver smock and the shining circlet and put them in her hands. Muriele carefully laid them on the bottom of the chest then replaced the rest of the clothing. She sighed with relief when she pulled down the heavy wooden top, closing everything inside.

"Come to my hut. We'll have a cup of hot chamomile. I made meat pasties, too." She clucked her tongue and shook her head in a wry expression. "I expected ye to need extra sustenance after being abed all night with such a virile man!"

Muriele blushed and hurried to pick up the soiled hunt clothing. From the placement of the sun, it was not as late as she feared. She'd still have ample time to wash and mend them afore the sun weakened.

On their way out of the keep, they skirted around the great hall. Everyone seemed unusually interested in watching her. The women looked envious and the men grinned as she passed. When she felt eyes boring into her back, she expected to find Magnus in the shadows, but did not. As she started to pull the great door closed behind them, she scanned the room.

'Twas Feradoch. Sprawled on a chair, his legs stretched wide in front of him, he peered from hooded blue eyes as he studied her. Slowly, his lips lifted in a pleased smile as if he'd found what he'd searched for.

Was an untried woman so obvious? In behavior, the lasses were more carefree. The married women didn't relax but watched their spouses. Some looked relieved, others angry if their husband pulled a servant girl onto his lap and whispered in her ear. When their husbands were nearby, there were painfully few matrons whose eyes gleamed with pleasure.

She remembered the loving glow in her mother's eyes when Muriele's father was in sight. After his death, it was a far contrast from Ragnhild's look when Baldor came near. If his back was turned, her eyes flashed with icy scorn or hot hate. If he approached her, all expression fled, leaving her soft brown eyes empty and cold.

Muriele had the one chance of happiness with Duncan. If ever she were to marry, she held no hope of finding the love Ragnhild had with her father Colban.

Today, the men looked like they stored their energy waiting for the games in the practice field to begin. The women enjoyed the light mood of a feasting day, watching as men wrestled and played Highland games.

Muriele was not one of them. She had to tend to her duties as on any other day.

"Lass, if ye dinna stop bumping into my heels, ye'll pull the shoes off my feet," Grunda grumbled as she entered the hut. "Fill the big pot with water to boil. Those clothes best soak in hot water to get the blood stains out."

Grunda knelt in front of her small hearth and built up the fire. Muriele wrinkled her nose when she dropped the clothing on the floor. Clothing reeking of day-old blood was sickening.

While they waited for the water to boil, Grunda puttered around setting her pewter cups and small wooden plates on the table. When the wash water was ready, it took them both to swing the iron arm away from the fire. Using heavy padding, they lifted the pot onto the floor. Grunda took a big wooden spoonful of soft soap and stirred it in the water. As Muriele added Magnus' torn plaid and her hunt clothes to it, Grunda poked them beneath the water with her wooden spoon.

"'Twill do." Grunda motioned her to sit. She collected the hot tea and meat pasties she'd kept warm on the hearth and set them on the table.

Muriele wrapped her chilled hands around the sides of the hot pewter cup. When she glanced up, Grunda stared at her with her arms crossed over her chest.

"Ye intend to refuse Ruthless?" Grunda blurted.

"I will be no man's piss-pot for his discarded seed! I was not born to be a leman. 'Tis not an honorable position."

"Aye, it is not. Though rightly named Ruthless, he's lived his life in honor. He does not strike me as a man who would offer a well-born woman such a thing."

"He would not have thought of it with Lady Muriele of Blackbriar, who had a dowry and honors to bring to him. I no longer have such."

"The first day I walked around him, sensing his character and his purpose in life, I saw the two of ye as one. In honor."

"A man who plans to take a wife wouldna force her to sleep aside him." Muriele snorted.

"Mayhap not at first." Grunda swirled her empty cup and studied the bits of chopped leaves.

"If a man doesna offer a handfast, I doubt he intends to wed."

"I know what I learned that day. Once he's had ye, he'll never be able to let ye go."

"I think ye misjudge his honor, Grunda. Gold and coins, lands and castles mean more to a man than any woman does. Without them, she is naught but a warm body to serve his needs."

Muriele could not keep the bitter words from spilling out.

She had no chance of the life she'd been born to.

She would settle for no less.

Magnus enjoyed Feradoch's companionship as they competed in the Highland games. Knowing this was the last of the fortnights they'd spend together, he wondered what they'd be doing this time a year hence. There would be no more long chases through the forests hunting louts who'd wronged a member of the Gunn clan, no more hunts competing together for the biggest deer, and no more nights of drinking and wenching until the sky lightened.

Trying to relieve the tension building by the hour, he played and he fought hard this day. He lost his concentration each time his thoughts strayed to the soft, naked arse snuggled against his warm flesh. Feradoch sensed the moment he did, and changed his strategy, slamming him against the hard ground and pinning him there.

"Ho, Ruthless!" Olaf's thundering voice rang out. "Did the wee slip of a woman sap yer strength last eve?"

The men howled lusty excuses for Magnus, each one painting a more lurid picture of him and Muriele abed. Anger built in him they would speak so of a woman far better bred than any of them. Was it the true reason for his ire? Or was it because nary a one of the supposed sexual exploits had occurred?

Magnus heaved himself up, tossing Feradoch back to bounce against the ring of men around them. He slid to the ground, ending atop a warrior's bare feet. The man blinked with surprise and tried to step back. He couldn't move his feet.

"I would welcome a hot arse warming my feet, but only one whose wet slit invited my toes to explore its hidden cave." He snorted and shuffled backwards, dumping Feradoch's buttocks in the dust. "Yer hairy ballocks tickle."

Feradoch slammed the heel of his hand down on the man's foot and shoved himself upward. He nodded toward Magnus. "Father, ye pricked a sleeping giant awake."

"Too late to be of value to me, brother. Ye already had me pinned to the ground for the count." Magnus conceded the match.

Laughing, Feradoch looked at him. But his eyes didn't show humor. Instead, scorn stared at him.

He'd sensed Magnus hadn't swived Muriele last eve.

As a youth trained under Olaf's hard hand, if a lass piqued his lust, he took her. He never lacked women to warm his bed. Or the forest floor. They were a necessity to fill a man's needs. After a battle, women were compensation for the wounds and trouble their men had caused him. Though his reputation as a ruthless warrior made them wary of Magnus' touch, they learned he wasn't the cruel man they expected.

Until the siege at Blackbriar, he took those he wanted, being cautious not to spill his seed on fertile ground. Once he'd explored Muriele of Blackbriar's bedchamber, he'd lusted after the lass whose scent permeated the clothing there. Afterward, no matter how comely, he didn't easily find satisfaction in other women.

He shook himself and motioned for Gille to dump a bucket of water over him. Where was Muriele? He had not seen other than glimpses of her as she hurried to Grunda's hut, her arms laden with laundry. 'Twas near time for the day's feasting. She would return by the time he bathed. He thought of the scarlet kirtle and pink tunic he intended to lay out on the bed. It would enhance the beauty of her hair and eyes.

His cock quivered in eagerness. After last eve, surely she had grieved her last over this Duncan. He envied the man who could cause such a beauty to mourn for him and deny Magnus his rights over her.

This night, willing or not, he would have her.

CHAPTER 20

MAGNUS LINGERED OVER A tankard of cold ale as he gazed down into the front bailey. He sensed Muriele before he saw her. She carried their clean clothing in her arms. Her long strides carried her to the steps leading up into the keep.

Damp, dark curls clung to her neck and shoulders. She had already bathed. His blood thickened as he watched until she disappeared from his sight.

Gulping down the last of his ale, he refilled his tankard then sat in the armchair beside the table. As her footsteps approached the door, his face stiffened in determination.

He'd not tolerate her resistance this eve. Had he not shown patience enough this last fortnight? By all rights, he should have beaten her when she left Kinbrace to search for her mother's body. He'd warned her. And surely, she'd deserved a hearty smack when she lied about leaving the bedchamber and stealing Grunda's knife.

He sprawled impatiently in the sturdy, high-backed chair and waited.

The door burst open and Muriele entered like a breath of summer. His nostrils quivered as the draft carried her unique scent.

"'Tis time ye returned," he said, his voice harsh.

"I waited until the feeble rays of the sun dried yer kilt, my lord."

"Ye are barely in time to change for the feasting."

"Change?"

"Aye."

Magnus pointedly looked at the bed where the scarlet

kirtle and pink tunic lay, a splash of color against the earthy brown covers.

"Are ye intent on selecting everything I am to wear?"

"Aye."

"Do ye not think I know enough to select my own garments?"

"I do. But I want to see ye garbed in striking colors. I think ye would pick others just to thwart my eye's enjoyment."

Muriele snorted. Loudly.

"'Tis most unladylike."

"When a lady is treated like a servant? I dinna think so."

Magnus heard the increasing noise of the great hall. He was impatient to join the feasting ... and to see her naked body as she changed.

"Come. Enough of this. Change yer clothing."

Her face took on a stubborn air. Her chin jutted out.

Magnus stood. He took one measured step toward her.

She blinked and backed up half a step.

"If ye want me to change, leave me in peace so I can put away the clothing I have in my arms."

"Then do so. My stomach grumbles." He sat back in the chair, his legs stretched out, ankles crossed.

"Why do ye not go below? I will follow."

"Huh!"

His gaze searched her face. The flesh between his brows wrinkled. He didn't trust her.

Muriele stared him down. He fidgeted, unwilling to miss the sight of her tempting flesh. Yet, if he didn't leave, she would learn her beauty held power over him. He tried another tactic. He would ignore her words and soothe her with aimless chatter.

"In the feast tonight, Ivan will do his finest work with the larger animals killed. I particularly favor boar."

He breathed a long gusty sigh and casually bent his knees and brought his right ankle to rest across his left knee. It allowed the heat from the fire to warm those parts of him in sad need of comfort.

When her gaze followed his movements and brought a rosy flush to her face, it pleased him.

She twirled and hurried to put away his clothing and her own. She still had her back turned when she spoke.

"Do ye have to stare at me?"

"Ye feel it? If ye dinna pay heed and change, ye will feel more than my gaze."

She sucked her teeth and slammed the lid of the clothing chest. This time, she didn't hesitate but kept her back to him as she pulled off her kirtle and smock. The peat fire was kind to her flesh, masking her scars in the wavering light.

He took a sip of ale to wet his mouth, for it had gone dry at the sight of her elegantly formed body. She was all fluid grace from fine-boned shoulders to trim ankles. His gaze followed down her form where it flowed in at her waist and gently flared at her hips. He hardened at the thought of running his hands down her warm flesh to cup her there. Above each plump nether cheek, a dimple made his lips purse thinking of tonguing each little dip.

He stifled a groan when the pink tunic shielded her from his view. All too soon, the scarlet kirtle followed. He sighed and vowed he would soon have her in his arms.

Naked.

Beneath him.

Muriele hurried with her dressing. He needn't touch her with his hands for her to feel heat everywhere his gaze traveled. Her stomach quivered with anticipation she determined to stifle. Her muscles quaked. She cursed herself for a fool. Though Duncan's kisses had stirred her blood, Magnus heated it without a touch.

She combed her hair and left it to flow down her back. Without a maidservant, she could braid it for the night but could not arrange it suitable for dining. She tugged open the chest and removed a silver circlet from the tray. 'Twould keep her hair in control. Taking a matching silver girdle, she belted it low on her hips.

"I am ready, my lord."

"Took ye time enough. I near fell asleep waiting."

Huh! How could he have been so restful when she felt

sparks flying with her every movement? If he'd watched her any closer, he'd have been dressing her himself. Or undressing her, more likely. The thought made her nipples itch and harden, her breasts swell and become firm.

"Why did ye not?"

"And have ye steal out of the room and be off to stir mischief?"

"I dinna cause trouble!"

"Nay?" Magnus rose from his chair, stretched his massive arms above his head and gave a loud yawn. "The first day at Kinbrace, ye caused me to hang useful men on yer behalf. Then ye convince a man to think ye such easy swiving he attempted to have ye right outside the bedchamber."

"I ne'er did anything such. If ye had allowed me my knife, the filthy lout would have kept his distance; else he'd have felt the blade shorten his randy staff."

"Aye. And I would have had another warrior less. At that rate, the garrison would be naught but old men and young squires."

Magnus threw open the door and started toward the stair well, not bothering to see if she followed. Sounds of laughter and deep male voices arguing the merits of a battle flail against armor floated up the winding stairway. As she passed the window slits, the sky darkened as clouds began to roll in. She shivered as cold air ruffled her hair and trailed damp fingers along her nape.

On making the last turn, she glanced over her shoulder thinking she'd heard someone behind her.

"Umpf!"

Air flew out of Muriele's lungs. She missed her footing and tumbled down the last two steps to bounce against Magnus. Her breasts cradled his head between them. To keep from sliding down his back onto the hard stone steps, she grabbed his massive shoulders.

"Well, now, my lady. Are ye so desperate for a caress ye'd resort to fumbling me in the stairwell? When we return to the room, I will give ye a tumble worth waiting for." His voice held a hint of a chuckle.

"I tripped. Ye well know I wouldna grab ye for any

other reason."

"Then why have ye not let go? Though I do relish having my head between yer lovely breasts."

Muriele shoved away from him and untangled the skirts around her legs. Furiously scrambling back up a step, she shoved her hair over her shoulders then righted the circlet near falling off her head.

Magnus waited at the foot of the stairs, his hand outstretched. She had half a mind to ignore it. After the expression in his eyes changed from a glint of desire to steely, black warning, she laid her fingertips lightly on his. He clamped his other hand atop it, forcing her fingers to curl into his clasp.

The hall was near overflowing, making it nigh impossible to follow a conversation. Especially if it was private. She could spot those who tried, for they were talking lips to ear, their eyes darting around to see who watched.

Women in brightly colored kirtles, knights in snowy white shirts and green and black kilts gathered close to the dais. Lesser soldiers and villeins stood talking around the trestle tables.

Vivid banners hung from the dark rafters and tapestries covered the whitewashed walls behind the Chief's table and the wall opposite the mammoth fireplace.

Chief Olaf, not attempting any form of modesty with his kilt hiked up baring his arse, warmed his buttocks at the fireplace. Muriele blinked as the glow from the fire highlighted the red hair dusting his nether cheeks. He wriggled his hips and leered at the woman standing beside him. She didn't even flinch.

Earthenware flagons of cold wine stood on the snowy linen cloths of the high tables, whilst ale or cider awaited the retainers and servants. Even the trestle tables had white cloths upon them, though not of the same quality.

Chief Olaf flung his arm in the air and beckoned Magnus forward. Feradoch lounged beside him, his shoulders pressed to the warm slate beside the fire with one leg bent, his foot braced on the stones.

"The lass has a sparkle in her eyes. Ye must have given her a good tumble," Olaf said with a lewd grin. As he studied her from head to toe, Muriele cringed at the glint of appreciation on his face.

The muscle beneath Feradoch's right eye twitched as his gaze, too, probed her.

"Aye. Her cheeks have the same rosy hue as her kirtle," he said in a slow, thoughtful tone.

Her gaze shifted to his face in time to see his lips tighten and his nostrils flare with displeasure. She noted Grunda, with her back to the fireplace, walk the length of the high table then stop for a breath or two. Muriele cocked her head, puzzled. From what she could see, Grunda seemed to smooth the tablecloth beneath Magnus' wine goblet.

Olaf reluctantly dropped his clothing to cover his hairy arse and made his way to his chair. Muriele started to pull her hand back, but Magnus refused to release his clasp.

When he led her to the high table, her feet dragged. She hadn't realized she'd dreaded sitting so near the lecherous older man until Magnus pulled back the second chair from the Chief's and helped her to sit. When he sat between her and his foster father, Olaf looked surprised for a moment, then grinned at Magnus' possessive manner.

Gille and a much younger page stepped forward. The small page held the basin as Gille poured warm scented water over Muriele's hands. When the youth's arms quivered with strain holding the heavy basin, Magnus slipped his hand beneath it to take some of its weight.

"'Tis a verra large basin, is it not?" He smiled at the boy and rescued the linen drying cloth as it near slipped from the youth's arm. When he moved to dry Muriele's hands, she started to take the cloth from him.

"Allow me to dry my own, Sir Magnus."

"I will decide what ye are allowed."

She near ground her teeth at his gruff warning. Forcing herself to relax, she let him pat her hands dry.

While the diners talked and finished their cleansing, a grizzled old man played such a rousing tune on the bagpipes her feet began to tap.

After several sips of wine Magnus coaxed to her lips, Muriele felt at ease with the knights and their ladies. Several women eyed Magnus, openly lusting over him with their husbands sitting beside them. Magnus seemed unaware of their scrutiny.

As he'd done the day before, Magnus took choice cuts served on silver platters and placed them on the trencher she shared with him. He took care to cut everything in small bites she could easily pick up with her fingers and place in her mouth without having to tear them apart with her teeth.

She thought the courses would never end. 'Twas a wonder they had not eaten everything from the last hunt. Gille kept their goblet filled with wine. After each sip, 'twas the custom to use a linen napkin to wipe the droplets of wine from where her lips had touched, but Magnus put his hand firmly on hers, turned the goblet and drank from the same spot. His eyes flashed a promise of something to come. Butterflies danced a frantic pace low in her belly.

By the time they served the last course of fruit pasties, sugared grapes, cheese squares, savory tarts and wafers, she contented herself with grapes and bits of cheese. Did Magnus never feel full? She watched as he wolfed down an apple tart in two bites and a multitude of wafers and cheese.

A beautiful young woman with hair as deep black as Magnus' own, wove her way through the crowded tables to where the musicians played. She turned and twisted, dipped and swayed in tune to the music. As she came close to the high table, 'twas apparent her filmy green clothing was better suited for the bedchamber! It left little to a man's imagination.

Muriele's eyes widened as the woman slithered to the floor where she writhed and contorted her body. Could she have extra bones in her body other women did not? When she brought up her legs and locked them behind her head, Muriele didn't need to touch Magnus to feel his body heat. With each of the dancer's sensuous moves, the air surrounding Magnus began to spark and near crackle as his body tensed, sending wave after wave of simmering desire. His face tightened, his breathing harshened as his lust built to a peak. The sensual woman teased

him alone, never taking her gaze from his face. She pursed her lips inviting kisses as she slowly straightened her legs and rose gracefully to her feet. Dancing and twirling, looking over her shoulder to keep her heated gaze on his face, she enticed him to be her invisible partner.

Though Muriele was not wise to the ploys of passion, she knew a dance of desire when she saw one! The more the girl slithered closer and thrust her woman's center seductively toward the dark knight beside her, the more Muriele seethed.

"The lass invites a tumble, Magnus," Olaf said with a lewd chuckle.

"'Tis not the place for swiving, Chief." Magnus shifted in his seat, loosening his kilt around his hips.

Muriele glanced sideways at his lap. The bastard had a raging cockstand! Heat pooled in her belly. She squeezed her legs together. Surely 'twas from anger. Why should she care if he swived the girl? Many women here would be very happy to tend his needs. Why, Sir Erland's wife licked her lips and her eyes grew heavy-lidded when she stole glances at Magnus! The woman didn't even try to hide her desire.

Olaf grinned and kept his eyes on the dancer and Magnus. Muriele was sure the knights sitting toward the end of the table were taking bets, for money passed hands. They looked from Magnus to the woman and then to Muriele. The ruttish men were betting he took them both to his bed this night!

Her temper erupted and got the better of her good judgment. She pushed against the table and attempted to slide her heavy chair backwards. She was near on her feet when Magnus' hand clamped her wrist.

"I dinna wish to leave, lady. Sit!"

"I wish to retire."

"Ye will wait until the Chief or I dismiss ye."

Never had anyone talked to her in such a way. She tried to wrench her arm away. He clamped her wrist harder. Knowing everyone at the table avidly watched them, she forced herself to lean closer so they would not overhear.

"Dismiss me?" She sucked in breath through tight jaws and

near hissed her words. "Ye think I must bide at yer pleasure until ye are ready to meet with her?"

"Calm yerself, woman." He brought the goblet of wine to her lips to force her to drink.

She reared her head backward.

"Ye think wine will make me as dough in yer hands? It will not!"

When he would not take the wine away, she took a big gulp then shoved his hand away. Wine dotted the white cloth like splatters from a killing.

Always before, she had been able to control her anger. Even with Baldor, she had learned to shut her mouth and find other ways to thwart him. But tonight she had little control. Her heart thumped. She had gone too far.

The taut muscles in Magnus' jaw jerked. As he took long, slow breaths, his eyes shot black sparks. When he fixed her with a hot glare, she thought it best to escape his presence.

Slowly, she rose to her feet. He did not move. Just stared at her. His eyes narrowed to cold slits. Promising something. What? The room became deadly quiet. No one moved. The dancer stood still, her eyes studying them.

Gille pulled her chair clear. She turned to her left, away from Magnus. When he didna move, she took a step, then two. 'Twas not until she reached the end of the table that she heard his chair scrape backward. She didn't dare look behind her. She walked as dignified as possible for a lady in a hurry. When she reached the doorway, his footsteps matched her own.

Not knowing where to go, she instinctively headed toward their bedchamber. When she started up the stairwell, she grabbed her skirts up to her knees and ran up the stone steps like all the wolves in the forest nipped at her heels. When she turned a corner, she hesitated. Listened.

Had Sir Magnus returned to the great hall? Nay!

He slowly climbed.

Each booted step rang an ominous warning.

Chapter 21

MURIELE BURST OUT ONTO the landing. She rushed past the torch flickering in its wall bracket, her eye on the doorway, her hand outstretched far ahead of time. Her heart thudded. It seemed she would never reach the latch.

She chanced a quick glance behind her. Oh, Saints! She wished she had not.

Sir Magnus stepped out of the gloom into the light as he stalked her, his steps measured, his lips set in a grim line. His large hands clenched and relaxed as if they longed to wrap themselves around her neck.

The length and tempo of his stride quickened, eating up the distance between them. Her heart thudded. She reached the door. Frantic knowing he was so close, she fumbled with the latch. With all her might, she shoved the door until it was open enough for her to squeeze through. Turning, she pushed with both hands, her feet anchored to the floor. It near closed. With a sharp, loud noise, his boot slammed against the outside edge. She was but a finger's width away from latching it.

He thrust it toward her. For all the help it did Muriele, she may as well have been an ant trying to stop a log rolling down a hill. Why, the dratted man did not even need to exert himself.

Relentlessly, the space widened as her feet skidded backward. Once he gained entrance, he took her by the shoulders, lifted her as if she was no more than a sack of feathers, and stood her several paces from the doorway.

He didn't speak. Though his skin was taut, his face was devoid of any expression. She had never encountered such cold, quiet anger. It unnerved her more than if he'd ranted and raved as Baldor had done.

With deliberate movements, he quietly closed the door and latched it. He stopped. Stared at her through narrowed lids. He must have read the defiant expression on her face for he lifted the wooden plank propped in the corner beside the doorway and placed it in the braces at each side of the doorframe. No one could enter or leave unless he allowed it.

Her heart pounded against her ribs so hard it would surely bruise itself. She had the urge to swallow, but how could she when her mouth was as parched as sun-scorched grass after a month without rain?

Why was she so hot? Never had the joining of her thighs felt like heated blood pooled there. And why did her skin prickle when he folded his arms, widened his stance and stared at her. He took his time, his gaze slowly covering every inch of her from her disarrayed hair to the tips of her shoes peeking beneath her skirts. When his gaze probed her breast beneath the scarlet kirtle, her nipples responded. The tunic and kirtle were of the softest cloth, yet their pressure against her nipples felt like scratchy wool. She had to force herself not to rub her palms across them.

Her face flamed when his gaze moved to stare where she felt the hottest. Oh, heavenly Saints! Her body wept for him. Magnus' nostrils flared. Could a man know when a woman was in heat, the way a dog could scent a bitch ready to mate? How loathsome to think in terms of animals. Yet it was appropriate. It could be naught but animal lust, untouched by the human mind and heart

Magnus' blood seemed to boil in his veins. His senses were so heightened he was aware of every quick breath Muriele took. He knew her breasts tingled when his gaze studied their form beneath the kirtle. She had unconsciously rolled her shoulders trying to put distance between her nipples and the cloth. From the look of distress a few breaths later, she must have felt her body dampen with anticipation.

His nostrils flared, anticipating the heady scent of desire

he would encounter when he trailed kisses from the dip in her belly to the soft nest of hair guarding her sex. He gritted his teeth as his cock swelled even more. He knew he wept for her as surely as she did for him.

Lucifer's horned prick! He would have to control his mind, else he would spurt his seed afore he even entered her.

"Take off yer clothes and get into bed," he ordered.

Without waiting to see she obeyed him, he turned his back and went to the table beside his chair. Someone had placed two goblets and a pitcher of wine, chilled from the looks of the sweat beaded on the outside, on the table. And the fireplace blazed to take the chill from the room. Neither wine nor the fireplace was Brian's doing. He knew Magnus preferred a cold room and seldom drank chilled wine.

Curious, he poured some into the goblet. Lifting it to his nose, he sniffed then took some into his mouth and let it roll around on his tongue, tasting it. 'Twas the same as at the feast below, but he would bet something enhanced it. He swallowed, feeling its warmth as it traveled down his throat.

He did not fear poison. Nay, 'twas something much more subtle. He had encountered it afore. It made a man or woman more, hmm, pliable. And eager. He swirled the wine around in the pitcher, thinking as he watched it.

Who wanted them to mate? Whoever it was could be no more eager than he was! Not Olaf. He believed they already had. Not Feradoch. His foster brother wanted Muriele for himself. Not Sweyn or any of his men … or women. He could near see the person who did. Her eyes would brighten and flash now where they had frowned on finding him up and about when the sun first rose.

He chuckled. Old Grunda. What did she hope to gain by his taking Muriele? Did she think he would petition the king for Muriele's hand once he had swived her? He had no need of her for a wife. 'Twas as likely to happen as bluebells pushing their bright blossoms up through the snow.

He smiled. Knowing Muriele's old friend approved of his lustful intentions was a hurdle he wouldn't need to clear. Had it been the other way around, he would not look forward to one of her dire forebodings. They too oft came true. Too oft? He snorted.

They *always* came true.

Hearing a soft rustle, he turned to find Muriele stood beside the bed still fully clothed. Instead of ordering her to remove her clothes, he poured a generous portion of wine into his goblet and walked over to her.

"Scarlet becomes ye, lady. From the moment ye put it on, I have thought of naught else but removing it."

When he held the wine out to her, she took it and sipped. He knew her thoughts. If she held the goblet and drank slowly, how could she undress? She meant to stall him. He hid a smile, for when he lifted his hand toward it she pulled back and raised it to her lips. He would let her sip enough to soothe her fears, but he didn't want her muddled.

Walking back to his chair, he removed his boots and stockings. Though he pretended to ignore her, he felt her watching him. He lined his boots alongside his chair and stood. His heavy sword belt wrapped twice around his waist held his kilt in place. He held onto the scabbard as he unbuckled and pulled the belt free. His kilt dropped to the floor with a soft rustle. He sensed rather than saw her turn her back as he finished stripping.

Naked, he padded over and stopped behind her. When he reached around her to take the goblet from her fingers, she startled.

"I see ye wish me to undress ye?" His breath fanned the hair falling over her ear. Bending his head, he trailed wet kisses on her long slender neck.

"Nay. I wish to leave my clothing on."

"On? If it be yer wish." He clucked his tongue with regret. "Hm, but it would ruin such beautiful clothing."

He put the goblet on the floor at their feet then reached up and lifted the circlet from her hair. He laid it atop the helmet stand then pulled her back against his chest. His hands reached around her and removed the silver girdle riding low on her hips. He placed it beside the circlet.

His fingers sought the laces at her bodice. Slowly, he pulled the ends. Over her shoulder, he watched the gap widen, displaying the pink tunic and the creamy breasts beneath. She jerked forward as if his body scalded her. No doubt, his engorged member pressed against her back made her uneasy. He nuzzled the back of her neck, inhaling the scent of her hair. She shivered then tightened.

"Muriele." Magnus whispered her name as he ran his hands from her shoulders down her arms. His fingers grasped her wrists, then, with both their arms, enfolded her in a warm embrace.

"Nay."

The word was more a groan than a whisper.

"Aye."

His right hand dipped unerringly down her tunic bodice to cup her left breast. His calloused palm rubbed the straining nipple as his fingertips prodded the plump flesh. Wanting to taste her, he bent his head and nibbled her earlobe, then laved it as he ran his tongue around the dainty shell of her ear.

He sucked her skin where her neck met her shoulder, gently drawing it into his mouth. So sweet the way she leaned her head to the side, yielding her neck to him. Her breast, warm and firm, filled his hand. When his fingers slid off, he gripped the nipple by his thumb and middle finger then used his forefinger to tease the tip relentlessly. His left hand finished untying the laces then pulled her kirtle off her shoulders, letting it fall to her elbows.

"Ye are so beautiful," he whispered between kisses as he nudged the pink tunic off her shoulder to join the kirtle. When he had bared her to her waist, he turned her in his arms to press her breast against his naked chest.

Muriele gasped at the feel of Magnus' hot flesh against her. Like the man himself, his body was hard and unyielding. She had expected it to be. His mouth swooped down, hungry and demanding, in a kiss that turned her body to fire and her mind to want it all.

She was no innocent about what happened between a man and a woman. Expecting to wed soon, she had yielded to Duncan after her father had promised her to him. Her only regret had been 'twas the only time, for soon after, Lord Colban had died.

Now, she felt her blood rushing in her veins, felt heat first in her breasts and then in the pit of her stomach. He moved back a space and hooked his thumbs in her clothes, sending them slithering down her sensitive skin to the floor. She felt strange, standing there naked, except for shoes and her stockings tied with ribbons above her knees.

Magnus pulled back further and trailed his tongue from the small hollow in the base of her neck, ever so slowly, down until it dipped into the hollow of her belly. His hands followed his progress down her back. When he swirled his tongue there on her stomach, he trailed one finger down the joining of her nether cheeks. Muriele trembled, wondering if he would dip between her legs and touch the part of her that burned so hotly.

Her fingers grasped his thick hair, wanting to hold to something. He looked up at her, his eyes hooded with lust, his breath deepening. He untied the ribbons holding her stockings and peeled them down. Grasping each ankle in turn, he urged her foot up enough to slip off her stockings and shoes.

As he stood, he brushed his naked body against hers, his hands hovering with but a breath between his palms and her flesh. His chest pressed against her long legs. He felt tremors begin from her shapely calves, up her quivering thighs. He halted, his lips playing with the soft curls protecting her womanhood, his hands now gripping her firm buttocks. Her fingers tugged at his hair, urging him upward. He attended her wishes. When the black hair feathering his chest brushed over her breasts, she sucked in a sharp breath.

"I throb for ye, Muriele. Dinna deny me."

Magnus stood, lifted her in his arms and near threw her on the bed, coming down atop her covering her completely with his massive body. Had she wished to move, she couldn't.

His smoldering black regard said *ye are mine. Only mine!*

Threading his fingers through her hair, he held her still while his mouth eagerly plundered hers. He groaned at the sweetness he found there. She tasted of sweet berries and tarts dripping with honey. When she kissed him back, her tongue followed his into his mouth. He growled his delight.

With one knee, he prodded Muriele's legs apart. 'Twas when his engorged tarse nudged between them her body began a veritable shower, readying for him. She opened her legs further as he placed himself there with a sigh.

Though his hips were trim, still the size of his body spread her legs further apart than she had expected. She wriggled and bent her knees, bringing her feet up even with his arse. What should she do? Was she to grasp her legs around his buttocks? Or should she be still?

Muriele had felt drawn to Magnus when she had first seen him at Blackbriar. She thought hate made her blood quicken, her pulses race. Mayhap it *was* hate at the time. Now Muriele's body thrummed with an emotion equally strong . . . hot desire.

His hand reached between them, his fingers parting the hair protecting her opening. One finger slid between her plump nether lips. She felt him searching, knowing he tested her to see if she was ready to receive him. She squirmed when his fingertip teased the small nub and sent a flash of desire through her. She thrust upward, inviting him. He played with her sex, making her near beg him to enter her.

Would Magnus be surprised when he took her?

Disappointed?

She would soon find out, for he nudged her opening and angled his hips as he started brushing his tarse against her eager flesh. Her hips rose slightly to meet him. She clutched his shoulders, her body tense and waiting. His size was more than she had expected.

His tarse was so full. So hard. Her heart raced, waiting for him to fill every bit of her.

Magnus held Muriele, savoring the feel of her supple body thrashing beneath him. Breath rasped from his lungs when his exploring fingers felt how ready she was. He circled her opening. She was hot. Wet.

Taking hold of his cock, he guided himself into her, entering slowly. He stopped to savor every little inch, his heart drumming faster and faster. He found no hindrance in his path. He hesitated for a moment, surprised. Yet, why should he be? She had shown evidence of having been in love with her suitor. Sharp talons of disappointment tore into his mind. He had wanted to be her first! Needed to be. Never had he felt such before. Jealousy filled him and he reacted.

He shoved hard. Fast. Punishing.

Driving her upward on the soft bed. Hearing her gasp, he tried to control his feelings. He had no right to feel betrayed. He moved in to the hilt and stopped. Burying his face in her neck, he took deep, calming breaths. He squeezed his eyes tight and counted, willing his heart to calm its racing. Once he knew he had control over his body, he relaxed.

She felt so right. A perfect fit. He increased his tempo until he was rocking into her. If she didn't come soon, he would disgrace himself. Wanting to feel the spot giving him such intense pleasure, he reared up on his knees and ran his finger through her curls until he felt himself at her entrance. His finger circled his cock, plunging and retreating in her flesh. He stopped, all the way to the hilt. He found her nub. When he teased it, she jerked and tried to make him move. He denied her. Held her hips immobile as she thrashed beneath him.

For certs, from this point on, he would banish all thoughts of her first lover from her mind.

He could stand no more or he would explode. He thrust and retreated, faster and faster. Then, of a sudden, fell forward on his elbows and held still to enjoy the feeling of being inside her. And to show her he was in control.

She tried to move. He lowered his body atop her to keep her still. She pounded her legs on his buttocks. He didn't budge. Her head pushed back on the pillow, straining. He nipped her neck then ran the tip of his tongue around the outline of her lips. She rooted for his mouth, much as a child searched for his mother's dripping breast. Finally, she begged. Pleaded.

"Please! Please!"

"Please what, Muriele?"

"Please, dinna make me wait!"

"Wait? For what, lady?" He gasped the words, still holding still.

"Ye torture me." She tried to arch her back, struggling to move beneath him.

"Please what, lady?"

"Let me find release!"

He reached between them again, circled and rubbed hard on her nub as his cock lunged rapidly. She exploded with rapture, her legs clamping his waist tight, her hands clawing his back as she convulsed beneath him. He felt her muscles ripple as she tried to milk him of his seed. He held tight to his control and waited until her quaking slowed. Finally, he pulled from her. He grabbed his engorged cock and gritted his teeth to keep from shouting as he spurted his release on her soft belly.

He would plant no seed until he could claim a child as his own.

Never had he felt the desire to conquer a woman as he had Muriele. Sweat dampened their bodies as he clutched her to him again. Finally, his cock stopped throbbing. When they both gained their breath, he rolled off her.

Strange he'd never cared whether a lass was a virgin or if she'd had a hundred lovers. Why did it matter who had breeched this one? He stared at the ceiling, wondering. Was it only Duncan of Dalbreak? Or had she taken lovers before or after him? The questions ate at him.

He gritted his teeth wanting, and yet not wanting, the answer. There was also the question of why she'd been so reluctant to wear the blue-green kirtle and silver smock. If it was so important to her, then why had she buried them at the bottom of her chest?

Muriele felt his tension and knew he wasn't pleased there would be no virgin's blood on the sheets. She had worried she might be ripe for breeding. She'd been mindless with passion. Too enthralled with the moment to protect herself. Thankfully, he'd not spilled his seed within her.

He surged out of bed and padded across the cold floor to the washstand. A pail always stood close to the fireplace, keeping water warm for scraping off the whiskers around his cheeks come the dawn. He filled the basin with it, dipped his fingers into soft soap and lathered his groin and sex. After he rinsed with the cloth, he dumped the water out the window opening then refilled the basin.

When he stood above her, he noted the wary look on her face. She held her palm upright, stopping him.

"I can cleanse myself, my lord." She pushed her hands on the mattress, ready to spring from the bed.

Magnus shook his head at her.

"'Tis the only way I know not to plant seed in a fertile woman."

"Aye, I have heard of such."

Muriele stood and held her hands out to take the basin from him. He again denied her, and though she would have liked privacy for such an intimate cleansing, he held onto the basin. She dunked the cloth then lathered it with soap. Feeling her face flush, she ducked her head and cleansed between her legs and belly. The musky smell of a man's seed wasn't pleasant. She thankfully rinsed her flesh then dried her belly with the edge of the sheet.

While he tossed out the water and put the cloth and basin back on the stand, she crawled between the covers and pulled them up to her neck.

"Why do ye hide yer naked body as if ye had been untouched afore this night?"

"I may not have been untouched, but I'm not used to any man seeing my bare flesh."

He strode back to the bed, his sex limp against his heavy ballocks. 'Twas the first time she'd seen his shaft totally lifeless, for even when she had stitched his leg, he had not completely subdued this part of him with a will of its own.

He threw himself on the bed, rocking them like a stormy night at sea then turned to face her. He bent his arm and braced his head in his hand. His probing gaze studied her as if he could see into her mind.

"Who breached ye first?"

Chapter 22

"Huh! Ye have no right to question me."

Muriele lips tightened. Turning her head, she refused to look at him. Had he asked her to handfast with him, she would have told him afore they made love. But, nay, he merely took what he wanted. It did not obligate her to tell him of her life.

"Nay? Ye are mine and have been since I conquered Blackbriar."

He narrowed his eyes at her and his lips tightened.

"Who was the first?"

She jerked her head back to glare at him. "Who was the first woman ye swived?"

"The blacksmith's daughter."

His answer totally surprised her, for she thought he'd ignore it.

"I demand an answer. Who was yer first lover?"

"There was no first *lover*."

"Dinna dare lie. Do ye think me so unskilled I wouldn't know a virgin from a lass who has made love afore?" He snorted and thumped his fist on his outstretched leg. "There was no hindrance when I entered ye. Not a hint of virgin blood. Ye were tight, but then only women who have birthed a child contain me easily."

"My *first and only* lover was Sir Duncan. When he came to my bed, we were to wed. There was no shame in it."

Jealousy pricked at Magnus the way she defended Duncan's actions.

"How often did he plow yer belly?"

Muriele sat upright and turned to lash him with a furious gaze. The randy lout went too far!

"A dozen times. A hundred times!" She stopped and drew in a breath and shouted, "Likely it was too many times for me to count! Is that what ye want to hear? "

Magnus fell back on the pillow and burst into laughter.

"As much as that, eh? Ye must have bred a castle full of bairns." With a chuckle in his voice, he raised his brows and asked, "Did ye name them by numbers?"

"There were no bairns," she muttered under her breath.

"Nay. And no other lovers. I'd warrant ye laid with him only once afore yer father died and Baldor barged into yer life."

She fell back on her pillow but didn't speak. There was no need.

Magnus regretted badgering her into speaking. The dreamy, satiated look had gone from her eyes, replaced with haunted shadows.

He gently brought the covers up to cover her shoulders made bare when she waved her arms around declaring she had taken countless lovers. He bunched his pillow under his cheek and watched her

"Lass, why can ye not bear to wear the kirtle?" He had no need to name which one. She would know.

"The color was his favorite. 'Twas to be my wedding dress." She turned her back to him.

He rose from the bed, pinched out the candles and quietly returned. He didn't touch her. She needed to sort through her feelings.

Though it had been painful for Muriele, he now knew all about her. From this night forward, he would read her thoughts and happenings from her face and eyes. Her life was out in the open.

At an early age, he had learned things unknown had a nasty way of causing disasters. Once he had taken control of the warriors of Kinbrace, he did not abide anyone keeping secrets from him.

His eyes widened in surprise. One person did! He had

forgotten old Grunda. He remembered glancing toward the table and seeing her put the pitcher of wine between their places. No doubt, 'twas she who also placed the wine in his room.

He would get his answers from her before she had time to think up some lie.

Magnus slept lightly, conscious of each move Muriele made. He wouldn't allow her to slip from the room and do something foolish. No doubt, when she awoke, she would regret surrendering to his lovemaking.

Before the first light struck the top of the eastern mountains, Magnus slid from the bed and belted a plaid around his waist. For a man of his size and bulk, he could move soundlessly. When he left the room and eased the door shut, he held his sword and shaft against his body, the near empty wine pitcher in his hand.

He didn't scratch at Grunda's door, nor did he rap his sword hilt against it. He took hold of the latch and shoved it open to bang against the wall, thinking to strike fear in the old seer's heart.

"What took ye so long, boy? I thought to see ye soon after Muriele slept!"

Had Magnus not been skilled in keeping anyone from reading his face, his mouth would have gaped. Grunda sat at her table, a pot of herbs steeping to her left and two earthenware cups and small plates waiting in front of her. A small pan sat on the stone shelf inside the fireplace, sending the aroma of hot scones drifting through the small hut.

He latched the door behind him, for the morning was damp and cold. It didn't bother him, but the old woman would mind the discomfort. He thumped the pitcher on the table. With both palms flat out on the wood in front of her, he leaned down and looked her in the eye.

"Did ye not think me skillful enough to bring Muriele beneath me? What drug did ye use to heat her blood?"

She grinned at him. "Naught but the simplest of herbs

which mingle well with wine."

"Why?"

"If the wrong man claims her, 'twill be as I predicted. Great harm will come to her, causing fathers to fight sons. Brothers to turn against brothers."

"Ye speak in riddles, old woman." He slapped the table and sat in the chair already awaiting him.

Grunda calmly retrieved the rolls and set them in the middle of the table. After pouring the herbal tea into their cups, she nudged one over to his hand.

"I have no wish to wed." He picked up the cup and let the heat from the brew warm his lips before he took a swallow. He was completely at ease as if he visited her often.

"From the time the child was born, I knew her destiny was with ye. I knew not who ye were at the time, but I saw yer face."

Magnus snorted and shook his head. Taking a bite of the scone flavored with bits of fruit, he sat back and waited for her to explain.

"When she fell in love with young Duncan of Dalbreak, I feared for her life. He was a good man. But not strong enough to keep her safe. 'Twas proved when the bastard Baldor captured and murdered him. Muriele near died, too. 'Twas an infection caused by a muddy cloth the beast slapped atop the terrible brand."

"The threat of Baldor no longer lurks."

"'Tis yer destiny, boy. Dinna fight it; glory in it."

His left brow rose. "Boy? Nay, my destiny is by my design, not writ in the stars or dreamt about by old women. A year hence, I return to Clibrick. I will wed for gain when the time is right."

She leaned forward, her arms on the table. Angry sparks seemed to radiate from her as she stared into his eyes.

"Ye were meant to rule Blackbriar with Muriele at yer side. Dinna be an eejit!"

"No one calls me such!"

Magnus surged to his feet. He widened his stance and slapped his hands down on the table on either side of Grunda's arms. Leaning forward until he was near nose to nose with the old seer, his voiced lowered to an icy whisper.

"'Tis good ye are an old woman, else yer headless body would now be twitching on the floor."

Grunda threw up her arms in frustration as he stormed out the door with barely controlled fury. His forceful exit caused the rickety door to swing wildly before it crashed shut with such vigor twigs and debris from the thatched roof floated down like brown leaves in the midst of autumn.

Grunda's unsteady hand brushed them from her hair.

Muriele awoke to a dark room, her back chilled, though something pressed against it. She didna have to look to know if he was present or absent. If he was anywhere near, her skin tingled and her heart quickened with a feeling of anticipation. When he was absent, she felt none of these. Naught but a pillow shared her bed.

She sat up, surprised her woman's place was sensitive, more so than when she had lost her innocence to Douglas. Was Magnus still angry he wasn't the first? What right did he have to care one way or the other? This had not been their marriage bed. Neither had he offered to handfast with her.

Throwing back the covers, she near fled to grab her warmest clothing. Once dressed, she hopped onto the edge of the bed to pull on heavy stockings then slipped her feet into her waiting shoes. Bringing the fire back to life took longer than it had to dress. She stood close to it, rubbing her hands together.

Once she had taken the chill from her clothing, she grabbed her wooden comb. Her anger made her wince when she encountered the knots he'd made in her hair. His great hands had wound her hair around them, anchoring her head to the bed while he plundered her mouth.

"By the Saints!"

Irritated, she near yanked a hank of hair out of her head. Each stroke became more aggressive as she thought how he had humiliated her to suggest she'd had a multitude of lovers. For sure, he'd taken more than his share of women. How many had he breeched and left for their future mates to berate them for it?

Finally, she was done. She gathered it in one hand while she secured a thin strip of leather around it. She must hurry and straighten the bed afore Grunda arrived.

Something had smothered her good sense. There was no way she would have allowed him to make love to her without honor. Since 'twas certainly not love words he'd spoken, their ardor must have been the result of a potion.

By what right did Grunda have to interfere in her life? Granted, she'd been with Ragnhild before Muriele was born, but the seer wasn't her parent. Sure as Hades, she wouldn't give Grunda the satisfaction of seeing the sheets.

Grabbing the coverlet, she tossed it and the blanket on the floor. When she flung back the top sheet, she saw the telltale signs of lovemaking. Muttering under her breath, she stripped the sheets off then shoved the soiled linens under the bed. She hid their absence by replacing the blanket and coverlet. Hearing soft footsteps, she composed herself.

She surprised Grunda and opened the door before the old woman reached it.

"Have ye come to inspect the bedding again this morn?"

"I have no need."

"Did ye think I wouldna be able to resist Sir Magnus after the potion ye put into the wine? It was easy to deny him."

Grunda chuckled and patted Muriele's cheek as if she thought her slightly demented. She eyed the made up bed over Muriele's shoulder.

"I already had the answer. He paid me a visit afore he met his men in the practice field." Her gaze scanned the room. When she didn't find what she expected, she uttered a pleased cackle. Bending over, she felt the floor under the bed and pulled out the laundry.

Muriele raised her hands high and muttered a curse under her breath then shook her head.

"Why do ye spy on me?"

"I told ye afore. In case ye are dense and didn't understand, Sir Magnus will be yer mate for life."

"Sir Magnus' only interest in me is what lies betwixt my legs!" She flushed making such a crude declaration.

"Ye both may think so. I know better."

"Ye forget. I am his servant. His seamstress. His laundress. I dinna doubt he thinks to add being his leman to the rest of my duties!"

"Humph!"

Grunda shook her head and went over to pull the coverlet, blanket and pillows into the middle of the bed then dumped the soiled sheets atop them.

"What are ye doing!?"

"Saving ye from falling over yer words when the laundress arrives to find a bed without sheets. Helen comes up the stairwell now."

Sure enough, afore Muriele could count to twenty, the rotund woman appeared in the doorway, her arms full of clean sheets and her face wreathed in a smile.

"Sir Magnus says ye are to be accorded respect and treated as the other knights' wives. 'Tis about time!" Helen dumped the clean bedding on the wooden chair and bustled about the room setting it to rights.

So, he wanted her treated like the other wives? He may as well have bellowed to the world she was now his favored leman!

"Esa, 'tis glad I am to see ye," Grunda said.

Muriele whirled around to see her friend looking uncertain as she stood in the doorway. Why did she hesitate to enter?

"Come, we will all go down to break our fast together," Muriele said, holding out her hand to her.

"Ye young lasses go ahead. I must visit the Alewife. She has been feeling poorly. I fear it willna be a good birthing."

With a waggle of her hands, Grunda hurried them along.

The two women were silent, for there was no privacy in the spiral stairwell. You never knew who might be coming up from below, or who could be behind you in the last turn.

Once they sat at what they began to feel as their favored table, they filled their wooden bowls with gruel, berries and honey. When they began to eat, Muriele remembered the night's activities and fought to keep any expression from her face. 'Twas good she had. Looking up, Feradoch's sky blue eyes stared into hers.

He smiled and nodded then glanced at Esa. His eyes squinted then lit. Esa tensed and her hands began to tremble.

"Why does he upset ye, Esa? He appears to be most gentle."

Esa shrugged.

Muriele glanced toward him again and watched him smile and laugh with the men at the table. He never seemed to demand having his own way. It was a pity Feradoch's complaisant personality hadn't softened Magnus' harshness.

"Does Feradoch leave at dawn tomorrow to return to the Morgan's at Clibrick?"

"Aye. He leaves for the last time. When he returns here, 'twill be for good." Esa sighed quietly.

There was a sound of resignation in the soft breath of air. Would this quiet, lovely woman miss him while he was gone? They were such opposites in looks they drew your gaze when they appeared in the same room. Esa was near as tall as Feradoch. Where he was all sunlight with his blue eyes, light skin and red-blond hair, she was midnight, with near black eyes, skin kissed brown by her ancestors and hair as black as a moonless night.

The day passed quietly. As if they knew each other's thoughts, they avoided the great hall at the noon meal and sought cold slices of beef and heavy bread in the kitchens instead.

The men eyed Muriele with open appreciation. They knew. Just by looking at her. And no doubt, Magnus strutted more than usual. Everyone had seen him stalk her when she fled the banquet last eve. He may as well have declared his possession of her afore the whole castle.

Whenever Muriele glimpsed him, she veered in the opposite direction. Esa seemed to understand. They worked in the herbal garden with Grunda, and when they finished and returned to the hut to clean their hands, Muriele heard Gille's light steps approaching. She rolled her eyes and called out for him to enter afore he needed to scratch at the door.

"I know, Gille. Yer helpless master orders me to return to wash his sweaty back," she said as she heard the door open.

Gille's eyes near popped from his head. His master stood no more than five paces behind him. Did the dratted man walk on clouds to annoy her?

"Not my sweaty back, lady. A most special part."

Magnus' deep, resonant voice flowed over her body like a heated waterfall. His eyes smoldered and his lips lifted in a wicked grin. How could he cause her body to respond with naught but his voice and the look in his eyes?

"Ye dinna appear to need help with anything, my lord," Muriele said. "Yer hair is still damp from washing and ye have donned clean apparel."

"Aye. And ye are as grubby as any farmer." He walked over to take her hands and turn them palm upward. "What good does it do if I lighten yer duties only to have ye work in the fields?"

"I wasna in the fields. The herb garden was in need of clipping. The days are over-warm. Ye can near watch the weeds sprout."

Muriele tugged her hands from his grasp and wiped them on the cloth hanging from her pocket.

"Ye look like a common villager. Return to the keep and prepare for the meal. I have no time to see ye dressed properly afore the Chief grows impatient."

"'Dress properly? Appear on time?' Muriele near shouted the words. She stiffened, hands on her hips as her eyes regarded him with withering contempt. "I dinna need ye to select my clothing, ye hulking oaf!"

Taking determined steps toward her, he regarded her with cold speculation. He halted only when his boots met the tips of her shoes. She dared not take a deep breath else, her breasts would prod his chest.

"As I said afore, I have no time at the moment. But this 'hulking oaf' will tend to ye later."

Magnus' hand shot out and grabbed her hair in his fist then pulled her head back, holding it still. He glared into her eyes then crushed her lips in a kiss unlike any he had given her. His teeth crashed against hers as his fingers on her jaw made sure she opened to him.

His tongue didn't play with her lips. It didn't explore. It conquered.

She shuddered and her knees quivered. She near crumpled. He stopped the kiss as quickly as he started it. Abruptly. Suddenly, he was gone, leaving her to sway and grab onto a stool near at hand.

She heard the door slam and felt the draft from it before she gained control of her seething body. If any other man had dared treat her so roughly she would have kneed his groin. Why did she turn to butter in Magnus' hands?

When Grunda chuckled, she turned and eyed her. The old seer approved!

"Ye have met yer match, Muriele, else why did he leave with nary a scratch or bruise on him?"

Grunda lips quivered just the slightest bit when she spoke. Why, she must have read Muriele's mind.

"Huh! If he thinks to tend to me later, he will have bruises and cuts aplenty," Muriele muttered her face aflame.

Esa stood, wide-eyed and uneasy. "Come. It's much later than we expected. We have time enough for you to bathe and wash your hair. I'll help."

"Ye have enough to do for yerself, Esa. I can manage."

"I can dress your hair. I'm good at it."

"If ye prepare in one room, 'twill be much faster." Grunda beckoned them to follow.

As they hurried to the keep, she laid out a plan whereby the two women could bathe and dress quickly. Muriele's hair would be the last thing needing tending. By the time they put her plan to work and were finished, the bedchamber looked like an army had tromped through it.

Grunda stood and regarded the two beautiful women, one so fair and graceful, the other dark and mysterious. She noted their physical differences were much like Magnus and Feradoch's.

Muriele wore a striking sleeveless green kirtle with bands

of golden-colored threads embroidered on the bodice and sleeve openings. A filmy, long sleeved smock the color of pale new leaves in spring flowed through the openings. Esa combed Muriele's hair, gathered it in layers and braided them in rows down the back of her head. The last was at Muriele's nape, where Esa tied it off with silken ribbons, leaving a hand's length of golden hair free. Wisps of soft curls trailed each temple.

Esa wore black and pale gray with her tightly curled ebony hair pulled back from her face and gathered with curved combs to hold it there.

Muriele's face and slender neck were pale wheat; Esa's features were striking angles and warm dark honey.

"Off with ye. I'll put the room to rights before Sir Magnus returns." Grunda opened the door and held it.

"I'll go first to be out of the way," Esa said as she started forward.

"Nay. Walk beside me." Muriele took her elbow. "Many thanks, Grunda. We'll be in time. I wouldn't want our lofty Sir Magnus to strain his throat bellowing for me."

"Watch yerself, lovey. Dinna prick his temper overmuch." Grunda's tone held a stern warning.

Chapter 23

"THEY ARE WELL INTO their cups from the sounds of it."
Muriele looked over her shoulder at Esa, uneasy hearing the rowdy men so early in the evening.

"The night before Feradoch returns to Clibrick, Chief Olaf provides special entertainment for him."

Esa hesitated, one foot hovering above the next downward step.

Muriele tilted her head and studied her friend's expression in the dim light. Esa's lips had tightened to a thin line and her eyes held a hint of fear. Surely, she didn't fear Feradoch. He would do naught to cause her unease. If not him, then Magnus?

When they stepped out into the open, Muriele grasped Esa's hand and brought her alongside. Occupied with comforting her, she paid no heed to the crowded room. Feeling a change in the room, she glanced around to find its cause. Her gaze clashed with Magnus' own. His intense stare roved from her head to her toes, appreciating what he saw — if one could count lust as appreciation. Feradoch, too, looked over the women as if judging their worth.

His gaze shifted to study Magnus. His lips tightened. What displeased him? Did he not like the way Magnus studied her and Esa? Mayhap he felt Magnus was crude to take advantage of his position as conqueror of Blackbriar?

Chief Olaf clapped his hands for quiet and waited until the room stilled.

"Ah, all that is sunshine and shadows rolled into two beautiful women." He slapped both men on the backs. "Fetch them. They will sit beside you. Our traveling musicians are from

Wales, as is Esa. After our meal, she will dance to their rousing music."

The closer the men came, the more Esa's fingers trembled within Muriele's grasp. Magnus' face was intent. Severe even. But then, when was it not? He was forever grim-faced. She could count on one hand the times she had seen him smile or even look at ease.

Her gaze turned to Feradoch. Hungry anticipation hardened his face when he looked at Esa. 'Twas not simple lust. More like a wolf before he devoured a plump hare. It was quickly gone, for now his features showed only kindness and the desire to please.

Magnus' warm, calloused hand separated hers from Esa's and placed it on his arm. The soft hair tickled her palm until he pressed her hand down firmly to grasp him. The heat of his bare skin and the hard muscles there sent shivers from her fingers to her shoulder.

Wearing a black sleeveless tunic falling short of his knees, his strong muscled arms and powerful legs added to his massive frame. He must have sensed the heat rippling through her. Though his face tightened, devoid of expression, his black eyes gleamed.

He was the vivid image of a magnificent unrestrained animal.

Did all of the Morgan clan run true to their motto, *with a strong hand*? If Magnus was any indication, they did. Her mind flashed back to last night. Strange. Those hands had been most gentle. If they had not been, his ardor would have caused bruising over every inch of her flesh. Her fingers jerked at the memory. He glanced down, his eyes heated with passion.

How had he known where her thoughts had lingered? Then, suddenly, all expression left. It was like dousing a light, hiding his thoughts in deep darkness.

"Aye, ye didn't need me to select yer clothing," he murmured. "No one would recognize the filthy little lass fighting in the bailey with dirt smeared over her face."

He thought her little? She was as tall as many men in the room.

"As beautiful as ye are, lass, be reminded. It will not matter to this hulking oaf. I willna allow *anyone* to speak to me with so little respect."

If he thought to beat her for what she'd said earlier, he'd best think twice. Though she might not have her weapons strapped to her thighs, her hands and feet would aid her in making sure he wouldn't remain unscathed.

They had arrived at the high table and talking quietly was at an end. He helped her to sit, but with every gentle touch, he reminded her of his tightly controlled power.

The meal passed in a blur, for entertainment accompanied each course. As before, Magnus cut the meat in small pieces and placed them on her side of the long plate. His own were much heartier.

There was little chance for conversation, for she refused to raise her voice loud enough for everyone to hear. Often she leaned forward and glanced at Esa. As the evening progressed, whenever she saw Feradoch whisper in the dark beauty's ear, Esa's face became frozen and blank, giving no hint of feeling.

Finally, a course of fruits, nuts, small hot rolls and sweet wine ended the meal. Olaf, more than a little the worse for drink, banged his goblet on the table and stood. His voice boomed out.

"Bring on the Welsh performers. It has been long since the wench Esa has performed for us."

Men banged their cups on the table and chanted for Esa. Their anticipation thrummed like a live presence in the air.

Five Welshmen danced their way into the great hall. Three men, their fingers blurring as they set the savage pace, pounded bone beaters on bodhrans, the old Celtic war drums of goatskin stretched over round frames. A fourth man played a wooden flute, the fifth a stringed instrument. As they leapt and played, Muriele's heartbeat quickened from the wild rhythm.

Esa shoved back her chair and stood, transformed. Shaking her combs from her long, tight curls, she freed her hair to whip about her face. Her deep voice rang out, dark and husky. When Feradoch made to touch her, she twirled out of his reach. In long, graceful steps, she worked her way around the table to leap into the midst of the performers.

The faster the musicians beat, the faster she danced and sang in the Celtic tongue. She warbled deep in her throat while she dipped and swayed, twisting her body to the primitive music. Muriele couldn't take her eyes off Esa — nor could anyone else in the hall. Magnus leaned forward, his eyes hot, the vein on his neck visibly throbbing. Every man's expression showed he wanted to throw Esa on the floor and rut with her.

Feradoch surprised her the most.

His face, normally so quiet and peaceful, filled with lust. His jaw twitched, his hands couldn't keep still. They reached forward then snapped back as he forcibly controlled himself.

Esa ignored everyone and gave herself over to the music. Where one tune ended, another immediately took over. Her voice and the music bounced off the rafters. Her heart and mind belonged to the musicians. Finally exhausted, she crumpled to the floor while the players leapt into the air, pounding out their last notes.

Muriele jumped up, thinking to run to her. Magnus grabbed her forearm, urging her back into her chair. She spluttered, wanting to argue that Esa needed her. He shook his head, slowly, warning her to stay still. She saw why.

Feradoch vaulted over the table and stalked over to the crumpled figure on the floor. His stance dared anyone to draw near him. Like a giant spider, he swooped down and plucked her off the floor. Her head dangled over his left arm and her legs rested over his right. He juggled her slightly until her head rested against his shoulder. Purposeful steps led him quickly out of sight.

Muriele thought he only sought to remove her from the great hall, but a chill passed over her when she spied Grunda watching. Her face was taut. Uneasy.

"Her dancing is as powerful as the strongest potion. There will be many bairns birthed nine months from this night." Olaf held up his wine goblet in a silent toast then laughed and threw a cloth bag of coins to the Welshmen.

If the behavior of the men at the lower tables was any indication of how potent the dance had been, Magnus believed Olaf called it rightly. In the darker reaches of the hall, men pulled servant girls onto their laps, and by their jerking motions, they had not waited to find privacy for a quick swiving.

His body had responded with eagerness. Thankfully, he had the freedom of his tunic. His cock was unfettered. He leaned over to Olaf and spoke for his ear only.

"At dawn, I ride with Feradoch as far as the foot of Loch Rimsdale. I wish to learn if the distant villages have had any problems with raiders since we killed the last group"

"How many of your knights will patrol with you?"

"Feradoch has six of his own retainers. I will take a like number."

Once Olaf nodded, Magnus turned to Muriele. "We go above. Now."

As if she dreaded being alone with him, a shadow passed over her face. She couldn't have used a more insulting name than a hulking *oaf*. Hulking he could forgive. His body *was* massive but well honed. But she'd meant it as an insult.

For certs, he wouldn't tolerate her calling him an oaf.

She would learn he was neither clumsy nor stupid.

CHAPTER 24

MURIELE'S KIRTLE LEFT HER arms near bare but for the thin leaf-green sleeves of the smock beneath. Ascending the stairwell, Magnus enjoyed the warm feel of her flesh while he guided her ahead of him. The closer they came to the top, the slower she moved. He didn't slacken his pace but required her to increase hers. By the time they reached their bedchamber, she was breathing heavily.

Seeming reluctant to enter the room, he lightly edged her shoulders. The room was warm, and Grunda had turned down the covers. A tray with cold pork, cheese, bread and a chalice of wine sat beside it. Again. He halfway expected to find the seer had slipped another potion into the wine. He'd check. If so, he would see Muriele did the drinking.

He didn't need any enhancement for his sexual appetite.

As he closed the door, he watched Muriele halt beside the bed. In the flickering firelight, she seemed to glow. He always thought of warm breezes and sunlit days when he spied her.

"Bare yer body to me," he ordered.

She didn't move.

"Ah, I am pleased ye wish me to undress ye. It will give me an opportunity to show ye how this oaf can easily strip a woman with nary a tear in her most delicate clothing."

When her hands lifted, he brushed her fingers aside with a sweep of his on and a stern look.

"Nay! Stand still. Dinna move."

He walked around her once. Then twice. Finally stopping behind her, he untied the silk ribbons holding the hair at her nape, being so gentle she could not feel him there. Once the ribbons fell free, he whispered his lips across the fine hairs of her nape.

Chill bumps covered her flesh.

He dropped the ribbons to the floor and began to slip her braids free, one slow row at a time.

Once her hair fell free, he ran his fingers through it, loosening and spreading it down her back. He nuzzled the wispy curls at her temple, touched his wet tongue inside her ear then blew just a hint of hot air over it.

She trembled.

He touched her shoulders then bent his knees as he drew his hands down the outline of her body, following it down to the floor. He eased the hem of her kirtle up, ever so slowly, until he brought it to her shoulders.

"Lift yer arms," he whispered at her left ear.

Slowly, she did and groaned softly. The garment came off and over her arms without disturbing her hair, better than any lady's servant could have done. He felt her tighten and knew she wondered how he'd acquired his skill.

He would tell her.

"Many women seek this clumsy oaf's hands."

'Twas like he had lit fire to her hair! She leapt forward out of reach and turned on him.

"This woman does not seek yer hands, clumsy or otherwise!"

"Ye may not seek them, but they will be there nonetheless."

He advanced toward her, watching her face. Her eyes narrowed and her mouth tightened as her temper rose. She was even more beautiful when the flush of anger warmed her golden face. When he was within a hand's reach of her, before he could even touch her, she turned and rolled, head over heels, across the bed and leapt to her feet on the opposite side.

So. She wanted to play? He vaulted over the bed. By the time his feet landed, she was gone again. This time, the table stood between them. If he feinted left, she was canny and responded in the same direction. He threw the table to its side and she sprinted behind the heavy armchair.

"Muriele! Come to me," he ordered.

"Nay!"

He grasped the chair's arms and tossed it aside. Instead of intimidating her, she lifted her smock, twisted sideways as if winding herself up, then twirled back again, her foot aimed at his middle.

"Uff!" The air burst out of him.

"The next time, 'twill be yer randy tarse," she hissed between near closed teeth. "Ye will need all yer lust-crazed women to soothe a battered shaft!"

"I'm warning ye, Muriele. Leave off; else ye will pay for it."

"Pay for it?" She sounded disbelieving. "Ye have already used me for yer pleasure. I have done naught but pay for being Blackbriar's heir. Ye can do nothing else to me."

He pretended to be unaware of her intent for her next move. Having watched her fight off the knaves in the bailey, when she kicked out again, he was ready for her. He caught her foot in his big hand and, careful not to cause her an injury, twisted it until she fell face forward onto the fur rug in front of the hearth.

She landed with a thud. He followed on his hands and toes atop her, allowing only the touch of his body against her, but effectively pinning her beneath him.

She caught her breath and tried to heave him from above her. He didn't budge.

"Get off me," she yelled.

"Why? I like the feel of ye." He grasped her smock and pulled it up to her waist then lowered himself and brushed up and down against her, letting his raging cock rub the seam of her buttocks. He stilled her struggles, pinning her legs between his and balancing his weight on his elbows.

She let forth a muffled string of words he couldn't make out. Nonetheless, he knew she cursed him.

"Enough! No woman should use such foul words."

When she drew breath to yell again, he lifted up, flipped her over and swiftly removed the smock. He stifled her words with his tongue in her mouth. He held her still, forcing her to accept his kiss. What started out as a savage way to halt her tirade, turned to soothing caresses instead. As he explored her teeth and inner cheeks, her rigid muscles softened. When he teased her tongue and tenderly drew it into his mouth, her breath hitched.

Much as he gentled old Bolt, he brushed his hands over her sides while murmuring soft, comforting sounds deep in his throat. Her legs relaxed. He reached between them and lifted his black tunic out of the way while nudging her legs apart.

Settling himself between them, he grasped his eager cock and rubbed its hot length against the petal-soft folds of her pleasure cave. And left it there. He held still. Relaxed his body and waited.

He felt her arousal begin for hot dampness teased his turgid flesh. Still, he didn't move between her quivering limbs. She became more sensitive to his touch. Trailing his hand from her collarbone down over her stomach to her belly, he felt tension and heat there. She jerked when his fingers delved through the curls guarding her cleft.

He burrowed a hand behind her buttocks and lifted her. Her legs lifted and locked around his back. When he entered her with a driving thrust, she was slick and wet.

"Hold on to me. The rug is too small," he whispered and guided her arm up around his neck. Her arms tightened with surprise when he stood up with her.

Now upright, he groaned when her weight took her down over him, not stopping until she surrounded him, flesh to flesh. She whimpered and writhed, for 'twas the first time his entire length filled her. His hands on her bare buttocks lifted her up and down until, with passionate cries, she pleaded for him to increase the rhythm.

He kicked the table out of the way and dropped her onto the edge of the bed. Standing with her torso resting on the soft bedding, he could watch her face as he thrust into her. Her head thrashed back and forth. Non-words spilled from her throat. With an iron will, he held his own pleasure under control as he fondled her breasts and feathered his fingers over her belly.

She locked her legs so tightly around him he could hardly move. Rubbing his fingers lightly over her tense belly, he felt the hard tremors of the muscles there and reached between them to stroke her swollen flesh. Triumph filled him on hearing her passionate cries.

He withdrew until naught but the tip of him stayed inside her steaming body. He refused to move though she strained to arch her hips up to him. Never had he made love to a woman as receptive as Muriele. Passion roughened his voice when he next spoke.

"Am I still a loathsome lout, my lady?"

Her muscles jerked as she tried to heave upward with her legs. He clamped his hands on her hips holding her firmly, refusing to allow more than his tip to penetrate.

"Answer me, Muriele. Am I still a loathsome lout?"

"Nay."

"Just nay?" He chuckled and circled a calloused palm over the tip of a straining nipple. "Nay, 'my lord' or 'nay, I am sorry'?"

She opened glazed eyes to glare at him. Passion battled her stubborn refusal to submit to him. With his gaze locked on hers, he trailed his fingertips from her breasts to the soft curls below. Everywhere his fingertips touched her glorious skin, chill bumps followed. Very lightly, he crept his finger near her nub again until she squirmed and strained.

"Nay, my lord," she gasped out.

"Was it so hard to admit ye misspoke?"

Magnus slowly entered and retreated, then increased the tempo until she was again on the verge of climaxing. Once more, he stopped after burying his arousal in her straining heat up to his groin. An evil twinkle flashed in his dark eyes.

"Enjoy the feel of me claiming ye whilst I rid myself of my clothing."

Muriele near screamed in frustration. His powerful cock filled her. Her muscles grasped him tighter. She could think of naught but wanting his manhood to bring her to completion. As he leisurely removed his clothing, she felt his hot gaze caress her body. Heat flushed everywhere he looked as if he touched her.

Once his clothing dropped to the floor, she wanted to feel

the steely strength of his body beneath her hands, the bunched muscles at his shoulders, his broad, muscled chest and the hard slab of his belly. She wanted it all.

She squirmed and beat the bed with her fists, frustrated.

Magnus' eyes deepened to flashing black as he held her gaze prisoner.

"Look and watch how I am loving ye," he whispered, his face tight with passion. His gaze lowered to where their bodies joined.

Heaven help her, she did.

He pulled back, slowly gliding his wet, slick erection from her. Even more heat pooled there. Surely, her flesh must be flamered now. Her body wept in anticipation, her belly quivered.

He lifted her hips, almost demanding she watch them make love. He thrust his tarse in just a small bit then stopped. Wetting a long forefinger with her juices, he ran his blunt fingertip around his thick arousal where her flesh joined his. He pulled back again. She thought she'd scream with need.

But, no, he didn't stop. He grinned and began his slow thrust again, letting her watch, nay, wanting her to watch and feel the building passion as his finger followed around his tarse, around her, making her aware of her body stretching to accommodate him.

She could stand no more. Her entire being pulsed with blinding passion. He thrust faster. She couldn't turn her gaze from his tarse, wet and slick, pounding into her now with soul-shattering intensity. Arching her back until naught touched the bed but her head, a chain of spasms tore through her body. She screamed as she exploded with it. As her body thrashed and fought for completion, one thought filled her mind.

She hated Magnus.

He had caused her body to betray her!

Magnus' heartbeat pounded so loudly in his head it near muffled Muriele's cry of pleasure. Had she not found release when she did, he could not have held off his own. Not a breath too soon, he jerked back and fell beside her on the bed.

"Lucifer's horned cock!"

He bent his head backward, his throat straining and sore. He held his breath. By God's love, he'd shouted the words for all to hear!

He groaned and clutched his pulsating cock. The way his seed spurted time and time again, surely 'twas enough to sire a hundred children.

Never before had he had such a powerful release. He gasped. Tried to calm his breathing. When he closed his eyes, all of his previous sexual encounters flashed through his brain.

Not once had he felt the way he had with Muriele.

Perchance the stories were true? Had her mother used some spell, which rendered men mad with lust? If so, she had passed her lore to Muriele.

He opened his eyes a slit. Muriele's face contorted as if she grimaced and clenched her teeth at the same time. Her flesh became mottled.

The daft woman was holding her breath!

Cautiously, he rose on an elbow and peered down at her. With eyes squeezed together, she muttered something. He leaned closer to her lips, afeared her violent climax had made her brainsick.

She whispered something again and again and gasped for air between each short burst. He leaned so close he could feel her breath on his ear.

"I hate him … I hate him … I hate him."

Relieved, he fell to his back and snorted. Loudly.

"Ye do?"

He propped himself up again and waited. Finally, Muriele opened her eyes and glared at him.

"For certs." She hissed the words through tight lips.

"'Tis a strange way ye have of showing dislike."

He trailed a fingertip over her lips. She swatted it away.

"Ye near burst my ears with yer hatred. Tsk! Think what an unholy noise ye would make should I truly pleasure ye."

He was out of the bed before her fist could meet his jaw.

Chapter 25

L ONG BEFORE THE SUN rose, Magnus entered the great hall and carefully picked his way through the sleeping men. They played a strange tune with their snoring and farting. Were they louder, they'd rival a badly played bagpipe.

The more canny warriors had parked their buttocks on benches early in the night and waited for their seatmates to drink themselves senseless. It took but a slight nudge to topple them to the floor, giving the winner a preferred sleeping spot.

The twelve knights who would leave with him came up from the bailey at the same time Magnus entered the room. Pages brought platters of hot food left from last eve, cheeses, fruits and fresh breads, enough to fill the travelers' bellies. When Magnus took his seat, Olaf and Feradoch eyed him with very different expressions. Olaf showed broad approval; Feradoch was coldly reserved.

"You look in need of sleep," Olaf said.

"I had plentiful rest."

"Plentiful? When?" Olaf grinned and elbowed him in the ribs.

"Most of the night."

"Ha! Your bedchamber sounded like the battle of Hastings took place there."

Feradoch fixed him with a disapproving stare.

"For sure, 'twas a battle of sorts."

Magnus extended his arms to stretch his shoulders, clench-ing and straightening his fingers as he did so.

"You don't look battle scared," Olaf said.

Magnus shrugged.

"I won."

He filled his wooden plate with cold lamb, hot bread, cheeses and a baked fish. He devoured them. Last night's bed sport had left him with a huge appetite. It took two full plates to appease his hunger.

He ignored Feradoch's cold frowns and kept his own face free of emotions. When it came down to it, his foster brother was the one who looked battle worn. Magnus had heard his footsteps going past his bedchamber way after the midnight bells for Vigils rang.

Disliking their scrutiny, he leaned forward to hand two small sealed scrolls to his foster brother.

"Deliver them to Chief Angus and Graemme first thing on arriving at Clibrick. I reminded Father I take over as first in command over the warriors. Graemme will train under me."

"Pfft!"

Magnus raised a brow and stared at Feradoch.

"I dinna think so. My brother's body looked to be as honed as mine."

"You have more work ahead of you than you expect."

Magnus shrugged and turned away. He looked forward to the next days they would ride together and wished to forestall an argument that would mar them. When Chief Olaf pushed back his chair, Magnus stood and raised his hand toward the knights.

"Come, we must leave if we are to ford the river Helmsdale afore nightfall." Magnus stood.

If the men hadn't eaten their fill, 'twas their own fault. The knights followed suit, though Feradoch seemed reluctant to rise.

Olaf buffeted him on the shoulder.

"Come, lad. The forest makes for slow traveling. No telling how many lawless bands will delay your travel. An unwelcome rain will make fording impossible."

"Aye." Feradoch chuckled and flashed a gleeful smile at Magnus. "Per chance Magnus will show us where the wild woman killed the boar intent on tearing him a new arse hole."

Magnus stiffened and glowered at him. Feradoch's blue eyes blinked innocently. Reminding Magnus of his carelessness didn't sit too well with him. It made him fear he'd also been lax in other areas.

He took great strides to leave the great hall. Men grunted and cursed when he shoved their feet out of his way, then clamped their teeth together when they saw his glowering face. When he strode through the keep's entrance and down the stairs, he took a deep breath of damp, clean air.

Muriele crept into his life as surely as that puppy the first year at Kinbrace. Until now, no woman ever distracted him. If one caught his interest, he swived her. If his cock rose with glee when next he spied her, he swived her again. None held his interest long enough to make her his leman.

Less than a year now, he'd return to Clibrick for good. He wouldn't take a leman with him. She'd be a distraction and complicate his duties as his father's first in command.

Sir Cormac, Magnus' knights and their squires were mounted and ready. Sir Erland's face looked as tired as Magnus felt. Hmm. 'Twas another reason not to allow a woman access to his mind and heart.

As Sweyn fell into step beside Magnus, he frowned. "Feradoch's men may be knights, but they are an undisciplined lot."

Magnus looked at their battered helmets, bits and pieces of armor, animal skins and kilts. All carried battle-axes and swords aplenty.

"Aye. They cling to the old Viking ways. They are savage fighters but hard to control."

"I wouldna turn my back on any of them," Sweyn warned.

Magnus stopped, his legs spread, his hands on his hips, studying the seeming confusion before him. Feradoch's knights milled about with their squires and horses.

"What do ye wait for? Do ye expect yer master to give ye a hand-up?" Magnus' bellow produced the desired results. The men speedily mounted and filed into line.

As he walked past the horse trough, his groin stirred, remembering.

Something about Muriele was different from other women

he enjoyed swiving. Was it her defiance that interested him? By Lucifer's fetid breath! She challenged his every move.

For truth, he had a *need* to conquer her. Even now, the satisfaction of seeing her passion filled face and hearing her breathless begging for release quickened his blood.

"Magnus, did you not satisfy your cock last eve?"

Sweyn's deep voice held a hint of laughter.

Magnus skidded to a stop and glanced down. As his unruly cock engorged, it pulled his plaid up along with it. Now, cock and plaid bobbed at his sudden halt, agreeing with Sweyn. Surely 'twas Lucifer who caused his tarse to have a mind of its own! He had no time to lust after any woman.

He was a warrior. A conquering warrior. One much feared for never losing a battle. He was not an untried youngling!

"I did. More than thrice." He growled with disgust.

"Hm. Do you think you should pour cold well water over it?" Sweyn chuckled low in his throat. "It's been many moons since I've had need of such."

Magnus brushed his hand down the front of his clothing, sending a message to his randy body there were more important things than swiving. He refused to allow another thought of Muriele to enter his mind.

All around them, stirrups groaned, leather saddles creaked and harnesses jingled. Restless horses tramped and sidled, impatient for a good run.

Gille stood whispering and cooing to Odin while clutching the reins in one hand and rubbing the great white horse's nose with the other. The way the beast behaved, the boy had a natural instinct for soothing him.

Brian took Magnus' claymore from a young squire and helped Magnus strap it to his back. When he mounted, he settled the claymore more comfortably then checked his weapons. Before he pulled on his Norse helmet, he patted his short sword at his side and the dagger strapped to his left boot. The squire would carry the axe and shield until Magnus had need of them. Satisfied, he nodded then studied his youngest squire's face as the boy passed him Odin's reins.

"Ye did a masterful job holding Odin still, Gille. Ye have gained more muscle in yer shoulders and arms these past days."

If the lad continued in his growth, he would have a body much like Feradoch. The bone structure was there. Every day, he became surer the boy was either Feradoch's half brother … or his son. It mattered not which man had fathered him. Neither would acknowledge the lad.

Magnus needed no standard-bearers today. Everyone in the eastern Highlands was wary of crossing him. He and his men would accompany Feradoch halfway to Clibrick. Once there, they'd turn around and return, stopping along the way to check outlying villages. In about a fortnight, they'd be back at Kinbrace Castle.

Olaf strode over to Feradoch and stopped, legs straddled wide, to give his son instructions in a hard voice.

"Make the most of these last days at Clibrick. Learn all their skills, their tricks with weapons. Angus will be unhappy to lose you. I've a good mind to keep you both when spring comes."

Olaf looked out of the corner of his eyes at Magnus and chuckled. 'Twas his usual lecture each year when they parted. He gave Feradoch a final grin before he moved to Magnus.

"Be sure you return in one piece. You'll not have Feradoch watching your back."

"Eh? Since when have I needed anyone to watch my back?"

"Not since you were ten and eight when the foolish lout thought to run you through while you took a piss in the woods." He laughed and slapped his thigh. "You lopped off his head without even pissing your boots."

"Then ye have naught to worry about."

"Rid the woods of any landless warriors. They'll be quick to take your head and steal the horses and weapons if you give them the chance."

The sun shyly peeked over the eastern mountains like a timid lass stealing a look at her betrothed. As it lightened the darkness to early dawn, Olaf slapped Odin on his haunches then bellowed with laughter when the horse reared in surprise. Magnus expected it and had the great horse in tight control.

With a solemn nod at the old man, he and Feradoch moved to the front of the line.

Feradoch grinned at Magnus. "I'll be first over the draw-bridge onto open ground!"

By the time they reached the barbican, the two men were in full gallop. The horses' hooves thundered, throwing dirt and dust in their wake until the air clouded.

Magnus leaned low over Odin's neck, urging him to greater speed. Evenly matched, neither man was willing to let the other win as they reached the wooden bridge.

Of a sudden, Magnus' nape prickled. Someone watched.

He had no need to look back. What a shame he hadn't the same instinct when he'd ordered the women of Blackbriar to pass in front of him.

Even amidst a violent summer storm, his body would know she was near.

'Twas Muriele.

CHAPTER 26

MURIELE STOOD OUTSIDE THE great entrance doors to the keep. Her hands clutched the wool shawl around her shoulders. Not for the first time, she wondered how men could go about without as much as a thin shirt covering their chest and back. True, they did have the end of their kilt thrown over one shoulder and tucked beneath the weapons belt at their back. Even so, most of their flesh was bare to the elements.

The early morning light was enough to see two men on their warhorses racing across the drawbridge as if they were carefree younglings playing catch-me-if-you-can. A burst of laughter floated to her. She strained in hopes she'd hear it again, for Magnus had never laughed heartily before. She knew it was he for a blur of white, surely Odin, streaked ahead of the other horse as they reached the end of the drawbridge.

A dozen knights and their squires trailed them at a canter. By the looks of their taut arms, she sensed they longed to let their mounts have their way and gallop after them.

How long would Magnus be gone? Hmpf! He'd not even bothered to wake her and say he was leaving. She would be grateful not to endure his unwelcome bed sport. Her cheeks heated with the memory of just how *unwelcome* her body had been throughout the night. One touch of his calloused fingertips on her bare flesh was enough to send heated throbs of anticipation betwixt her thighs.

The thought of it made her cross her legs as if she had a sudden need to pee. She startled when Grunda's voice spoke softly behind her.

"Dinna worry. He will return within a fortnight. Sooner if

he can. His dreams will plague him and make his sleep restless."

"Worry? I welcome having him gone. Even more welcome would be his not returning."

"Tsk!" Grunda sucked her teeth. One bony finger prodded Muriele's shoulder. "Ye'd best pray the Devil is too busy tormenting souls to hear ye."

"Tsk yerself! I dinna care if he hears me. With Magnus gone, he canna be ordering my every move."

Grunda shook her head. "Be careful for what ye wish for. One day Lucifer might send Magnus on a needless journey. Then ye'd learn just how much ye longed for his return."

Muriele grasped the wool beneath her chin, warding off a sudden gust of cold air. Clouds were creeping in over the mountaintops to the east. She'd hoped for a warm day to work with Grunda on the herb garden. She could even take a stroll through the orchards picking up pears, plums and apples. Ivar the Stout's wife would be pleased for the fresh fruit to make pasties.

"Come back to the hut. Barley broth is warming by the fire and fresh baked scones. I have yer favorite raspberry sauce to trickle over them."

Muriele's stomach growled reminding her she'd eaten little last eve.

When she turned to follow Grunda down the stairs, her muscles reminded her of Magnus' appetites of another kind.

Muriele's days passed painfully slow. She and Esa spent much of their time together. After they had mended all of Magnus' clothing and their own, the only outlet for their energy was to work in the herb garden with Grunda. They helped the old seer gather herbs and make potions. Muriele didn't have enough to keep her mind occupied, nor ample exercise to work off the energy of her healthy body.

At Blackbriar, her mother had trained her to take over the responsibility of a keep when she married. She had been busy from sunrise to sundown. Once abed, she'd had no trouble sleeping.

Now, her nights were restless. When she did sleep, she awoke with heavy breasts and heat throbbing through her woman's place. She spent half the night pounding her pillows and pretending she enjoyed having the bed to herself.

One day, after they had bathed and dressed and were awaiting the evening meal, Muriele sat cross-legged on the bed. Esa walked around Magnus' big chair, studying it from all sides. Finally, she flashed a bright smile at Muriele and plopped down in it.

"Ow!" She sprang up and rubbed her buttocks. "What a monstrous hard chair! I'll sport bruises on my nether cheeks."

"When Magnus lounges there, he always looks comfortable."

Muriele slid off the bed and went over to try the chair. Forewarned, she eased herself down on it.

"Ugh!" She murmured and tried to scoot to the chair's back "Never have I sat in a more troublesome seat. Mayhap because the chair is overlarge?"

She gave up searching for a comfortable spot and stood. She took her pillow from the bed and placed it on the chair before she sat again.

"Ah. Much better."

She wriggled around and sighed again. Her muscles were sore from spending the morning on her knees tending the smaller plants.

"Magnus sits on his bare arse when his kilt rides up in back. Ye would think it would be a discomfort to his, uh, dangling parts," Muriele said with a wide smile.

"Surely he finds it as hard as we do?"

"Aye, 'tis likely. He often leans forward with his elbows on his knees. Do ye think perchance he tries to cup his stones betwixt his thighs?" Muriele paused then snorted, "Pah!"

"What is it?"

"I am a fool to think about *his* comfort. He destroyed every comfort I had."

"I think the blame lies with Lord Baldor. Sir Magnus warned him to surrender. All in Scotland know when Sir Magnus speaks they'd best heed his words."

"True. But because of him, I'll never make a suitable marriage. Why could he not have been content with killing Baldor? Did he have to ruin me, too?"

"I am sorry for it. Everyone at Blackbriar paid for Baldor's stubborn pride."

"Aye." Muriele's shoulders slumped. "I was trained from a child to run a keep. To be a lord's wife. He stripped all from me. He forces me to be his servant. His leman. He didn't even offer a handfast." She flushed. "I'll always hate him for it."

Seeing the haunted look in Esa's eyes, Muriele was shamed for being so insensitive with her friend. She remembered her unease when Feradoch had stalked over to Esa's body crumpled on the floor. He had seemed triumphant. Like a man who claimed the spoils from a war fought for his amusement. Grunda's face had set in grim lines when she watched.

Muriele swallowed, uneasy. Was Feradoch forcing Esa to be his leman?

Fortunately, for Magnus, dark clouds overhead waited until they crossed the Helmsdale River before they pelted the travelers with showers so cold as to be near hail. He didn't complain. They'd had several encounters with men too thick between the ears to be wary of attacking them. A good fight loosened their muscles and warmed their bodies.

Glancing behind him, he saw why the fools had been so bold as to attack. To a stranger, the bedraggled men appeared harmless, too hefty around the gut to put up a good fight. Few weapons showed. What the attackers hadn't seen was the quantity of swords, flails, war hammers and knives beneath the wet plaids.

Whenever they stopped and watered their horses, the men rummaged through leather saddlebags to find tidbits saved from their last meal. As they chewed on stale bannocks, they tended their weapons with dry cloths.

The thick canopy provided by the dense forest gave them some protection. Thankfully, the clouds finally emptied. Looking ahead, he spied an area large enough for a good-sized camp. When daylight started to wane, Magnus called a halt.

A small stream ambling alongside provided water for drinking and perhaps a quick bath, while plentiful branches and ferns were available to build lean-to shelters for the night. He would relish sleeping without rain dribbling into his ear and seeping through his wet clothing.

"What do ye think, Feradoch? Are ye ready to rest yer bones?"

"Huh! It'll take more than a night," he said with a wry smile.

"Aye. If we build a round of fires, it should be ample warmth to dry our clothing."

He turned in the saddle and gave orders for the squires and servants to hunt dry kindling for fires then branches and ferns to build shelters. The knights would see to their own horses. He motioned Brian off when he stepped over to take Odin.

"Nay, I'll see to him. Tend yer own mount."

Sweyn and Magnus led their animals down to the stream where they both stopped to drink. At the same time, Odin drank then threw up his head and shook it, neighing softly.

"Nothing like a cold drink when ye're tired, eh, boy?"

He stood and rubbed Odin's neck and shoulders while the great horse drank his fill. When it snorted and stepped back, Magnus led him to the campsite and removed his saddle.

"Ye must be glad the day is done. If ye could speak, ye'd have demanded I hie myself off yer back and walk, would ye not?"

Odin shook his head and snorted. Magnus chuckled as he began to rub him down.

"When ye rear and buck, are ye trying to tell me so?"

He stopped and patted Odin's neck, then scratched between its ears. While brushing the horse, Magnus kept up a steady stream of soft comments, telling Odin what a valued, stalwart steed he was.

When he spread the saddle blanket over its broad back to ward off the night's chill, Feradoch laughed behind him.

"You treat the horse like he is your leman. He's naught but a foolish animal."

"Hmpf! A warhorse is nay foolish. In battle, he has saved my sorry arse and struck down opponents I couldna reach with my sword. Do ye not value Thor?"

"He carries my weight," he said and shrugged. "The beast responds to commands because he knows my whip stings and my spurs prod him if he doesn't. I don't waste foolish words on him."

Thor snorted and pawed the ground trying to get at Odin. Impatient with the black horse, Feradoch yanked on the reins and led him to the far side of the fire where his knights had tethered their own mounts.

"That one gives nary a thought to anything living unless it eases his comfort," Sweyn muttered behind Magnus.

"He has changed since we returned to Kinbrace."

Magnus frowned, disliking that he'd noted the difference throughout this last visit. Never before had Feradoch uttered such sly comments about Clibrick under the guise of an innocent, smiling face. And though Magnus had chosen to ignore them, his instincts told him 'twas a good thing this spring would see the end of their fostering.

By the time Magnus and Sweyn had taken a quick dunking in the stream, several good-sized fires chased the chill away. Within the warm circle of fires, servants had built drying racks out of sticks and spears then placed the damp plaids over them.

Magnus and Sweyn wiped cold water off their naked bodies and walked over to stand in the circle. Magnus bent at the waist and reached his arms over the glowing heat to rub them dry.

"Dangle your randy cock any nearer the flames and you'll not be swiving the witch's get when you return." Behind Magnus, a man sniggered and belched. "Her rosy lips look ample for a big, burnt cock. Cold well water will cool her mouth when you pump your seed there."

Magnus stiffened. His flesh was no longer chilled but near aflame. His fists convulsed with suppressed rage. Loathing welled like bile from his belly. He slowly turned. 'Twas one of

Feradoch's knights. The fool grinned and held up a beefy hand to thrust his middle finger in and out of his mouth in vulgar imitation, all the while sucking and making noises like a lass near a climax.

He near bit his finger off when Magnus' left hand flashed out to clamp steely fingers around his hairy neck. Grabbing the knight's left wrist, he twisted it backward and up between his shoulder blades. One fierce blow from his bare foot to the backs of the man's legs sent him to his knees, squealing like a stuck pig.

Hardened warriors scurried backward. Growls, as chilling as an angry wolf's, rumbled from Magnus' chest and spilled from his twisting lips. His breathing rasped. He steadily forced the knight's face toward the hot embers at the fire's edge.

The screech of a sword drawn from a sheath filled the air. Magnus ignored it.

"Come now! You canna harm my man over a jest," Feradoch protested.

Magnus paid no heed.

"Hold back!" Sweyn ordered. "'Twould be unwise to meddle with Magnus after the fool stoked his rage."

Magnus felt Sweyn's bare leg touch the side of his hips. He heard him draw his sword.

Steadily, Magnus forced the knight's nose toward the hot embers, near burying it there. The man screamed and jerked. Magnus held his thrashing body firmly while he counted to five. He leapt to his feet, pulling the dolt up with him. Still clamping the howling man's arm, he shoved him to the stream. A swift kick to his arse propelled him into the icy water.

"Dinna ever stick yer nose in my business or mention the lady again. If ye do, 'tis yer cock I will singe!"

At the bellowed words, birds already abed for the night, rustled branches as they took flight.

The knight spluttered and tried to crawl out of the cold water.

"Fool! Keep yer nose beneath the water to draw the heat out."

Magnus turned to find Sweyn still guarded his back, though there was no need. His men stood close by wearing grins. He thought to see Feradoch's knights armed to the teeth.

None had drawn a sword.

Faces solemn with admiration, nodded

He grunted. He retrieved his near-dried kilt and gathered it around his waist. He went to sit beneath a gnarled oak tree, his back against the trunk, facing the camp.

With half his attention on the men and their duties, he puzzled why his temper had flared so quickly. The knight's comments were no worse than usual for men gathered together. No doubt, at times he had been as coarse himself.

He clamped his teeth. He knew why.

When the man made his obscene gestures, he had seen Muriele forced to such a position.

The oaf had no right to make such odious remarks about her. Even though she no longer had money and a castle to inherit, she'd been the daughter of Blackbriar.

He shook his head, ridding himself of her face. Muriele meant nothing to him.

She warmed his bed. Sated his body.

He had no need for her other than those duties.

Once he made his final return to Clibrick, he would seek a bride to bring him wealth and lands.

He would never see Muriele again.

Pain flashed through his chest so quickly he thought he had imagined it.

It could be naught but a need to belch.

Chapter 27

DURING THEIR DAY'S RIDE, hapless hares, unfortunate enough to show themselves, were now boiling in iron pots. When the mouthwatering aroma drifted to him, Magnus was sure his pain had been from hunger.

Now he'd cooled his anger, he joined Sweyn beside the campfire. Feeling dry, warm ground beneath his arse, he sighed with comfort.

Soon, a servant brought stew to Magnus and Sweyn. As was his custom, Feradoch joined them.

"If we had not forded the river when we did, we'd never make it across now," Sweyn said.

"Aye. It'll be a sennight or longer before the water lowers. 'Tis good we have other business to attend." Magnus filled his wooden spoon and without waiting for the food to cool, swallowed it. As it went down, warmth spread through his chest.

"Clibrick is too peaceful."

"Peaceful? Is that not why we rid our lands of lawless knaves?" Sweyn asked as he scraped up the last of his stew.

"'Tis better to have villagers fearful of their betters. They demand less," Feradoch said. "I prefer ridding villainous louts from the forests on Gunn lands." He swung his spoon back and forth as if wielding a double-headed axe. "Heads roll much farther on flat, hard-packed earth."

Ah! At first sight of them when Magnus rode out with Feradoch, the Gunn villagers ran into their huts and shuttered their windows. Magnus had oft thought they feared him because of his reputation as ruthless.

Could it be it was not from him they ran?

After a restless night, the foster brothers parted ways the next morn. They thumped each other on the back, as men who do not like to show affection oft do then left on separate paths.

Feradoch had not ridden more than half a day when he found signs of travelers ahead of them. He stopped to peer from atop a small hillside into the valley below. A small party journeyed westward. Flashes of bright colored clothing and the glint of light off well-kept weapons aroused his curiosity. He tracked them until near dusk then closed the distance between them. When they charged out of the forest, they found the party bore King David's livery.

"Hold!" Feradoch held up his right hand, his sword pointed upward. "By God's graces! How can you be so careless to let someone overtake you? Do you not know the Highland's abound with thieves?" He shouted at the men. "Who is in charge here?"

An elderly monk, his cheeks quivering with fright, advanced his horse a pace.

"I am. I deliver a missive from King David to the Chief of Clibrick."

What could King David want with his foster father? 'Twould be easy enough to find out.

"Ye are far off the trail leading to Clibrick." He lied to the monk with nary a twinge of regret.

He watched the men's reactions. 'Twas apparent they didn't know the area for they looked surprised and didn't argue with him. Since dusk fast approached, Feradoch ordered everyone to make camp for the night. He spoke quietly to his own men, and once they settled for the night, offered to share their meal. He always carried well-stocked canvas bags with him, but he didn't bring them out until he and Magnus parted ways. 'Twas one of the secrets he and his men kept to themselves.

After plying the monk and his guards with wine, he wove a story of how dangerous the area had become.

"The way ahead is fraught with lawlessness. Whilst I and my men can reach the castle in safety, you will surely be slain by landless knights."

"Once they learn we are sent by the king, will they not let us go in peace?"

"They kill first without thought as to whom they slay."

"Your own party is at risk, also?"

"As you can see, we travel lightly with naught to tempt thieves. Your fine weapons alone are enough to lure an attack."

"But I must deliver a missive to Chief Angus. Place it only in his hands, the King said."

The monk acted more like a lass than a man did for he chewed his upper lip and his eyes pled like an untried virgin. Feradoch stifled a snort and smiled.

"Well, now, you have naught to worry about." He leaned close to thump the man's shoulder. "I am Chief Angus' son. My hands are as his hands, so to speak. I will safely deliver your message to him while you return to safety. It will be best for all around."

Feradoch refilled their cups and chuckled. Often lasses told him they likened his appearance to the Angel Gabriel come to earth. Now, he used his looks to manipulate the King's men. After frightening them with tales of brutal killings in the area, he soothed them with sincere words and biblical quotes.

"How does a peaceful man such as you travel with safety?" the monk asked.

Feradoch waved his hand at the warriors surrounding the campfire. They scowled and were so heavily armed they appeared to have sprouted weapons from their skins.

"My men protect me, a lone man. But they are not enough to keep a large party safe."

Afterward, it was easy to convince the monk he could safely give Feradoch the missive.

At first light, he sent the monk and his men back from whence they came. He had no qualms about reading King David's message. When he learned the King intended to marry Muriele to the man who conquered the infamous Lord Baldor of Blackbriar, he threw it in the campfire and immediately made plans to thwart him.

In his early years at Clibrick, he had made friends with Bruce, a young man studying under the tutelage of the castle's old priest. Whenever Feradoch grew bored with swiving a woman, he turned her over to the lustful young man who didn't care the cast-off lass bore Feradoch's "eye" brand on the hairline above her nether lips.

When Feradoch was ten and seven, he decided the priest was unnecessary. Who would question the death of an old man in his sleep? One moonless night, he straddled the sleeping man and clamped his hand over the shriveled lips while he pulled the pillow from beneath the priest's head. It was over quickly.

He rather enjoyed it. It gave him a raging cockstand. The dying man was stronger than he had anticipated; when the priest bucked and struggled, trying to throw him off, it was like being astride a reluctant virgin.

From then on, Bruce heard confessions and became Chief Angus' scribe. He quickly passed on interesting tidbits to Feradoch. For a price.

It would be simple for Feradoch to enter the castle walls secretly in the dead of night. He would have Bruce write two missives. One supposedly from Olaf stating he wanted an immediate end to Magnus' presence at Kinbrace. Feradoch would deliver the other to Olaf when he returned to his home. In the missive, Angus demanded Olaf order Magnus to return to Clibrick to wed.

Bruce had access to the Chief of the Morgans signet ring. Feradoch had stolen his father's before he left. There would be no questioning the messages. No questioning the priest, either.

After the midnight mass the day of his return to Kinbrace, a sharp blade across Bruce's neck would see to it he'd not be spilling secrets to Magnus about Feradoch's secret activities and his bountiful supply of reluctant whores.

Several days later, Feradoch and his men reached their destination. Between the shore of Loch Naver and the sharp rise of Ben Clibrick, the castle rose atop a lone foothill. Lush forests on the mountain behind the castle surrounded its back. On the north side facing the loch, they had cleared the land leaving it a green meadow. The wind blew wild flowers of every color in graceful waves, as if they were a continuation of the sparkling water of the loch.

Small villages dotted the landscape below as far as the eye could see.

Feradoch's lids narrowed; his lips thinned.

He sat taller in his saddle.

One day, all this would be his.

"Another sleepless night, Magnus? Ye look ready to spill blood at the drop of a feather." Sweyn stepped backward out of his friend's reach.

"Sleep? 'Tis not from lack of sleep but because of it."

Magnus deep voice sounded gravely as if he had shouted all night long. He rubbed briskly at his face, hoping to release his mind of the dreams plaguing him each night.

Since that wet evening when Feradoch's man had spoken so crudely of Muriel, each night he relived the times he had swived her. The dreams were all but real. 'Twas as if he hovered in the air above the two bodies watching their sexual struggle to best each other. On awakening, he found he had even spurted his seed.

In his dreams, he heard every sweet sigh, soft moan and cry of ecstasy spilling from Muriele's lips. He felt every kiss he'd fluttered over her naked flesh and watched his fingers tweak her nipples and caress her breasts. He felt his tongue lave those same turgid tips afore he suckled.

He teased and tormented her body and brought her into wave after wave of tension. His buttocks rammed his cock into her until she begged him for release.

When he emptied his seed, he threw himself off her and sprawled on his back. Shock jolted through Magnus. It was not him he watched atop the lass. The faceless man snaked an arm beneath Muriele's waist. He pulled her tight to his side. Triumph radiated like a red aura around him. As his gaze met Magnus', fire sparked like torches from where there should be eyes.

Lucifer's putrid farts!

Blast his cackling, bloody lips!

Magnus felt an unholy urge to wrest the faceless bastard from the bed and sling him from atop the highest tower of Kinbrace. His fingers twitched, wanting to grip Muriele's golden hair and wind it round them until her face was against his.

Then he would strangle her.

Enraged, he awoke as quickly as a bolt of lightning striking the earth.

Magnus shook his head; his lips curled in anger.

Those close to him suddenly had cause to tend their personal needs deeper into the line of trees.

He could not blame them.

He hungered for a bloody fight.

For killing.

Chapter 28

MURIEL, TOO, WAS PLAGUED with troubled sleep. No matter how she prepared the room afore she climbed into bed, she was either too cold or too hot.

Huh! She was lying to herself. No sooner did she close her eyes than Magnus stole into her dreams as stealthily as a fox crept atop wet leaves to pounce on a fat grouse.

Their nights together were so real it near made her believe he was a sorcerer. As she drifted off to sleep, his scent floated on the air. The bedchamber, the bedding, especially his pillow, smelled of leather and spices.

His warm, muscled arms enveloped her, and she inhaled deeply to capture his tantalizing essence. The coarse hair on his chest tickled her breasts and tempted her fingers to ply through it from his collarbone down to his thrusting nipples. She'd fingered them, liking their hardness and the light hair springing around them.

He would sprawl on his back and urge her to explore him. What better way than to straddle him as he had done her? She could trace the hard muscles of his chest, and run her palm lightly over the hair there and down where it narrowed to that exciting place. She rose on her knees and, avoiding touching him with her woman's place, traced the line leading to the mass of curls around his maleness. Sitting back on her haunches, she admired his shaft jutting like an imposing tree surrounded by black wheat.

He would take just so much teasing before he would grasp her waist and toss her on her back. She was always ready for him. Closing her eyes, she could concentrate on his filling her bit by bit.

His laughter warmed the skin at her throat when she tried to lock him in her arms, her legs around his hips. Still he slid away into nothingness as dawn crept over the sleeping land.

After a night spent with his incredible hands and lips tormenting her, she awoke throbbing and near ready to scream from frustration.

He never allowed her to climax.

She sat up in bed, the covers falling around her waist. Frustrated heat rose to her face. She grabbed Magnus' pillow, placed it over her crossed legs and pounded it with her fists until tiny down feathers floated in the air.

Grunda came into the bedchamber like a March wind shoved her through the doorway. Her eyes twinkled when she saw Muriele surrounded by a cloud of feathers.

"I told ye 'twas best not to voice a wish, else Lucifer might grant it! Do ye still welcome Sir Magnus' absence? He may not be here to order ye about, but I ken ye miss his bed sport more than ye are willing to admit."

"Miss him? How can I miss a man I dinna like?"

"Aye. Ye keep telling yerself so and one day ye might believe it."

"I do believe it. He gives me no choice but to share his bed."

"Then why do ye bear the same look as Flori and Ingirid?"

"Huh! What do ye mean?"

"Ye didn't suspect? I thought their dislike of each other would have made ye curious." Grunda clucked her tongue and tossed her a warm robe, which Muriele deftly caught.

"Suspect what? They are fashious with each other because they are so different." She wrapped the robe tightly around herself then slid off the bed into her shoes.

Grunda snorted. "Who can be more different than Esa and ye? Ye enjoy each other because ye dinna share a man."

About to splash cold water into the basin, she spilled it on the floor instead.

"Ye ne'er were so gawky afore." Grunda shook her head. "Have ye ne'er noted the women follow Magnus wherever he goes? They near drool on the back of his kilt."

"What? Does he …?" Muriele's breath caught in her throat as she awaited Grunda's answer.

"He did. Afore he took ye into his bed."

"They are welcome to him." She turned her back to hide her flushed face.

"Then why are ye so restless? I'll wager ye haven't slept half a night since he left."

"I dinna feel at ease in this chamber."

"Hmpf!"

Grunda ambled around the room, straightened Muriele's wooden comb and the boar's hair brush on the washstand then rearranged the pots of soap on the shelf below. Deliberately slow, she hung Muriele's cloak on a wall peg Magnus had installed for her.

"I ken the tapestry pillow ye made had naught to do with him?"

"It did not."

Grunda snorted again and looked toward the fireplace.

"It cushions his chair."

Muriele settled her clothing around her shoulders and hips, allowing the yellow smock to peek through the slits of the dark blue kirtle.

"I made it for my own comfort. And for ye and Esa when ye visit."

"Then when Sir Magnus arrives on the morrow, ye will remove it?"

Muriele's head bobbed up as she tied a braided rope girdle to ride on her hips. She took a deep breath, no longer dreading the day for its sameness.

"'Twould be childish to do so."

"Esa is below. She waits to break her fast with ye."

"Won't ye come with us?"

"Nay. I only came to tell ye I'll be visiting the Alewife. She's feeling poorly. I ken her man samples too much of her brew. She drops out one bairn then fills with another within a month. She's well into her eighth month, yet she still sickens throughout the day."

"Should I come along?"

"Nay. When time for the birthing, I'll need yer help."

Grunda flicked her hand at Muriele to go before her as they left the room. At the foot of the stairwell, they parted ways as Grunda headed to the keep's outer door. Muriele had no need to search for Esa. She waited at their favorite table.

"You dinna look like you have slept well this past night," Esa said.

"Ye, too?" Muriele rolled her eyes at her friend. "Grunda questioned me as if I was yet a youngling. She says I have the same look as Flori and Ingirid." She leaned her head toward Esa so she could whisper. "Did ye know they have had bed sport with Magnus?"

"Could ye not tell?"

Muriele shook her head. She glanced up in time to see both women sat across the room. Together. If eyes could shoot barbs, the floor of the keep would be slippery with Muriele's blood.

"I dinna know how to deal with this."

She lowered her head and concentrated on stirring her porridge and buttering a cold scone. Never before had she reason to feel shame.

"Keep your head tall and don't flinch. Clear your gaze from all thoughts so they can't read your mind."

"Ah. That is what Magnus does. I canna read his thoughts." She hesitated. "Except angry ones."

"He learned early to guard them."

She glanced up at Esa and realized 'twas as hard to read her eyes as it was to discern Magnus' thoughts. She knew so little about her friend and didn't want to cause her distress by asking. Did she love anyone?

Grunda thought she was Feradoch's leman, yet they never noted one another in the great hall. The night Esa collapsed after dancing was the only time she had seen him touch her. She remembered how tense his body had been. He wouldn't have taken advantage of Esa's weakened condition, would he? Stinging on her lower lip reminded her she treated it as if she gnawed a bone.

At Clibrick Castle, Chief Angus and Graemme studied Feradoch. As Feradoch lounged in his seat, he watched his foster father push a hank of silver-streaked hair behind his ear. Small creases formed between his brows as he the studied the small parchment on the desk.

"Your father calls an end to sharing our sons. He asks I order Magnus to return. That he has caused trouble. Why did he not simply send him home? I expect he shared his thoughts with you?"

Feradoch watched the Chief's face, pleased he had not doubted the forged missive. Angus was still tall and lean, his silver temples his only concession to age. He and Magnus looked much alike, except the father's brown eyes sparkled when he laughed.

"Aye."

Feradoch lowered his gaze and fidgeted in his chair. Finally, he sighed and his eyes filled with compassion when he looked up.

"Chief Olaf tires of righting the damages from Magnus' ruthless ways. He has turned the villages and nearby castles against him."

"Heh!" Graemme scoffed.

He stood behind his father, arms folded across his chest. He leaned his shoulders against the wall as one foot slammed the stones behind him to steady himself. His tense body vibrated with the need for action. And from the look in his eyes, Feradoch would be the target.

"He says naught about it in his missive."

The gaze from Graemme's burnt-almond colored eyes bored into Feradoch's, seeking the truth behind his benign features.

"Truth be told, my father is as afeared of Magnus as the villagers. Your brother flies into a rage over imagined slights. Father will be aggrieved I said anything, but I kenned you wanted an answer."

Feradoch blinked and a guileless smile spread on his lips.

"Aye." Chief Angus sighed and leaned back in his chair. His eyes brightened with expectation.

Resentment churned and boiled in Feradoch's soul. If it took substance, its foam would rise up and roll from his lips as he screamed scathing words of loathing.

How could Angus prefer Magnus! Feradoch had lived here most of his life. *He* should be the favored one! His wily brain and skills were far superior to this man's hulking son's.

"I will have need of you for the next sennight, Feradoch. Then you will be free to go."

"I am always at your command whenever the need arises." Feradoch smiled fondly at the Chief and left the room.

He near gloated. The Chief had taken his story easily, but for a moment, he'd feared Graemme had seen through his ruse. Far from a weakling, this younger son was nigh as formidable as Magnus. Their difference was their personalities.

Where Magnus was hard and unmovable in his beliefs, Graemme tended to be open in his opinions. Of the two, Feradoch was more wary of Graemme, for he looked far beyond the obvious and searched out the lowliest of details.

Feradoch's time at Clibrick could not pass swiftly enough. Had he his way, he would leave at first light. The sooner he arrived at Kinbrace, the closer he would be to claiming Muriele's wealth as his own.

Prickles of excitement awoke Muriele to total darkness. She hugged Magnus' spare plaid around her shoulders, added a block of peat to the banked fire and brought it to life.

After she tended to her needs, she washed and splashed her face with cold water from the pitcher. Shivering, she sat on the cushioned big chair and curled her legs close to her hips. Sighing, she tucked his plaid tightly around her feet and watched the flames. Though she tried to stifle it, she yawned so widely she was sure she could have put her fist in her mouth. Grinning at the thought, she decided to rest her eyes.

Earlier that night, Magnus had decided there was no need to sleep on the damp ground when Kinbrace was just short hours away. They would reach there not long after the midnight hour. It would be time enough to sleep, or swive, depending on a man's inclinations.

Magnus intended to swive, to erase the dreams of someone else seizing what was his.

Silently, he entered the room. By the fire's light, he saw Muriele cuddled in his chair, clutching his plaid around her. His face softened then tightened with desire. After ridding himself of his clothing, he washed with the water at the washstand. With care not to wake her, he lifted the sleeping woman in his arms then sat down slowly.

What the . . . ? Prepared for hardness, he instead met a pillow of some kind. Realizing how harsh the chair had been, he sighed and enjoyed the comfort.

To savor Muriele's beauty, he eased off her cover and exposed her creamy skin He explored the beauty in his lap, wanting to imprint on his mind it was he, not that infernal bastard in his nightmares, who held her.

He played with all the sensuous areas he knew most excited her.

Her dreamy sighs and quivering belly gladdened his heart.

She squirmed and her legs relaxed and opened, causing his cock to dance with glee.

When her fingers clenched the hair on his chest and yanked a surprising handful, his randy member wilted!

Magnus gripped her wrist to keep her from wrenching every hair off his body.

"I take it ye dinna like being awakened with love sport?"

He somberly awaited her reply.

Muriele frowned and shoved against his chest to sit upright. She glanced down and saw she sat naked upon the wool covering Magnus lap. His naked lap.

"How long have ye been here?"

She tried to drag an end of the wool up from the floor to cover her.

Magnus promptly shoved it down again.

"Long enough to know ye missed me."

He looked pointedly at her swelling breasts jutting their pink tips at him.

"'Tis from the cold, naught else."

"Then we must cover them to keep them warm."

He gently cupped her breasts in his big hands, then swirled his rough palms over them, watching her eyes all the while. He felt her tension build and knew she would fight it. He didn't give her a chance.

Never had he known a woman with such rapid response to his lovemaking. He took full advantage of it, and before she could build her defenses against him, she was grasping his shoulders and moaning as his mouth swooped to plunder hers.

For the next sennight, Magnus spent a portion of each day searching out Muriele when she least expected him. She might be picking fruit from the orchard when she heard Odin's hooves approach. If she tried to run, he grinned and gave pursuit. If she hid behind a haystack, in an empty stall in the stable or even behind a tree, he searched her out. The clever horse seemed to turn on a spot. For truth, Odin seemed to enjoy this people's game, for when he reached Muriele he nuzzled the back of her neck and bumped his chin on her shoulder.

One day, when Magnus caught Muriele by surprise, every-one stopped in their tracks on hearing Magnus' laughter floating from the orchard. But a moment later, a commotion at the drawbridge distracted them.

Feradoch and his knights galloped through the gatehouse into the front bailey near trampling Gille.

"Out of my way, fool!"

Clouds of dust and clumps of sod flew in the air when the

knight and his men hauled back on the reins. They looked like they had ridden for days with little sleep. Did they flee an army about to raid the castle?

Gille, knowing his master was in the orchard with Lady Muriele, took off at a run, yelling at the top of his lungs.

"Sir Magnus! Sir Magnus! Sir Feradoch has returned!

Muriele's sweet begging in Magnus' ear made his chest swell with such strong emotion it nearly overcame the physical pleasure he was feeling. He rose up on his knees ready to bring her to completion and froze on hearing Gille yelling and thrashing through the low-hanging branches.

Muriele gasped when Magnus abruptly withdrew and sprang from atop her. Grabbing his shirt from an apple tree branch, he jerked it so hard the branch whipped back and forth and tumbled ripe apples to the ground. Muriele jumped to her feet, dodging the fruit and fumbling in her haste to straighten the kirtle over her naked body.

Unfortunately, it twisted below her creamy beasts. Before Magnus could reach out and aid her, the squire skidded to a stop in front of them.

Gille gulped and diverted his eyes as Magnus grabbed his kilt off the ground and tossed it around her shoulders.

"Go back to the bailey, lad. If they ask, tell them I will be there shortly." His voice was still husky with passion.

Grasping Gille's shoulders, he swung him around then gave him a light shove.

He turned back to Muriele with a wry smile, regretting their interruption. "When ye are ready, count to thirty and make yer way to the keep by way of the cookhouse," he said as he lifted his kilt off her shoulders.

While gathering it around his waist and belting it in place, he watched out of the corner of his eye as she hurriedly straightened her garments. By the time he slammed his short sword into its sheath, they were both presentable.

Except for Muriele's hair. He had made a fine mess of it when they were making love. Anyone seeing its disarray would know why. She ran her fingers through the long curls, tidying them.

"The ribbon. I can't find the ribbon," she muttered as she bent down and frantically rustled through the leaves.

"Ah, because ye canna see behind ye." He grinned and plucked it from its hiding place half inside the back of her dress and half out.

Magnus handed her the red silky ribbon she'd earlier woven in amongst her braids.

"Go, else they'll come looking." She nodded at him to hurry.

He gave her one last glance then couldn't resist winding a silky curl around his finger. Quickly, he caressed her breast then ran toward the keep.

"Ho, Feradoch! Has tragedy stuck Clibrick?" His mind raced from one thought to another. Had his father died? Had someone slaughtered his family? Or were they safe but under siege?

Magnus' long strides took him across to where his foster brother was still pulling his leather bag off his saddle.

A look of triumph flashed through Feradoch's blue eyes and near turned them darker. It disappeared behind a somber mask.

"Nay. All are safe. But I relay an urgent missive from Chief Angus."

He grabbed the leather bag and held it tight to his chest as if he expected Magnus to wrest it from him.

"Come, boy!" Chief Olaf called. "Have ye caused trouble at Clibrick and they sent ye packing?"

Feradoch bristled. His lips lifted in a feral snarl. It was like his father to expect the worst from him.

"Chief Angus loves me as his son. He grieved to see me leave."

"Then get yourself in here and let's hear this news he sends."

Olaf led the way into the keep. Being near time for the noon meal, he shoved people out of the way in the great hall. If they didn't move fast enough, a swift kick to their shins hurried them on.

As Olaf and Magnus took their seats, Feradoch stood, his

shoulders back, a look of triumph lighting his face.

"It seems Magnus' father has called an end to our long arrangement," he said as he pulled a rolled parchment out of his bag.

When Olaf reached for it, Feradoch stepped out of his reach. He stiffened and his nostrils flared as he stared at the entranceway. Magnus' gaze followed where his foster brother looked. Muriele came into the room, her hips swaying with her long-legged walk. From her soft-eyed look, flushed face and rosy lips, all but a novice at love sport could tell she had been thoroughly tumbled.

Feradoch fists flexed. He started reading the missive, not taking his eyes from Muriele. Magnus scowled. How could he know what the message said unless he had opened it earlier and learned it by heart?

> *Magnus, return in haste to Clibrick. I have contracted a betrothal with Nell, daughter to our neighbor Blanding. The ceremony will take place immediately upon your return.*
> *Her father is in ill health and wishes to assure himself of the nuptials afore he dies. Nell is his only heir, so you will have all once he is gone. I think the choice a favorable one, for you seemed smitten with her when you were a lad.*
>
> *Angus, Chief of the Morgans.*

Feradoch's face gleamed with satisfaction.

"The missive is addressed to me! By what right had ye to open it?"

Magnus grabbed the parchment and glanced quickly through it. He held fast to his building rage, keeping himself from throttling Feradoch for overstepping his rights.

His foster brother's face smoothed to a sympathetic smile.

"I feared you would not tell the lady Muriele the truth of it."

"Ye think I would leave without telling her why?"

"Nay. I feared you would force her to Clibrick."

Magnus stared at him in disbelief.

"If she traveled with you, she would believe you did so because you intended to make her your bride," Feradoch continued. "She is a lady by rights and should not be your leman at Clibrick."

He shrugged away from Magnus and withdrew another message from his bag intended for Chief Olaf. He had not broken the seal to this one.

Olaf opened it and frowned. "It mentions no wedding only that he wishes an end to our arrangement. He asks I send you to him with much haste."

Magnus tried to make sense of it all. When last at Clibrick, his father had made no hint he contemplated a betrothal for him. It was unusual, too, for he would know Magnus would resent having his bride chosen without his say.

Nell wasn't at all suitable as his wife. Why, the girl was afeared of her own shadow! He shuddered to think of a bride who cringed whenever he entered the marriage bed.

He wanted sons! He'd learned if a woman was frightened, she couldn't conceive.

"Sweyn, see the men are ready to leave at dawn in two days."

The fidgeting boy on his left reminded him. "And see Gille is properly outfitted for a long ride."

He looked around the hall, searching for Muriele. She stood near the doorway as still as a frozen waterfall in the dead of winter. Until his gaze collided with hers.

At first, Muriele appeared stricken. As he watched, her expression changed to accusation then snarling hatred.

She was gone in a swirling blur of color.

CHAPTER 29

MURIELE SLAMMED THE DOOR to Grunda's hut, her face drawn and white. Her body seethed with hatred. She reached inside the fake pocket in her kirtle, and with a flash, her dagger streaked through the air and embedded in the far wall with a thud. Magnus had returned it to her only two days before. How she wished she had buried it in his cruel heart.

"I take it ye are upset with Ruthless?"

"I hate him!"

Grunda cocked her head. Her gnarled fingers gripped Muriele's chin and she turned her rigid face first to the right then to the left, studying her. Her dark brown eyes softened with sympathy.

"Hm. This morn, hearing yer pleas for Magnus to take ye, I likened yer feelings to be more on the tender side."

"Ye were spying on us?" Muriele was dumbfounded her old friend would do such a thing!

"Nay." Grunda released her chin and gave her a soft pat on her shoulders. "I had an uneasy feeling that soon I would be in need of a powerful sedative. I was making an elixir with mandrake to have on hand."

"It doesn't explain how ye heard us." Muriele huffed.

"'Tis quiet here. Though my hands were busy, my ears were free to hear a great deal said around the castle. Now. How can ye wish to put a knife through Magnus' heart when ye were filled with lust for him this morn?"

"That was afore Feradoch returned to announce Magnus must make haste to return to Clibrick and be wed."

"Then ye also hate the proposed bride?"

"Nay. She has no say in who she marries."

"Her father then?"

"He is near death." She shook of her head. "He only wishes to see her safely wed."

"Ah! So ye think Magnus knew aforehand and kept it from ye?"

"Aye! The lying bastard."

Muriele talked as she paced so quickly anyone watching her would think the floor burnt her feet. She stopped for a step and snorted. Loud.

"I mean no more to him than any whore who followed his camp."

"He does not look at ye like he would a whore. His eyes follow ye wherever ye go. In my visions, I have not seen him married to another."

"Ye must have seen false then. By the sound of his father's summons, all that remains to seal the marriage is his rutting presence.

"He leaves to make a favorable alliance while I am forever ruined. I regret I didn't kill him before he climbed between my legs!"

"Tsk! Ye'd have missed learning bed sport at the hands of a master."

"What good is it to me? Except to increase my value as a whore!"

"Stop calling yerself a whore. Ye are a lady of breeding."

"Ha! A *lady* of breeding with no holdings or honors. What man of like breeding would wed a woman with naught to offer? One he knows was a plaything of the most dreaded man in Scotland. I am naught but tainted flesh."

"Come. Sit with me." Grunda beckoned her to the table. "I have food enough for the both of us. There's no need for ye to see him until yer temper cools. I dinna think Chief Angus would take kindly to having his son returned across his horse."

Mutton stew simmered in a pot, and from the growls coming from Muriele's gut, she knew the lass had not eaten since dawn and now night was falling. She soothed her young friend with words and food — and with a sleeping draught in her ale.

Come morning, Muriele would be in a more peaceful frame of mind. Grunda still believed Muriele was fated to be Magnus' mate for life. Something had gone amiss. It would take time to discover what it was and set it to rights.

Shortly before dawn, a fist banging on Grunda's door awakened them. When she swung the door wide, the Alewife's drunken husband stood there weeping and blubbering. All they could gather from his jumbled words was his wife was trying to birth the bairn and there was so much blood he was afeard she was going to die.

Both women gathered herbs and potions they thought needful, a bundle of clean cloths, a thin blade and a heavy blanket. He led them out the postern gate, for he had told the guard his plight.

When they arrived at the village hut, they feared they had not the skills to save either the woman or the babe who refused to be born. They worked all day, using every trick Grunda had learned and those Muriele had acquired through her mother's midwifery. In near constant pain, the woman screamed her heart out. The bairn's head bulged at the opening then retreated. It refused to venture into the light of day.

Late into the next evening, they were sure the Alewife had not long to live. Grunda gave her a small portion of the sedative made from mandrake to ease her.

"Grunda, the bairn is overlarge and tearing her flesh. Mother once delivered one such as this by cutting the skin at the bottom of the birth path to aid the head and shoulders to pass through."

"Do what ye must. The bairn is too feeble to fight any longer and the Alewife is beyond feeling. We will lose both if we dinna get the bairn out."

Muriele put the thin blade in a small pot of boiling water. Neither Grunda nor Muriele had any idea whether it was day or night. Focusing on helping the suffering mother took all their attention. Truly, they must have been there a long time. Grunda's hands trembled and she had difficulty rising from the stool beside the pallet.

Muriele wasn't too pleased with her own hands. They were not steady and she was plagued with unease. As when Baldor refused Magnus' final terms, the heavy feeling of pending disaster surrounded her.

She splashed cold water on her face and let it trickle down her neck while she scrubbed her hands again. Wrapping a clean cloth around her right hand, she plucked the knife hilt from the side of the pan and held the blade upward until it cooled. She only hoped the woman stayed unconscious until she could make her cut.

Taking a deep, calming breath, she knelt at the foot of the pallet. Grunda and the woman's sister bent the Alewife's legs and drew them up to her waist and outward. They were in luck, for the bairn had withdrawn enough Muriele, with careful precision, used the blade's tip to open a small line at the base. She placed her hands around the outline of the bulging head and was gratified to feel the tension giving way.

"When ye feel her muscles harden for another push, place yer hands alongside the bairn and urge him downward. Once his head is clear, the birthing will near be over." She took a deep breath and let it out quickly.

Just then, the woman moaned and her eyes opened wide with pain.

"Push!"

When she called out the word four more times, the bairn was free. She left it to Grunda to clear the boy's mouth for its first feeble squalls while she attended to the rest of the birthing. When Muriele and the Alewife's sister had the woman bathed and on a fresh pallet, Grunda had cleansed and swaddled the boy. She put him to his mother's breast to nurse while her husband watched over her.

Muriele tottered on her feet, too tired to make the trip back to the castle. She wrapped herself in a blanket and curled up on the earthen floor. When she closed her eyes, she had wits enough to realize it was late night and more than a day had gone by.

Her last thoughts were how much time had passed since Feradoch delivered his hateful news?

CHAPTER 30

IT WAS NEAR MORN when Magnus stumbled up the stairway and entered his bedchamber. He and Feradoch had exchanged heated words about him breaking the seal to Magnus' missive and reading it aloud.

It wasn't like his father to do such a momentous thing in Magnus' life without consulting him. But then, he had not asked his feelings when he fostered him to Olaf, either. Magnus didn't object to the betrothal as such, but he would have preferred a bride with more heart.

"Muriele?"

He hadn't meant to shout, but her name echoed around the room. He stumbled toward the shadow of the bed. He'd never noticed the floor being so uneven before. He near fell when he crashed his left shin against the corner of the heavy chair.

"Shite!"

Had Muriele moved the chair so she'd hear him enter?

"Why did ye let the fire die? I canna see."

He tottered when he reached the bed and bent to feel for her.

He chuckled as he fell forward, landing across soft woman's flesh.

"Sorry. Didna mean to crush ye."

Soft hands tugged at his arms, helping to pull him further onto the bed. He sighed, happy for the help. He must have dozed for a moment, for the next thing he knew, he was sprawled on his back with Muriele straddling him.

He fumbled with her breasts and frowned. They were flatter than last eve. And they seemed misplaced on her chest. Had he squashed them further apart when his weight fell on her? He tweaked her nipples then rolled them between his thumb and forefinger. He scowled. He was such a clumsy oaf for having injured her. Her nipples seemed swollen to twice their size.

She was brazen tonight, for she took his wrists and tried to shove his hands aside. He decided to let her have her way. What would it hurt to let her have control on this last night? His throat ached at the thought.

She rose up and took his cock ... no, 'twas strange she *grabbed* his cock, near hurting him ... and held it upright to settle down onto him. When she firmly seated herself and began to rock, she leaned forward. Her hair brushed his cheek, tickling his nose. He went to swat it away, and when he did, a different scent floated from it. No lingering aroma of apple?

He grabbed a handful of hair. He sniffed. Loudly.

Roses?

He grabbed the woman's shoulders and tried to unseat her. She held on, fighting back, grinding against him. The damned woman tried to force him to spill his seed!

He heaved up, toppling her off the end of the bed.

"You fool!" She shrieked then jumped up.

He was as sober as if someone had emptied a bucket of snow on him. Before she got halfway to the door, he dragged her back by her hair. Finding a lighting stick on the mantel, he held it to the hot embers then lit the candle on the table.

The woman he held was the blond bitch who could always coax life into his cock, even when he was near death.

But no more.

His member cringed and fell limp. Disappointed. He felt sorry for his cock and patted the dejected thing in an attempt to soothe it.

"Ingirid. I dinna recall asking ye to my chambers."

"The slut who fights like a man did not see fit to spend your last night with you. I took her place." Her lip jutted out in a sulk.

"Go! Before I lose my temper and beat ye all the way down to the great hall!"

Ingirid grabbed her clothes off the floor. As she passed through the doorway, she wriggled her bare arse at him, letting him see what he was missing.

"Get!"

She slammed the door behind her.

Magnus held the candle high and looked around. Muriele's things were still against the far wall as they had been before. Where could she have gone? To Grunda?

He would retrieve her. Dizzy again, he lurched halfway to the door. Could he find Grunda's hut in the dark? What if he couldn't make it that far and fell asleep on the ground, his head cradled on a mound of horse shite?

Having a lucid moment, he turned and slumped down on the end of the bed. He was a man betrothed to another. By rights, he was as good as married. It would be wrong for him to take a leman until his bride was increasing.

He tried to blow out the candle, but the determined thing kept coming back to light. He'd fix it. He smashed the palm of his hand down on the wick and nodded when the room darkened. Falling back on the bed, he reached for Muriele's pillow and shoved it beneath his head. He rubbed the side of his face and nose on it, sniffing the apple scent. He still had some hours to sleep. On the morrow, he would search her out and demand she wait until he was free to continue as they had been.

He nodded at the cleverness of his plan. It shouldn't take but a sennight or two to sire an heir.

His last thoughts were he was wise to seek his bed. 'Twas so much better than dirt and warm horse shite.

"Are you going to sleep the day away?" Sweyn's voice near startled Magnus off the bed.

God! His head was as if filled with ant-sized blacksmiths pounding away on their anvils. The foul taste in his mouth made him wonder if he *had* ventured out and fallen asleep in the courtyard.

"Thought you would need this," Sweyn said as he shoved a cup with a foul-smelling potion at him. When Magnus did not take it, he added, "Dinna stare at it. Drink it down!"

"What happened last night?"

"Happened? Ye were a fool to let Feradoch coax ale and wine in your gut until you near fell off the bench."

"I could not have been too unhinged. I found my way to the right bed, didn't I?"

To assure himself he was in his own bedchamber, he glanced around quickly. And moaned. Even his eyelids hurt.

"After Gille and I shoved you up the stairwell and near carried you to the room."

"How late is it?"

"Well past the noon hour. I tried to awake you earlier, but you were stubborn."

"Ah."

Magnus nodded and winced for the movement. Then he saw Sweyn's right eye was swollen and bruised.

"My work?"

"For certain it wasn't Gille's."

"Should have let me sleep."

"We leave at first light on the morrow. I thought you would need time to gather all your belongings from the past. I've two carts ready."

Sweyn looked around with frowning disapproval. He untangled a sheer smock from the sheets and raised a brow.

"I thought Ingirid lied when she spread the word you spent your last night," he paused to repeat word for word her boast, "ramming your 'huge and hard as granite cock' in her pleasure cave."

"I didn't. When I learned who it was, I sent her from the room."

"Too late to do aught about it now. Her words are all over the castle." He clamped his jaw together as if he would have liked to lecture further about it.

"Have ye seen Muriele? Her things are here, but she hasn't been in the room since early yestereve."

"Nay. She slept in Grunda's hut." He eyed Magnus and frowned. "Afore dawn, when I found you slept alone, I went to see how she fared. Neither woman was there. Their pallets looked rumpled as if they'd left in the middle of the night. No one knows where they are."

"Lucifer's moldy arse! I forbad her to leave the castle walls!"

"Humpf! It seems to me, you no longer have the right to forbid her anything."

"She is my property. Olaf gave her to me as a prize of war."

"And now he's taking her back since she canna leave with you."

Magnus' stomach roiled. The vile potion Sweyn mixed to relieve his head's aching did not agree too well with his belly.

"I intend to send for her once my bride increases."

Sweyn looked at him in disbelief. "And you expect the lady Muriele to happily join you and be your leman? Where did you misplace your brains? Betwixt your balls?"

Magnus felt sick. He barely made it to the window opening in time to spew, not caring if he showered anyone who happened to walk by beneath him.

When he stood away and turned, he spied her cloak hanging on a peg and her clothing trunk against the left wall.

His chest ached and his throat felt like a hen had lodged an egg behind his Adams apple.

Muriele stood atop the landing at the entrance to Kinbrace's keep. An early morning breeze fought to sweep back fog creeping relentlessly from the forest. It moved like ghosts on silent feet intent on swarming over the castle and taking all within to their soundless world.

Her eyes burned. She blinked to clear her vision. 'Twas only because she was wearied to the bone. She and Grunda had slept little, not daring to leave the Alewife unattended. They packed her betwixt her legs as tightly as they could, trying to staunch the steady stream of blood. They had near given up on saving her when the stream eased to a trickle.

She tried to swallow past the growing lump in her chest.

Her breath hitched.

No one needed to tell her. She felt Magnus' absence much as she would know if someone had cut off her right arm in the night.

Magnus left Kinbrace without so much as a single word to her. The heart-wrenching passion they'd shared all those days and nights had meant naught to him.

He would not return. She felt it in her bones. No matter what Grunda said about them fated to be life partners. Magnus likely rode as fast as the wind, goading Odin on to greater speed in his haste to return to Clibrick and claim his rich bride.

She bitterly hoped his betrothed was so repulsive he'd need to swive her in the dark of night. She doubted he would care. He would be content with her ample dowry, thriving castle and fertile lands.

All the possessions Magnus wanted — all the possessions Muriele no longer had.

To keep her dignity, she straightened her slumped shoulders and stood tall.

To keep her sanity, she let scorn spread like molten oil to thaw the frozen pain in her heart and fill the emptiness within her.

Her heart leapt when warm arms surrounded her and pressed her back against a massive chest and hard body.

Magnus had not left without her!

A warm cheek pressed against her face and a soft voice spoke in her ear.

"He was not a proper mate for you, my sweetling."

She stiffened and pulled forward, immediately aware her heart had not quickened as it did when Magnus was near. Feradoch's arms immediately softened and released her.

"I did not mean to frighten you, Lady, I only offered comfort."

Muriele swung around, holding a shawl tightly under her chin. Feradoch's gentle blue eyes gazed down at her with empathy. A gust of cold wind loosened a lock of her hair and whipped it across her face. Through softened lips, he murmured soothing sounds as he slowly reached out to secure it behind her left ear.

"I feared it would sting your eyes. I hope I dinna offend you."

"Nay." She looked down, not knowing how to talk to a man who had kept his distance since she had come to Kinbrace.

"I watched for you."

A slight crease formed between her brows as she tilted her head to look up at him.

"Why? Was there a need?"

"Aye. I kenned there was."

Feradoch's red-blond hair blew softly back from his beautiful face. His misty blue eyes looked sad and hesitant, like he debated on how to say his next words.

"Do not believe all the sly whispers Ingirid has spread about last eve. She has been jealous of you since you arrived through the gates."

Muriele stiffened.

"What possible rumors could she have spread? All the time I have been gone, I have been with Grunda tending the Alewife's difficult lying-in."

"Not about you, my sweet lady." He pressed his lips together and shifted his feet looking like someone who regretted to impart hurtful news. "She claims Magnus forcibly carried her to his bedchambers and used her so often she fears she will be increasing."

Hot, searing hate filled Muriele. She pretended her face had turned to stone to keep all emotion from showing. Gritting her teeth, she forced out of her mind the picture of Magnus rutting so mindlessly with Ingirid he spilled his seed within her.

That hurt the worst. Even in his most passionate frenzy, he'd always managed to withdraw at the last moment to come on her bare belly.

"Thank you, Feradoch. It was kind of you to warn me aforehand. It truly doesn't concern me. She was welcome to him. I'm glad he can no longer bend me to his will."

She stepped to the side, indicating she wished to enter the keep. He swept her a bow and reached around her to pull open the heavy door.

Muriele nodded her thanks and calmly made her way

through to the great hall. It was later than she thought, for many people were already preparing to break their fast. A flash of color drew her gaze as Esa hurried toward her and took her elbow. She steered her to their far corner where the table was empty.

"Where were you? Did you hide from Magnus' leaving?" She looked worried and upset.

"Nay. The Alewife had need of me. Magnus did not."

"The dust of his leaving has just settled."

"He must have been anxious to start."

"He didn't look to be. Feradoch rode out with him as usual. They galloped through the barbican and over the drawbridge, but for the first time in many years, Thor pulled ahead. They parted ways at the edge of the forest."

"He left no word for me. Just rode away as if I had never been."

Esa put an arm around her shoulder. It was fortunate she had, for Ingirid entered the room holding on to Flori's arm as if she was so very tired she could not walk on her own. She made sure everyone's gaze was on her when she seated herself at the high table. She did so gingerly as if it pained her. Her loud "Oh!" and then sighs of suffering added emphasis to her plight.

The high table had half as many chairs as before, since Magnus' knights and their wives had departed with him. Feradoch scowled at the woman and she bowed her head as if embarrassed. Huh! Slim chance of believing that! Muriele had heard the woman danced naked whenever the coins offered were high enough.

"Come! No sense in yer eating this gummy porridge when I have prepared a pot just the way ye like it," Grunda's voice said at her elbow. "There is plenty for three. By the pale faces of ye both, ye need a day to relax and be in the sun and fresh air."

Muriele and her friend were more than willing to escape the stuffy hall and the sympathetic looks the women threw her way.

That morning was the start of a new life for her. She and Esa broke their fast with Grunda from then on. The three became such close friends they seldom appeared separated.

Olaf did put a restriction on their friendship, however. He insisted both women sit at the high table for the noon meal and the evening repast. He placed Muriele to his left between Feradoch and himself and Esa to his right. He boasted he had the two most beautiful women in the castle at his sides.

Feradoch was an attentive partner, always assuring she had the best portion of foods offered. He knew her favorite was roasted pig. Sometimes, he went hunting early in the morn to spear a pig and bribed the cook to prepare it for the noon meal.

He wooed Muriele like a most earnest swain. Each day he rode out as dawn broke and found the newest, most unusual blossoms and brought them to her. Sometimes, her offering for the day would be a smooth river rock with unusual, brilliant colors.

For the first time since her father died, Muriele relaxed and let life sweep her on. She refused to think of Magnus, and when she did, it was to picture him wed and walking with his adoring bride clinging to his arm. Her hate for him grew more each day.

Whenever the weather permitted, Feradoch took her for rides along the shores of Loch Badenloch. For her safety, he brought guards to ride ahead and behind them in case there was any danger of lawless thieves. He wanted her to ride a magnificent black mare sired by Thor, but Muriele had grown fond of Bolt and insisted on riding the gelding.

The more at ease she became in Feradoch's company, the tenser Esa appeared. When Muriele asked her friend if she preferred she not accept his attentions, Esa's troubled eyes looked as if she longed to impart something. She would hesitate and say, "He is not all he seems."

Magnus had been gone near three sennights before Feradoch passionately ventured a suggestion heartily approved by Chief Olaf.

He took Muriele out into the moonlight and they strolled amongst the birch trees and listened to the night noises of owls, crickets and various creatures. They reached a small stream where brilliant stars lit the sky above.

She felt the strength and the hard smoothness of his

muscular arm as they walked. He put his hand atop hers, lightly caressing it. When he stopped, he gently grasped her shoulders and turned her to face him. She drew back apace, for she felt his body heat as he brushed against her.

"Dinna be alarmed, my love. I mean you no harm."

"I am not afeared, my lord."

"I have talked with my father, and he is most pleased about what I propose."

She parted her lips to speak, but he stopped her.

"Shh, my love, wait to hear me out." He cupped her left cheek as gently as a mother would her bairn's head.

"Since the fall of Blackbriar, you have lost your position, your castle and keep, villages and honors which would have been passed to you as your dowry had Baldor died of natural causes."

"I know only too well what I have lost," Muriele replied. Why did he feel it necessary to remind her of it? She stiffened.

"It grieves me to mention it, but your having been the plaything of my foster brother destroyed any chance of your making a suitable marriage."

She jerked backward, pulling away. He intended to take over Magnus' position as her lover? Never again would she be any man's whore!

"Hear me out, sweet lady. From your face, I see you misjudge my intentions."

A moonbeam shed light over his pale beauty, showing kindness softened his face.

"We have no priest at Kinbrace and dinna expect one until next summer." He hesitantly ran his fingers through her hair then cupped her head with his big palms, tilting her face up to look into her eyes.

"I have loved you from the first sennight you came to the castle. Father regrets having so callously given you to Magnus. 'Twas cruel of my brother to hide his coming betrothal when he returned to Clibrick.

"What does …?"

He silenced her again, rubbing his thumb across her

soft lips.

"I care not that you have no lands or manors. No coins or wealth to bring to a marriage. I propose a legal handfast for a year and a day, or until the priest returns to Kinbrace so we may repeat our wedding vows before God."

Muriele stared at him, struck dumb. He could have any woman in the Highlands, yet he offered for her knowing she had nothing to bring into a union?

While she was still stunned, he pulled her into a soft, non-threatening embrace. When his beautiful face lowered, his lips were soft and gentle as they moved over hers, and then feathered light kisses on her cheeks, her forehead and neck. He didn't venture for more intimacy but slowly released her and awaited her reply.

Chapter 31

WHEN MAGNUS CAME TO the rolling hills outside Clibrick Castle, he and Sweyn paused at the same area Feradoch had stopped to gloat over someday seizing the lands below.

The wind blew strong, heralding a gusty rainstorm in late afternoon. He took deep breaths of the Scots pines in the lush forest of Ben Clibrick behind the castle. Hearing a faint sound, he glanced atop the foothill where the castle rose facing the loch. A lone rider charged over the drawbridge, his sword uplifted and waving in the air. Magnus broke into a grin seeing long, black hair flying in the breeze. He kicked Odin to a gallop, holding his shield but not bothering to draw his sword.

When near abreast, Graemme struck out with the side of his sword, landing a clamoring blow on Magnus shield. They both burst with laughter as they tussled until they fell off their horses to land and roll together on the soft ground.

"Sir Sweyn! Save him. My master hasn't drawn a weapon. The man will kill him as sure as my master loped off heads to save me!"

"No worry, Gille. They won't hurt each other. Much. Most likely a few bruises," Sweyn said dryly.

"But, but …!"

Hearing the distress in the young squire's voice, Magnus held up his hand at Graemme.

"Hold, brother. The lad is newly in my service and not used to anyone getting close to me."

Graemme's burnt-almond colored eyes searched out Gille. When he saw the youth's red, worried face, Graemme's eyes crinkled at the corner and his sensual lips lifted in a wide grin.

"Did ye never have a brother to wrestle with, lad?" Graemme leapt to his feet and ruffled Gille's hair. Turning back to Magnus, he held out his hand. "Come, old man, I'll help ye up."

"Heh! Best be careful else I'll toss ye into the loch."

Graemme vaulted onto his horse at he same time Magnus mounted.

"Come. Father is anxious for the truth of what goes on at Kinbrace."

They started out at a gallop. By the time they reached the castle, the other knights and their wives were behind them. The only men who lagged were riding the small highland horses pulling the carts.

The enthusiasm of everyone gathered to greet him surprised Magnus when he slid off Odin. He'd spent very little of his life at Clibrick. Feradoch was the one who grew up here, yet they didn't seem to regret his leaving.

"Son!"

Chief Angus' tall form loomed in front of him. His piercing brown eyes studied Magnus' face before he enveloped him in a hug, which would have crushed the bones of a lesser man.

After their greetings, Angus sent both his man and Sweyn off on a needless errand.

That he held back on allowing anyone else in his solar except Graemme surprised Magnus. What could be so secretive he wished no one else to hear?

Angus waited as a servant pored each a pewter goblet of chilled wine then nodded at him in dismissal. He and the two brothers sat at a table overlooking the loch.

"I'm glad to have your return, son," Olaf said as he held up his goblet in salute.

"Aye!" Graemme agreed. "And I dinna believe for one heart-beat ye were so cruel Olaf wanted to rid himself of ye."

Magnus near choked on his swallow of wine.

"What? What foolishness are ye talking about?"

Angus studied Magnus' face then frowned. "The missive from Olaf requested, nae, *demanded* your return to Clibrick.

Feradoch delivered it."

"See, father! I told ye the man lied through his teeth."

"Feradoch? Lie? What lie could he tell about me?"

"Oh, at first he appeared reluctant to tell us why his father wanted ye gone from Kinbrace," Graemme explained. "Huh. He spilled it quickly enough after a few questions. He claimed ye terrorized the villagers until they were so afeared of ye they hid in their huts whenever ye rode close."

"Aye," Angus added. "He claimed not even Olaf could control your savagery."

A sickening lurch spread through Magnus body as he began to wonder what purpose Feradoch had for fabricating such a lie. His voice was so low, both men had to lean close to hear him.

"Did you write me a missive for Feradoch to deliver?"

"Aye. I welcomed your returning home. Neither Graemme nor I believed you had turned savage."

"You didn't send this particular summons to me?" Magnus took the folded parchment out of his tunic pocket and handed it to his father. "It was written by the hand of yer scribe, the young priest."

Graemme rose and leaned over his father's back as they read the words together.

"What!" They both exploded at one time.

"Where in the pits of Hell did he get such an idea?" Angus stared at the writing. "It is Bruce's writing, for sure, but none of it is true."

"Send for him to explain himself!" Magnus' muscles tightened so tensely he felt he'd likely explode.

"Impossible." Angus shook his head, his eyes sad with understanding.

"Why?"

"A guard found him dead late on the day Feradoch left." Graemme swallowed. The muscles in his jaw twitched. "We thought by his own hand. He clutched the bloody knife that slit his throat."

"And old Father Anthony?"

"He passed on in his sleep several months ago," Angus said.

"When last I was here, I thought he was traveling through the villages doing his good work."

"I failed to mention it to you since your stay was so short."

"Was Feradoch here at the time he died?" Magnus felt bile rise up in his throat.

"Of course. He was on his knees all night in the chapel. He prayed for God to take the old priest's soul straight to heaven. Tears ran down his cheeks."

Magnus put his head in his hands, his elbows on his knees.

"How could this be Feradoch's doing! Never have we quarreled. He treated me as a true brother. He was even jealous of you, Graemme."

"Yet before he returned, he made you sound like you had run amuck for the past years, but he and Olaf didn't want us to know of it," Chief Angus said.

"The only reason I can think of is he was so jealous he wanted to be rid of you. To keep you away from Chief Olaf."

Magnus could easily believe it. Feradoch wanted his father to himself, and Magnus couldn't blame him. But, Satan's balls! To murder a priest ... perhaps *two* priests?

There were so many unanswered questions they spent days going over them in their talks.

The castle ran smoothly with the transition of Magnus to his father's first in command. There was no hint of jealousy on Graemme's part.

He missed Muriele. More so with every night that passed. His dreams were again plagued with making love to her. Now when he was ready to release his seed, strong hands grabbed his shoulders and tossed him across the room. He hit the stone wall and crumpled. Somehow, someone tied him to a ring on the wall. He could only watch as Feradoch crawled on all fours from the foot of the bed and straddled Muriele to claim her. Instead of moans of pleasure, she cried out in pain. He awoke in a sweat and paced the rest of the night away.

He reasoned Feradoch kept to Esa and dark-haired women with dusky skin whenever he was at Kinbrace. Muriele's hair was much like sunshine filtered through the leaves of a willow tree, and her skin was golden. Also, she was a strong woman, one who would never attract Feradoch.

Magnus shook off his worries and decided before the next day ended, he would send a spy to learn how Muriele and Grunda fared.

The next day it dawned on Magnus that several of the village girls working at the castle avoided talking to any man. When night came, he pulled Graemme aside and they went up on the keep to watch the moon streaming down on the loch.

"I've noted several women refuse to meet our eyes."

"Aye. At least six of the prettiest stay away from all men. Two have asked father if they may enter a nunnery. He refused, saying they were not suited for God's work but for breeding bairns. They ran, crying, and didn't ask again."

"I knew it was a lie!" Magnus struck a clenched fist on a merlon, making small chunks of stone filter to the ground.

"What was?" Graemme asked, sounding afeared of hearing the answer.

"Feradoch accused me of branding women at Kinbrace when in blood lust after battle. Supposedly, I used an 'eye' above their thatch of hair. The 'eye' would insure no man would take them with it looking on."

Even in the gloom of the night, he saw his brother's face lose its color. His eyes looked tragic as he slumped against the wall and sat on the hard stone.

With a hitch in his muffled voice, he gave a hint of his pain.

"It started with one girl I swived often. Of a sudden, she refused to look me in the face or allow me close. She only allowed Feradoch near. Time and time again, it happened and no matter how I questioned them, no one would say a thing."

"Come morn, we'll speak with father about this."

The next day they broke their fast in their father's solar. They talked about the shame of what Feradoch had done to the women. Angus said if they refused an offer of a goodly sum and a chance to wed one of the men-at-arms, he was at a loss how to help them.

Graemme offered the best solution.

"We will have the midwife talk to each of the women. If they refuse a large dowry and marriage to a good man, they may prefer a nunnery. If so, we will pay for their place there. The church will be grateful for the dowries and the women will be safe from scorn."

Magnus paced the room. He remembered Esa never looked at another man and seemed reluctant to accept Feradoch when he was there. He cringed, knowing the same had happened to the beautiful Welsh woman.

He couldn't get Muriele out of his mind. If he closed his eyes, she was there, her eyes pleading with him. Feradoch had changed the most after she came into Magnus' life. Chill bumps traveled up his back. His scalp crawled with tension. He sat down and began to talk to his father and brother about the fall of Blackbriar and the woman who should have inherited it all.

They all came to the same conclusion. Feradoch had watched his chances and made his plans early on. Getting rid of Magnus was only the beginning of something far greater, but they knew not what. They had not long to wonder, though, for a commotion at the front gate drew them to the window.

A messenger with a small escort had arrived at the castle. A squire held Kinbrace's standard high for all to see.

They galloped up to the steps. With a sinking heart, Magnus saw Olaf's own commander. Something dreadful had occurred. He leaned far out the window and bellowed loud enough for everyone in the courtyard to hear him.

"Sweyn, in all haste, escort Sir Hakon to the Chief's solar!"

Chapter 32

MURIELE'S HEART POUNDED THE later it got at the banquet. The handfast had been over quickly. It required only that they stand side-by-side in the middle of the great room, her right hand in his left held high, as they vowed to live as man and wife for the length of one year and a day.

If at the end of the year, one or the other was displeased with the union, they need only to declare it so. If the woman was increasing or a child had been born, then the one breaking off the union forfeited the child to the other.

Her stomach became queasy. Feradoch insisted he move into Magnus' old bedchamber with her. His reason was sound, for it was a large room. When she suggested they replace the bed, he snarled at her. It was the first time he had been aught but loving and pleasant.

The thought of making love in Magnus' bed felt sinful. It didn't help that Grunda had fought her about the union with Feradoch. She still claimed Magnus was to be Muriele's partner for life. Though Muriele repeatedly told her Magnus was marrying another for her fortune, Grunda muttered they were fools.

Muriele shifted in her chair. Feradoch had been drinking steadily. His left hand crept to her lap to rub her thighs close to her center. When she tried to hold his hand still, he gripped her wrist so tightly pain shot up her arm.

He surged up from the chair, still holding to her wrist.

"'Tis only fitting the entertainment end with a dance to stir the blood afore my lovely Muriele and I go above for bed sport."

He dropped her hand and clapped his hands, hard. Five musicians entered, the same Welshmen they'd had before. When

Esa didn't stir beside Olaf, Feradoch shoved back his chair, went to her and dragged her chair backward.

"You will dance for my union!" He wound her hair in his fist and forced her to rise.

"Feradoch! What are ye doing?" Muriele rose and grabbed him by the shoulder. He shook her off.

Esa twisted away, spewing words in the Welsh tongue. Muriele was sure she cursed him in her native language, for hate shot from her eyes. When he lifted a hand to strike her, she twirled and vaulted over the table to be in the midst of the musicians.

Feradoch turned back to Muriele and shoved her back into her chair.

"Never interfere with what I do, lass. You are too young to understand."

He picked up his wine and gulped down half the goblet without stopping. He lounged back in his chair as if nothing troublesome had happened. Olaf frowned and shook his head, his eyes disapproving. Her new mate stiffened with resistance, but he clamped his teeth together.

Once he had started drinking heavily, he no longer resembled a gentle man. His nostrils became pinched, his cheekbones prominent over sunken cheeks and his lips thinned to a hard line. Kindness no longer shined from warm blue eyes; they peered frostily beneath drooped lids.

Muriele barely recognized him.

He didn't take his gaze from Esa as she danced. A hard, roaming hand searched down her leg then tried to pull up the skirts of her kirtle to fondle her bare flesh. Horrified, she shoved it away.

He turned to her with a leer. She didn't have time to think before he picked her up as easily as if he lifted a bairn and threw her over his shoulder. The room erupted in laughter and hooting about the impatient groom. All the blood rushed to her face, and his hard shoulder beneath her stomach near made her lose what little she had eaten.

Bellowing to one of his men to follow them, Feradoch

started up the stairway. He ignored her pounding on his back, asking him to let her walk. After he threw back the bedchamber door and carried her through, his man closed it behind them. No doubt, he stood guard outside to see they were not disturbed.

With the look of a triumphant warrior ready to sample his captive, Feradoch stood her in the middle of the room then backed away.

"I did not tell you how beautiful you are today, my love. You look like a fey creature of the forest with flowers wound amongst your curls. Ye willna sprout wings and fly through the window will ye?" He grinned at her, his face calm and looking as angelic as ever.

She didn't know what to make of it. Had her own nervousness made her read crudeness into his actions in the great hall?

"I doubt my fanciful wings and I would fit through the opening." She felt herself blush.

Standing there, she didn't know what to do. Should she undress? But a squire had lit the fireplace and it would illuminate her back.

Oh … Saints … in … Heaven! After the first sennight of bed sport, Magnus had never mentioned her ruined back.

Once he had abandoned her without a word, she had focused her hatred on him. With it and Feradoch's instant wooing, she had forgotten her scars.

She gulped to keep from spewing.

But surely, no one who had wooed her so lovingly would take offense at it.

Would he?

"Will it put you more at ease if I remove my clothing first? You will see you have the perfect mate. One who is as manly beautiful as you are as a woman."

Her heart sank. He kept his gaze fixed on hers as he slowly removed his kilt and folded it. He sat and pulled off his boots and left his leggings on. When he bent to pull his shirt over his head, the bunching muscles of his shoulders were as impressive as Magnus'.

She crushed her thoughts to a halt right there! The men

were nothing alike.

Blond hair encircled his male nipples, already hard buds. His handsome face and virile chest with golden hair sprinkled over it made him look ethereal.

'Twas when his eyes heated and he untied the string to his leggings and slowly lowered them over his hips to fall at his feet, she gulped. His legs were long and lean. His, uh, manhood was surrounded with golden hair, his penis long, his balls heavy and tight.

He put his arms out to the side and slowly turned, showing her his magnificent back, narrow hips and tight buttocks.

Nay, she had it wrong. No angel would produce a cockstand! He was more like a magnificent Greek god. Never would she have thought the male body beautiful. There could be no other name for Feradoch's.

Suddenly she heard his deep laughter and realized her mouth gaped open like a landed fish. She flushed, for she had been staring.

"Your turn, my beauty. We are evenly matched."

When she stood frozen, he came over to her.

"You need help with your undressing?"

"Nay. But it is hot in here. Could ye bank the fire and blow out the candles?"

"What? And miss seeing you unwrap your lovely body? Never!"

She looked over at the bed and saw someone had drawn back the covers. She doubted it was Grunda. She had dreaded the moment when she had to lie on the bed where she and Magnus had made love. Now, she could not get there soon enough and draw up the covers to hide between them.

Moving close to the bed, she started to unwind her hair and remove the chain of rose flowers and green leaves. She placed them on the armor stand. When she lifted her kirtle up and over her head, she laid it on her clothing chest.

Like him, she sat and took off her shoes and stockings. She left naught on her body but the sheer smock. Using her fingers, she combed through her hair, spreading its wealth over her back. She stood and let him look his full. She knew her rosy nipples were easily seen and the thatch of wheat-colored hair covering her woman's place.

"Beautiful. As I pictured you."

His cock swelled even tighter and its eye began to seep. His breathing became raspy and impatient.

Muriele slipped beneath the sheet to lie on her back.

"What's this?" His eyes narrowed. "You canna be shy. Not after you were well-used by my foster-brother."

He came close and tossed the sheet to the foot of the bed.

"Up! I want to see all of you down to the littlest bit of flesh of your nether lips."

He grabbed her hands and pulled her to her feet. When she hesitated and didn't pull the sheer smock off, he reached out with both hands and tore it from her body.

"Put your arms wide as I did." It was no request but a hard order.

She did as he said.

"Turn for me. I wish to see your delicate arse."

She didn't move. Suspicious now, he narrowed his eyes to mere slits and studied her.

"You have something to hide."

His breathing grew heavy with anger. His face again changed to all sharp angles. Not a glimmer of kindness lit his eyes. He grabbed her wrist and twisted it up between her shoulder blades, turning her around.

Deadly silence fell over the room.

He had seen her back.

A scream of rage shrilled from his lips as he slung her to the floor. When he did, his hand hit the sharp side of the nearby helmet stand.

"Your Devil's mark cut me!" He brought his hand to his mouth and sucked the blood away. He put his foot on her hips, holding her to the floor while he looked her over. "Magnus never wanted you; else he would not have thrashed your back."

"It isn't a Devil's mark. Let me explain," Muriele sobbed with shame as he ground his bare foot into the small of her back.

Frost came from his voice as he flipped her over with his foot. She didn't dare rise seeing his wild face.

"Look at what you have done. Even seeing your beautiful breasts canna make my cock rise."

He looked down at his limp member, circled it with his hand and briskly pumped himself. It failed to swell, but lay limp.

"I willna be cheated of my marital rights."

He went over to fling the door open and gave orders to the man standing there. After slamming it shut, he picked up his belt and came after her. He stood over her, winding it around his right hand. She leapt up. He slung her back down and the belt began to fall. When she tried to struggle to her feet, he put his foot on her buttocks and continued.

Muriele clamped her teeth together to keep from screaming. 'Twas what he wanted to hear, what made him feel powerful. All savage men were alike. Baldor was most pleased when she screamed in agony. Never again would she give voice to her pain.

She'd spend her days in Hell before she would give another man that pleasure.

CHAPTER 33

MURIELE'S BEDCHAMBER DOOR FLEW open. The guard thrust Esa into the room with much kicking and cursing from her and sweating and grunting from him. When he shoved her to the center of the room, his eyes widened in horrified disbelief on seeing Feradoch, naked and sweaty, beating his bride.

"Keep your mouth shut if you value your tongue! Get out of here. Don't come again, no matter what you hear. They are naught but women who must be taught a lesson."

He slammed the door on the retreating man's back.

Esa became a wild woman when she spied Muriele trying to push herself up off the floor.

"You fiend from Hell! You've near killed her."

She flew at him, her fingers arched like cat claws. When Esa went for his face, he grappled with her and held her wrists together as he ripped her clothing off. For the first time, Muriele saw a branding worse than hers. It was an obscene eye above Esa's sex.

"'Tis her doing. She put a spell on my cock! It willna swell at the sight of her. You will pleasure me. When I have a proper cockstand, I'll teach this Devil's Spawn a lesson."

He forced Esa to her knees, grabbed her face and shoved it against his limp sex nestled amongst a thick tuft of golden hair.

"Suck!"

Feradoch's growled order sounded like a ravening wolf. He ground his sex into Esa's face. When her teeth clenched shut, he used his iron fingers on her jaw and forced her mouth open. Ramming his cock between her lips, he began to pump. His hands knotted in her thick, curly hair and forced the rhythm he wanted.

Esa scratched and clawed at his stomach.

"Let her go!" Muriele pushed up to her knees then to her feet. She grabbed a heavy boot and beat him on the back with it. He didn't flinch.

Finally, he howled in anguish for Esa clamped her teeth on his swelling cock. Fisting both hands, he struck her temples a crushing blow. She fell at his feet.

Blood ran down his limp penis. He kicked her in the face then grabbed her legs to straighten her out. Straddling her, he wrapped his long fingers around her slender neck and squeezed.

"You filthy Welsh whore! You'll die for that."

As he strangled her, she tried to claw his face. He shook her, striking her head on the floor.

Sobbing, Muriele climbed on his back. She bit his ear and tried to gouge his eyes. He gave a mighty twitch like a bear annoyed by a hunting dog. She flew off him and hit the floor.

She picked herself up and grabbed her eating knife off her clothing chest. He saw her and swerved sideways. The blade entered high on the back of his left shoulder. One hand left Esa's neck long enough for his massive arm to swipe Muriele away. She hit her head on a bedpost.

"Whore! You'll wish you were Esa. I'll enjoy swiving you until you are dead."

Esa's arms and hands weakened until they fell limply beside her. He shifted his body and rose up on his knees. Unthinking, he exposed his nether parts.

Seeing her chance, Muriele steadied herself, drew back her right leg and kicked out as hard as she could ... her foot struck his balls with a goodly force. She felt their hard roundness smash upward.

Feradoch gave an eerie, high-pitched howl. He bent in half and released Esa to clutch his sex, gasping and puking. Blue eyes wide with shock, his gaze clashed with hers.

They silently promised her death would be long and slow.

Muriele shook her head at him, denying him. She caught sight of the large earthenware pitcher on the washstand. Jumping to the middle of the bed, she reached for it and scrambled back.

Feradoch released one hand from cupping his sex and lunged at her. He grabbed for her foot as she jumped off the bed. She was too agile for him. She circled him, fast. Still gasping for breath and puking, he couldn't keep up with her twists and turns.

Holding the pitcher above her head, she used all her body to crash it down on the back of his skull.

"Ye slimy bastard from Satan's privy! Go back to Hell!"

He stilled as if frozen. Blood seeped from his scalp and turned his sun-gold locks a dull red. He didn't speak, didn't look to be breathing. He crumpled beside Esa.

Muriele hoped she'd killed him.

She stared at the man she had once thought as caring and loving. Never would she have believed him to be so evil. She should have known. 'Twas said Lucifer had been the most beautiful of God's angels.

Crying, she held Esa's head cradled on her lap, her tears falling on the lovely, dark-skinned face.

Something alerted her. The door opened with a light rasp.

God help her! The guard had returned. He would run her though with his sword. She wrapped her arms around Esa's head to protect her from further damage.

"Love, dinna fear. Only I noted the guard run out the back of the keep like the devil was after him. Once he left, I seized my chance to come up."

"Oh, Grunda. He killed Esa because she tried to help me." Muriele clamped a hand over her mouth to stifle the wail threatening to rip her throat apart.

"Come. Let me see. She may not be dead."

Muriele carefully slid from beneath Esa and tenderly laid her head on the floor before she scrambled to her knees.

Kneeling, Grunda put her ear to Esa's chest and listened. "She yet lives. Come. Hold her head up for me."

While Grunda took a small vial from her pocket, Muriele carefully lifted Esa's head and shoulders.

"What is it?" she asked, eyeing the vial.

"If he mistreated ye, I thought to use it on ye." Grunda shook her head. "She will sleep so soundly as to appear dead until I give her another potion to arouse her."

"It willna harm her?" Muriele wrung her hands.

"Nae." Grunda looked around at the bloody belt, the over-turned furniture, the clothing strewn on the floor and the linens trailing off the bed. "Olaf will want to keep this quiet for 'tis obvious Feradoch intended to murder ye both. He will simply discard her in the woods and pretend she met her fate there. I will watch for her."

She took the hem of her cloak and blotted away the potion drooling from the sides of Esa's mouth.

"What will I do? They will hang me."

"Ye must get far from here. Yer blade did little damage. 'It will be days afore we know if his head is badly injured."

Grunda grinned and looked questioningly at Muriele when she saw Feradoch had frozen with one hand clutching his balls.

"It'll be some while afore he uses his tarse to again bedevil another girl." She grinned at Muriele. "Ye look to have had a good aim."

"It seemed the fastest way to stop him."

"And the most fitting." Her face took on a worried frown. "Let me see yer back."

"'Tis not too bad. Baldor did much worse."

She turned and kept from flinching when Grunda's fingers touched her swollen skin.

The spaewife grabbed a small jar of cream they'd made for keeping Muriele's face smooth and healthy. She spread a generous portion on her back.

"We must hurry now. Ye'll need to wear yer hunting clothes. They will last the longest."

Muriele flung open her chest and pulled out the sturdy clothes. Grunda helped her ease on the oversized shirt then settled it gently against her back. She helped her finish dressing then tossed a pillowcase at her. Muriele shoved two extra garments in it.

"Dinna forget yer warm cloak." Grunda grabbed it off the

wooden peg and eased it around her shoulders.

The old seer searched through Feradoch's clothing. Finding a small bag of coins tied to his belt, she shoved it inside the heavy cloak's pocket.

"Tell Esa it was my fault when she comes to." Muriele took one last look at her friend, reluctant to leave her.

"Come!"

They slipped out of the room and quietly closed the door.

"Luck is with us. The Alewife's brother stands guard at the postern gate this night," Grunda whispered. They stood in the shadows beneath a tree as she eyed the wall walk above the gate. "While ye were getting Bolt, I told him to take his time relieving himself behind the stables. He didna ask questions. And he will never speak of it."

She shoved a bundle filled with provisions into Bolt's old saddlebag and tied a rolled up blanket, plaid and Muriele's clothes behind the saddle.

"Ye are well-armed." She was so quiet she was near silent. She'd brought Muriele's weapons from her hut.

Muriele nodded and patted the full quiver of arrows slung across her back and the bow hanging from her shoulder. She quickly flipped up her skirts to assure the old woman she was again carrying a sheathed knife attached to each thigh.

Grunda kissed her cheek then opened the postern gate as Muriele mounted.

"Go quietly, love. Once ye make the woods, ride like that Devil in the room is after ye."

Muriele nodded. Hate bubbled in her heart for all Magnus and Feradoch had destroyed in her life. She vowed never again to believe another Highlander. She would make her way south to the border country. Her spine stiffened as she eased Bolt through the opening. She glanced back with a quick wave at Grunda who silently closed the gate.

Muriele kept the horse to the shadows of the castle wall until she came to a dark area nearest the woods. She patiently waited until a cloud covered the moon then silently walked the horse in the shadows until they disappeared in the line of trees. She breathed a sigh of relief at the silence from the wall walk. No one had seen her.

Chapter 34

THOUGH IT WAS A cold day, Magnus was clothed in naught but the kilt bunched at his waist and boots. Even so, one thought caused sweat to slide down his backbone. He refused to give words to it in his mind.

On the landing outside the Chief's solar, Magnus listened to the clatter of Sweyn and Sir Hakon's boots as they jogged through the great hall and up the staircase.

Was an army attacking Kinbrace and gained access? Had Chief Olaf met with an accident or been killed? Why did they not send Feradoch instead? Sweyn and Olaf's commander cleared the last step.

"Hakon."

The commander nodded solemnly as they grasped each other's arms in greeting.

Chief Angus and Graemme stood awaiting them in the solar. Servants had brought pitchers of wine, cheeses and bannocks from the servants' stairwell to refresh the travelers.

Hakon was dressed in the old ways, much as Magnus as a lad had first laid eyes on him. Animal pelts covered his torso. A massive leather belt anchored a heavy wool plaid gathered at his waist, and brown leather boots covered staunch, muscled legs up to his knees. He had also armed himself to the teeth. A short sword and a dagger hung from his belt, two protruded from his boot tops and a claymore rode across his back.

His heavy brows lifted asking permission as his hand gripped the hilt of the claymore.

"Of course. Ye have no need of it here," Chief Angus said.

Sweyn brought over a small table and placed it beside the

commander. Hakon propped the long sword against it, then removed his other weapons and laid them on the table's top with a sigh. They were not his only means of defense. If the man stripped himself bare, no doubt they would find other weapons hidden on his person.

Magnus couldn't stand the tension any longer. Better to know what it was than speculate on every gruesome detail crossing his mind.

"What tragedy has befallen Kinbrace?" Magnus pulled a chair close so he could watch the man's face.

Olaf's commander retrieved a rolled missive from beneath his animal pelts and somberly handed it to him.

When Magnus' fingers folded around the parchment, he felt a crushing foreboding. He stared at it and took a deep breath. Still he didn't open it. He grasped a full goblet of wine and drained it then slammed it back on the table.

He stiffened and wiped all expression from his face as he untied the roll then broke Olaf's seal. He leaned forward and spread the missive on the table.

He read aloud. The first sentence made his heart sink. The next required him to dredge up all of his years of hard-earned battle skills to show no emotion. His voice faltered but a heartbeat.

> *Magnus of Clibrick, I call on ye to honor yer blood oath with my son, Feradoch of Kinbrace.*
> *Feradoch and Lady Muriele of Blackbriar were hand-fast in a ceremony on September 10. The same night, she stabbed Feradoch in the back and felled him with a heavy pitcher against his head. By the time ye read this, he will likely be dead. His leman, Esa, was also murdered. She was lying beside him. I ken Muriele killed them in a jealous rage then disappeared.*
> *'Tis time to call on ye to honor yer oath. Find her and bring her to Kinbrace.*
> *'Tis fitting she be hung and her body left for the vultures.*

Magnus couldn't move. He stared at the writing, thinking he couldn't have read it correctly.

"Where did this killing take place?"

"In your former bedchamber. Feradoch took it as his at the handfast."

"Muriele would not have wanted anyone there when they sealed the handfast. Why was Esa in the room?"

"Shortly after they retired, Feradoch ordered a guard to fetch Esa." Hakon frowned. "When we questioned him, he stammered and wouldna say anything other than Esa resisted entering."

"Did he hear anything while he stood guard?"

"He said his master was in a fury and ordered him to leave." Hakon shifted in his seat. He wouldn't meet Magnus' eyes.

Magnus blurted out, "Muriele was a warrior woman who could defend herself, but never would she kill without reason. And Esa? She treated her as a sister!"

"I dinna ken it." Graemme blurted out.

Magnus took hope at an idea. "If Muriele is missing, 'tis possible someone entered the room and committed the murders then kidnapped her. Not even Muriele could get the better of Feradoch." He frowned and thought some more. "How was Esa killed?"

"Throttled."

"Throttled?" Chief Angus looked puzzled. "Was this Esa a small woman? I canna believe a woman strong enough to choke another."

Magnus picked up his argument. "They both are tall. And Esa was every bit as muscled as Muriele. How could Muriele have overpowered her and held her down long enough to kill her?"

"Aye," Hakon said. "I voiced the same questions. Feradoch came to long enough to say Muriele had done it all."

"Came to?"

"The old spaewife tended him. Stitched the wound in his back and the flesh on his head. Then she, too, disappeared."

Chief Angus scowled. "This spaewife? Did she examine the lady also?"

"She had no chance. Chief Olaf had Esa's body tossed in the midst of the forest. He claimed she belonged to some witch cult for she had a strange brand above her, uh, nether parts." He blushed and cleared his throat. "I didna see it."

"'Twas *his* doing!" Incensed, Chief Angus surged up from his chair. "By all that is Godlike! Do the Gunn's not believe in burying the dead?"

"Nay, Chief, only ones they consider *deserving*," Sweyn said. He made a wry face. "They dinna bury many. They made much fun of Magnus and me for putting them all beneath the ground."

Hakon looked at Magnus then down at his feet. 'Twas apparent to Magnus he disliked his duty.

"Chief Olaf ordered I rest but one night and return with word ye have already set out to capture the lady Muriele."

Magnus frowned. "She can't have traveled far afoot."

"Och! She isna afoot. She took old Bolt from the stable, since he is also missing."

Magnus' brow rose at this. Why would she take the old gelding instead of a warhorse in his prime? "Sweyn will see to your comfort for the night."

Graemme slapped both hands on the table as he, too, bolted up from his chair. He looked at his father, his face determined. "I go with Hakon back to Kinbrace. Something doesna feel right. Lady Muriel is a woman of breeding, not some common slut who would kill over a man having had a leman. Afore my brother hunts her down to hang, he must have proof she murdered without reason."

"Aye." Chief Angus sighed and nodded. "I would not have an innocent woman's death heavy on my son's heart."

"Father, ye canna stop this. I have been honor bound since the day ye and Olaf had us swear a blood oath together. If the happenings prove true, I must fulfill it no matter the cost."

Hakon cleared his throat. "Chief Olaf insists ye deliver her unharmed so he may have the pleasure of, uh, witnessing her punishment."

"I leave at first light. When I find her, I'll bring her back. She won't be able to hide the truth from me."

Magnus hardened all thoughts of Muriele in his mind. From this time on, she became a stranger, one who killed her new mate and mayhap her best friend. He would hunt her as he would if a filthy lout had killed Feradoch.

He knew he would find her. His instinct had always told him when she was near. It would aid him in tracking her. But he could not stop the sickening chill spreading through his body.

"You're nae going alone," Sweyn said.

"Muriele is a canny hunter and can move about the forest in silence. I will track her fastest alone. Two horses are easier heard than one."

"Aye. Still, you're nae going alone," he repeated.

"I order ye to stay. The Chief needs ye here." Magnus looked at his father to get his support.

"Huh! I dinna need Sweyn. He goes with ye. I wouldna have yer anger surface and have ye do something unthinkable."

Magnus gritted his teeth and threw up his hands. There was no arguing with the chief of the Morgans. He was even more stubborn than Magnus himself.

Thunderstorms came in over the Loch and swept away dawn as easily as a servant used her broom made of twigs to remove debris from the keep's steps. But the ominous darkness did not stop the travelers.

Four knights accompanied Graemme to Kinbrace with Sir Hakon. Magnus stopped growling about not needing a guardian and was grateful to have Sweyn as company in such a miserable undertaking.

Their saddlebags overflowed. Oiled hides covered the rolls of blankets and supplies Magnus deemed might be necessary when they captured the lass. He wiped Muriele's name from his mind and concentrated on ignoring memories of their time together.

Between the noise of the drawbridge lowering and the shrieking of the portcullis rising, it was useless to speak. As the drawbridge thunked to earth, Graemme gripped Magnus' shoulder.

"Dinna believe all ye have heard, brother. Living these years with Feradoch, I dinna trust *anything* about him."

"Not even his death?" Magnus' eyes held surprised questions he had no time to ask.

"Nay. Not even his death," Graemme shook his head. "'Tis the reason I ride to Kinbrace. I will search out the truth of it all."

"Take care, brother. The Gunns are easily angered when questioned."

Magnus thumped Graemme's shoulder and turned to bid his father farewell. The two brothers mounted and rode over the drawbridge. Graemme and Hakon's men turned east, and Magnus and Sweyn south.

The lass was clever. She would have left Kinbrace and headed west first then make her way south to the Lowlands. The weather had already turned colder. In another month, winter would be upon them. A man traveling alone would find it difficult to hunt his own food, find shelter for the night and avoid the churls and varlets searching the forests for easy takings.

'Twas unlikely the lass could survive alone.

His jaw twitched and icy dread prickled his back remembering the sight of Lady Ragnhild's body when he and Sweyn buried her.

Chapter 35

WHEN SHE ENTERED THE dark forest, Muriele didn't stop. She was familiar with the paths and knew where to avoid every dip in the ground. Bolt might be old, but he had a warrior's heart. He sensed her fear and trod carefully.

Once they were far from Kinbrace, she followed Loch Badenloch south until a glimmer of moonlight showed her a place she had crossed often when hunting from Blackbriar.

Bolt was reluctant when she urged him into the cold water, but her murmurs close to his ear and constant pats on his cheek soothed him. Her clothing seemed to draw up the water, for she was soaked to her waist when they finally reached the other side.

Fortunately, she had pulled her cloak high around her breasts and kept it dry. Shivering, she dismounted. She hated to lose any time, but reasoned she wouldn't be able to save herself if she caught an ague and fell where her pursuers would easily find her. She stripped and wrung as much water from her clothing as possible then put her hunting clothes back on. She tied the rest to the saddle horn, and when she gained the saddle, she spread the warm cloak around herself making sure to cover Bolt as well.

Fear told her to travel straight south, the shortest route to the Lowlands. It might be the shortest, but it would also be the most obvious. Likely, the Gunns would head to Blackbriar believing she would seek familiar ground.

She took a deep breath and made her plans. If she headed southwest to Dalmore, west again to Lairg then east to Tarbott, they would not expect that. Though she'd never been very far from Blackbriar, she'd heard men talk of their travels and knew how to make her way to the border.

She kept to the path for the first days, going as fast as Bolt could. When he began to tire, she went far into the woods, found a stream and let him drink and rest before they continued. Late each day, any time she spied a cave she drew her short sword and made sure of its safety then took refuge in it.

Food was easy enough to come by. When she stopped for rest and water, there were hares aplenty deep in the woods. She retrieved her arrows and kept her kill for cooking when it was dark enough no one would see the smoke. The next day, she ate what she had saved from the night before.

Several times, she thought someone trailed her. She stopped to listen, and if she heard anything but regular forest sounds, she got off Bolt and put her ear to the ground. On hearing horses' hooves, she took the reins and walked deep into the trees.

Bolt might be an old horse, but he was quick to learn. After several days, if she put her arm on his neck and urge his head downward then touched his forelegs gently with her foot, he settled on the ground. She gathered branches and leaves and used them to cover the horse and herself so prying eyes would see only the cluttered forest floor.

She could swear the faithful horse held his breath as much as she did.

The Gunns would expect her to circle around the high mountains when she came to one, but she tried to do what they wouldn't expect. Once high enough, she made sure she and Bolt weren't visible and scanned the countryside as far as her eyes could see.

How many sennights had she been gone? She no longer awoke at night with the urge to wail like a halfling. Her clothing had more than a few rents. She had no way to mend them. When she needed to wash, she stopped long enough to bathe, beat her garments on a smooth rock and wring them as dry as possible.

Attaching her wet clothing to the back of her saddle, it was nearly dry by the time the sun lowered. She alternated her hunting clothes with a woolen kirtle she slashed down the center to cover her legs as she rode astride.

Each day seemed colder than the last. Wearing her plaid wrapped around her as the men did, she carried her weapons close to hand. She avoided close encounters and worried most about lawless knaves. They traveled silently and gave little warning.

Afore she chose a spot for the night, she climbed the highest tree and scanned the treetops around her. If a flicker of light or a stream of smoke wound its way through the leaves, she walked Bolt in the opposite direction.

One night, she found nothing out of the ordinary. After picking the small bones of a grouse clean, she banked her small fire. Content, Bolt grazed on lush grass close to a stream.

When she noted his ears twitch and his eyes flicker, she sat quietly. Eyes watched her. She drew her legs closer to her body, seemingly getting more comfortable. Her hands on her thighs looked relaxed, and they were — for she had only to curl her fingers around the hilts of her daggers strapped to her legs.

"Och! I ken them wood sprites done left us a gift."

Muriele smelled the bearded man before she saw him step from behind a nearby tree.

"They be special kind. Look at the fine horse!"

Another man, equally as filthy as the first, appeared from the woods. He eased slowly up to Bolt and reached to take his bridle. Bolt's head flashed. Much to Muriele's surprise, he bit the hand when it came close.

"Aggh!" The man backed away. "Ye son of Satan!"

He kicked out at Bolts legs. The old horse snorted and stomped. Rising up on his hind legs, he twisted and struck out with his hooves. He hit out until he knocked the man to the ground then proceeded to stomp on him. Surely, the man's screams would alert anyone for a league around! She expected to hear horses crashing through the woods as other varlets sought them.

"Ye'll pay fer my friend's death, ye scrawny witch!"

The filthy churl was near atop her, his hands reaching for her hair. When he bent over, Muriele brought both hands up, a knife clutched in each, and struck as hard as she could. One blade entered his chest, the other struck up below his right collarbone.

He fought, clawing for her throat. Fire raked across her cheek as his mangy nails tore her delicate skin. She kicked and twisted. Visions of Esa's struggle to breathe made her fight the harder. If she gave up, no one would be there to pull him off her in time. Grunting and shoving, she forced the knives deeper. Finally, he went limp. She took great gulps of air, turning her face away from the greasy head resting on her shoulder.

The sickening smell of blood made her swallow back vomit. She had no time to be a helpless woman! With a great heave, she rolled him off her.

Scrambling to her feet, she pulled hard to remove the knives from his body. After wiping them on his filthy clothing, she checked the second man. Both were dead. She listened to the night sounds. All was quiet. Moving from tree to tree making an ever-widening circle, she looked for their camp. She came across a small fire, nearly died out. Cautiously, she felt the ground around it. Still warm. She covered the dying embers with dirt to make sure it didn't burst into flames again. Two grungy blankets assured her. The eejits had been alone.

Making her way back to her campsite, she dragged the men deeper into the brush. After covering them with their filthy blankets, she found branches and leaves aplenty to hide them. Once she finished the chore, she waded in the stream fully clothed. As she stripped, she soaked the blood from her clothing.

She paid special attention to cleaning her stinging face. As she smeared a salve on her cheek, she thanked Grunda silently for adding as many salves and unguents as she could to the supplies she'd prepared for her.

Putting on her dry outfit, she doused the fire and dragged a branch around to hide any footprints. She even covered Bolt's hefty pile of shite.

"What a masterful horse ye are, Bolt. Ye must have been a warhorse in yer younger days to fight like that!" She hugged his neck and checked him over, making sure he was unharmed. She quickly saddled and readied him.

"Come, my braw old man. We must leave."

Taking his reins, she led him into the stream. In a short while, her feet felt near frozen. She ignored it. Bolt hadn't rested enough to carry her.

She kept her eyes on the moon's movement. When she knew they were far from where they'd stopped, she scanned the sides of the stream looking for caves. Luckily, she found one near hidden by small trees.

'Twas lucky, for it would make a warm place for them to sleep.

The next morning, she discovered it was a perfect spot to rest a day. She searched along the streams banks and the damp woodland for moneywort. When she found a cluster of the rounded leaves growing in pairs along the stems, she collected enough to make a poultice for Bolt's front legs. Tearing strips from her smock, she wrapped them tightly around his forelegs and tied them there. Given a day of rest, Bolt would be strong enough to carry her again.

As Muriele traveled farther south, she hoped the Gunns wouldn't come this far searching for her. The weather was so cold she feared she and the horse would freeze during the night. She wore breeches and her hunting jacket and gathered the warm plaid around her waist. Pulling her hair tight behind her head, she tied it with string then bound her head with cloth cut from a heavy chemise. Anyone who didn't study her closely would think she looked like any young man. For certs, she was tall enough to pass for one.

The next village she came to, she dismounted and strolled with long-legged steps to the closest hut. There she found an older man and his wife. He was struggling to chop wood with one arm. His left looked to have been injured and not yet healed.

When she approached him, her voice surprised her. It was as husky as Esa's from not talking above a whisper for so many days. She offered to look at his wound and treated it with her salves then suggested she cut wood in exchange for food and a night in their lean-to for Bolt and herself.

When the old woman called her inside to share their meal, she learned another elderly couple was hoping to find someone to travel with them and their newly widowed daughter to Dumbarton. They had family there but were afeared to start out on their own. The old man's hands were unsteady, and he could no longer forage for food nor protect the women.

'Twould be easy to lose herself amongst several people, for she would be seen as a male of the family. The next morning, the couple happily accepted her offer. They would leave in two days time.

She cut plentiful wood for the injured old man and hunted for both families. When they left, Muriele was satisfied the kind souls would have enough firewood to last a fortnight or more, and food for the next sennight.

On the journey to Dumbarton, Muriele avoided conversation. Pulled by a strong, brown horse used to working in the fields, the women and old man rode in a cart filled with their meager belongings. Muriele and Bolt led the way, ever watchful for other travelers. The narrow, dirt road led from north to south. Whenever they heard someone approach, Muriele helped pull the cart to the side for other travelers to pass.

Once they were out of the way, she disappeared with Bolt into the woods. When she returned, she said she'd had to piss and didn't want to offend the young lass.

She lost track of the days. Finally, they arrived at Dumbarton where the family convinced her to stay a fortnight. The farm was well isolated and she never ventured far from it. Bolt needed the rest more than she did. She waited until his legs were sturdy again before riding further.

When she left, she took to the forests for towns and villages were much closer in the Lowlands. A sennight later, she came to several small villages within leagues of each other. She ventured close and found she was on the road to Raptor Castle near the English border.

'Twas late in the day and Raptor was less than a league away. Bolt had been failing of late, and she had walked for the last two days. She stayed inside the edge of the woods, for Bolt couldn't move quickly enough to leave the road to hide. She hoped to watch who came and went from Raptor at night and at dawn. Surely no one from Kinbrace thought she would make it this far. It would do no harm to be certain.

Bolt began to quiver as if in pain. Thinking he may have brushed against thorny vines, she walked around and checked his unsteady legs.

"What is it, Bolt?" She patted his neck and smoothed her hands over his body, soothing him as best she could. Her heart raced when he hung his head and seemed too tired to lift it again.

"Please, old one, be all right. Ye are my only friend in this world. Everyone else is gone." She couldn't stop the tears flooding her eyes. "Let's lie here for the night. We'll be out of the way and ye can have a long night's rest. We're near the border and will be safe soon."

Muriele quickly unsaddled and urged him down on his side as she had taught him. Once he was down, she grabbed handfuls of grass to tempt him and laid it in a pile. Finding a stream, she brought water back in a small wooden bowl she'd made her first sennight away from Kinbrace.

Sitting on the ground, she lifted Bolt's head onto her legs and held the grass to his lips. He made a few half-hearted attempts to nibble then gave up. She rubbed between his eyes and crooned to him, then dribbled water in the side of his mouth. He swallowed but shook his head wearily.

"You dinna want to be bothered, eh, old fellow? Rest then. Tomorrow ye'll have a stall with hay and oats and all the things ye have missed these months. I'm sorry. So sorry. I should never have taken ye from Kinbrace."

All night, Muriele talked and rubbed Bolt, soothing him as best she could. She pulled off her head covering, letting her hair free. At daylight, thinking no one would recognize her at Raptor Castle, she put on her worn-out kirtle. Twas the last of her garments except for the filthy hunting clothes she'd not been able to clean since Dumbarton.

Her stomach grumbled. Yester eve, she'd eaten the last of a hare she'd caught and had not been able to hunt since. She kept up a steady murmur of words to Bolt, not paying heed to what she said until she realized she prayed Bolt would pass on easily. He didn't seem to be in any pain, but she knew he wouldn't live. His breathing became more and more labored. Just afore the sun rose, he gave one last snorting breath and was quiet. Bending over, she put her cheek against his, letting her tears flow freely.

But she didn't cry for herself. She cried for Bolt ... for Grunda ... for Esa.

Murmuring fervid curses, she prayed God had sent Feradoch straight to Hades and that Magnus would soon join him there.

ChAPTER 36

"THE LASS COVERED HER tracks well."

Magnus grunted at Sweyn's remark. 'Twas said so often he bit his tongue to stifle a surly reply.

"Aye, she has. If not for the vultures swarming over Ben Alder, we would have lost her."

Magnus shuddered at the images flashing through his mind — Muriele dead, her body being devoured by the great vultures. He had needed to swallow back vomit surging to this mouth.

The closer they had come to the site, the slower they'd approached. When they came to where the birds fed, the scavengers took flight with a great whoosh, some diving at them trying to drive them away from their feast.

Magnus heart had thumped and cold dread swept through him. When they came close and saw the skeletons were too large for a woman, his heart calmed. Examining the corpses, Sweyn discovered long strands of wheat-colored hair clutched in one mangled hand.

The men had come upon Muriele, but had not taken her by surprise. She had killed the one clutching her hair. Something had crushed the other culprit's head. Bolt had reverted to his battle training and trampled the man sneaking up on him.

They searched around, unknowingly circling as Muriele had done. When they did not find any signs of a horse having ridden away, they knew she had gone into the stream. They followed it south, searching the banks until they found the cave. The ground showed the two had spent a day or two resting. She had been thorough on covering her tracks, but they found a charred stick where she had cooked a hare, its small bones scattered around.

They traveled, east to west, for two months before they came upon a village where the people remembered a slim lad with wheat colored hair riding a tired old horse. The lad had been kindness itself, mixing elixirs for an old man's stomach ailments and hunting food for those whose larders were bare. All denied it was a lass. How could one be so tall and skilled at hunting? And who but a lad could throw a blade and bring down a hare in mid-leap?

They combed the countryside until winter snows stopped them at an old inn in Glasgow.

"We have scoured near all of Scotland and still have not found the lady, Magnus. Why do you not leave her in peace? She has found safety somewhere. We should let her be."

"I have told ye why every day for near a year. I made a vow and willna break it!"

"You are blind to honor an oath to Feradoch. He is not worthy."

Magnus surged out of the chair, knocking it backward. His hands reached for Sweyn, but at the last moment, he stopped himself.

"No matter the reasons, I canna break a blood oath," he bellowed.

After everyone scurried to the other side of the room, he sighed and ran his hand over his face. He no longer wore a defined mustache and short beard framing his lips and chin. It had grown so long he felt more bear than man. No wonder people veered from his path when he approached.

Once the weather warmed and the roads were passable, they set out again. Every now and again, they learned of a slender lad with a caring heart. The description of the horse assured them 'twas Muriele on Bolt.

Sweyn seemed to get the most information out of the villagers, for good reason. One look at Magnus made people lower their heads and shuffle as fast as they could seek their huts. When they rented a room at an alehouse in Dumbarton, they stumbled upon their best lead.

"If you expect to scour the towns around Glasgow," Sweyn commented, "you'd best dress like a braw Scotsman, else people will think you a stinking Viking come to carry off their women."

"Huh! Ye dinna smell so sweet yerself."

"Aye. But I have a kindly face whilst you look like a wolf with a beard."

Sweyn walked over to the innkeeper and asked about a bathing tub, for the streams were naught but ice. The man thought him a dafty Highlander, for no one took a bath this time of year. They were welcome to use the tub in the barn if they heated their own water.

They dragged the tub into an empty stall near to their horses. By the time they finished scrubbing off their mud and grime, they were grateful straw covered the dirt floor.

Magnus stood naked before a polished metal square propped atop bales of hay. He honed his knife and started cutting the beard from his face until the hair around his chin was no longer than the width of his smallest finger. It took longer to scrape his cheeks clean, and trim the moustache framing his lips down to his chin.

Just as Magnus began to use the tip of the blade to scrape between his lower lip and chin, Sweyn spoke up.

"Best be careful else you'll ne'er be able to pucker-up for a proper kiss!"

Magnus cast a baleful eye at him. 'Twas a mistake because he nicked the rim of his lip and blood welled.

"Told you to be careful."

"Dolt."

He took a handful of water and splashed the blood away before he finished.

"I never would have thought you could look crueler than you did when we left Clibrick," Sweyn said.

"I dinna look cruel. Older, mayhap."

"Ha! Your face looks as taut as a ravening, black wolf stalking its prey, your body as lean as one and your muscles hard as yonder post holding the roof over our heads."

"Ye are fanciful."

"Not when I see eyes as black as burnt wood with naught a flicker of life reflected there."

Magnus snorted but his temper exploded when he wrapped and hooked his belt around his clean plaid. The cloth slithered down his hips, hesitated a bit when it caught on his cock then fell to the wet straw.

"Lucifer's putrid bowels!"

Leaving the bundle of wool around his feet, he grabbed his knife and, taking the very tip, dug it into the belt's leather to make a new hole.

"Your temper is more apt to spark, too."

Magnus turned a murderous glare on him. Sweyn's tongue stilled. For a minute.

"I think we should return to Clibrick and find a lusty lass for you to wed. One who'll swive your brains out. That should keep you in a better mood."

Magnus' knife whistled past Sweyn's head and landed in the wall behind him. Sweyn quirked his brows and grinned.

"Aha! Your aim is off, too."

In the village outside Dumbarton the next morn, they heard of a man, his wife and daughter who had arrived in Dumbarton with the aid of a young lad. They had convinced the lad to stay with them for a sennight before he moved on. They went from hut to hut until they learned the family had moved in with relatives at a farm close by

Before the reached the hut, Sweyn looked at Magnus and cleared his throat.

"We may learn more if I do the asking."

"Ye think they'll tell ye their secrets more easily?"

"Old ones are likely to be timid around a man looking like he'd rather throttle them than smile."

"Huh! If ye think ye can ask the right questions," Magnus muttered.

When the approached the farm, two women working in a garden jumped up and ran into the house. The men took one look at Magnus and quickly backed away. Sweyn, a bright smile on his face, put them at ease. Magnus looked around the yard and saw they'd been chopping wood. He shook his head at the uneven cuts of the logs. He picked up an axe leaning against a leafless tree and nodded toward them. Sweyn soothed the men as he went inside the hut where the women huddled out of sight.

It didn't take Magnus long to stack a large amount of firewood near the hut's door. He found swinging the axe helped relieve the horrendous pictures flashing in his mind since Chief Olaf demanded he keep his vow.

He couldn't sleep at night without seeing Feradoch atop Muriele making violent, passionate love to her. Had he kept Esa as his leman and caused Muriele to fly into a violent rage and kill them both?

After every muscle in his arms and back ached and his body ran with sweat, the oldest man timidly came to ask him into the house for food. Magnus was careful to smile, which was easier now he'd worked some of the anger out of his mind. The four men sat at the table while the women served them barley soup and freshly baked brown bread.

Magnus kept his conversation to the towns they had been through and the unusually cold weather. Not long afterward, they were on the road again.

"I ken I asked the right questions. They told me the lad had wheat-colored hair and was strong. Also, the horse was old and the lad called him Bolt. The lad also said he was making his way to the border country."

"She would not think I would hunt for her this far."

"Aye. Likely not." Sweyn looked at Magnus and shook his head. "What is eating at you? It's rotting away at your mind. If you dinna speak of it, you are likely to go barmy afore the month is out."

Magnus glanced up, seeing the kindness in his mentor's eyes. Always he had told Magnus the right advice when he went through harsh times with Chief Olaf. Likely, he could help him see what had gone wrong now.

"Before we left Rimsdale, I thought Muriele cared for me.

I planned to send for her after I wed."

"You told her you planned to make her your leman!" Sweyn looked shocked.

"Nay. I had not the chance. She disappeared with Grunda and didn't return afore we left."

Sweyn looked up at the sky and shook his head. "You planned to ask a lady, a lady of good breeding and background, to move into a hut and be your whore?"

"Not my whore! My leman."

"As far as she is concerned, 'tis no different. I know you believe everything Chief Olaf taught you as a lad. Because he *gave* the Lady Muriele to you as a spoil of war didn't make it right. When you used her, I thought you planned on asking the king for her hand after you straightened this betrothal out with your father."

"After I learned father's arranged betrothal was a lie, I still knew he wanted me to marry for land and a fortune. I was waiting for the right time to tell him about Muriele. There were more pressing matters with raiders, if ye remember."

"Aye."

"Never has a woman matched me in hunting and riding. And she was far better at knife fighting than many of my own men."

"I think your Father would have been impressed with her. Likely, he would have given his consent."

"Do ye think Feradoch lied because he was in love with Muriele?"

"Ha! He never loved anyone but himself." When Magnus was silent, he added, "I dinna believe it happened how they said. It does not sound like something the lady would do."

Instead of easing Magnus' mind, he had more questions than ever.

Finally, around the next turn in the hill's path, they could see over the tops of the trees below. In the distance, the darkest, most imposing castle Magnus had ever seen, sprawled within curtain walls that seemed to go on for leagues.

The menacing structure could only be Raptor Castle.

They spent a fortnight in an alehouse in Coldstream, learning of the happenings at the nearby castle. It wasn't until they'd been there long enough to buy everyone ale and a meal, plus lose a plentiful amount on table games, when people began to talk freely.

One eve, Sweyn sat at the lone table in their room, his fingers drumming on the scarred wood. Magnus slouched on the narrow bed, his legs spread and elbows on his thighs as his hands slapped the sides of his head in frustration.

"Lucifer and all his warty devils! Everywhere we go, we arrive too late."

"Why do ye not leave her in peace? By all the Saints, she is in a convent in Northumbria. If we cross the border and forcefully take her from there, we will likely start a war."

Magnus ignored him and switched the subject.

"Never have I heard of a man as heartless as Chief Broccin of Raptor Castle." Magnus threw up is arms in disgust. "He makes Olaf look like a saint."

"Aye. He does. After Broccin beat his son Ranald and destroyed his face, he threw the dying lad into a cart and had him abandoned at Kelso Abbey." The muscles in Sweyn's cheek twitched with disgust.

Magnus thought of the years he had lived under Chief Olaf and considered himself lucky.

He began to pace the room, slapping his right hand against his thigh in anger as he spoke.

"The whole countryside must have been shocked when Chief Broccin's eldest son was killed on the morning of his wedding. The old bastard wasn't about to lose the thriving castle and rich honors his daughter-to-be would bring him. Though he discarded the dying son like so much horse shite, now he wanted him back. He didn't care that he'd become a monk. It was easy to petition the Pope for a special dispensation — accompanied with plentiful gold coins."

"My drinking companion said the monk refused to leave."

"He had no choice. With the Pope's blessing and Chief Broccin's army gathered to raze Kelso, Ranald had to return to Raptor. He left a life of peace to sire Broccin a grandson."

"Muriele would have been there when he returned. I'd be willing to bet she took it all in stride." Magnus could see her quietly adjusting to the changes.

"Were it not for all the turmoil, the lady could easily have been wed by now and out of your reach. As it is, Ranald is her protector. He visits her to see she is safe. She'll never leave the convent. There is also a knight from Hunter Castle who visits the first day of each full moon."

"She's a canny lass," Magnus said slowly. "She knew I'd follow and take her back."

"Uh huh. What better place for safety than a convent?"

Magnus kept silent. His mind worked thinking on one plan, rejecting it, and then bringing another to mind. He refused to give up.

"If they are like most convents and abbeys, wayfarers may enter for the night." Magnus decided how he could capture her. "We go to Crookham in Northumbria. 'Tis close to the convent. I will find what I need to enter and spend the night. When I leave, she will be with me."

His heart sank knowing if his plan worked, he'd likely be taking Muriele back to a terrible fate. The only way he could be free of his blood oath was if Feradoch did something that nullified it.

His shoulders slumped.

No chance there.

Feradoch was long dead by now.

Chapter 37

Nine Months Earlier

MURIELE'S LEGS WERE SO numb after cradling Bolt's head all night she couldn't have jumped up and run if Lucifer himself was astride the horse whose hooves edged ever closer to her.

Prepared to meet Magnus's vengeful eyes, she summoned all of her anger and hate over everything that happened since she first laid eyes on him.

Her gaze met the black eyes of a helmeted warrior studying her. No cold accusation stared back at her. Instead, interest and understanding did. His lips smiled, hesitant at first, then broader.

She shook her head, trying to clear her thoughts. The man before her was not Magnus, but the leader of a patrol from Raptor Castle. She knew he was their leader, for while the rest of the men were alike in their dark clothing, he looked like fall leaves in the forest with his yellow tunic and red cloak.

He dismounted slowly and murmured softly to her.

"Lady, 'tis naught else ye can do for yer faithful companion."

When she didn't reply, he bowed and started over.

"I am Moridac, son of Broccin of Raptor Castle. We will give ye shelter there and our men will return to bury yer horse. 'Tis likely fitting, for he must have been a most loyal steed."

He motioned for one of his men to lift Bolt's head as he took her hands and helped her to rise on cramped legs.

"Would ye tell me yer name, Lady? Were ye thrown from yer keep when raiders took it over?"

"Lady Muriele," she blurted without thinking. She nodded, for he spoke true.

She felt filthy alongside the elegant man who smelled of sandalwood and spices. He seemed to sense her hesitation for he tried to put her at ease.

"We will return to Raptor Castle. Lady Joneta, my aunt, will see to yer care," he said as he mounted his horse. One of his knights lifted her to sit behind him.

Muriele was too heartsick to make any protest. She had survived the months it had taken to reach the border. Perchance someone from Raptor could help her cross over into Northumbria.

She'd find safety at the Convent of Mary Magdalen. It stood southeast across the ragged border from Kelso Abbey. Though she had no money, perhaps her skills would be of enough use to them to allow her to stay. To avoid Magnus' vengeance, she would gladly tend the ill, hunt, work in the gardens or clean floors — whatever it took to be safe from him.

Lady Joneta was a kindly woman. Though Muriele tried to avoid anyone seeing her back, Joneta glimpsed it and immediately made excuses to send everyone from the room. She did not press her to tell her of her life. She brought her a beautiful kirtle and smock stored away after the Chief's wife had died.

As if the bath and clothing had been magical, her confidence returned. When she walked into the Chief of Raptor Castle's solar, she was once again what she'd been born to, a lady of breeding.

Chief Broccin's gaze immediately settled on her, his expression as hungry as a starving man looking at a juicy, rare side of beef.

The next months, Muriele felt comfortable with life at Raptor Castle. She made friends easily. Soon after she arrived, Moridac died in a hunting accident on his wedding day. Muriele wasn't the only one surprised when Chief Broccin left with an army and returned with Moridac's identical twin Ranald.

Muriele watched Ranald over the next months and found he was the most faithful man she had ever met. She didn't see the disfigured right side of his face repulsive. She and his wife became fast friends, as did his bastard cousin. When Muriele saved Ranald's pregnant wife from a certain, gruesome death, he gave the Convent of Mary Magdalen a fortune to house Muriele for the rest of her life.

She was happy there, tending the herbal gardens and the dispensary. Ranald's cousin visited often trying to get her to marry him, but she always declined. She never told them from whom she fled, but they knew she was terrified of someone stalking her.

As always, when evening fell and any travelers happened to seek safety for the night, she watched from a hidden spot on the dormitory rooftop. Tonight, when wealthy strangers came through the gateway, she studied them. The man wore a bright green tunic and a red cloak with yellow lining and colorful Saxon clothing. He reminded her of Moridac. His wife rode behind him. Instead of brazen clothing, her kirtle was fawn colored. A forest green cloak had a wide hood, which she'd pulled low over her face to protect her from the night chill. A male servant followed the proper distance behind them.

Their backs were to Muriele, but from what she could see in the shadows, the tall man's hair was black as burnt wood, tied behind his head with a thin length of leather. His manner and clothing spoke of good breeding. When he swung down from the horse, he lifted the woman as if she weighed little more than a child. It was no small feat, for his wife was near as tall as he was. Muriele imagined the muscles flexing in his powerful body, making heat streak to her lower belly.

Putting his arm across his wife's shoulder, he turned to kiss her cheek, showing a full beard cut short. Something about the strength of his jaw caused her heart to pound.

She was having fanciful thoughts because she had long been without real bed sport. But, dream sport she'd had aplenty. Each morn she awoke with an ache in her heart. In dreams, Magnus was a tender lover, but before the dream ended, he cruelly dragged her from the bed to a post in the center of the room. He tied her hands above her head then called out to someone in the hall.

Feradoch entered, though he was naught but a faint shade of himself. He handed Magnus a whip with three tails and urged Magnus to start her punishment for killing him. To her shame, she sometimes awoke screaming. Had Feradoch wielded the whip, she'd have bit her tongue off before uttering a cry.

She shuddered and quietly made her way through the dark shadows. She was anxious to seek her room before the sisters could escort the woman into the same hallway housing women not married to God.

Breathing a sigh of relief, she slipped down the passageway and entered the peace of her room. 'Twas sparse, for truth not what she had known all her life. One single cot with a stuffed pallet, a small table, a wooden stool and a corner table with a basin and small pitcher of water for washing. A few pegs on the walls held her meager wardrobe. She had no need of fancy kirtles, smocks and cloaks. She had only finery enough to dress appropriately for expected visitors from Raptor.

The Abbess and all within the convent protected her attempts to remain hidden. Whenever visitors arrived and she took to her room, the sisters brought food to her until she came out on her own.

Hearing a light scratch and a whisper on the other side of the door, she put her ear to the wood. A young girl working in the kitchen brought her green pea pottage, brown bread and water for her evening meal. Keeping her face hidden, Muriele opened the door wide enough to accept the tray. With whispered thanks, she quickly closed it.

Seeing the loving couple below had sickened her heart. She forced herself to eat the soup, for she'd regret not doing so in the morning. After months at the convent, her clothing hung loose. Whether it was the small portions of food or from the exercise of working most of the day, she neither knew nor cared.

Once done, she performed her nightly cleansing and, after praying on her knees, she slipped naked between the sheets and thin blanket. Two things she truly missed — plentiful water to bathe and warmth through the night.

She listened to the night sounds of women entering their cells to sleep without their mates. Sometimes she heard giggles. No doubt, an ardent husband was stealthy enough to find his way to his wife's bed.

She smiled at the happy sounds and though she had not thought she'd be able to sleep this night, she relaxed and dozed off. Sometime later, another door whispered closed and she knew the man had enough bed sport and returned to his own cot.

The bells of Lauds heralding dawn had not yet sounded when, hearing a slight rustle beside her cot, Muriele awoke.

Before she could scream, a hand clamped over her mouth. When unyielding fingers dug cruelly into her cheeks, terror near drove her wild.

CHApTER 38

"CEASE FIGHTING ELSE I'LL throttle ye and leave yer body for the good sisters to find."

Magnus!

Recognizing the cruel voice, she struggled and fought. He straddled her and sat on her belly to keep her still. After stuffing her mouth with cloth, he tied a strip around her head to hold it there.

How could she not have known it was Magnus last eve when she'd watched the 'loving' couple she'd envied? She'd ignored the flash of hot excitement that had always sparked through her when he was near. She'd been celibate for a year and thought it was because of the stranger's superbly formed body.

Magnus shifted and hauled her out of bed with his arm clamped around her waist. When he pressed her naked back against him, his body beneath the soft fabric of his clothing was iron-hard as it had always been. She kicked backward at his shins, and then stomped down with all her might on the top of his feet while she tried to claw the gag from her mouth.

It hurt her. He didn't flinch.

He grabbed her wrists and kept tight hold of her.

"What should I do?"

A woman's soft voice. Muriele's eyes adjusted to the dim light before dawn. She was as tall as Muriele herself. Her heart sank knowing why the woman was there. Their show of love when they entered was a pretense. He needed a woman to take her place and delay the convent from finding out he had taken her.

"Remove yer clothes and help me dress her."

Though not above a whisper, Magnus' voice had hoarsened.

The woman laid the forest green cloak on the bed and quickly pulled the fawn kirtle over her head, along with a cream smock.

"Are ye sure this be yer runaway wife?"

"Did I not tell ye she was? Dinna question me."

He put his mouth close to Muriele's ear. "If ye dinna want to see her harmed, stop fighting. I'll kill her if I have to."

The coldness in his tone convinced her he meant every word.

He shoved her forward and told the woman to slip the smock over Muriele's head. When she did, her forced Muriele's arms through the sleeves. As he pulled the smock down her back, his hand brushed along its length. He stilled. Holding her with one hand, he felt quickly over her back. After he'd pulled the smock down past her buttocks, he nodded to the girl to lift the kirtle. Now they had the way of dressing her, it went quicker.

Magnus bound her wrists in front of her. The bells for Lauds rang, calling the sisters to Mass. He snapped his fingers for the cloak. Standing her before him, he put it around her shoulders and tied the ribbons at her neck. He ran his fingers through her hair. His head jerked up to study her when he felt its length. His hands searched over her head as if he could not believe her hair barely came past her shoulders. In another circumstance, it would have felt like a caress.

Not today.

He pulled the hood up over her head and down low over her face.

Watching the woman putting on Muriele's clothing from the night before, he nodded.

"Dinna let anyone see yer face. Keep behind the door and tell them ye are ill disposed and dinna want anyone to get sick." He frowned and looked at Muriele.

"Have ye an eating knife?"

She'd be damned for a sinner before she'd make anything easy for him. She ignored him. He studied her eyes, expecting them to give her away by the urge to look toward its hiding place.

"Look around. See if ye can find one."

"No place to look, really. She has no trunk and barely any clothing."

She stared around the room then went to the table. On one end, she found the small drawer hidden there. When she eased it open and saw two daggers there, she gasped.

Muriele near gasped with her, for when she bent to pull the drawer open, a pale shaft of moonlight spread across her hair. How clever of him. Magnus had chosen the lass to help in his hateful plot not only for her height, but her hair was near the color of Muriele's.

Magnus grunted. Keeping hold of her, he stalked over to the cot and threw off the pallet, exposing her short sword. He hooked its sheath on his belt beneath the bright red cloak. One dagger he hid in his boot top.

"Saints! Why would a woman need such protection? 'Tis enough to arm a man!"

He handed her the second dagger.

"Take this. As soon as we leave, cut yer hair to match hers. In case someone should come in unaware, keep yer back turned so they dinna see yer face."

He reached in a pocket of his green tunic, brought out a leather bag of coins and tossed it on the table.

It would soon be time for everyone to break their fast. Muriele hoped Magnus knew naught of the convent's routine.

He did.

"We must leave afore someone comes to the hallway and discovers me with my *wife*. If I learn ye didn't obey me, yer family willna get the cows and plow horse I've arranged for them."

Magnus gave the girl a withering stare as warning. Putting his arm around Muriele's waist, he forced her over to the door and listened before he opened it a crack. Cautiously, he eased his head out to glance up and down the hallway.

"Latch the door behind us."

He hurried Muriele out of the room. She'd hoped he would become lost, but he seemed to know the inside of the convent as well as she did. No one was about until he forced her to the big door leading out into the courtyard. A knight stood there enjoying the sunrise. He looked at them and smiled.

"Ye leave early. Restless night, eh?"

"Aye. We mean to take advantage of an early start." Magnus voice sounded friendly, but he cut off all further conversation. "There's my servant now. Enjoy the rest of yer travels."

He hurried her down the stairs where three horses awaited. Sweyn had come with him! How could this kindly man aid him in such a vengeful quest? He came over with the three horses they'd ridden on the eve before. All three looked swift. All she'd need is a bit of luck when he put her on the horse. If someone had trained the horse well, she could make it rear and throw her to the ground, exposing her bound hands and the gag. The Abbess would recognize her hair. Even if Magnus were still able to remove her, they would send word to Ranald at Hunter Castle.

Magnus soon dashed her hopes.

When Sweyn handed him the reins, Magnus murmured to him, "Hold tight to her until I'm mounted. She'll try something foolish if given the chance."

Once Magnus seated himself in the saddle, Sweyn lifted her up to Magnus' waiting arms. He shifted her to ride across his thighs, her head against his right shoulder and his arm securely around her waist. She tried to make eye contact with Sweyn to plead with him to help her, but he avoided looking at her face.

"She's lighter than she was. They must not have fed her very well," Sweyn muttered.

"Humph! More likely her guilty conscience kept her from eating."

Magnus wrapped her cloak tightly around her and pulled the hood lower over her face. Likely, for the Abbess and the guards' benefit he spoke in a normal tone.

"'Tis a cold day, love. We canna have ye catching a chill now ye're increasing. Lay yer head against my shoulder and try to sleep." He pressed her head against him. In a threatening whisper, he warned, "Keep it there else ye'll regret it."

Magnus urged the horse toward the gateway with Sweyn leading the third horse.

"Mother Abbess. Thank ye for the night's lodging."

He handed the Abbess a silk bag of coins, all the while keeping Muriele's head tight to his chest.

"My blessings to your wife, my lord. May you have many children to brighten your years," the abbess said with a smile.

Muriele stiffened. Many children indeed. He wouldna see any children, for she'd ne'er be such a fool as to swive with him again. But then . . . a man would be most vulnerable when his cock was urging him to comfort it! She'd kill him the first chance she could.

The men pulled the heavy, wooden gate wide and Magnus cantered the horse through the opening. Muriele tried to fight and squirm, knowing this was her last chance for anyone at the convent to see her. His steel arm around her waist tightened until it was so painful she became still. He kicked the horse into a faster gait and then into a gallop. She could barely hear the chilly words he spoke in her ear over the pounding noise of the horses' hooves.

"Ye little fool! Who do ye think would win out if one lone woman and two old men tried to stop me? Eh?"

Muriele quieted, knowing the truth of it.

The only deaths she could stand on her conscience were Feradoch and Magnus' own.

Magnus steeled himself to ignore the warm arse pressed so intimately between his thighs. 'Twas bad enough his balls were like two large, hard stones he was sitting on, but his deranged cock didn't care Muriele had murdered two people in cold blood. It well remembered the ecstasy of the spasms her hot, slick body squeezed around him as she climaxed. It swelled and near exploded when her hood blew back and the clean, sweet smell of apples drifted from her skin and hair.

'Twas all that moat scum, maggot ridden Lucifer's doings!

He yanked her hood up and anchored it between her head and his chest. If he couldna smell her unique scent, he could pretend she was any woman he captured to take back for justice.

They had ridden as fast as possible until the mountain road

became too steep and the horses labored. They had no need to hide, for no one would know she was missing for a sennight or more. 'Twas swifter to use the best roads headed west toward Galashiels. By the time anyone picked up their trail, they would be well into the Highlands and beyond their reach.

His stomach turned and vomit near surged to his mouth when he thought of handing her off to Chief Olaf. He knew him too well. He would insist Magnus carry out the punishment as part of his oath. He steeled himself not to think of putting a noose around the lovely neck he had nibbled and licked his way up to the sweet spot beneath her ear … where the thick knot of the noose would rest.

"'Tis well past the noon hour. If we don't stop soon, I'll piss myself," Sweyn said as he drew alongside him. "You can change horses and give this one a rest."

Startled from his thoughts, Magnus stared at him and then nodded. They would pull off the road where they were close to water. Sweyn had filled a canvas bag with bannocks made of oats, a loaf of hard brown bread, dried meat, and a round of cheese, some apples and nuts.

If they kept up this pace, they would reach the Highlands sooner than he expected. 'Twas easier to travel a straight route and not bounce all over Scotland much like a Highland cow weaving after eating soaked grass beside a still.

His arse would thank him for the chance to take his weight off it. He turned his horse's head left to leave the road and follow the sounds of rapids on the other side of the trees. They used caution as they approached, for he didn't want to encounter men who lived in the woods after falling into disfavor from the men they served.

"All's clear," Sweyn said softly, looking at Muriele.

He dismounted and came over to take her from Magnus' arms. When Magnus moved his arm from where he'd clamped it around her waist, his hand brushed the side of her breast. She cringed as if something repulsive had touched her.

Once Sweyn had her, he held her shoulders until he was sure

her legs would hold her upright. She twisted her head, throwing off the hood and looked him in the eye. With her bound hands, she motioned toward the cloth tied around her mouth.

"Take it off," Magnus said. "But the first time ye raise yer voice, lass, I'll stuff yer mouth with soiled clothing."

She answered with a glare then turned her back on him and looked at Sweyn.

"May I go into the bushes to, er, tend myself?" Her face flamed.

"Let her, but stay within a tree's width," he told Sweyn.

She opened her mouth to speak again, but he waved her off.

"Nay. Ye can tend yerself with yer hands tied."

She turned and entered the woods where Sweyn led her. He had no need to go after her for she returned in good time. Without so much as a glance at Magnus, she strode over to the rocks beside the rapids and lifted her clothing to kneel on the wet rock. Though it was agonizingly slow, she cleaned her hands and did her best to put water on her face.

Magnus stared at her. She reminded him of a dog trying to wash its face after wetting its paw then rubbing its eyes.

"By Odin!"

Magnus stomped over to her and untied her hands. When he freed her, he felt a flash of guilt. Her skin was aflame and rubbed raw around the prominent bones on top of her wrists. Why hadn't she said something?

Fool! How? He'd not given her a chance to say a word after he woke her in the convent.

He guessed she'd give him an earful now. He hardened his heart not to believe a word from her mouth.

CHAPTER 39

MURIELE WAS GRATEFUL TO be away from Magnus. Every breath she took, his scent reminded her of the many nights she had lain with her head cuddled beneath his chin. His beard now covered more of his face. He looked like a different man. Even harder. One who had stifled all feelings of empathy.

His name as Ruthless had taken over his mind, his being. He no longer looked like the man she'd fallen in love with. Saints help her! 'Twas the first time she'd admitted her feelings for him ... before he left Kinbrace without a word to her. If he had beaten her, she wouldn't have felt more degraded. By his silence, she had become a nithing to him.

Too lowly to confide in — good only for his cock's pleasure.

Now, she didn't want to speak to him. She feared all the hurt, the abandonment, would break through and she wouldn't be able to control her urge to kill.

Part of what had happened afterward was her fault. She'd let the hurt make her vulnerable to Feradoch. How could she not have seen in his eyes that hatred filled his beautiful body. His pretense that all he wanted to do was protect, comfort and love her had all been a lie.

As Feradoch courted her, she'd been so confident of his goodness she hadn't even thought about her ruined back. For the man who prided himself in having everything lovely, the sight of her flesh must have been truly disgusting.

Grunda had tried to warn her. She thought 'twas only because her old friend had seen falsely into the future and believed Magnus and she were fated to be together forever.

Esa's face as Feradoch choked her never left Muriele's mind

for long. At every one of the many Masses at the convent, she'd prayed Grunda had been able to save her. And she had added prayers of forgiveness for killing Feradoch. Would she go to Hades for trying to save her friend? If so, she knew Lucifer would use Feradoch as his minion to torture her for eternity.

She shuddered.

Sweyn came to put an apple, a hunk of cheese and brown bread on her lap then sat a pewter cup of cold water beside her leg. She drank the water but ignored the food. Why eat to keep her body alive when she would hang in a sennight or so?

She stared off into the bushes, watching the birds, squirrels and wildlife flitting from one tree to another. They looked so carefree she envied them. She spied a fat hare behind the two men, his body still and scrunched down to avoid notice. At any other time, she would have used her bow and arrow to supplement their food. Now she kept silent, hoping the creature could slip away unharmed.

"She's nae eating, Magnus," Sweyn said the following evening.

"When she gets hungry enough, she will."

Magnus couldn't help glancing at Muriele. Her face was thinner than it had been. Her shorter hair suited her. Where it was wavy before, now it was curling at the tips. A frisky breeze blew a wispy ringlet to tease her eye. When her arm lifted to shove it aside, her flesh was all sleek muscle.

"She hasn't said more than a few words." Sweyn looked at him from the corner of his eye. "I thought she would plead her case with you. Did she say aught all day?"

"Nay. Not one word. She avoids even looking at me. I have asked her repeatedly why she killed Esa and Feradoch. She stiffens and ignores me. No matter what I ask her, or how I ask her, she looks away."

"Huh! Can you blame her? I think you should hear her side of the story. Graemme believes Feradoch wasn't as he appeared."

"My foster brother was a good warrior. He enjoyed a battle

and didn't mind a little bloodshed."

"Aye. Graemme talked to me many times on our visits. He told me of his doubts. Feradoch did like battles, but he also liked battles with his bed sport. He becomes passionate only when he inflicts torment on his partner."

Magnus shook his head. "Esa has been his leman for many years. Do ye think she would have allowed such?"

"What choice did she have? Have you never wondered why she kept to her bedchamber for a sennight each time he returned to Clibrick?"

"She grieved over his leaving."

"You're blind, man. Grunda made frequent trips to her rooms with unguents. When she walked by me, I could tell her pockets were full."

"Ye are yammering. The simple fact is Muriele killed them both. If he'd treated Esa ill, she'd not have let Muriele handfast with him."

He bolted to his feet, and while Sweyn replaced the food in the bag, he readied the horses. Thinking of her in Feradoch's arms sent harsh streaks of anger shooting through his mind.

Muriele sat quietly, ignoring them. He noted she finished the water, but she'd not taken a bite of food.

"Do ye want to take the apple with ye?"

She shook her head but didn't deign to look at him. She wanted to pout. Let her. Afore evening fell, she'd be asking for food. When he lifted the food off her lap, he felt her body heat through her clothing. Remembered passion went from his brain to his stones.

After the horses made one last trip to the stream for water, Magnus untied her waist from the tree. She held out her wrists and waited. The rope burns looked angrier than ever. He hesitated then bound her more loosely. Once they were farther away, he would have to allow her to pick herbs or find whatever she needed to make a healing paste for them.

"Sweyn, may I ride the spare horse?"

"Ye may not," Magnus interrupted, "until we reach the Highlands."

He mounted the second horse, and before she could take another breath, he again held her firmly across his thighs. His arm didn't clamp around her as tight as before. Holding herself as straight as possible, she avoided leaning against his massive body.

He did not intend to stop to sleep for the night. The full moon was bright, and he planned to make good use of it to speed their travel. When they reached the Highlands, they would need to move slower over the high mountains where a horse could easily place one hoof too near the edge and topple it and the rider over a cliff.

For two days, they traveled near full time. He continued to question Muriele. She continued to treat him as if he was invisible. During the middle of the night, they stopped to tend and rest the horses and eat whatever game Sweyn happened to bring down with his bow during the day. A small fire late into the night would go unnoticed.

Magnus again tied her to a tree while they tended the horses and prepared food. She drank only water and ignored the grouse Sweyn cooked on a spit. When Magnus saw she intended to go hungry the first two nights, it didn't faze him. He offered her food to Sweyn and, when he declined, ate it himself.

They banked the fire and took turns sleeping. Magnus untied Muriele and had her stretch out beside him, a rope around her ankle tied to his wrist. She shrugged away when he attempted to cover her with her cape and did it herself. If she so much as moved in her sleep, he felt it.

They were up and riding again long before dawn broke.

Muriele was bone tired and hungry, but she could put up with it. When she'd fled Kinbrace, she'd been much more tired and hungry. She got used to it then, and she'd get used to it now.

When Sweyn took her up on his horse, she relaxed more. Leaning against him to rest wasn't repugnant to her. The only problem was he also tried to get her to talk. How insulting! They thought she'd callously murdered Feradoch for having a leman. And to blame her for Esa's death was more than she could stand.

Even if Magnus knew the reason she'd stabbed Feradoch, he still wouldn't change his vow. The pig-headed fool. How did he think she had the strength to strangle a woman as tall as Esa and murder Feradoch at the same time? Hadn't they reasoned that while she tried to kill one, the other would have stopped her?

She'd believed she loved Magnus until he'd proved he'd thought so little of her he'd not told her of his father's plans. Had he explained, mayhap she would have understood. She'd have gone on with her life and not been easy prey to Feradoch, who treated her the way knights at Blackbriar used to treat her. He'd even courted her by entertaining her and giving her small gifts of flowers and such.

After Baldor, Magnus and Feradoch, she'd be a fool to trust any man. Even Sweyn. When he asked questions and tried to get her to speak about her life after they'd left Kinbrace, she turned her face away and kept her thoughts hidden.

On the fifth night, the men did as usual. When Sweyn took watch and Magnus slept, clouds rolled in, masking the moon. Muriele had twisted and turned each night on purpose to accustom Magnus to feeling the tug on his wrist. At first, he jolted awake and stayed alert, watching her 'sleep.' Each time she deliberately moved, he startled less. Finally, this eve he did no more than grunt.

She'd studied the knots for three days and knew with any luck at all, she could untie her end. Feverishly, she set to work on freeing herself. Her fingers were sore from digging at the knot, the flesh scraping off now and then. She was in the shadows of a tree, and Sweyn's back was to them as he sat watching the dark woods between them and the road. He didn't notice when she reached out to gather wet leaves and bunched them beneath her robe.

Silently, she slipped away. In the safety of the dark woods, she glanced back to see her robe looked like she still slept beneath it. She knew Magnus would awaken when it began to rain and they'd find her missing. They wouldn't look for her close by, but would spread out.

Careful not to leave a trail, she went a short way until she found a perfect tree to climb. Pulling the back of her skirts forward between her legs, she tied them around her waist with the ribbon she'd taken from the cloak's neck. She was up and near the top of the tree with time to spare before the rain started.

When it did, it didn't start easily, but in a downpour. She hugged the big trunk, her legs wrapped tightly around it when it began to sway with the wind. She heard Magnus and Sweyn calling her name and thrashing through the woods. When they didn't find her right away, they returned for the horses.

Dratted Satin's evil eyes! She'd hoped they'd walk in ever-widening circles long enough to put distance between them and the horses. Then she could race back, take one horse, saddle the other and lead it. She'd carry the saddle and trappings of the third horse, leaving it bare.

She soon heard hoof beats and knew they'd decided to hunt her ahorse. Now the bastards worked in two widening circles. Sweyn started before Magnus. If Sweyn missed spotting her, 'twas a chance Magnus would see her on his turn in the same area.

Muriele grappled with the tree swaying in the wind. She hugged it for all she was worth as Sweyn rode beneath her. He was very thorough, his eyes constantly looking around for her.

"Lass, you'll freeze out here alone," Sweyn called.

He rode a little farther.

"You have no weapons, no food. Come out from your hiding place," he called again.

She kept her lips clamped shut. She'd sooner die in the woods than hang by the hands of a man she'd thought she loved!

When he widened his circle, she near sighed for there was quiet for a while. Then Magnus came close. The rain had slowed, but the wind had picked up. It tore at her hair, her clothes.

The wet droplets crawling down her back against the ridges of her scars felt like creeping spiders. Shuddering, she tried not to think about it for spiders were the one thing she dreaded most. Once, playing hide and find with a friend, she'd gone below in the dungeons of Blackbriar. Her friend wouldn't think to find her there! She'd no need to. When Muriele had spied the spiders looking like they were starting to scamper toward her, intent on eating her flesh, she had screamed so loud she'd alerted the whole keep.

Hearing Magnus stop below her, she bit her lip to keep silent. Cautiously moving her head only enough to look below, she watched him back up his horse and stare at a limb close to the ground. Something bright fluttered from amongst the wet leaves. He leaned over on his saddle to pluck it off.

The tie she'd used on her skirts! When had it come lose? She'd been so conscious of hanging on to the tree and trying to keep her clothes from flapping, she'd not even realized it had come free.

He held still. Looked all around him. He studied the ground and thought. She could imagine his frown when he bent his head.

God no! He looked up at the closest trees. Watching. Turned in his saddle and studied those behind him.

He straightened and sat rock still.

"Come down, Muriele."

His rough voice said her name like it was a curse. She didn't answer. Mayhap he was only hoping she was somewhere close.

When he slowly raised his head, he dashed her hopes to Hades and back. He must have the sight of an eagle to find her in the heavy canopy, for his cold, black gaze stared into her eyes.

When she didn't move, he put his fingers in his lips and whistled for Sweyn. In a short time, he arrived towing the extra horse as if it was an extension of his arm.

"You found her?"

For answer, Magnus looked back up at her.

"Come down," he demanded.

When she again didn't answer or move, he sighed. Handing his reigns to Sweyn he spoke loud enough for her to hear.

"I have half a mind to shake the tree till she falls like a ripe apple. It would save me the trouble of taking her to Kinbrace."

"Ye can't do that!" Sweyn sounded shocked at the sugges-tion. "The tree is the tallest in the forest! She'd fall to her death."

"Then, if she falls when I pry her arms loose, catch her or

not. It's up to ye."

He hoisted himself to stand on his saddle then swung up to the closest branch. Rather than have him touch her, Muriele gave in.

"Sweyn, tell the ruthless bastard to wait."

"For what? For ye to grow wings and fly into the sky?" Magnus said with contempt.

He stood on a branch close to the trunk, tested his weight on it and moved up to the next.

Muriele's legs near cramped when she released the trunk. She unclasped her arms and pulled her skirts free. 'Twould be cumbersome climbing down with their weight clinging to the branches, but she had no choice. She put her foot on the limb below her, and then the next, and the next, slowly making her way down. She was ready to go to the branches above and to the left of Magnus when she heard a sharp crack.

Of a sudden, the footing beneath her was gone. She grabbed for something to hold onto but missed. Broken limbs tore at her body in all directions.

By the Saints, she hurt. She was afire from the scratches and scrapes. Even her cheeks felt torn. She hit the back of her head on a thick branch, making her eyes blur.

Her clothing snagged and ripped, but nothing slowed her descent — until she slammed against something hard as steel.

'Twas the last she knew for a while.

Chapter 40

Magnus's breath caught and his heart halted when Muriele started falling. She was too high and out of his reach for him to aid her. He grabbed a limb and clenched his fist around it; put his left foot on another spot to his left. Leaning out as far as he could, he snatched her plummeting body out of the air.

He swayed and near lost his balance. The tree branch groaned.

Taking deep breaths, he listened as Sweyn directed him where to place his feet the rest of the way down to Odin.

Muriele was so limp, he feared she'd broken her neck when she'd hit her head. He felt Sweyn's hands on his booted feet, guiding them to the saddle.

"There are no lower branches. Steady yourself and pass her to me," he advised. To narrow the distance, Sweyn stood in his stirrups.

Keeping one hand on the tree, Magnus bent his knees until Sweyn's waiting arms lifted Muriele from him. Once he had her, Magnus slid down into the saddle.

"We've got to go back to the camp. She may be seriously hurt."

His calm voice surprised him. Inside, his mind raced as fast as his pulse. He took Sweyn's reins so he wouldn't have to move Muriele. It was slow going, for he had to pick his way carefully to lead all three horses.

"We're nearly there. I hear the rapids."

They carefully picked their way through the next stand of trees and came out onto the clearing where they had slept. After Magnus spread a blanket and they'd placed Muriele on it, he hurriedly started cutting her clothes away. Sweyn looked for bits and pieces of dry kindling on the ground where they'd slept and soon had a fire going and water heating. He searched through his saddlebags and took out a jar of ointment he carried in case Magnus was injured.

Magnus' hands gentled as he felt over her head and found a swelling bump in back. Mayhap she'd be out long enough he could tend her injuries.

Touching her naked body brought back memories of every time he had run his hands over her supple form. His body responded though he tried to discipline his mind to ignore what he felt with his fingertips. Even unconscious, she groaned and her nipples responded when he accidentally brushed too near them.

His blood pounded, painfully filling his cock and making his stones so firm he had to spread his legs to ease them. How could a mere woman make him forget all his body discipline? Before Muriele came into his life, he could be abed with Flori and Ingirid and still have control over when he allowed his cock to stand high or forced it to be patient and let them coax his passion.

Carefully using his blade to help him, he pulled splinters from her chest and arms. Thankfully, the cuts on her face were clear of wood. He used his cloak to shield her from Sweyn's eyes, though for the life of him, he didn't know why he cared. He washed her wounds with hot water then slathered them with the foul-smelling ointment.

He finally asked his friend's help to turn her over, for he needed him to hold her head steady.

"Holy God in Heaven!" Sweyn's eyes filled with pity on seeing Muriele's back.

Magnus gasped and pain squeezed his heart. 'Twas not the bloody cuts, nor did he think her back unsightly in any way. Nay, it was not either of them.

These scars were from a different beating. Alike. New.

Someone had flogged her with a wide belt embedded with sharp studs. Not someone. Feradoch. For ceremonies, he wore a magnificent belt with colored jewels fastened on it. Muriele's flesh bore the jewels' imprints in three, long stripes.

"The bastard beat her after their handfast." Sweyn's voice was heavy with horrified disgust.

Magnus covered her firm buttocks, for she twitched and started to come to her senses. He wished she would not. He needed time to understand what could have happened.

"Why wouldn't she tell me? Every time I questioned her, she refused to answer even 'aye' or 'nay.'"

"I canna believe she killed Esa and Feradoch out of jealousy. No woman treated so cruelly would want the man," Sweyn's eyes were soft with pity.

"Aye. Knowing him, he'd never have released her from the handfast. He must have isolated her where she couldn't escape. For all the Chief's faults, he wouldn't take kindly to Feradoch's mistreating a lady of breeding."

"Unfortunately, he didn't consider Esa a lady and looked the other way," Sweyn said.

Bitterness in his voice drew Magnus' attention. How could he have missed anything so obvious? Sweyn's eyes had lit with pleasure whenever Esa danced at Olaf's bidding. When the music faded and Feradoch triumphantly carried the sultry woman from the room, his entire face was expressionless.

Muriele groaned, bringing their attention back to her plight. Though bruised, her back had few cuts.

He cupped her head in his hand and held it tenderly as he rolled her onto her back.

"Fetch me the green tunic and the black cloak," he asked Sweyn.

When his friend handed the tunic to him, he folded it to pad the ground beneath her head. Taking the elegant cloak, he spread it over her and tucked it in at the sides. The day was turning cool again. He gave a wry smile. She wasn't in any shape to escape again, but if she did, they would easily see her creamy skin in the darkest forest.

"What have ye done to the lass?"

The demanding voice came from the thickest trees

behind them.

Magnus reached for his bow and arrows, while Sweyn's sword rasped from its sheath.

Graemme used his claymore to thrust aside branches impeding his progress.

"How in Hades did ye approach without us hearing?" Magnus asked.

For answer, Graemme whistled. Loud. His obedient steed sounded like an army pushing through the trees. He came over to nuzzle Graemme's shoulder, begging him to stroke his neck.

As Graemme affectionately patted and praised the big beast, he frowned down at the girl on the ground.

"She's more comely than any lass ye've ever bedded. From the looks of ye when ye tended her, she must be Muriele of Blackbriar."

"Aye, she is."

"I thought ye described her with long hair the color of ripe wheat flowing down her back? Did ye cut it as part of her punishment?" His scowled with disapproval.

"Nay. It was as we found her in the convent."

"And her injuries. Have ye caused them in any way?" He fingered his claymore as he advanced on his older brother, his lids narrowing. Magnus sprang to his feet.

"The reckless lass escaped during the night and climbed atop the tallest pine in the forest. While forcing her down, she fell halfway. I plucked her to me as she plunged by."

When he realized he was making excuses to his younger brother, Magnus scowled.

"How did ye find us and why are ye here and not at Clibrick or Kinbrace?"

"To keep yer sorry arse from making the worst mistake in yer life."

Magnus frowned and his body stiffened at the disrespectful way his brother was talking to him.

"And that is?"

"Believing anything out of the lying mouths of the Gunns." He reached in his pocket and pulled out a packet of cut up leaves to toss to Sweyn. "Do ye think ye can brew these? I dinna know about ye two, but I'm cold and wet from chasing two steps behind ye for days now."

Magnus motioned them to move to the other side of the fire so Muriele would not awaken. She seemed to be breathing smoother and he hoped she was in a natural sleep. Once they sat cross-legged on the ground with hot cups of herbal tea in their hands, Magnus became impatient.

"Ah, I feel warmer already," Graemme said.

"Ye'll feel warmer still if I snatch ye off the ground and pound my fists into yer pretty face! Start talking."

"Well, at Kinbrace I learned Feradoch wasn't dead. They wouldn't let me near him to see how badly injured he was. Olaf said he was at death's door, but I didn't believe him. I watched at night and saw a woman going into his room. Once all was quiet, I put my ear to the door and listened." He snorted and cursed. "No man near death can fuck with such abandon."

"What did ye hear?"

"Fortunately for me, he was drunk and talked more than he should. He told his whore he intends to force Muriele to marry him and take her straight to Blackbriar and establish himself there. He said the King wouldn't do anything about it once he did the deed. Then he plans to make her sorry every day of her 'short' life for running from him."

Magnus' hands clenched in his lap. "Did Chief Olaf believe Feradoch was dying?"

"Aye." He stopped and frowned. "I kept an eye out, and when the Chief went to see his son, I peeked in the room. It was darkened and Feradoch gasped and cried out in pain and acted like he was at death's door."

He grinned at Sweyn. "I think I make a very good spy."

"Did ye find anything about Grunda and Esa?" Magnus leaned forward watching his brother's face.

"After the men and I left Kinbrace, we asked everywhere and couldn't find the old woman."

Magnus' shoulders slumped and he wiped his hand over his face.

"It didna stop me. I remembered ye told me Muriele had lived deep in the woods. We hunted the woods until we found them. When old Grunda saw me, she held tight to an old, rusty sword until she realized who I was."

"How in Lucifer's maggot-infested brain did she know who ye are?"

"I dinna ken. She walked circles around me, staring, then grunted. Said I was the younger son of Clibrick. The one with compassion and brains to think." Seeing Magnus' insulted expression, he laughed so hard he snorted.

His laughter was so infectious, Sweyn joined in. Scowling, Magnus waited patiently.

"What did ye learn there?"

"She told me Feradoch had beaten Muriele because she was not perfectly formed and he couldn't consummate the handfast. He sent the guard to bring Esa to tempt his cock to rise. When she resisted, he strangled her. Muriele tried to save her but kenned she was too late."

"Kenned?" Sweyn straightened.

"Aye. She yet lives. Grunda gave her an elixir to make her appear dead then rescued her from the woods. She lives with her. I left my men to protect them."

Magnus heard Muriele stir and jumped to his feet. The little fool was trying to escape again! She had gathered the robe about her and was trying to stand.

"Did the blow to yer head make ye an eejit?"

"Esa is alive? Ye have seen her and Grunda?" Her hoarse voice asked Graemme. She ignored Magnus as she stumbled closer to the men sitting by the fire.

Graemme rose and came to bow in front of her. "'Tis an honor to meet ye, Lady Muriele. I have heard of yer good deeds from everyone at Raptor Castle."

Muriele's blush put color back into her pale cheeks. She swayed and Magnus reached out his hand to help her, but she shrunk from him.

Graemme studied her face and he shook his head. "If ye rest until dawn, we will be off to Clibrick. Ye will be safe there with my father and Magnus to guard ye."

"If yer brother has any say, he will return me to Chief Olaf."

Magnus knew he would never take her to Kinbrace, but there had to be a way to honor his vow. How, he didn't know yet. He stayed silent. Unmoving.

When Muriele shunned Magnus' help, Graemme scowled at him and helped her back to her makeshift pallet. Sweyn took her a hot potion, and as soon as she finished it, her eyes closed and she was fast asleep.

Chapter 41

MURIELE SLEPT SOUNDLY FOR the first time since leaving the safety of the convent. When an early rising bird sang to his mate, she blinked her eyes open. Sweyn was already cooking porridge.

Magnus and Graemme must have slept beside her. She remembered waking and feeling glorious heat. Whether she turned to her right or her left, she'd snuggled against a warm, hard back. Both had already risen and taken the opportunity to wash the travel from their bodies. They'd just come from the water and stood at the bank with water streaming from their hair and down their backs. They didn't know she had awakened and took time to stretch and enjoy being naked before they donned their clothing.

She blinked. Aye. Their bodies were much alike.

In all things.

An irksome bug landed on her nose, walking up and down as if it owned the flesh on which it trod. Hoping they would not notice, she raised her hand to send it on its way. Before she could stop herself, she groaned in pain. Her shoulders felt every bit of the strain she'd used to hold her weight on the branches as she fell down the tree yester morn.

Graemme's burnt-almond colored eyes twinkled with humor when they met hers. Why, he knew she'd been awake all the time! He was near as tall as Magnus with black hair lightened with hints of brown. His nose was not as strong as his brother's was and he didn't wear a beard. He must scrape it from his face daily, for dark shadows showed beneath his skin. The biggest difference between the two was their lips.

Graemme's were wide. Sensual. They softened just looking at her. Overall, he was wickedly handsome as he came over to greet her.

Magnus' lips were full. Hard. Aye, Magnus was just as handsome, but in a dark way. He reminded her of his standard. A snarling black wolf's face on a background of gray. As he glared at his younger brother, his lips curled back from his teeth much like a snarl.

"Ye may go into the woods to dress," Magnus all but growled at her as he handed her a tunic. "We must make good time leaving here afore anyone learns the lady in the convent is not ye."

She waited until they turned their back then bit her lips as she rose from the hard ground clutching the cloak around her. She made quick work of tending to her needs and dressing, before she went to the loch to splash her face.

Graemme must have brought much-needed provisions with him, for the aroma of baking flat cakes made her drool. She had not eaten for days thinking 'twas better to starve than to accept food from a man who thought she would murder for senseless reasons.

Hmpf. Not that she *wouldn't* kill. She could and did so swiftly when it warranted. Had Feradoch died, she wouldn't have regretted it. But now Graemme had proven she'd had just reasons for trying to kill Feradoch, they were not taking her to Kinbrace. Still, she would need her strength to defend herself at Clibrick.

Graemme looked at the comely lass and could tell she used all her will to walk without limping on aching legs. Sweyn had told him of her refusal to eat and of her climbing the Scots pine in her bid to escape yesterday. Now he understood the tales he'd heard of her from the villagers around Raptor Castle.

"I saved the biggest oat cake for ye, Lady," Graemme said as he held it out to her.

She hesitated then thanked him and took it. Magnus scowled at her but she ignored him.

"Sweyn, may I ride today?"

"Nay." Magnus came over and lightly ran his hand down the back of her head. She pulled away from him. "The swelling is still there. Ye ride with me."

Graemme looked at his brother's scowling face and shook his head. What ailed the man? As far as he could see, the lady had reason aplenty to be angry with him. Knowing Magnus, he'd probably never told her he loved her. And with his hardbound honor, likely he didn't explain why he had to leave her at Kinbrace. Graemme snorted as they prepared to leave. If his father had truly picked out a timid bride for him, would Magnus have blindly wed her?

He watched Sweyn lift Muriele up to Magnus' waiting arms. He caught a flash of tenderness pass over Magnus' harsh face when his arms closed around her. 'Twas so quickly gone, if he'd blinked, he would have missed it. Why did Magnus hide his love from her?

Lucifer's crooked teeth! He didna even realize he loved her! Pity for his brother filled him.

They traveled swiftly for two days, riding into the night as they had before. Graemme led the way with Magnus and Sweyn following. Magnus still refused to let her ride the horse saying the jarring could scramble her brains. Once they reached the high mountain ranges, they stopped at dusk. Sweyn and Graemme were able to hunt while Magnus refused to let Muriele out of his sight. Because he couldn't trust her, he told Graemme.

Humph! He lied. 'Twas because he feared losing her.

After the third night, Muriele was strong enough to ride her own mount. She ate more each day, always accepting food from Graemme and Sweyn. Magnus had stopped offering knowing she would refuse all aid from him.

The day finally came for Graemme to leave them and go east to fetch Grunda and Esa to Clibrick. Sweyn kept cautioning him on how to handle Grunda so the old seer didn't throw a curse on him. When he mentioned Esa, he nearly begged Graemme to treat Esa with tenderness.

As Graemme rode off at the break of dawn, Muriele felt the first excitement in many moons. She knew she would see her friends afore a fortnight passed.

When he was out of sight, excitement changed to calm as she mused over her reception at Clibrick. Chief Angus raised both Graemme and Feradoch. Which one of the men took after him? Was he as calm as Graemme? Or was he deceitful like Feradoch?

Clibrick Castle was beautiful as the sun began to set. Golden rays of light danced on the waves of Loch Naver and bathed the massive castle in a warm glow. Ben Clibrick behind it looked dark and threatening. She could almost imagine gremlins and ogres hiding behind trees, waiting to pounce on the castle inhabitants if they went beyond the castle walls.

The portcullis was up and Chief Angus, his man Fergus, and the knights and their wives already awaited them in the front bailey. When his father came to greet Magnus as he dismounted, he held his arms wide and enveloped him in a bear hug for the first time in his life. At first, Magnus was stiff and startled, then softened when his father murmured, "I am thankful to have my *real* son back."

When the Chief's eyes went to Muriele, they widened in surprise.

Muriele had bathed at dawn and washed her hair. Wispy curls blew from her temples and teased her eyes. When she brushed them away, the sleeves of the large tunic dropped back to her elbow revealing the healing rope burns on her wrists and the bruises and cuts from her fall.

Chief Angus' lips tightened and he glanced quickly at Magnus before he courteously reached to help Muriele dismount. She could have done it by herself, but it was so pleasant for a nobleman to treat her as a lady again.

"'Tis an honor to have you as our guest." His face grew taut when he saw his son's stony expression. "As long as I am Chief of Clibrick, you have a home with us. Come, my housekeeper will show you to a room where you can rest before the noon meal."

He motioned to a plump, kind-faced woman who hovered near by. She beamed and bowed at Muriele then started chattering as she led her into the keep.

"Guest?" Magnus asked.

"Aye. Guest!"

"I must honor my vow, though I dinna intend to return Muriele to Feradoch." Magnus jaw jutted stubbornly.

"The King wouldn't allow it."

"Why do ye say so?" Magnus asked as he followed his father into the solar.

"The King sent armed escorts with his messengers." He went straight to his table and picked up a thickly rolled parchment. "You'd best be seated afore you read it."

Fergus, with a big grin on his face, poured goblets of wine and Sweyn passed them around while Magnus read.

"What!" Magnus jumped up and started pacing the room. "So this is the reason Feradoch lied. Why he planned a handfast with Muriele."

"Aye. He hoped to see she increased quickly so the King would have to give her and Blackbriar to him," Lard Angus said.

"I am to marry Muriele in all haste? Blackbriar needs to be rebuilt and I am to hold it in King David's name?"

"You read it rightly."

Magnus stiffened. His thoughts churned. In the Highlands, a handfast was as good as a marriage. He couldn't marry her. Olaf would see it as another treachery for certs!

The thought of having Muriele as his wife made his blood race. He doubted she would consent to it, though, for she would not meet his eyes and edged away from him when he stepped close. The whole time he carried her on the horse, her body vibrated with tension until she slept. It was only then he let himself relax and glory in the feel of her in his arms.

He wanted Blackbriar. Had wanted it before he overthrew Baldor. He hadn't known how much until now. That it came with a bride who could fight for herself made the prospect even more appealing. She would be a helpmate in running Blackbriar. And he would be close enough to curb Olaf's lust for acquiring more land.

He determined to have her whether she was willing or not.

Two days later, Muriele looked suspiciously around the Chief's solar. Magnus and his father were there, as was Sweyn and Fergus. Standing alongside the fireplace in front of a dark tapestry, she had not noted the brown-clad priest until he moved over to stand beside Magnus. She frowned and turned to the Chief.

Why didn't he speak? He had been cordial and talked easily during their meals in the great hall. He'd asked all manner of questions and seemed pleased with her answers. Today he looked uneasy. Magnus appeared sterner than ever! Ah, she knew. The priest was his doing. Anger stirred in her belly.

"Ye have brought a man of God to question me?" She put her hands on her hips and glared at Magnus. "Is it your *honor* troubling ye so? Even though Graemme told ye what truly happened, ye still dinna believe me?"

She turned and faced the young man who shifted his feet. Why was he nervous?

"'Tis obvious ye dinna want to ask the questions. There is no need. You want to know if I planned to kill Feradoch of Kinbrace? I did not plan it. I had no need. But after what happened, I did try to kill him. The only thing I'm sorry for is I did not have a better weapon. If so, I'd have run him through or slit his throat — anything to stop him from choking Esa. If he had died, I would not waste one minute of remorse over it."

"Er, nay. It was not. But confession would be good for your soul." The young man's face flushed.

She frowned at him, ignored Magnus and turned to the Chief.

"Then why did ye summon me?"

Angus sat back in his chair and looked at Magnus. Since his son wouldn't speak, he did.

"The priest needs to know if the handfast was, um,

consummated before the events that followed."

"It is no one's business but mine."

"'Tis very important that we know," the priest said.

"I fail to see why. But nay, it was not consummated."

"Ye were in love with him. He was in love with ye. Why did he delay?"

Muriele face flamed. Her mouth worked but the words wouldn't come above a whisper. The priest could not hear and asked her to repeat it.

"He said no matter how beautiful I was he could not swive a woman with a back as disgusting as mine."

She started to run for the door, but Magnus caught her elbow. She tried to shake him off. He held tight.

"Can Esa vouch you did not have bed sport with him?" The Chief's voice softened.

Humiliation caused her eyes to well with tears. They wouldn't let her leave until they heard it all. She lifted her chin and swallowed back her shame.

"Do ye want me to strip naked and show ye why he couldna touch me without another's help?"

She shook off Magnus' hand. She reached up and started tugging at her clothes, beside herself with shame and grief she'd kept banked for so many months. Magnus caught her wrists and held them against his chest. She shoved at him but he didn't let her go.

"I was branded by my loving step-father. He lashed me too. Because he couldna take me, Feradoch added his own particular pattern amongst the others. Giving pain helped him to harden. Even so, 'twas not pleasurable enough to ignore the ugliness of my skin."

Strong arms pulled her against a hard chest. Magnus cupped her head against his shoulder and rubbed his cheek on her hair.

She heard the men talking about the handfast. Shamed she had broken down in front of them, she stifled her sobs.

"We agree, then. She did not set out to murder either Feradoch or Esa," Magnus said.

"Aye! Ye canna condemn a woman for wanting to gut the

bastard." The sound of Sweyn's outraged voice near bounced off the walls.

"I am satisfied the handfast was not consummated, therefore it is not legal. She is free to wed." The priest solemnly looked at Magnus and nodded his head.

"The ceremony will be held Sunday, in four days time." Chief Angus smiled.

Surprised, Muriele shoved Magnus so hard he rocked back on his heels.

"What! Free to marry? And what ceremony?"

Angus dismissed the priest. After he was gone, he told Muriele they'd had a messenger from Olaf saying that though she'd tried to kill Feradoch, he still lived. She must return and honor the handfast. If she didn't, they would wrest her from Clibrick Castle by force.

But since she had convinced the priest it wasn't a legal handfast, she was free to marry as the King ordered.

"Marry who? And when did he order this?"

Magnus thought it best to answer her questions from back to front.

"Kind David has written ye shall marry and return to rebuild Blackbriar. He sent orders a year ago, but Feradoch stole them. Another well-guarded messenger arrived several months past and King David demands the wedding take place as speedily as possible."

He hesitated before he answered anything further.

"Marry who?" Her eyes narrowed and her chin jutted.

"He specifically stated the man who conquered Blackbriar must marry its heir."

"You?" She shouted.

"*Me.*" Heavy determination resounded in that one word.

"Nay!"

"Aye. Ye will!"

Magnus stalked from the room before she could say another word.

Chapter 42

"**N**AY! I WILL NOT!"

Muriele shouted as Magnus heaved the door shut. His father patiently waited for her to stop pacing.

When her tempo slowed, the Chief spoke quietly.

"My son seems a hard man, one who could never soften toward anyone. It is my fault. I had misgivings about fostering him in Chief Olaf's keeping. Magnus is harsh and rigid because he grew to manhood under a tyrant. Had I known how cruel Olaf would be, I'd have done battle rather than go through with the oath."

"'Tis a pity he suffered such a harsh childhood. Still, I'll not forgive him leaving me in Feradoch's brutal clutches." Muriele's chin jutted in determination.

"Ye know ye have my friend's love?" Sweyn said. He sat sprawled on a chair, his legs stretched out.

She scowled. "Aye, sure he has. As much as Feradoch's. They show their love in agonizing ways," she said with scorn.

"I saw Magnus' face when we tracked hovering vultures to the top of a mountain. His face was sick with fear until we found the bodies were men. He knew they'd attacked you when he saw a horse had crushed one's skull. 'Twas a feat Bolt performed when he was still spry enough for battle."

She nodded. "If he loved me, he'd know I wouldn't murder without just reason. And he'd have left me at peace in the convent."

"Magnus relaxed for the first time in months when he learned ye were safe within their walls. He couldna leave ye there. He had to honor his vow."

"Aye. His vow. If Graemme had not found Esa and Grunda, yer friend who loves me so much would have hung me with his own hands." Determined to end the discussion, she headed for the door. "I willna marry a man who loves in such a way. The King will have to find another husband for Blackbriar."

Her long strides took her out of the room. The door shook when she slammed it.

Though she took her place at the high table between Magnus and Angus, she shunned talking to Magnus. He served her with courtesy, always careful to select the best food for her. He refilled her wine whenever the goblet was half-filled. Knowing she preferred the crust, he burnt his hands tearing off the ends of the hot loaves of bread.

He didn't force her in any way. He spoke softly. If she didn't answer, he didn't get angry. He patiently treated her with respect. Though his former lovers at the keep eyed and flirted with him, he ignored their efforts.

Magnus face was a dark mask of determination. The marriage would happen on Sunday whether she consented or not. 'Twas the only way to keep her safe from Feradoch.

On the third day, she could no longer ignore the preparations the castle workers were making for Sunday. The keep's seamstresses worked around the clock preparing kirtles and smocks to replace the ones left at Kinbrace.

The knight's wives all took delight in Muriele's open personality. Though she missed Esa, they kept her days from being lonely.

As the sun was directly overhead, the gatekeeper's horn sounded three times. Someone who belonged to Clibrick approached. Muriele ran to the window and saw Graemme. Surrounded by swarthy warriors, Esa and Grunda rode hanging onto their rider's waists.

She tore from the room, her heart beating with happiness at seeing her well-loved friends.

"Esa! Grunda!" She called out as she ran down the steps into the bailey.

She stood impatiently switching from one foot to the other until they galloped through the barbican and pulled to a halt in a cloud of dust.

"Grunda, I feared so for ye. If Chief Olaf found out ye helped Esa, he would have hunted ye down." She enveloped the old woman in a tight hug.

"After stitching the Devil's spawn, I left in the darkness of night. The fools took Esa where I thought they would. I quickly gave her the potion to bring her to."

"Esa! Ye are more beautiful than ever. Is yer neck healed? Ye are able to talk and sing?"

Esa's throaty laughter answered for her. "If you had not fought so hard, I wouldn't be doing either."

They hugged like two sisters long deprived of each other.

Sweyn stood nearby. His eyes searched over Esa for any lasting effects of Feradoch's mistreatment. When Muriele moved aside to let him come close, he took Esa's fingers and bowed, placing the top of her hand against his forehead, pledging himself to her.

Esa flushed and smiled. Without Feradoch looming in the background, mayhap Sweyn's love would bear fruit.

Magnus strolled over and buffeted Graemme on the left shoulder. "What news from Kinbrace?"

"We must talk immediately."

When the women headed to Muriele's room, she motioned her new Clibrick friends to come with them so they could become acquainted. When Fergus came to the room later and asked Grunda's presence before Chief Angus, she thought it strange.

In the Chief's solar, the commanders of the castle awaited Grunda.

Magnus introduced his father. Since she was the eldest and wisest of them all, they sought her council.

"Pfft! Ye want something. Come out with it."

"Graemme tells us Chief Olaf and Feradoch are preparing to besiege Clibrick if we dinna return Muriele to them."

"Graemme is a wise young man. Aye. They plan to force a

marriage between Feradoch and Muriele. If they get possession of these, they will be able to."

Grunda reached in the pocked of her old kirtle and brought out heavy purple velvet wrapped and tied with a purple silk ribbon.

"They belong to Muriele and Blackbriar." She shot a withering glance at Magnus before continuing. "When this young fool left Kinbrace without vowing his love for Muriele, she returned them to their hiding place for safety. She didn't have time to retrieve them when she fled Olaf."

She put the purple satin on Angus' table and untied it, letting the material open. Lying on the velvet were two rings.

The men stared at Ragnhild's wedding ring with the trinity knots and the blood red stone between them that Muriele's father had given his bride.

The second ring was Lord Colban's given to him by King David when he bestowed Blackbriar upon his friend. 'Twas heavy gold carved with Celtic designs and set with a large bloodstone from Iona.

"King David willna allow any man to marry Muriele without having these rings as evidence Blackbriar belongs to them."

Magnus let out a long sigh. "Those rings were what the King meant when he said the next Chief of the castle and his wife would be wearing two sacred rings."

"Aye. Muriele's wedding ring will be her mother's; her husband will wear Lord Colban's."

"Grunda, we need yer help," Magnus said. "Do ye still believe we were fated to be mates?"

"Any but a fool would know it. Pfft! And ye certainly behaved like one."

Grunda took his shoulders and stood him apart from the others. She stared at every feature in his face, looked him over from head to toe then walked around him several times, studying him.

"Ye haven't changed."

"A wedding is set for tomorrow," Magnus said. "'Tis the only way to keep Muriele safe, but she refuses to say the vows.

I will need yer help during the ceremony."

"She will wed with ye tomorrow, have no doubts. She may be angry on Monday, but it will be too late for her to change anything — if ye make haste with the, uh, consummation."

Magnus knew better than to question the old seer. He certainly didn't want her anger directed at him and striking his cock off with a lightning bolt!

While the castle prepared for the coming battle with Olaf, the keep prepared for the morrow's wedding.

Muriele was determined to stay mute at the wedding ceremony. She was none the wiser that it was beyond her control.

Sunday morn the sun rose without a cloud to dim its glow over Loch Naver. Dew sparkled on the fields of wild flowers, making them look magical as they danced in the breeze.

Grunda's face, when she came to wake Muriele, appeared years younger, for her eyes twinkled and her smile shone with happiness.

"Dinna look so pleased with yerself, Grunda. The preparations have been a waste of time. I told them it is for naught. They think I'll see the Magnificent Ruthless waiting with the priest and swoon with desire."

"Yer calling him magnificent is right. He rose early to greet the Morgans who live close enough to attend." She rolled her eyes and grinned. "I'm thinking Graemme will have to guard his brother to keep all the lustful lasses from locking him in a room and lifting his tunic to have their way with him."

"Ye are getting foolish in yer old age," Muriele said and grinned.

"I brought ye some mulled wine to stiffen yer spine, since ye seem so afeared of wedding."

"It will be a very *loooong* ceremony. Magnus will stand afore the priest 'till his beard grows white. I'll not repeat the vows."

Muriele took the pewter drinking cup and sipped. She wouldn't admit it, but her hands and feet were icy. Whenever she thought of defying Magnus in front of everyone at Clibrick, her stomach churned.

What if he became violent?

The door opened and Sweyn held it for Esa to enter, then handed her a tray.

"I come bearing food for the bride. And for the rest of us. Sweyn has been most helpful," she said happily after the door closed behind her.

Muriele swung her legs over the side of the bed and slipped on a robe as Esa placed a tray enticingly filled with hot scones, butter, cheese and porridge with fruit and honey, on the table.

Muriele relaxed and ate between sips of her wine. She felt much better with her stomach filled. Butterflies there had settled and she felt more confident. The women kept her so busy time flew. She bathed and Grunda washed her hair for her. Once they wrapped her in a drying towel, Esa soothed her by combing and drying her hair with a silk cloth to make it shine.

"Dinna drink too much else ye will snore when 'tis time to repeat yer vows." Grunda teased as she filled her wine cup.

"I will not be repeating any vows," Muriele said and smiled. She felt relaxed and became interested when Esa talked about the guests she had met.

"'Twas strange. When men came over to talk with me, Sweyn always seemed to have a reason for them to meet someone else."

"Strange? Are ye blind, Esa?" Muriele's laugh was close to a giggle. "Ever since I arrived at Kinbrace, Sweyn has been in love with ye."

"Sweyn?" Esa stopped combing Muriele's hair and blushed. "Let us get you clothed afore they come banging on the door with their sword hilts."

Muriele studied Esa as she and Grunda held up a shimmering midnight blue, long-sleeved smock for Muriele to slip over her head and arms. Next to come was a sleeveless sky blue kirtle so sheer the dark smock gleamed through. Four silky ribbons tied the front and back of the kirtle together. The shining blue material flowed through the openings like wispy clouds.

Grunda wrapped a long gold girdle low around her hips several times then linked it so the ends hung in the middle. A blood red stone hung from a clasp at the end of each gold chain.

"Where did this come from?"

"It seems yer Ruthless has acquired many magnificent pieces in his years of battle."

"Take it off. It should be saved for his wife." Muriele felt frantic. She couldn't take jewelry from a man she had no intentions of marrying.

"Nay. It is where it belongs," Grunda said.

The old woman's soothing voice calmed her. Strange, but it did feel like it belonged to her now.

They had no sooner put the final touch of winding flowers through Muriele's hair than they heard Sweyn's impatient tapping on the door. Esa went to open it and blushed when he smiled at her.

Chief Angus entered and held his bent arm up for Muriele to place her hand there. "I have come to escort you to the church, lass. I hope you dinna object if I take the place of your father?"

His warm flesh through the cloth made her feel calm and assured. She smiled at him as they left the room. She hardly noted when they left the keep, for it was an unusually beautiful day.

When they reached the steps of the small chapel at Clibrick, the number of people lined up on either side of the walkway amazed Muriele. The colorful tunics and kirtles caught her eyes, but one person stood out amongst all the rest. He calmly waited beside his brother at the door to the chapel. Magnificent was an apt expression for his silver and gold embroidered tunic and a sleeveless scarlet robe made of silk. His shoulder-length black hair was different from how she'd seen it before, for a braid at each temple accented his commanding face. His moustache and beard framing his lips and chin were clipped close. Not a hair was out of place.

The closer they came to him, the harder her heart beat. 'Twas strange, too, for she heard a voice soothing her. She looked around, but no one was close. Only Esa and Grunda walked behind her.

How did they reach him so quickly? He hadn't taken his black eyes from her the whole time she came toward him. She felt his tension coiled so tight he looked as if he was ready to spring on her at any moment.

When Chief Angus took her hand and placed it in his son's, Magnus' fingers closed gently around it. It felt comforting. Everything passed in a blur. She dreaded the time fast approaching for the vows. She stiffened. He cupped her hand in both of his, patting it. She heard a voice in her head soothing her.

Things are as they should be. Your parents are watching from above and want you to be safe with Magnus. Accept him. He was born to be your mate for life.

Graemme came to stand close to the priest. He carried a yellow pillow. She startled when she saw the familiar purple velvet cloth spread open on it. Candlelight on the jewels sent rainbows flashing on the cloth. Was she imagining things?

Magnus watched her beautiful face as she put her hand into his. It felt warm, not icy like he had feared. He turned and nodded to the priest for him to get on with the ceremony. He'd already warned him to be brief.

It was. The poor young priest recited all of the preliminary words as quickly as he could. He looked confident when he asked if there was any man who could show just cause why they may not wed. Had there been an objection, he wouldn't have heard it.

He skipped from there to ask Magnus if he would have Muriele to be his wedded wife, to love, honor and cherish her, forsaking all others.

"I will." His answer was strong enough for every person to hear.

His grip tightened on Muriele's hand when the young man turned to Muriele and repeated the same words to have Magnus as her wedded husband.

She tilted her head to the side as if listening. A slight smile wavered on her face and she nodded without speaking. He felt waves of energy around her and glanced behind Muriele to see Grunda. She fixed her gaze unwaveringly on the back of Muriele's head then gave a slight nod.

"I will." Muriele's voice sounded dreamlike.

The priest turned to Graemme and blessed the rings. Afterward, he handed Magnus her mother's ring to put on her hand.

He took her left hand, repeating the ring vows on each finger until he slid it onto her ring finger.

Muriele looked at her hand, puzzled, then shrugged and smiled at him. The priest handed her father's ring to her and gave her much the same vows to repeat, except when she placed it on his ring finger she hesitated and looked at the priest. He repeated more strongly, "With this ring I promise to obey."

Magnus thought she would finally balk. He looked at Grunda as Muriele stared at Magnus hand. Grunda didn't take her eyes from Muriele, but her lips moved wordlessly.

Muriele sighed and slowly said, "With this ring I promise to obey," and seated it over his knuckle.

The rest of the ceremony was over swiftly. When the priest nodded, Magnus turned Muriele to him and kissed her gently.

The kiss was soft and pleasant. The heat coming from Magnus' body spread welcome warmth through her limbs, reminding her of standing before a baking oven on a cold day. She took a deep breath of his familiar sensual pine scent and sighed.

Chief Angus welcomed her as his daughter-by-law by hugging her and kissing her cheek. Graemme, too, did the same, but his kiss was more intense. No doubt to tease his brother? Esa hugged her and Grunda cradled her as she would a youngling.

When she said, "You did the right thing. He will protect you always," Muriele jolted. 'Twas Grunda's voice she'd heard during the ceremony.

Magnus and the crowd flowed swiftly back to the keep, for the wind flowing over Loch Naver began to turn the day chilly. There was much laughter as everyone hurried up the steps into the warmth of the great hall.

From the moment Magnus had put her mother's wedding

ring on her finger, she had felt a calm peace flow through her. Lord Colban's ring looked right on Magnus' competent hands. She shivered at the thought it might have graced Feradoch's elegant finger before she found out what a snake he was.

Tables and benches filled the great hall. White clothes and flowers were at every long table, silver trenchers and goblets served the knights and guests while warriors and archers were to use bread trenchers. Food was plentiful and prepared with the utmost care, much as she had known at Blackbriar.

Magnus must be pleased, also, for a soft smile lifted the corners of his lips. His eyes sparkled. The evening flew with entertainment between each of the courses brought to the tables. She felt a little uncertain of herself from having partaken of so many toasts from well-wishers.

Muriele frowned as flashes of memory at her meeting with his family several days ago. She heard herself yelling, "Nay." Unease pricked at her mind. Why had she given in so easily? He had left her without a word of his feelings a year ago. Had she given up her pride to be with him? Or was her fear of Olaf and Feradoch the prime reason?

"'Tis time for ye to go above, Muriele."

Hearing Magnus husky whisper in her ear, panic near over-come her.

Flashes of the rapacious look on Feradoch's face, the hate in his eyes, came back to haunt her. What if with the scars he'd added to her flesh, Magnus found her back unsightly? She clutched the table, her knuckles whitened. Her right hand slid slowly toward Magnus' eating knife.

His hand covered hers and drew it away. He gripped her chin and turned her face to him.

"Go above, wife."

She didn't want to go above. When she did, he would follow her. Fear tightened her chest. If she displeased him, he would turn on her.

It would be more torturous than a beating by Feradoch.

Chapter 43

MAGNUS FELT HER FEAR and patted her hand. Her father's ring was very noticeable on his finger. She stared at it, and somehow, it must have reassured her for her hands relaxed. He stood and helped her to rise. When Esa and Grunda led her from the room, he sighed with relief.

What if she had screamed "Nay!" as she had yesterday? Or, worse yet, pulled a dagger on him in front of their guests? It sickened him to think he would have to force Muriele to make their marriage complete.

No one knew how much time they had before Chief Olaf and his army arrived. In order for their wedding to be legal, the priest must verify they had consummated their vows. If not, Feradoch could claim prior possession to her.

Graemme came to sit beside him and grinned. "Never have I seen ye so tense about bedding a lass, brother!"

"Ye dinna know my new wife very well." Magnus snorted then shook his head in shame. "She has drawn a dagger on me more than once. Ye'd be tense as well if ye had to search for weapons afore ye bedded yer bride."

"Hm. 'Twould be a bit awkward," he admitted. "How will ye go about it?"

"While we were being wed, Gille searched the room and through her things. He took them to Sweyn for safekeeping." He grunted and shook his head. "She had acquired a veritable arsenal."

"I canna imagine the beautiful lass being able to wield a blade," his father said.

"Get her angry or cause her to fear ye and ye'll see for yerself."

"Surely she couldn't have concealed any on her person before the ceremony? Ye should have naught to worry about," Graemme said.

"Ha! She wears a blade strapped to each leg. If she is naked, it will be easier. If not, I will hold her in my arms and kiss her, all the while smoothing my hands over her body."

"And if ye find nothing?" His father asked.

"It doesn't mean she is not prepared. When she isn't looking, I will check beneath her pillow and the floor under the bed."

Graemme tried to smother a laugh, but it came out more of a cough. "The night will nigh be gone by the time ye swive her."

"Ye wouldna think it so funny if ye were in his shoes," Angus said. "Have ye not thought the last time his bride was to be bedded, the man rejected and shamed her? He beat her without mercy?"

Graemme nodded. "Aye. Ye will have to go easy with her. Ye canna let her memories cause her to fight ye."

"Well, son, you had best complete your duty afore daylight comes." Angus patted his shoulder and smiled.

"Aye, and change yer scowl to a smile afore ye enter yer chamber." Graemme had lost his teasing smile. His face was serious now.

God knew he was more than ready to take Muriele. All this long day, his loins had been afire. But it was important he took her in the right way. If he came to her in weakness, their marriage would begin with her having the upper hand.

He shook his head as he ascended the stairwell. He would be gentle, but firm. She must know from the start she was now his property to do with as he liked. If he didn't want her to go about with a blade strapped to her leg, then she would not. He needed to be keep her on a tight leash or she would never obey him.

It was unthinkable!

His hand was on the latch afore he knew it. He pressed his

lips together and opened the door. His chamber at Clibrick was thrice the size of Kinbrace's. A peat fire burned in the hearth giving light to half the room, the rest was in shadows. His bed stood at the far wall between two massive windows with wooden shutters pulled tightly closed. It was overlarge, giving more pillows under which to hide a weapon. He did not require much in a room other than his bed, a table with two chairs, a washstand, and a large armchair by the hearth. He had ordered a cabinet made to hold her clothes instead of pegs on the walls.

Muriele and Esa stood beside the bed. Esa had her arm around Muriele's shoulder and patted it. She gave him a stern glance.

By Lucifer's snotty nose! Did she think he would enter and throw Muriele on the bed to have his way? Although, that's what his tarse was begging him to do.

Grunda smiled at him. "I brought the wedding mead yer father's Alewife made for ye." She poured a goodly amount into two pewter goblets tooled with wedding knots. She put one hand to hover over each goblet, threw back her head and shut her eyes. Wind whipped through the room, though the door and shutters stood closed. In the strange voice she used when seeing the future, she spoke.

"Harm was done to the daughter of Ragnhild's blood. It will be as she vowed. Clans will suffer. Fathers will fight sons. Brothers will fight brothers. All is split asunder, never to be as it was afore!

"Yer body will crave only yer wife from this night hence. She will swell with yer first son within a moon's passing. Make no mistakes in the days to come else ye will lose all."

"Enough of yer foretelling, old woman. Yer words are enough to shrivel even a cock made of steel. If 'tis sons ye want me to plant, be gone with ye." His voice was harsh with impatience.

As Grunda cackled with laughter, the strange turbulence stopped.

"Come, Esa, we had best leave afore he shrivels to naught but a nub."

After the women left, Magnus stared at Muriele as if he had never seen her before. His face grew taut with desire and his body near pulsated with the need to lie atop her.

"The deed must be done tonight. We can celebrate our wedding in two ways. If ye fight me, I will use force. If ye dinna, I will be gentle as possible for one of my size."

He stared into her eyes. Did he try to read her thoughts?

"Ye remember when we had bed sport afore? Never did I hurt ye and I dinna want to ever cause ye pain. When the time comes, I will cause Feradoch to regret every harsh touch on ye."

She watched his eyes, his face, and read naught but honesty there. This last caused her to relax. She had no need for the blades hid beneath her pillow and under the bed, nor the short sword under the feather pallet. She'd hidden them afore the ceremony.

Grunda had made her a sleeveless robe made of the thinnest green fabric. It had no ties, no way to hold it together except her hands. She glanced down and realized though they were on the far side of the bed from the hearth, every line of her body was visible to Magnus' dark eyes.

She fumbled for the opening and pulled each side across herself, trying to be less visible. Magnus shook his head. Slowly. Then came to put his hands atop hers. His thumbs flicked her fingers, letting her know to let the robe go. She did.

Her skin prickled, became sensitive. She stiffened, not wanting him to remove the robe and demand she show her body to him like Feradoch had done.

He sensed her thoughts, for he dropped her hands and turned to the table. Picking up a goblet of mead in each hand, he held one out to her. She took it, though she had downed more wine at the table today than she ever had. With all the different courses, it had been a long meal.

He drank, his eyes darkening to midnight as he watched her over the rim. She gulped half of hers, wondering if she should speak. Perhaps not, for the only word repeating in her head was "Nay."

She doubted it would cause him to be gentle.

Was he reading her mind? His gaze bored into hers so intently she thought mayhap he could.

He put his cup down. She backed up, expecting him to seize her. Instead, he took off his scarlet robe and tossed it across the back of the armchair. He kept his gaze on her, his movements slow.

The braids at each of his temples seemed to make him even more commanding. He looked natural with them, like they belonged beside his face. When had he taken off the gold chain belt and his sword? She blinked.

Magnus didn't attempt to take off his silver and gold tunic. Sitting on the edge of the bed, he pulled off his boots. When he lifted one leg to pull off his boot, she saw his heavy balls resting between his thighs. Only the base of his prick showed. She blushed, knowing the silky top was looking toward his head and not his feet.

"Would ye refill our mead, wife?"

Muriele hesitated. The word 'wife' had sent a warm spot to her belly. But to do as he asked, she would have to turn her back to him.

"Please, my wife?"

He'd tended her back in the forest. He wouldn't be surprised at how much uglier it must now be. She filled the cups, but before she could turn and hand his to him, the warmth of his body near touched hers. Her belly quivered. The empty spot between her legs contracted, craving for him to fill it. She squeezed her legs together trying to ignore it.

Magnus hands rubbed down from her shoulders to her fingertips, caressing her with their warmth. Pressing himself against her back, he took her hands, crossed them beneath her breasts with his as he wrapped her in his arms. She felt his warm breath on her ear as he moved his head down to brush his cheek against hers.

She twisted in his arms. Took his braids in her hands and pulled his face down so she could feel the smoothness of his bare skin and the soft hair framing his upper lip and chin. 'Twas like his lips were within a small frame, accenting them. They looked very sensual today. His kiss proved soft and inviting. He opened his mouth and gently probed her lips with his tongue. She parted them for him to enter. The deeper the kiss, the harder she pulled on his hair. Finally, he lifted his lips.

"Let us drink the mead and gaze out at the loch. 'Tis beautiful in moonlight." His voice sounded harsh with passion.

He handed her a cup, led her to the window and opened the wooden shutter. The evening breeze blew in, but she didn't care. It truly was a beautiful sight. Without speaking, they drank the mead. She felt his gaze on her and wondered why he didn't look at the water? 'Twas silly of her. He'd seen it in the moonlight many times.

When had he taken their empty cups? While she still stood at the window, he went over to bank the fire then came back. He closed the shutter, and in the dim light, she watched his shadow as he removed his tunic and dropped it.

Her breathing quickened. She wished she could see his magnificent body. He padded softly over to her. His thumbs lowered her robe off her shoulders and arms and let it slither down to her feet. She took a deep breath, remembering all the nights of lovemaking they'd enjoyed at Kinbrace.

Muriele was more than ready for him when he began kissing her. He picked her up and coaxed her legs around his hot body. She clung to his shoulders and her breath caught as he lifted her buttocks and both hands started playing with her sex. One hand squeezed her buttock while the fingers of his other explored around her nether lips until her juices began to flow.

Putting his longest finger into her hot body, he explored around then inched a second finger in. He plunged so fiercely it lifted her. His other hand came to join in the play, working itself between their bodies and finding her hard nub. He rubbed then squeezed gently. She contracted around his fingers and groaned. He rubbed harder and faster, smearing her wetness around her opening.

She begged. "Please!"

He had to know what she wanted! When his cock didn't

enter, she grabbed a braid in her mouth and tugged.

"Vixen!"

He rubbed hard on her nub until she squirmed and kicked his back, tried to find his prick, but he didn't let her.

"I am the master, my love."

Magnus pulled her nub with just the right pressure and her body quivered and shook in a fierce climax. Her body grasped his fingers in an iron grip. He plunged deep and waited until her spasms weakened.

She gasped for breath and expected him to put her down, but he did not. He started over. She was twice as sensitive as before, and in a few short breaths was near to pleading again. This time, he lifted her buttocks and lowered her slowly onto his steel-hard cock. Though she was weeping for him, the year without sex had tightened her pathway. When he filled her, she could think of nothing, could feel nothing, but his steel-hard prick inside her.

Each time, he built her to a pitch then stopped and soothed her only to begin again when her quivering slowed. She was about to scream when he walked over to the bed. Her arms and legs tightened and clung to him as he crawled with her until he reached the center of the bed. Once there, she loosened the iron grip of her limbs and settled on the sheets.

He pounded inside her, rocking her until her head met the headboard. She thought her mind had exploded for a bit there, for light came through her eyelids. Or it could have been the fireplace, for Magnus didn't cease his rhythm. After a few breaths, it was dark again.

When he finally allowed himself to come, he didn't pull out as he had at Kinbrace. Plunging all the way in, he spurted his seed. Her body's spasms milked him of every drop.

Sweat covered them both when he finally pulled out and fell to her side. He held her close and put her head on his shoulder.

They didn't get much sleep. In fact, if she started to drift off, his tantalizing hands awakened a new excitement in her. He took her in a variety of ways, each of them as satisfying as the last. She drowsily thought being on top was her favorite, for he had allowed her some control. But she knew he meant this night to be a lesson she would remember.

In a most delightful way, he showed her he was in command

They fell asleep as the sun began to rise.

"Ye are up early, brother. Hunger must have made ye leave the bed with such a beautiful wife still fast asleep."

Magnus plucked a bannock from the kilt gathered above his belt and wiggled it at Graemme. "Had two of them already. Check the knights' equipment while Sweyn and I see to the warriors."

As he walked away, Graemme laughed and called to him, "Ye best adjust the end of yer kilt to cover the claw marks on yer back!

Magnus shrugged. They wouldn't be noticeable amongst the old scars there. He had worries far more pressing. He expected Chief Olaf and his army to appear at any moment. They posted lookouts throughout Ben Clibrick at their back 'Twas the most likely way to attack the castle since an army could hide in its lush forests. Loch Naver was to their front. Their sides were low hills down to the waters of the loch.

When Magnus joined him, Sweyn had already started checking the warriors' weapons as they stood in two long lines. If a sword didn't cut a blade of grass they held out, the warrior had to hone it again. They checked the chains and wood handles of the morningstars, the shaft on the war hammers, studied the points on the spears and the feathers on arrows and the strings on bows. They immediately fixed anything appearing to have any weakness.

Magnus ignored the men's teasing about his back. He didn't mind. His wife was the only woman he had ever swived who matched his passion with fervor. He smothered a grin. They would truly be startled to see her telltale marks on his arse!

Who would think such an elegant woman could be so wanton?

When they had done all they could, Graemme and his father joined Magnus beside the well as the two young men doused their heads with cool water.

Chief Angus cleared his throat when Magnus finished and draped the damp drying cloth around his neck to cool him down. He met his father's dark gaze and tilted his head.

Angus nodded before he spoke. "The priest can truthfully tell Chief Olaf and King David he personally saw the vows consummated last eve."

"I heard the door opening and its closing. Had Muriele known, she would not have taken it lightly." Lightly was putting it mildly. He was glad she had been in the throes of passion; else, she would have torn into him with teeth and claws!

"Er, are ye sure ye made yer bride swoon with joy last eve?" Graemme's eyes widened.

Magnus looked behind him and saw his bride charging toward him like a Valkyrie ready to collect his soul and fly it to Valhalla.

Before she was halfway to him, he felt her fury.

"What right did ye have to take my weapons?"

Muriele skidded to a stop, frowned briefly at his father and brother and came so close to Magnus her nose near bumped his chest.

"A man shouldn't get his toes cut from beneath the bed when he climbs onto the mattress. Nor should he have a finger severed when he puts his hand under a pillow to grab the end of the bedding whilst striving to satisfy his wife's hearty appetites" His lips twitched at the corners. "Did ye plan to clip my tarse with yer short sword under the mattress?"

"Deny me my weapons again and ye'll find yer stones missing one morning." With hands on her hips, her eyes shot angry sparks at him.

"That seems quite harsh. Gille took them to hone and polish the blades. Ye have neglected yer weapons since I last saw ye." He rubbed his chin as his dark eyes somberly studied her. "But I am quite fond of my stones, large as they are. With such a dire threat to them, I am inclined to have yer weapons added to the armory."

"Do so and I'll acquire others." Her chin jutted stubbornly.

When her stomach growled from hunger, it spoiled her determined demeanor. She blinked and blushed when the men laughed at her surprised look.

"Come, 'tis time for the noon meal. Everyone else has already gathered and they canna eat until Father's seated," Graemme said. "After yer *active* night, ye both need sustenance."

"Aye, love. Ye must build up yer strength before night falls."

When Muriele gasped, Magnus laughed. His brother and father looked at each other and smiled at the hoarse sound.

It was near two years since they had heard him laugh.

Chapter 44

At nightfall, Magnus guided Muriele to stand on the fur rug before the fireplace so he could enjoy the firelight dancing over her velvety skin.

"Let me," Magnus brushed Muriel's hands away and began to untie the laces on either sides of her tunic. "Unveiling a woman, piece by piece, is an aphrodisiac."

Proving it, he removed each item of clothing with his lips, teeth and tongue. His breath rasped when her smock lingered on the hardened nipples of her creamy breasts. With his tongue, he flipped the cloth over the nipple, closed his lips over the turgid flesh and gently aroused it with his teeth. Not wanting to neglect the other breast, he did the same. When her smock slithered to her feet, his lips trailed from her chest down her soft skin. His tongue's tip dipped in her navel, teasing it while his hands reached up to tweak her nipples, letting them know he had not forgotten them.

Feeling his hot tongue on her taut belly, her legs quivered. His lips caressed over the hollow where her legs joined.

"Ah, so soft. So sweet."

He gripped her knees and urged her legs to open. She grasped his shoulders, no doubt fearing she'd lose her balance and topple over.

Cupping her buttocks, his lips explored amongst the blond curls there. She jerked when his nose moved aside the curls hiding her hard nub. He groaned as his lips closed over it. Softly, he plucked it then tormented her by swirling his tongue around and around it. When he drew it into his mouth and gently scraped it with his teeth, her hips thrust at him. She needed more than gentle kisses now.

Hands that had been rubbing and squeezing her beautiful nether cheeks, reached between them to plunge his fingers in her center while his mouth did its magic. When he removed his fingers, he widened her stance and explored her with his tongue. She gasped and tried to pull back. He didn't let her. He wanted to taste her skin from head to toe. She was so sweet. Like hot honey.

Muriele tangled her fingers in his hair, not knowing if she wanted to pull him away or bring him tighter to her. Shamefully, she knew the answer. She rocked against him, keening low in her throat. Quivering now, she thought the torment would never end.

Swiftly, he grasped her waist then pulled her down to the fur rug beside the fireplace. Kneeling, he pulled her legs on either side of him, lifted her body to meet his tarse and thrust all the way, bringing a sigh to her lips.

Spread beneath him with his heavy-lidded eyes gleaming at her, she felt wanton. He stared at her body. Watched his tanned hands exploring her breasts. She watched him watching her, and the tight look on his face was enough to make her convulse with her climax. She reached for him, wanting him to cover her, but he did not.

As her climax slowed, he turned her on her stomach, reached an arm under her waist and lifted her to her knees. She tried to fight him. Her back was bare to his eyes. The fire's light was bright and he'd see every ugly mark of Feradoch's belt.

"Shh, let me."

One hand reached to her shoulders and forced them to the rug while he slowly entered her from behind. She felt vulnerable. More so than at any time in her life. For the first time, she felt his power over her mind and body. Knew he more than matched her.

His hand traced each mark. His thrusts became faster and he adjusted her so she was no longer on her knees but flat on the rug, his one hand beneath her sex holding her up to meet his thrusts.

His lips kissed the scars imprinted by the wicked belt. She felt his tongue lathe the shameful brand from her stepfather. He slid his face over it and up to her shoulder. His mouth opened wide and he clamped his teeth on her right shoulder beside her neck. It didn't hurt. He didn't mean it to. It was a sign of possession as they both released their passion. When he spurted his seed into her, she felt it more than at any other time.

His climax went on until he filled her. Reluctantly, he slowly withdrew from her body.

When she rolled over on her back, he had already risen and brought over a basin of water and a cloth. He rinsed off his tarse then knelt. She would have taken the cloth from him, but he shook his head. Nay, he wanted to do this.

'Twas strange allowing him to do this woman's job. The man everyone feared as Magnus the Ruthless was as gentle as a troubadour when she least expected it.

He put the basin aside to lie down beside her. With his arm under her head, her back tucked neatly against him, they slept.

They must have slept much of the night, for daylight came quickly. Magnus stirred, uneasy. Jumping to his feet, he went to the shuttered window. Muriele awoke, hearing shouts from the guards upon the curtain walls surrounding the castle. When she reached the window, she saw why.

The mimic of dawn came from the west, shining light above the hill leading down to the waters of the loch. Magnus gave out a bellow to the guards below to sound the alarm.

Coming toward them was Olaf's army riding through the night. Every man bore a torch aloft as he galloped his horse through the shallow water where the loch met land. Water splashed, the torches making the droplets as brilliant as jewels. The horses stepped high as they charged toward the castle.

Magnus threw on the tunic he'd dropped on the floor earlier, picked up his sword and wound his belt around him until it hung at the right level.

"Get dressed and strap on all yer weapons. Gather the

women into the great hall and stay close to Esa and Grunda. I'll send the older men who can no longer fight on the walls. They can still use their weapons."

"Can't I help on the walls? I have my bow and arrows, and you know my aim is accurate."

"Nay! I need ye here to protect the women and the aged. Dinna show yerself to Olaf unless I call for ye."

"But ..."

"Obey as ye vowed!" He grabbed his claymore propped against his wooden cabinet and was out the door.

She'd obey him as long as it was reasonable. If she could help, he would just have to accept that. She dressed in her oldest kirtle, one much like the one she'd had on when climbing the tree. It gave her legs freedom to run or jump astride a horse if need be.

She stood by the window as she strapped her two knives on her legs and her short sword around her waist. Watching the happenings below, it looked like Olaf and his men were flying over the water. They shouted Viking war threats or curses. She didn't know which. Carrying torchlights, they appeared warriors from an ancient age!

Animal pelts covered their shoulders; leather belts held scanty bits of wool around their waist. On their stocky legs, they wore animal hide boots up to their knees, the fur against their skin. They carried torches in one hand and spears and swords in the other.

Olaf was easy to spot with his fiery red hair long and shaggy around his shoulders. He dressed as his warriors. She had never seen him thus. A man who had once looked like an ordinary Highlander now looked like a savage.

Feradoch, too, was visible. He was the only warrior to shun his heritage. She snorted, knowing he felt himself too comely to cover his body with ugly clothing. His hair blew like a silky, yellow pennant in the wind.

Only the soldiers following Olaf and Feradoch wore their Viking helmets. Those riding behind them were without armor on their heads, but round leather shields hung from their arms.

They carried bows and full quivers across their shoulders. Claymore's across their backs. Did they expect an easy capitulation from Clibrick?

She knew what they thought. Olaf would convince Magnus to hand over herself and Esa. Because of his terrible vow! Her stomach churned. She looked toward the helmet stand. Olaf's ancient helmet he'd given Magnus at the blood oath was gone! She prayed he would not wear it. It would only serve as a reminder of what he had vowed.

The sun had risen before the balance of Olaf's army had splashed onto the beach afore Clibrick Castle. Magnus was not surprised at their numbers, for he'd trained many of them. Never had he thought he'd live to regret forcing them to be skillful.

He did now.

Not a word came from Olaf. He calmly set up a camp of tents spread clean across the far opening close to the waters of the loch. He walked out onto a large layer of rocks on the water then stood staring out over Loch Naver. He seemed sad to Magnus. As though he didn't like being here.

Olaf wore only short wool around his middle and animal pelts covered his chest. He'd left on his skin boots, not caring waves splashed up on them. His shaggy, reddish hair flew away from his face, and his beard ruffled in the stiff breeze. Did he close his eyes and savor the feel of the sun and the mist on his face?

Magnus tore his eyes from his foster father and joined Angus and Graemme with their three commanders. They had talked over and practiced all siege preparations since they'd first learned Muriele had fled Kinbrace. Archers and slingers defended the walls at each embrasure, ready to step behind the merlons when fighting began. They were a massive show of force letting Olaf know he wouldn't have an easy time of it.

Even the women and children had been busy. Muriele and Esa had gathered them in the great hall. The women brought every piece of clean cloth they could use for bandages. They tore them in strips and rolled them in balls, following Grunda's instructions. The older women were in charge of the children. They took them up to the third floor where the windows were too high for arrows to reach.

While Esa kept the women occupied, Muriele and Grunda gathered herbs for cleaning, healing and lessening the pain of wounds. Later in the day after all preparations were completed, Muriele made sure the women armed themselves with their eating knives. They brought down the oldest children and all went out into the baileys where she told them to collect the biggest stones they could find and build piles of them to keep a ready supply for the slingers.

She watched from a tower window looking down at the front barbican where Magnus, his father and Gramme stood. Olaf and Feradoch rode their horses close to the walls, showing they had no weapons. Having lived with Angus through most of his life, Feradoch knew Chief Angus would never order Clibrick warriors to attack unarmed men.

Muriele shivered when she heard Chief Olaf's thunderous voice.

"Angus, meet us on open ground. Unarmed. As we are. We fathers have shared our sons. Surely we can settle this vow without bloodshed between us."

Magnus stepped in the open embrasure above the barbican. With his hands on his hips, his head held high, he looked half Highlander and half fierce Viking.

"We agree. We can settle this peacefully when all the facts are known," he answered.

She watched, horrified as Chief Angus and Magnus went down to the barbican door and laid their weapons aside. The guards opened the iron-studded door enough for each man to pass through, and then slammed the oak beam down on the supports. Every archer on the walls nocked an arrow and aimed their weapons at the two Vikings.

They no sooner approached the men than Feradoch started making demands.

"As your blood brother, you must honor your oath to avenge me. The witch-woman Muriele killed the lass Esa. She …"

Magnus held up his hand for silence. "Esa isna dead."

"She is. I saw her dead body myself and had her disposed of in the woods," Chief Olaf said.

"Look atop the barbican." Magnus turned and bellowed, "Sweyn, bring Esa forward!"

Sweyn reached behind him and took Esa's hand to bring her to stand at his side. She glared down at Feradoch with such contempt he flinched.

No one could mistake the dusky beauty nor fail to recognize her throaty voice.

"I live, though Feradoch tried to throttle me. Had Muriele not stopped him when she did, Grunda wouldn't have been able to save me."

Olaf called to Sweyn, "Have the lass turn around so we may see 'tis truly her."

Esa put her arms in the air and stood before an embrasure. She turned slowly, several times, letting them see her unmistakable tall body and black tightly curled hair. She stopped when Sweyn took her shoulders and gently put her behind him again.

Olaf looked his son in the eye, but Feradoch broke the contact. Olaf's shoulders were a little less straight. A crease formed between his eyes.

"So Esa lives! The witch Muriele still has to pay for trying to kill me!" Feradoch shouted.

Olaf's eyes chilled as he looked at Angus. "Esa doesn't matter. Keep her. But Muriele must return with us. Your son will honor his vow else I will topple this castle to the ground till naught is left but stones."

"Esa matters," Angus said. "Because she lives, she and Grunda told us what occurred that night. Feradoch thrashed Muriele with his belt and tried to kill Esa. I canna call what Lady Muriele did was treachery to my foster son, but defense for herself and her friend.

Feradoch stepped belligerently forward, his nose almost meeting Angus' own. "They tell you lies, old fool. She was born with the mark of a knife's blade betwixt her shoulders. Could anyone but a witch cut with a blade made of skin?"

He straightened and showed a small scar on his arm then stepped back.

"Ye are daft!" Magnus near snorted with disgust. "Her stepfather's to blame for branding her. And ye are to blame for thrashing her. The stones on yer belt left unmistakable scars on her skin."

Olaf frowned at Feradoch then looked back at Magnus. "There is no blame in a man thrashing a woman. But it is treachery when Muriele tried to kill him on the night of their handfast."

Angus spoke up. "There was no treachery. She didna stab him for the beating but was trying to save her friend. Think on it. I have a priest inside the chapel. We will ask him to help settle this. What say you we cool our tempers and meet again afore nightfall?"

Feradoch scowled, ruining the beauty of his face.

"Nay, we settle it now. Send for the priest!"

"As you wish. Fergus, send Father David to us."

ChAPTER 45

MURIELE WAITED WITH ESA at the solar window where they could see the clearing beyond the castle walls. When a knight escorted the priest to the two Chiefs, she wondered if Olaf had thought of some ploy to force Magnus to return her. How she wished she were the witch they claimed. If so, she'd turn herself into a mouse and scurry close to overhear them. Her stomach sank. Mayhap she should make plans now to escape from the castle.

As she quietly threaded her way through the women in the solar, bits and pieces of the women's whispers drifted to her. It seemed some thought she should return to Kinbrace. As many of them knew Feradoch, they were fearful if the Gunns won the battle, they and their families' lives would become a living Hell. Those who Feradoch had branded and forced to be his leman wanted Chief Angus to fight and drive him away.

Below in the clearing, young Father David listened closely to Feradoch. The priest's face was pale, his expression earnest. Magnus hoped he wasn't afeared of the Gunns' fierce appearance. He certainly looked it.

"Uh, hmm, I agree. I do not believe there is anything wrong in beating a woman."

Feradoch's face brightened with triumph.

"But," the priest continued, "the weapon for punishment should be as church law stipulates. A stone-riddled belt, no matter how beautiful, is not the same as a twig as large as your thumb."

"Shite on you!" Feradoch shook his fist in the priest's face.

The warrior guarding Father David shoved himself between them.

Feradoch didn't care that he cursed at a priest. "There still is her crime of trying to murder me." He looked at him with scorn. "You hide like a scullery maid. Step forward like a man. There is no church law saying an eating knife is not a weapon!"

Father David took the warrior's arms and urged him to move aside.

"Nay. It is a weapon, truly. But Lady Muriele used it in defense of saving another soul." He looked around at all of them. "Of the men you have killed, surely there were many you did to save someone else."

Olaf grabbed his son's shoulders to keep him from attacking the priest. Feradoch near frothed at the mouth on hearing Muriele defended. When they were far enough away, the Chief shook him and whispered fiercely.

Feradoch's eyes gleamed with triumph when they returned.

"Father David, we have a religious problem for you to solve. The Lady Muriele and I declared a handfast on the night she fled. She should be returned to me and honor her holy vows." His chest expanded with triumph. His smile became evil.

Father David ran a hand over his cheeks and mouth. He looked to be searching for the right words before he spoke again. Finally, he took a deep, shuddering breath.

"The Lady Muriele told me with Chief Angus, Sir Magnus and the castle commanders as witnesses, the handfast was not consummated. She has been absent from you for more than a year, most of the time sequestered in a convent with no other men. Just two days past, I joined Lady Muriele and Sir Magnus as man and wife by the holy sacrament of marriage."

"What about …." Chief Olaf started.

"I myself observed the marriage consummated. Thoroughly, I might add." The priest's blush was so red all his blood must have gone to his face.

Feradoch screamed and leapt at Magnus. Magnus' heart lurched. Where had his foster brother hidden the knife? It must have been within a pocket of his bright blue tunic.

Magnus raised his right arm to defend himself. When Feradoch struck, their arms clashed. Magnus shoved as hard as he could, deflecting Feradoch's aim. The blade grated against the top of Magnus's collarbone and ripped through the flesh of his shoulder.

He jumped back, then crouched and waited for the next attempt. When his father and Chief Olaf tried to step between them to intercede, he would have none of it.

"Dinna intrude!" Magnus yelled. "We will settle this."

The two fathers moved back. Both armies bristled with arrows already held in taut bows, waiting for their Chief's signal.

Olaf shouted and waved at his men to stay away. Angus put up his hand toward the battlements in a hold gesture. The priest grabbed his cross and started feverishly praying.

Muriele had already found a way to leave the castle. When the negotiations had begun, several of the men guarding the postern gate had run along the wall walks to watch the men below, leaving fewer guards. She had just taken her opportunity to slip out when she heard the men on the barbican shouting.

She pulled her skirts up above her knees. Her long legs and fear made her run as fleet as a doe. She skidded to a halt behind the priest. He jumped near out of his robes when he heard her panting breath behind him.

"Nayyyy!" She screamed and ran toward Magnus, her short sword in hand.

Chief Angus grabbed her arm and swung her back to him. His iron vise around her kept her still, though she struggled like a woman accursed.

"Dinna distract him, daughter. He will fight his own battle and not thank you for interfering."

How could he be so calm? Her heart fluttered and jerked until she was near dizzy from its haphazard beat. The men grappled on the ground. Magnus' left hand clenched Feradoch's wrist holding the knife. Feradoch was able to twist his arm enough Magnus lost his hold. He sprang back and crouched, circled and watched for an opening beneath Feradoch's weapon.

Whenever Feradoch struck out with the knife, Magnus ducked and dodged avoiding it. Blood covered the front of his clothing and dripped to the ground. Muriele whimpered and bit her tongue to keep from distracting him.

Finally, Magnus sprung at Feradoch and grabbed his arm again. Feradoch kicked Magnus' leg and topped him onto his back. The muscles in their sweaty arms strained as Feradoch's blade aimed for Magnus' neck. Where they were near equal in their wresting skills, it forced Magnus to use his left hand, weakened from the shoulder wound.

Feradoch used his body's weight to force the knife closer until the tip was near Magnus' throat. Feradoch snarled and ground out words filled with hate. "All these years, you stole my father's love. You deserve to die, you bastard!"

Magnus grunted and gave a mighty heave with his legs until they rolled over. Now, 'twas Feradoch's back on the ground.

Muriele couldn't see the blade between them. Where was it? She tried to jerk away from Angus. She had to help. She'd plunge her short sword in Feradoch's neck. But her love's father held her firm.

The men grunted and strained. Suddenly, there was a gurgled cry. Neither moved. Blood seeped from between them and spread on the ground.

Muriele dropped her weapon and pulled away to run toward the still bodies.

Their eyes filled with horror, the Chiefs walked slowly to the blood soaked ground.

She didn't know what to do. Tears streaked her face as she looked up at Olaf and then Angus, pleading for their help. They carefully lifted Magnus enough to see the bloody, tangled arms.

The blade rested between them.

Olaf moved to Magnus' legs and looked at Angus. "Take his shoulders. I'll take his legs. Put him on his back."

The priest had to help, for Magnus' inert body seemed to weigh twice as much. When they separated the two men, blood covered them both. Their chests didn't move.

Were they both dead? Had they mortally wounded each other?

The Chiefs knelt on the ground beside their sons, facing each other. Their gazes met in sorrow.

Muriele keened and bent to press herself against Magnus. Her tears dripped on his handsome face sending the blood there into rivulets slowly coursing their way down his cheeks.

He no longer looked the ruthless warrior.

With all vitality gone, his face was gentle, his body lax.

"By all the Saints!" Muriele screamed at him, "Ye canna leave me. Ye canna!" She balled up her fist and struck him a mighty blow on the chest. "I'll hate ye the rest of my life if ye do!"

On her knees, she crawled close and pressed her body against him. 'Twas as if they were in bed and she wished him to suckle her. Lifting his head on her arm, she pressed his face to her chest.

Sobs tore at her throat. Suddenly, a sigh of air whispered against her breast. She put her cheek against his and faint words gasped from his lips.

"Canna breathe."

She looked down at her left breast pressed against his nose and mouth. She near dropped his head in fear she'd suffocated him.

"'Tis like I prophesied," Grunda's voice sounded beside them. "I warned ye! Fathers would fight sons, brothers would fight brothers, but ye wouldna heed Ragnhild's words. Ye were both father to each young man. Ye loved the two in your way. Now ye may be left with but one."

The Chiefs looked at each other in sorrow. Olaf felt his son's chest. "His heart no longer beats. I will take him to my tent and prepare him to take home for burial." He looked at Magnus, worry in his eyes. "There will be no war over this. It was no fault of Magnus. See you do your best for him, old woman."

Men were already running out of the barbican carrying two litters. Olaf accepted their aid in placing Feradoch's body on one. Kinbrace warriors solemnly carried him back to the army of tents by the water.

Graemme took Muriele by the shoulders and lifted her from Magnus so they could take him into the castle and a proper bed. She followed the litter so closely she near stepped on the heels of the bearers.

Once he was on their bed, Sweyn cut away his clothing. Grunda cleaned the shoulder wound with a preparation made of moneywort then quickly stitched it closed. During the tussle on the ground, Feradoch's knife stabbed near Magnus' lung but his ribs deflected it.

Father David stood at the foot of the bed and prayed while Graemme and Chief Angus were there to provide anything the two women called for. As they had done with his leg, Muriele and Grunda worked together. As fast as Muriele knotted a stitch, Grunda cut the thread, closing the wound from inside and then the outer skin.

When they finished, Grunda used compresses made from harebell roots to staunch the bleeding and keep the flesh from turning foul. Sweyn held Magnus' head up for her to spoon an elixir of monkshood into his mouth. 'Twould dull the pain and keep him asleep.

All they could do now was pray and wait.

Chief Angus sent for the priest to come to the solar, for he sought understanding.

"I know Feradoch brought this terrible time upon us, but I am partly to blame. He lived with me since he was a lad. It was my fault if I did not teach him proper values. I thought I had. By the way he died, 'tis obvious I failed."

"You did your best. Graemme is a credit to you. Feradoch was a man who had to go his own way, whether good or bad." He paced the floor and stopped to study Angus. "Will Chief Olaf accept my prayers over his son?"

"Aye. I think he will. He is hurting and in conflict. Like me, he loved both men, though one more than the other."

Father David came back in the middle of the night. He found Chief Angus with his shoulders slumped, waiting for him beside the fireplace in his solar. The priest told him Feradoch had no killing injuries on his body. It was God's will that his heart had given way and stopped beating.

By dawn, not a hint of the army at their gates remained.

After a fortnight of careful nursing, Magnus healed enough to sit up in bed. If Muriele left his side, he tried to wait patiently for her return. If she didn't come when he expected, his bellows echoed from one end of the keep to the other. Old Grunda had assured them their first child would be born on the ninth month after their wedding. 'Twas clear to all Magnus couldn't stand to have his wife far from his side.

epilogue

WITH MAGNUS RECOVERING, CHIEF Angus sent an impressive escort with Father David to deliver a missive to the King. He wrote a full report of all that had transpired between Clibrick and Kinbrace Castles. He also assured him Sir Magnus and Lady Muriele would take residence at Blackbriar within a month.

When Magnus and Muriele arrived at her former home, she was ecstatic with joy. She had to look closely for the stonemasons had painstakingly repaired the damage done by the Kinbrace trebuchets and catapults.

"Aye! The new kitchen, blacksmith's station, stables, weaving huts … they have rebuilt everything necessary to the successful running of a castle. We'll comb the villages for workers. Within a fortnight or two, no one will know a battle occurred here." Magnus grinned as he saw his brother, hands on his hips and a pleased smile on his face, studying the castle.

"Blackbriar is every bit the size of Clibrick!" Magnus walked up beside Sweyn and elbowed him in the ribs. "Now ye will be living in one place all year, there is no reason to delay a wedding."

"Huh! If I could get Esa to say aught but 'Nay'"

"Mayhap ye should enlist Grunda's aide? She did a masterful job overcoming Muriele's objections." Magnus grinned, watching Muriele and Esa hurrying across the great hall heading above to the living quarters.

"This was my parents' rooms." Muriele showed Esa around the bedchamber and solar, then took her to see her old rooms. "I want you to move into my old chambers here where we can be close."

"I wouldn't feel right having such a room," Esa hesitated as she stared at the lovely furnishings.

"Dinna be a fool, Esa," Grunda said from the doorway. "This room is perfect for two."

"Two?"

"Aye. Ye and Sweyn. 'Tis about time ye put him out of his misery. He knows of Feradoch and yer shameful secret, and loves ye as ye are. Not often in life do ye find two people who love each other and are able to wed. Dinna be a gowk and fight it. 'Tis fated ye be together."

"Aha! Listen to her, Esa. Once she has decided ye should mate, 'tis best not to resist!"

"Well, now we have settled everything, I must see to my cottage and gardens. A young woman from the village has been tending them and wishes to learn to be a healer." Grunda flicked her fingers at them and breezed from the room.

Before the evening meal, Magnus waited impatiently as Muriele finished her own ablutions and dressed.

"Come, love, I need yer final decision on something."

"Since when have you asked my aid with anything?

He scowled at her, warning, "Don't get used to it."

He refused to answer any more questions as he led her below the castle where the former barons and their wives lay entombed. It was a huge room and very beautiful, much like the inside of an abbey. Magnificent stone arches and angels with widespread wings lent an air of peace one felt when in a sanctified place.

On a marble base, Lord Colban's tomb, with his stone effigy carved on top, held the prominent spot in the center of the huge room. Stonemasons had enlarged the base so a tomb equally as beautiful joined his. Muriele's tears started to fall as she realized Magnus had ordered Ragnhild's body brought and placed next to her beloved husband. Their likenesses were so well done she ran to kiss their faces.

Magnus followed, putting a comforting arm across

her shoulders.

"The sculptor couldn't finish carving your mother's ring, for he'd never seen it. With your consent, tomorrow he will make a drawing of it and the carving will be complete."

Muriele turned and hugged her arms around his neck. She leaned back and blinked away her tears so she could see into his eyes. Never did she dream Magnus the Ruthless could have such a tender expression. He truly loved her as much as she loved him.

He had finally realized few things in life are totally right or wrong.

There are many shades of gray.

Look for these intriguing romances in
Sophia Johnson's Raptor Castle Series

Available Now
Book 1 *FORBIDDEN*

Brother Ranald of Raptor Castle, a scarred monk in Scotland's Kelso Abbey, has a fearsome temper that causes objects to fly about, turn still waters stormy and candles to light with but a look. In the peace of the abbey. He controls his rage and fights his forbidden desires, but what would he become in the secular world?

'Tis his greatest fear when his father arrives with an army to force Ranald to return to Raptor Castle and wed. This monk turned man must now become husband and warrior.

Book 2 *SEDUCED*

Letia of Seton Castle is as beautiful as she is capable. Famed for her skill at training archers and slingers, she is used to commanding the castles defenses when needful. Married to elderly Baron de Burgh, she has never birthed an heir.

She must protect her castle and people when Maud and Stephen's battles throw England into anarchy. She sacrifices all when her husband devises a plan to save Seton Castle from ruin when he dies.

'Twas a simple plan with very few steps to follow: Capture her enemy, seduce him, bear his child and save her people. But falling in love was not in the plan.

Book 3 *RUTHLESS*

The Morgan and Gunn clans in the Highlands of Scotland have been feuding for longer than anyone can remember, until the chiefs decided to foster their sons with each other.

Before Magnus of Clibrick Castle and Feradoch of Kinbrace

Castle exchanged places when they reached their seventh year, their fathers ordered them to swear a blood oath that each would uphold the peace when they became men. Once they are grown and return to their own strongholds, should either man be felled by treachery, the other will seek vengeance for the deed.

Years later when the Gunn's call Magnus to honor the oath, he never expected to hunt down and hang Muriele of Blackbriar, a bewitching woman he captured and fell in love with when he besieged her castle.

Coming Soon
Book 4 *SURRENDER*

In the Taming of the Shrew, Katharine met her match in Petruchio. She was fortunate not to be in Elyne of Raptor Castle's shoes. When Elyne goes toe to toe with Graemme of Clibrick Castle, he checkmates her every move!

Graemme is not the harsh man Magnus is, but a vow made is also sacred to him. Elyne keeps one step ahead of him and leads him a merry and sometimes treacherous race before he gets the better of her.

But all is not laughter. Someone plots to kidnap Elyne, and when he tires of her, he will delight in killing her.

Author's Note

Dear Readers,

You'll recognize Muriele as the lovely woman from *Forbidden* who catches Raik's eye. You knew she was deathly afraid and hiding from someone in the Highlands who was chasing her across Scotland. She was so desperate for a strong warrior to take her to an Abbey in Northumbria she tried to seduce Ranald to take her there.

In that scene, I planned for Muriele to be somewhat wicked and immoral. Huh! I was going to kill her off toward the end. But she stomped her feet (Oh, my poor brain!) and took on a life of her own. She wanted her own book, and if I planned to kill her off, she wasn't going to go along with it. I had to go back and rewrite her scenes. Only then did she behave. I had her character wrong and she didn't like who I'd thought she was.

I had a deal of planning to do to get her to the Abbey and leave her in safety. She almost died aiding Catalin and Elyne when they were escaping to the Abbey. Ranald paid a fortune for the Abbess to keep her safe, even though Ranald had no idea from whom he was protecting her.

She appears again in *Seduced* when Raik tries to convince her to marry him so he can keep her secure.

So, with all that exposure, she *had* to have her story told.

It was fun having the wicked Feradoch manipulate honor-bound Magnus into hunting down the love of his life, knowing his oath will force him to hang her.

Oh, and you don't know it, but you've already met the hero and heroine to *Surrender*.

As in the Blackthorn Trilogy, please keep in mind that it is not always possible to use only words appropriate to the time. I kept the dialect down to few characters. If any word puzzles you, check The Glossary Pages in *www.sophiajohnson.net* or write me.

I'm always happy to answer any questions.

About the Author

Well, Rats! I'm tired of author biographies being in the third person. This one is going to be me talking to you. I'm a native Floridian born in Key West, FL. That makes me a Conch (pronounced conk), not a Florida Cracker. I spent my first six years in Panama Canal Zone. Many people have told me that when I'm nervous I have a bit of an accent that isn't quite southern or Floridian. That's because I learned to speak in Panama. It was stronger in my teens than it is today, but sometimes it sneaks out.

In Key West, I loved sitting beneath a coconut tree and daydreaming. My other siblings swim like fish. I'm the only one who can't swim worth a hoot. That's because I spent more time on the sand than in the ocean. The sound of the surf and the wonderful briny smell of the Atlantic would almost put me to sleep. But my daydreams kept me alert. I spent a lot of time, too, swatting mosquitoes and brushing sand off my arms.

Wherever we traveled, my father would refer to the people we saw and ask us, "Have you ever wondered how terrible life would be if you were that person?" The first time I remember was when I was six and we were walking by some very poor and obviously ill people. If we stared or drug our feet, it earned us a sharp rap on the head with his knuckles. That quickly straightened us up!

When I had free time, I always had my nose in a book. One day I was reading a Civil War story and it started me thinking what I'd do if I awoke one morning in some strange bedroom and someone came in and called me by another name? Even worse, what if I found I'd traveled back through centuries?

How would I react if I was the character I was reading about?

Now you have the secret to my writing. I always get into my characters' heads and ask, "What if …?"

I wouldn't be able to resist the men in my tales. And I'm not a very strong person. *snort* In fact, I'm a bit of a wimp. That's why I make my heroine's character the woman I'd like to be. Uh, huh! If I didn't, when Magnus stalked Muriele up the stairwell, she'd have squealed like a stuck pig!

My Tag Line is "Love Through the
Ages," the theme of my novels.

www.sophiajohnson.net

READER REVIEWS

I have not added reviews of The Blackthorn Trilogy because there are so many on Amazon.com for *Always Mine, Midnight's Bride and Risk Everything.* Kensington Zebra didn't advertise the books as a trilogy because they came out with the last one first. But I named it The Blackthorn Trilogy because a trilogy is what it was. The first book, *Always Mine*, sets the whole story into motion.

The Raptor Castle Series should be read in the proper order, because you'll learn the secondary characters from one book and follow him/her to the next.

FORBIDDEN

Jamet "bsmrk" *****
I didn't think that this was possible to surpass *Always Mine (Zebra Historical Romance)* an intense love story or *Midnight's Bride* a love story of delightful innocence or even *Risk Everything (Zebra Debut)* but with *Forbidden*, the first of the Raptor Series, Sophia Johnson has out done herself. From the first *Forbidden* grabs you and doesn't let you go until the end which in itself segues into Seduced so well and leaves you so anxious to read this next book.

"Stacy" *****
I am a lover of medieval historical romance books and came upon Sophia Johnson's Blackthorn Trilogy …. Sophia blew me away and took me far away to a medieval castle with some very sexy and sensitive warrior leading men and their feisty heroines! I loved the Blackthorn Trilogy and couldn't wait to

get more of what Sophia delivers: entertaining, amusing and downright sexy books! The first book in the Raptor Castle series "Forbidden" sizzles!

Brenda Ollis *****
If you have read any of Sophia's books, you know that she is an exceptional historical romance author. I read the three books in the Blackthorn trilogy and loved them. ... I didn't think she could top the last three. Well, have no fear!! I read "Forbidden" and could not put it down. Sophia has outdone herself with this first book.

Suzanne Canada *****
I love her characters - strong, handsome, sexy men and lovely, adventurous, brave ladies all interwoven in a story with twists and turns, ensuring I couldn't put her books down. This first in her new Raptor Castle series, "Forbidden", certainly did not disappoint! The handsome and mysterious Ranald and his lady Catalin, along with the other intriguing characters in the story, again kept me ignoring housework and family!

Lauren "llwotb" *****
I love the writing that Sophia Johnson creates. I have read the Blackthorn series and have just finished *Forbidden* for the second time. Her characters are strong and I wanted more. Hopefully her next books will be out sooner than later.

SEDUCED

Captured by Raptor
BooksRfriends2 *****
Seduced is the second book in the Raptor Castle Series. If you read book one (*Forbidden*), this continues with Raik's story. Warin De Burgh, the Baron of Seton Castle, is ill and his time is limited …. The Baron has a plan that includes Raik of Raptor Castle, but his beloved wife must agree. It will not be easy to convince her since Letia and Raik do not like each other. If you like historical romances you will want to add this series to your library.

Seduced
Cigram33 *****
Amazing read. So entertaining and informative of the times that the story was set in. I am looking forward to the next offering. CJM

Wonderful
Tisha *****
I love this book along with all Sophia's other book. She is by far my favorite author of Medieval romance novels. I can't say enough about them.

A Mesmerizing, Sexy Seduction
"Stacy" *****
Sophia has outdone herself with SEDUCED! I LOVED IT!! ... A great and entertaining read full of humor and the perfect, feisty seductress.